SEVEN TEARS OF HEAVEN
A VALENTINE INVESTIGATION

First Published in Great Britain 2024 by Mirador Publishing

Copyright © 2024 by Joe Talon

All rights reserved. No part of this publication may be reproduced or transmitted, in any form or by any means, without permission of the publishers or author. Excepting brief quotes used in reviews.

First edition: 2024

Any reference to real names and places are purely fictional and are constructs of the author. Any offence the references produce is unintentional and in no way reflects the reality of any locations or people involved.

SEVEN TEARS OF HEAVEN

A VALENTINE INVESTIGATION

JOE TALON

ALSO BY THE AUTHOR

The Lorne Turner Mysteries
Counting Crows
Money for Old Bones
Dead of the Winter Sun
Salt for the Devil's Eye
Bad Waters Run Deep
The Alchemist's Corpse
The Spirit Glass

Novellas
Forgotten Homeland
A Meeting of Terrors

A Dale Valentine Investigation
For Whom the Willow Weeps
Seven Tears of Heaven
Novella
A Prison of the Mind

Coming Soon
The Dead Also Have Secrets – Lorne Turner
And
An Agony of Lies– Dale Valentine

Your Free Book Is Waiting

When the police offer you a deal to escape prison, you take it. Right?
Dale Valentine, understands the system, he once wore the uniform, carried the warrant card.
Now, he's just a tool for the police as they hunt the worst criminal gang that London has seen in a long time. It's Dale's job to infiltrate, manipulate, and report back to his handler, Lauren Kennedy.
Only this job might just end up with him dead, and sixteen girls sold into slavery if he can't figure out how to save them.
Impossible odds become normal as Dale earns his freedom and the future he craves away from the dark streets of London.

Get a free copy of the prequel
Here:
A Prison of the Mind on Story Origin

~ *Prologue* ~

JOANNA KEPT HER BACK STRAIGHT as she marched up the hill with her shopping bags. The hessian handles bit into her soft palms, but she never put them down. Pushing through this kind of pain made her feel oddly alive and as if she could achieve something for herself. A litre of organic almond milk, vegan cheese, some rather nice and locally sourced fish, with a range of local vegetables loaded her strong shoulders. Walking from the health food shop in the High Street of Glastonbury up to her house in Leg of Mutton Road meant tackling one of the larger hills in the area, but it helped maintain her fitness. A habit developed during a difficult childhood in Georgia, the Southern United States.

Once she reached her house, she planned to spend the day in quiet contemplation. The last few weeks, well months really, had made her realise her life needed to change. She'd never understood why, but after her mother's abrupt departure just before her eighth birthday, her father had taken total control over his daughter's life. He combined her very expensive education at an exclusive Swiss academy, with holidays spent among his right-wing loony friends learning to shoot, self-protection skills, survival skills, and more shooting.

She'd hated it. At twenty-one, she'd finally escaped his clutches. Despite all the advantages his money gave her, Joanna knew a gilded cage when she saw one, and hers had diamond studs all over it.

Her freedom had, of course, been an illusion. One she'd recognised more clearly with every passing year. Here, in Glastonbury, things really changed. He wanted her home. He'd paid off Ocean for a start, who'd returned to the States. She'd thought Ocean had more integrity, but just like all the other men in her life, her father's money meant more than her love.

The tears made the pavement blur, and she blinked them back. Self-pity didn't suit her, and she'd wallowed long enough. Over the last year, since that mad night on the hill with the broken church, she'd felt time slipping through her fingers. She loved the weirdness of Glastonbury, but she had to move on.

Joanna knew someone was watching her, and it wasn't just her father. She'd seen men in a large SUV on the quiet residential road sat for hours, waiting. Then there were the times, especially over the last few weeks, where she'd caught sight of a figure in a black hoodie and cap hugging the shadows. Joanna knew the signs. Her father had done something similar when she'd moved to New York for a year. He'd hired heavies to protect her and a local detective agency to follow her about, to report any lovers and close friends. She'd been twenty-two and attending Julliard. Finally, losing her place because of the pressure from him had cost her too much of her soul.

At twenty-five, she wanted it back. She just needed a plan. She needed to vanish. In recent months, she'd syphoned money from her bank account, that her father controlled, and she'd hidden it as cash. Once she had enough, she'd set about finding a fake passport, not as hard as it should be, and she'd taken delivery last week. All she had to do was make sure *they* didn't see her leaving. That would be tricky.

Ditching the watchers needed a very specific skill-set. Running was only part of the plan. It was also about remaining hidden in a world full of digital footprints. Just one good CCTV camera and she'd be lost. Mission failure. Not something she could contemplate. The consequences would be too terrible.

Back in New York, one of her closest friends had, quite suddenly, thrown themselves out of their fourth-floor window. It had been three days before the end of term and the friends had decided to move to Los Angeles together to become actors. Losing Wes still caused her to weep uncontrollably if she thought about it too much. That's why she'd escaped here, to this backwater in England. She wanted to heal in a place that had no connection to her father, or to America, and had the depth of spiritual history that could lead her to a new life.

When she reached the house, she didn't see the SUV or the person in black. After unpacking the shopping, she went into her living room and stared out of the window at her incredible view. A band of rain swept over the distant fields, soaking the valley once more. The wind made the glass bend just a little, and she placed a hand on the shuddering pane. She'd miss this place. This view. The beautiful English countryside was just a breath away.

Turning, she sighed. Time to think about what to take and what to leave. Looking at the pile of books beside her favourite chair, she began to throw some into the keep pile, and some into the recycling pile. When she reached a series of leaflets, she shook her head. The handsome Indian face made her grimace.

"Yeah, you're a creep." In a fit of sudden anger, she tore the leaflet up and scattered the pieces. Then she picked up one of the books the creep had written, and she meant to do the same until the doorbell went.

"Maybe I'll use you as a fire starter instead," she told the book, tossing it onto the floor. Though the thought of burning books made her shudder. Yet another reason to stay away from the US right now.

The doorbell went again.

"Alright," she called. "I'm coming."

Putting on the chain, she opened the door and peeked through. "Hi," said her visitor. "Remember me?"

Joanna's eyes widened in surprise. "Sure. It's good to see you."

At least I think it is, she thought. Joanna released the chain and opened her door.

~ *Chapter 1* ~

DALE WINCED. FROM THE CORNER of his eye, he saw Milly hit the mats hard. Returning his attention to the group of four orange belts he needed to teach, he tried not to react to the struggling form of his assistant. She rolled onto all fours to regain her feet. The brown belt, a woman about Milly's age, had a hint of contempt on her face. Milly's grace lay in her mind, not in her body, and the brown belt enjoyed making it obvious.

Interfering in the dojo wouldn't help Milly in the end, but Dale wished the sensei running the class would stop pairing the two women up. As stubborn as Milly could be, everyone had a breaking point, and he'd noticed her private tears after the classes they'd taken together. Her new red belt put her at the beginning of her martial journey, and Dale knew she'd reach black belt given the patience of a good teacher, but only if she felt progression happening. Not if she faced humiliation in every class.

He'd discreetly ordered a special gi—the uniform for the dojo—so she didn't have to fit into the cheap suits new students wore. Making it a gift, a reward for completing their first lesson together, had encouraged her to stay the course to her first grading.

This, though, this endless battering from the higher belt, would be enough to end the courage of most students. Maybe that's why the dojo didn't have many female members. It saddened him. A good sensei knew how to draw the best out of their students and modified their teaching styles to each recruit. Or that's how he'd always trained and taught. Maybe in a class of a hundred students it was different, but here, with just fifteen, a teacher should be more personal, more aware.

They'd found the karate class, and an aikido class, in Wells. Far enough from Glastonbury for Milly to feel she wouldn't be in any danger of training with people she knew. The karate classes were going okay. They comprised of punching and kicking at Milly's stage. She might not be high with her kicks, but damn, she was fast with those hands.

The aikido proved to be more brutal. An excellent class from a martial point of view, not so good if you wanted to preserve your self-confidence and limbs. His eyes flickered to the clock, almost time, and he felt relief. Everyone shared the simple ending to the lesson with bows and thanks in Japanese. As he watched Milly head towards the changing room, pulling her tumble of red hair down to hide her face, he decided to take a little revenge.

"Rachel," he called out to the brown belt, who laughed with a couple of the young men. "Can I make a suggestion?"

She smiled and sauntered over, her black gi, the brown belt and her lithe body making it obvious she thought of herself as a warrior. "Sure, Dale, I'm happy to chat any time."

The slight flirtation did his ego good until he remembered the state of his assistant, and now friend. He took friendship seriously.

Too seriously, you old fool. The voice of Ringo haunted him less these days and Dale didn't quite know how he felt about the change.

"When you move in to complete ikkyo, your initial strike isn't martial. You're lazy with it and you're lazy with your rear hand before the elbow control comes in. If you are grading soon, and I am on the panel, then I would like to see an improvement," he kept his voice light, but her eyes burned with anger at his correction.

"Then perhaps you can teach me, sempai?" she ground out. Her hand ran through her short, peroxided hair.

For the next five minutes, Dale instructed her on the best way to strike with both fists to soften her opponent before the takedown to the floor. When she relaxed into the training, he struck. He came in hard and fast. She retreated, eyes wide, as she fell back into her bad habits. The elbow lock failed. He reversed the technique and took her to the floor. Hard. The air woofed out of her narrow chest. He almost put a knee in her back, then held it. He wanted to humiliate her a little, not break anything. In a dojo, gender shouldn't matter. He ought to treat her the way he would a man who acted like a bully, but he'd never quite achieved the equality necessary to really pile into a woman. He held her firmly by the elbow and wrist instead.

Then, in his hard South London accent, he hissed, "Women need to support women, not humiliate them. You'll have enemies in this life you can't fight, but she can. She's far cleverer than you are. Don't bully people in the dojo because they don't fit your stereotype. There's always someone bigger and better than you." He rose without discernible effort and hid the wince it cost him to show off.

Listening to Rachel curse up a storm as he walked away didn't improve his thoughts on this dojo, but it did give him a sense of childish glee. When he changed, not bothering with a shower in the old-fashioned changing rooms, he realised he'd done little to help Milly. She wouldn't thank him for making Rachel hate her even more deeply.

Once outside, he found his friend slumped against the wing of his beloved Audi A7, fiddling with her phone. The long mass of red curls kept an effective screen between her and the other students, leaving the dojo. He watched them sneak looks at the 'tubby kid in the school yard'. Dale had done his share of bullying kids like Milly when he'd been at school and in the police, but a few hard years in prison taught him a lot about vulnerable people.

"Hey, you did well," he said, pinging the doors open.

Milly grunted and climbed into the car. She hadn't lifted her eyes off the ground.

"Maybe we should try that small dojo in Street?" he said. "It's not the aikido I'm used to, but that's not a bad thing. What do you think?"

Milly looked out of the passenger window. "Maybe."

He didn't want her to give up. It would do more damage to her in the long run than she could possibly imagine. "Milly, women like Rachel—"

"Leave it," she said in a monotone.

"I think it might be—"

"Leave it, Dale. I'm fine."

He drummed his fingers on the steering wheel as they waited at another set of temporary traffic lights. "I'm not."

The road out of the smallest city in England always sported more traffic lights and 'temporary' diversions than anywhere else he'd lived. Admittedly, that was only Peckham, HMP Wormwood Scrubs and Glastonbury, but still, it made it impossible to enjoy the drive.

She glanced at him, the red nose and swollen eyes telling him all he needed to know. They wouldn't be returning to the Wells dojo.

"It's not alright, Milly. This is meant to help people, not hurt them. That's down to bad management and I'm not okay with it."

She didn't speak, just gazed back out of the window.

"I'm sorry," he murmured.

He heard her take in a deep breath and she wriggled in the deep leather seat. "You know what she does for a living?" Milly said unexpectedly.

Dale flicked on the car's headlights and windscreen wipers as the rain started up again. "No, what?"

"She works in the supermarket as a checkout girl." Milly looked at him. "Do you know what I do for a living?"

He chuckled. "I've a fair idea, but why don't you tell me?"

"I chase down bad guys. I'm a private investigator with a successful practice that works closely with the local police. I am a clever woman. The weight is a problem. I know that, but I'm getting it under control and it's working." Milly took a breath and nodded in affirmation. "This time it really is working. She might never be more than a checkout girl, and although that's a job that needs doing and those guys are amazing for their patience, right now—I'm far more successful." Milly faced forwards, hair pushed back over her shoulders. "I got this."

Her defence of people who work at checkouts in supermarkets made him smile. That was Milly, social equality and justice for all, even if they were behaving like total bastards. Dale didn't bother hiding his smile. "You have got it. So, you wanna try the new dojo or not?"

"God, yes, please. I really don't want to go back to that place. I hate it."

He chuckled. "Okay, I'll give them a ring and explain."

"Remember, when we get back, you have that Skype call with Mr Wolski."

Dale groaned. "The American."

"The American."

He sighed. The man wanted Valentine Investigations to find his missing daughter. She'd been gone three weeks. Not long in the scheme of things, but Mr Wolski couldn't motivate the police to do more than just open a file. People moved on rapidly in the transitory communities that made up the divergent populous of the rural town, making it very difficult to find a missing person. The police in Somerset had many priorities that didn't always involve tracking down adults who took drugs and go to wild parties. Dale had spent over an hour already trying to explain to the man that he'd be wasting his money, but this father wanted his daughter unearthed. Hopefully, that remained a metaphor, rather than a gruesome fact.

It disturbed Dale a little, the way the man spoke about his adult child. As if he had a right to know her every thought and action. Dale took the case, but mostly because he found himself worried about Joanna Wolski if her father found her before he did.

"I always thought people from a place like Savannah would be relaxed, a bit laid back. This bloke is like a rattlesnake on speed."

Milly chuckled. "He's a powerful man in Georgia. I guess he expects us to jump in the same way they do over there."

"Flashing dollars at me doesn't necessarily mean I bow."

"You're lucky to be in that position," she said quietly.

Dale knew it. He'd grown up dirt poor, made a lot of money being a police officer who worked with the criminals of Peckham rather than against them. Then lost it all during his arrest and conviction.

After that, he'd done a man a favour and now he had several lucrative investments and actual capital that needed investing in something sensible. He'd bought the cottage on the main road in Glastonbury and the car, started the business, and now he wanted more roots in the area. He figured buying another house might be a good idea, but did he really want to be a landlord?

"Can you be there to take notes while I talk to Wolski?" Dale asked.

"I'm supposed to be going out," she said. "But I can cancel."

He glanced at her as they drove into Glastonbury and hit another set of lights. "A date?"

She shrugged and gave a brief nod, but her skin betrayed her. Colour flashed over the pale surface. "I can cancel." The blush made him grin.

"No, Milly. You need a life outside work," Dale said, pulling out around the roadworks.

"You don't have one."

A truth he didn't know how to resolve. "Yeah, fair enough." His thoughts wandered to DI Lauren Kennedy and the gears in his head slipped and spun, going nowhere.

DETECTIVE INSPECTOR LAUREN KENNEDY STIFLED a groan as she lifted her damaged leg to force it to bend, trying to ease the growing pain. If she'd known how long she'd suffer after being shot, she'd have made more of an effort to get out of the damned way of the gun-wielding paedophile.

Rubbing her eyes, she tried to focus on the paper files and the digital report. Sleep in her new flat had proved elusive. Not because the flat was the problem, Lauren knew her job was the problem. She lived over a clothes shop in Glastonbury High Street. Her sitting room smelt of the incense leaking up from the shop below, and the stream of steam-punk and Goth customers amused her endlessly. The downside of living in the flat dawned on her after she'd paid a hefty deposit and signed the lease. She lived in the heart of Glastonbury's chaos. Every alternative lifestyle drifted about the busy main street at all hours. After years of living in London, the street noise shouldn't bother her, but since the shooting Lauren realised she jumped a bit too easily at shadows and creaks.

Right now, she sat in her tiny office at the back of the Street police station and stared at yet another cold case file. She had a horrible bleak feeling creeping up her spine and starting to rattle around in her head.

The file told a sad story. Ten months before, the body of a young man had been found on the seafront of Burnham-on-Sea, known locally as Burnham.

He'd been tucked up behind the RNLI Lifeboat Station and sea wall. Scratches covered his naked skin. They'd come from the lad running naked through heathland, according to the forensics' report, but no obvious fatal wounds that indicated murder. At twenty-five, the young man had life rolling out before him, but then it was gone. The report told her the victim consumed a toxic mix of illegal substances. They thought this, and the winter weather, meant his system closed down, and the cause of death was exposure. No one found his clothes and despite several appeals on local radio, in the news, and with leaflets, no witnesses had seen his arrival at the long esplanade in Burnham.

Her job?

Find the people who sold the drugs found in his body, and how the young man ended up on the seafront. He hadn't died by accident. Someone had drugged him. The body had perimortem bruising indicative of a confrontation before death. Were the drugs forced on him, or did he cause a fight before he died?

Originally, the coroner had called the death accidental, but several of the man's cases were being reviewed after two major mistakes on his part. It mattered to families how their loved ones died, and what is written on that last piece of paper that bookends the birth certificate. He'd misjudged two drugs' deaths, and the families had challenged his decision in court. It had left the police with the job of double-checking his work on other similar cases. That, combined with Lauren's predecessor being a bigoted prick when it came to the local alternative scene, meant several cases needed an overhaul.

The body of Sonny Collins had been tucked tight between the little RNLI station and the wall. With the bad weather keeping many off the seafront; it had taken several days for someone's dog to find the slim man. He'd obviously crawled into the space, hoping to find some kind of refuge.

The records showed a surviving family, comprising a mother and twin sister. They'd identified the remains. She needed to speak to them; or the mother, at least. Opening old wounds with these cold cases tortured Lauren each time she had to do it.

Pulling her lower leg back manually, she groaned at the pain in her thigh and back.

"You okay, Guv?" asked the newly promoted Detective Constable Ryan Matthews. They'd saddled the poor man with being her DC for the moment, though Lauren wanted him to be reassigned to gain experience in Bristol or Taunton.

"Yeah, just feeling ninety-years-old in one leg."

He grinned. "You need to exercise differently, Guv."

"What's that supposed to mean?" she asked, heading off into defensive mode without thinking about it.

Matthews rarely took offence, but having met his mother a few times, Lauren knew why. The woman had a tongue on her like a razorblade. "It means—I've seen you at the pool. You're swimming like a shark, putting the leg under too much pressure. You need to swim like a…"

Lauren's eyes narrowed. "Be careful, DC Matthews, you're still on probation."

Matthews' grin widened. "A sleek, sun-warmed, lazy salmon."

She huffed. "Good save. I've a mother to call, then visit. I'll need you to drive."

"Sure thing, Guv. If you're making a rellie call, then I'll go make us a cuppa. Listening to those is horrible."

"Coward," she shot at his back as he walked away.

Smiling, she returned to the file. She enjoyed Ryan Matthews' company; he took orders without a quibble and enjoyed learning about the job. He wouldn't be bullied by the others in the station into covering up inappropriate behaviour, and he understood the importance of teamwork.

She picked up the piece of paper with the details of Mrs Collins and her children, Sonny—deceased, and Eliza, the surviving twin sister. Father, also deceased for over ten years, had no criminal record.

"What a cursed family," Lauren muttered.

Aware she was prevaricating, Lauren picked up the phone and dialled. The family home was in Weston-super-Mare.

The phone rang five times before a woman's voice said, "Hello?"

"Mrs Collins?" Lauren asked. She couldn't tell much about the woman from that one word.

"That's right," Mrs Collins said. Good enunciation, well-educated then, and with no Somerset burr.

"My name is Detective Inspector Kennedy. Can I have a moment of your time?" Lauren kept her voice light, soft, understanding. At this point, some people broke into noisy tears, others went stony with their silence. One even slammed the phone down and another ranted at her for a full five minutes about how the police failed to find her daughter's killer.

"You can," came the hitched response. The soft sound of a body lowering to a chair came to Lauren. "What do you want?"

"Mrs Collins, as you know, your son's case has now been passed onto a team that is re-examining the coroner's decision of accidental death, especially considering the previous Senior Investigation Officer. We know, during the initial findings, you were worried. That perhaps we'd made some dismissive decisions about the evidence. We are here to deal with these older cases that we have yet to solve."

"You mean cold cases?"

Lauren hated that phrase. It made her feel the cold of a grave. "Yes," she admitted. "Though, I'd rather think of them as unsolved."

Silence at the other end.

She hurried on. "Would it be possible to arrange a visit to discuss your son's case? I only have reports and they're a little clinical, as you can imagine. I'd like to talk to people who remember Sonny, who can tell me what he was really like. It helps me build a personal profile that can lead to new insights."

"Oh," a hint of surprise. "That's… Well, yes. It would be lovely to speak to someone about Sonny. It's been almost a year and I feel like…" She paused, and Lauren heard the battle that must be happening in the mother's heart. "I feel like people think I should have stopped mourning by now. Just another dead druggie. Do you know what I mean?" For a moment, she sounded lost and broken.

"Yes, Mrs Collins, I'm afraid I know exactly what you mean," Lauren spoke from the heart, hoping her sincerity came through.

"I'm home most days, so whenever it suits you, Detective Inspector

Kennedy." Mrs Collins had gathered her resources and put her armour back in place.

"Then I shall come to visit tomorrow, and we can review your son's file together, Mrs Collins. Perhaps we'll learn something new." Lauren's hand ached. She gripped the phone too tightly in an effort to keep her voice even.

"I'll be here," said Mrs Collins.

~ *Chapter 2* ~

DALE ALLOWED THE FATHER FROM Georgia to rail against the ineffectiveness of the British police until he'd had his fill. There might well be many problems in the police force, but he knew damn well they had the same types of issues in the US. At least in the UK, you only dealt with a single entity. This man wanted everyone from a sheriff to a marshal to go out hunting every male varmint until they found his daughter.

"Mr Wolski, I think I should stop you there," Dale said to his computer screen, trying to keep his expression neutral. "Our local constabulary has done a thorough job of tracking down your daughter. The fact they can't find her does not necessarily mean she's in trouble. I need you to be aware that she may just not want to be found."

He added silently, *I don't blame her either.*

"Well," Mr Wolski said, "I'm not convinced, Mr Valentine. So, I will hire you and if you refuse to take the job, I'll find one of your rivals."

Dale kept his face impassive with effort. He knew full well Wolski couldn't find another local agency. Dale ran the only one in Glastonbury. There were others in Bath, Bristol, Exeter, and even Taunton, but he specialised in the small rural communities of the Levels and Sedgemoor. He was also one of the few who was ex-Job with strong connections to the local police.

"That's your prerogative," Dale said, sounding more English by the syllable. "However, we'll do all we can to help. I know you want Joanna's current whereabouts, but if I find her, I'll be seeking her permission before I give you a location. I'll tell you if she's alive and unharmed, but if she doesn't want to be found, that's her right."

The older man, with iron-grey hair and the face of a furious eagle, calmed somewhat. He stroked the well-trimmed white goatee, and his piercing blue eyes relaxed their grip on Dale. "Fine, I can work with that for now. I want reports with your invoices and if I think the two don't tally? Well, Mr Valentine, we'll have ourselves a problem." The threat slipped out too easily, as if he was used to pushing people around and expected compliance.

Dale worked hard to keep the irritation out of his voice. "I'm sure you'll be more than happy with our services, Mr Wolski. I'm aware it's early evening for you, but it's late here, so for now, I think we've covered enough ground. If you think of anything else I might need to know about Joanna, then email me the details. I have her photo, last known address, the key's location and alarm codes, and her personal details."

"Fine, we'll speak soon, Mr Valentine." Wolski killed the call.

Dale sat back and rubbed his face. "You're going to be fun," he muttered at the blank screen. It showed a still of his bird table, and the robin who'd decided he owned the entire garden. The novelty of having the extensive garden still hadn't worn off, despite the need to retain a team of gardeners to help keep control.

He made notes in a new file called, *Joanna_Wolski_MISPER*, while her father's words still rattled around inside his head. Milly could catch-up in the morning.

Apparently, Joanna had been missing for several weeks. She always video called her father on a Sunday morning, while she ate lunch and he had breakfast after his long run. She'd email if she couldn't make the call and he'd do the same. He'd received a cryptic email on the 21st of October saying she'd call when she could and not to worry. It hadn't worked, of course, he'd panicked, and when she missed the next call, he'd gone into full anxiety mode. He had called Scotland Yard in London then gradually worked his way down to the locals in Taunton, then the tiny police station in Street. Dale thought about calling Lauren and asking what she knew about Joanna Wolski.

He sighed, knowing a conversation with Lauren could well become more complicated than he wanted this late in the evening.

They'd gone out to dinner a few times, the spark fizzing between them until the drive home, where it died. Somehow the jigsaw pieces weren't fitting together anymore, and Dale didn't understand why.

"Bloody stop," he muttered to himself, throwing his pen away as he realised the damned thing had made endless circles on an overpriced electric bill. He had solar. How were they charging this much on an estimate? "Phone Lauren in the morning." He pushed away from the office desk, but picked up Joanna Wolski's photo.

Turning towards the darkened window, he held the photo and studied the young woman's face. She had a wild tumble of raven black hair, very pale skin that harked back to her mother's Irish heritage, and wide, large blue eyes. A smile lifted the full red lips, but it didn't reach her blank gaze. She looked, to Dale, to be haunted. He frowned. This girl needed finding. Those eyes were keeping secrets that she kept locked inside; was she hiding them from her father?

Walking from the converted barn to his cottage, Dale once more pondered Wolski's version of events surrounding his daughter's disappearance.

The young woman came across as a true Glastonbury trust-fund hippy, only with an American accent. All the photos Wolski sent to Valentine Investigations had her willowy form clothed in long flowing skirts and jumpers woven from soft wools. Not the cheap mixed stuff the poor of the parish wore while begging outside the supermarket. This was mohair and angora, according to Milly. The long, slim neck wore pendants and pentagrams with fine chains, not strips of cloth or leather. Her black hair reached her waist in a curtain of ribbons any gypsy fortune-teller would envy.

He also had photos of the boyfriend. A blond surfer dude with broad shoulders, tanned skin and the health of another wealthy American, this time from California. Dale would need to talk to Ocean—a real name, apparently—at some point, but the boyfriend had returned to the Sunshine State after a fairly horrible eighteen months of damp English weather.

While Dale cooked a veggie bolognaise for his dinner, he tried to sort through the timeline he'd been given. Joanna arrived in Glastonbury almost two years previously, knowing the town's reputation as a place to explore the vast reaches of a person's psyche and to heal a person's soul. Growing up in Peckham, on the hard London streets full of gangs and violence, Dale found it hard to understand this side of his adopted rural town, but he was learning. All Joanna had wanted to do was study at the feet of healers, mystics, gurus and explorers of the universe. Coming to the UK had been a compromise with her father, because he'd thought it safer than India.

When Ocean left Joanna almost six months ago, Wolski noticed an increased decline in his daughter. She'd loved the wrong man, and Wolski had tried to convince her to come home. The change in his bubbly, free-wheeling child became more pronounced four weeks before she'd vanished and Dale knew, even though it was unspoken, that Wolski feared she'd taken her own life.

Dale feared it too, but the police had been to her house and found no evidence of it. They'd also seen a clear indication of her packing in a hurry. Joanna was twenty-five years old. If she didn't want to call home for a few weeks, then she didn't have to. With limited resources, all the authorities could do was a welfare check and add her to the expanding database of missing persons. Every police officer in the area had a description of the woman, so they'd done their part.

The thing worrying Dale the most about Joanna's vanishing act was obvious. A clear decline in her happiness and the deep connection she had to her father. Wolski made it sound like they were the heart and soul of each other. Dale found it slightly disturbing, but he had no connection to his father at all, so family dynamics often confused him. Joanna's mother had moved to a commune in Florida after she divorced Wolski, and apparently, hadn't had contact with her daughter for almost seventeen years.

His phone rang just as he served up the fresh pasta. Putting the call on speaker, he said, "Aren't you out on a date?"

Milly said, "What did Wolski say?" Her voice sounded distant, as if she were on speaker as well. Dale knew she wouldn't do that unless she was alone and somewhere private. Like her bedroom in her parents' flat over the Green Man café.

"I'm guessing the date didn't go well?" Dale persisted.

"It was fine," she said. "What did the American say?"

Dale poured his sauce over the pasta. "I'm about to eat. Can we talk about it in the morning?"

"I guess," Milly said, though he heard the disappointment in her voice.

"Milly, I love your dedication to the job, but…"

"Fine," she huffed as if he'd interrupted her evening, rather than the other way around. "Ryan wants commitment from me."

"And you're not sure?"

"No."

"Because of Sully."

Silence.

He knew he should fight it, but he couldn't help himself, her predicament amused him. Milly's love life had gone from zero to one-hundred in just a few days over the summer, and she did not know which way to jump. In one corner of the ring, DC Ryan Matthews, a fine, upstanding young man. In the other, the damaged, ethereal Sullivan or Sully to his friends, who worked in her parents' café.

Finally, she said, "I'll see you in the morning."

"Sure. We'll check Joanna Wolski's place. Then we need to see which parts of the Glastonbury alternative scene interested her most."

"Sounds like a plan." Milly hung up.

Dale frowned at his phone as he forked Pennie into his mouth. She'd had a bad day. Since meeting her, Dale had worked hard to keep Milly at a distance, to keep everyone in his new life at arm's length, but since the shooting in the summer, things had changed. He'd allowed himself to start feeling connections to people and places. He loved his cottage and its garden that backed onto the abbey grounds. The Tor, rising from the surrounding flatlands, like its mythical history, still wove through the town's core. The strange cacophony of independent shops filling the main street with crystals, dragons, mystical books and so much more.

New people in his life had changed him as well, and he let them. The carapace that helped him survive in Peckham, then during his service in the Metropolitan police and finally in prison, was now softening. It scared him. Everyone he'd loved back in London had died; his grandparents and Ringo. He thought he'd be alone forever, and he'd grown used to the idea. Welcomed it even. Until Milly came into his life, and now he had a friend. Someone to worry about.

THE FOLLOWING MORNING, THE SHORT drive from his place to the café took longer than it should have because of tractors and cyclists on roads meant for medieval wagons. Well used to London traffic, Dale had more patience than most. Also, the interior of his Audi A7 always made life more comfortable. As he drove down the High Street he saw a tall, blonde woman with a pronounced limp leave the Green Man café. Lauren, his Nordic nemesis. She saw him moments before he pulled up on the pavement, parking illegally. He slid the window down for Lauren to speak to him, letting in a blast of cold air.

"Morning, sunshine, and what are you doin' in these 'ere parts?" she asked in a deep copper's voice from some ham Victorian play.

He grinned. "Well, officer, I plan on robbing the bank and spending the proceeds on women and beer."

Lauren laughed. "Good to know. I'll wait for the call out."

Milly appeared from the doorway of the café.

Lauren turned and winced as she caught her leg in a way it didn't like. "You two off to make the local police look bad?"

"We're hoping so," Milly said brightly. "Misper, right, Guv?"

Dale nodded, leaning over the central console to see the women. "The American, Joanna Wolski. You seen the file? Apparently, your lot did a welfare check."

Lauren shook her head. "Not my case. I'll have a nose, though, to see if anything pops up. I've a meeting with a grieving mother, so it's going to be a long day." She looked at Milly. "Ryan's coming with me, if you want to give him a message?"

Milly shook her head and Dale watched her face close down. "No, we saw each other last night. It's fine." She climbed into the car and sank into the soft bucket seat. Lauren closed the door.

"You're welcome to come up for lunch or supper, or something," Dale said to Lauren, "if the grieving mother is too much."

Lauren smiled and nodded. "Thanks, I might take you up on that. It's a reasonably fresh cold case, so the emotions are still very raw."

She tapped the top of the car and Dale drove away.

"Where are we going?" Milly asked.

"Leg of Mutton Road," he said, trying to sound Somerset rather than London. "Who thought that was a good name for a street?"

Milly laughed. "Probably an abbot of the abbey. They used to own everything in the area." She wore her hair pinned back, the chaos of red curls caged, at least until the wind blew. So, for once, Dale could see her face clearly.

"You okay?" he asked.

"Yeah, I'm just not sure I'm cut out for this relationship malarkey. It's bloody hard work." She studied her hands in her lap. "He's very nice, but I can't stop him mothering me. You know?"

"The word 'nice' is usually a killer for me, but I'm an unmarried philanderer, so maybe my opinion shouldn't be the one you ask for. Besides, a caring man is good, right?"

"It can also be a controlling one." She murmured, "Sully isn't like that."

"Sully can barely look after himself, never mind mother you."

She chuckled, the mood around her softening. "That's part of his magic."

Dale refrained from commenting, despite seeing the clear writing on the wall in ten foot high graffiti for poor Ryan. If Sully had 'magic' and Ryan had 'nice', then Sully won. It might take a while for Milly to see it, but she would. Sully didn't offer the easy option, but Dale had learned Milly never took on easy for its own sake.

He pulled up at the junction to Rowley Road, and they left the warmth of the vehicle. Dale grabbed his thick woollen coat from the back and Milly huddled into her huge rainbow cardigan.

She squinted and muttered, "Damn, that wind's bitter."

The view, though, in Dale's opinion, was impressive. The houses behind him must have a spectacular outlook over the smooth lands of the Somerset Levels. Even with the late autumn turning to winter, the fields and hedges rolled off into the distance like a vast green sea. Dale breathed in the clean air, ripping off the flatlands and closed his eyes. He took in the smell of wet air. The rain having filled the rivers and sent flood warnings through the small, scattered communities. They'd rather flood the villages and farms than the towns. It didn't sit well with Dale. The poor in these isolated places paid a heavy price.

"She rented this place," he said, looking at his phone. It showed a house sat on the ridge with a sharply sloping garden and a balcony for its owners to fully enjoy the endless beauty of the wide valley and distant peaks that led up to Pennard Hill.

"Wow, she really is a trust-fund baby," Milly said. "That place must cost over a grand a month to rent."

"According to the bank statements that Wolski sent over, it's almost fourteen-hundred." They started up the path. The steps cut into the hillside and drifted in a lazy curve around a large flowerbed before heading towards the front door.

He half expected Milly to be huffing behind him, but her training and the long walks she now took with a neighbour's dog were paying off. She breathed normally beside him. Once they reached the house, he nosed around a concrete statue in the shape of a fairy, then found the fake stone. He logged in the number Wolski gave him and retrieved the key to the house. Long ago Joanna proved she couldn't be trusted to leave the house with her keys, so there was always a spare set in the garden, wherever she lived. Dale considered it madness, but then he'd grown up in a place that could strip a car of its wheels within minutes without setting off the car alarm. Mostly by removing the entire car.

"Time to see who Joanna Wolski really is," Milly said as they opened the door to the house.

~ *Chapter 3* ~

MILLY STEPPED OVER THE THRESHOLD, the smell of a neglected house overwhelming her for a moment. The air escaped as if desperate to move on to fresher places, ridding itself of the musty, gone-off stain. She glanced down at the carpet, covered in the vomit from the letterbox. Pizza flyers, circulars and bills. She stepped around them for the moment, surprised no one had tidied up since Joanna's disappearance.

The navy carpet obviously hadn't seen a vacuum cleaner in a while and cobwebs hung, broken and dusty, in every corner of the ceiling. "She'll have lost her cleaning deposit," she said as she watched Dale head off into the house, his big form turning into a shadow as he entered a darkened kitchen.

"Damn me," he called. "No one has emptied the bins in the kitchen, either. Wow, it stinks in here." He blinked and pulled a face as he reappeared. "I think we need to tell Daddy Wolski his daughter was a bit of a baggage."

"I'm not sure that'll translate into American, Dale." Milly opened another door. The living room. She stepped inside and gasped. The view over the valley was even more spectacular. "I could live here."

"Not on what I pay you," Dale said, coming in behind her.

"True. Can I have a raise?"

"No."

"You're mean," she said, giving him a light punch in the arm. With great difficulty, she dragged her eyes away from the valley and concentrated on the room itself.

Large, fairly modern, with pale walls of a nondescript apricot and a nice pale suite of sofa and two armchairs. In the corner, away from the view, sat a modern television with all the usual clutter. A fireplace dominated the wall adjacent to the view. A sleek modern Swedish log burner sat, on a wide tiled surface that obviously used to be a nineteen-seventies' gas fire. Next to the French windows that led to the balcony, two smaller chairs stood, and by the dents in the cushions, appeared to be well used. A pile of books stood on a small table. Nothing had seen the right side of a duster for a long time.

One thing stuck out. It would in any home. A series of torn pieces of paper. Not ripped and twisted for the fire, but ripped and thrown about in what must have been an emotional state. They were scattered all over the carpet near the pile of books. Several more books lay in a pile to one side, many of them discarded, a tiny pyramid of wordy nonsense.

Milly bent to read the spines. "They're all on esoterica."

"I can't find a novel anywhere," Dale said. "But there're loads of the Avalon Times in the kitchen."

She joined him, more familiar with the local alternative newspaper than she'd care to admit. They gave it away to customers in the café, the small free press making money from advertising rather than sales. The decorative font on the front and the headline *Avalon, the home of aliens*, made her smile. Flicking through the pile, she said, "There are none from the last two months here."

"Take them with us. They might give us some information later," Dale said.

He poked about in the debris on the floor, took a few photos, then used his pen to move the pieces around. Opening the fireplace, he stabbed in the ash. He glanced about and noticed a series of tread marks on the thick carpet. Big boots had dug in and changed the pile in places. Also, they'd disturbed the dust. He tried to remember what police issue treads were like. They didn't seem to be familiar, and an odd circle appeared in the place the foot arch would be, like a faint logo imprint. Police boots had no logos.

He pointed them out to Milly, and she snapped some photos, just in case changing the image profile could reveal a hidden secret.

"Something happened here, and it wasn't good," he muttered as she left the room.

Milly went in search of a bag to put the newspapers in, heading to the kitchen. "Oh, God."

"What?" Dale barked, alarmed.

"The smell, you were right," she grimaced, holding her sleeve to her face.

She heard the evil chuckle from the living room. Rather than worry about the newspapers, she headed for the cupboard under the sink and found the bin bags. Milly then headed to the fridge, the bread bin, and the compost bin. She had to hope the different moulds and rot wouldn't join to form some great terrible golem of rotting vegetables and gone-off fish.

Holding the bag at arm's length, she found the key for the backdoor and threw it outside. "Sod the recycling," she muttered. Opening a window in the kitchen, she allowed the cold air to sweep through the small room. Then she realised what she'd thrown out.

Finding a cloth bag for the newspapers, she headed back to the living room. "I found some gone-off fish in the fridge."

"Oh, that's the smell," Dale said, pulling apart the pile of books and flicking through them.

"Yeah, but that's not the point. The house might not be sparkling, but I find it hard to believe a woman like that would leave fish in the fridge to rot."

Dale glanced up at her and sat back on his heels. "You're right." He frowned. "She left in a hurry and probably thought she'd return soon enough to clean it up. This lot," he waved at the debris on the floor, "tells me she was in a temper about something."

"Or someone was in a temper with her," Milly added quietly.

Dale rose. "Exactly. She wouldn't leave it like this either. The cobwebs, the dust, I understand leaving that. It's boring work and not something you notice if you're sliding into depression. The state of the kitchen and these torn leaflets are telling us something else. I'm worried about her, Milly. I thought this was another rich kid having a tantrum with daddy, but there's something wrong."

"There's also something in the kitchen I want to show you," Milly said.

They trailed back to the colder, but fresher smelling room. Milly pointed to the kitchen unit near the cooker. "Two glasses."

Dale approached. He bent and peered at the rims. "One with lipstick, one with gloss or lip balm." He reached into his pocket for a plastic bag.

"She left in a panic."

"Indeed." His dark eyes flicked to hers. "Go check the bedrooms. You remember how to search like a police officer?"

She nodded. "I also remember what you said about searching like a criminal as well."

His grin pleased her. "Go to it, Sherlock."

Milly climbed the stairs, nicely carpeted, and headed for the first door. Bathroom, a good place to begin her search. First, she opened the sink's cabinet. Inside she found tinctures, remedies, a box of paracetamol for genuine emergencies, and some makeup—vegan, of course. Despite the fish in the fridge, Joanna obviously didn't want to smear animal goo on her face. The small dark bottles lined up neatly contained alternative medicines for stress, anxiety, agoraphobia, and panic attacks. Milly recognised the names, because she'd been using the same potions for years. They'd also used the same practitioners by the looks of the labels. She sighed. Whatever scared Joanna Wolski, it left the young woman feeling vulnerable for an extended period.

She pulled at the plastic bath panel, to make sure no one used it as a hiding place, and behind the cleaning products. She also upended the box of organic cotton sanitary products. She found nothing stashed in a place few men would ever check.

Leaving the bathroom, but more aware than ever of Joanna's state of mind, she went into the main bedroom. Bohemian chic came to mind the moment she stepped over the threshold. A sense of Joanna trying to recreate a Moorish tent with too many colours. Milly headed to the bedside cabinet. The room had obviously been searched by the police. None of the drawers were closed and the wardrobe looked like it had vomited clothes everywhere. She thought about the boot prints Dale had found downstairs. Maybe the police hadn't done this search? That made more sense, and it added to the mystery.

She nosed through the bottom of the wardrobe, and found a set of expensive suitcases, but no holdall. Would a woman like Joanna have a holdall? Or a rucksack?

With care, Milly went through the small drawers and found nothing unusual except for the size of the vibrator and too few knickers and socks. However, her eyes were drawn to a flyer and a book, both of which had the same font and colours as the torn papers in the living room. The title, *A Dawn Awakening of the Soul*, matched the flyer stuffed inside as a bookmark and a handsome young man, probably of Indian extraction, stood looking soulfully at the camera. He held prayer beads wrapped around long hands pressed together in prayer, wore a tunic that could be of Muslim or Hindu design, and a dark beard that was neatly styled.

"Where have I seen you before?" she asked the sincere face on the book cover. Both went into the bag. More rummaging under the mattress revealed a Canadian passport. Milly flicked it open, frowning hard. Joanna Wolski looked up at her, but that wasn't the name on the detail page. Lying on her back, Milly wriggled under the bed as far as possible considering the size of her chest, and saw cash. A lot of cash stashed between the mattress and the wooden slats that acted as bed springs.

She put the passport into the bag, but left the cash. She found nothing else of interest, except for the fact that Joanna enjoyed spending money on herself. The place reeked of privilege. The jewellery box alone held more 'magical' healing necklaces, bracelets, belly chains, anklets, and other items than Milly had seen in the shop next to the café.

Joanna wanted to be saved, but from what? The world, herself, her father? Did it matter? An uneasy feeling crept over Milly. Joanna Wolski's privileged life held dark secrets. Mixed with an obvious decline in her mental health, at least according to her father, and some pretty terrible conclusions could be drawn. Milly knew conclusions weren't facts, but they needed to find this young woman, and fast.

She went through the other two rooms, but they were obviously for visitors and held nothing personal. Downstairs she joined Dale, who sat in a chair looking at the pile of books. They all now lay on the floor in neat rows.

"What was going on in this girl's head, Milly?" he asked, his tone grave. "There's something very wrong here. We have no obvious signs of violence, like a smashed door or window, but we have a disturbed mind." He glanced up at her. "Those glasses worry me. There's no sign of booze in the house, or weed come to that, but one of those glasses has a strange residue in the bottom. Did that happen the same day she went missing? If so, why put off the regular calls to her father several days before buying the fish? And what the hell was she looking for in all these books?" He waved a hand at the titles in front of him.

"She's a seeker of the mysteries. My guess? The modern world held no charm for her, and she wanted a richer life. She wanted to explore her mind, soul and perhaps her past lives." Milly picked up a book about meditation and travelling through those very journeys. "But that's not all, Guv." She fished out the passport.

Dale took it and looked for the information page. "Oh shit."

"Yeah. It's obviously a fake, but it's very good."

"She was running."

"If so, where is she now? There is a pile of money under the mattress and that passport. She left here without her safety net. How much trouble is she in to vanish like this?"

Dale handed Milly back the fake passport. "It looks terribly lonely for a young woman." His conclusion came with a sigh.

Milly shrugged. "Maybe, but she'd have been part of the community here, which makes me think we need to talk to the people in the community centre. That's the place most out-of-towners go for information about the alternative scene in Glasto."

Dale rose without a discernible effort. "I agree." He glanced at her. "Find anything else?"

"I think I might have." She pulled out the leaflet and the book. "Look, there's more from this guy down there." She pointed to the pile of other titles Dale had dug out of what might be the discarded pile and the torn paper on the ground. "She's a fan. Or was."

"And he came to Glastonbury." Dale pointed to the white box on the back of the leaflet with a sticker on it detailing a meeting. "It was at the community centre."

"Yep."

"Okay, we're done here. Let's close up the house and head back to the office. I'll email Wolski and let him know we're going to hassle the police. This needs escalating to a priority. I'm deeply worried about this girl."

"We'll keep the passport quiet, right?" Milly asked.

Dale nodded. "Oh yes. We aren't telling daddy dear about that."

LAUREN AND RYAN STOOD BESIDE her small red Kia Rio and breathed in the cold air coming off the Bristol Channel. They weren't visible from the house, which Lauren took to be a blessing. She really needed a moment to detox from the last two hours of her life.

"Fish and chips for lunch?" she asked into the well of silence between them.

"God, that would be amazing," Ryan admitted. "I knew CID would bring me up close and personal with more grieving families, but…"

Lauren breathed out, long and slow. "Yeah, I know. It can be intense. That was a bad one. She's a broken woman."

"It's just so sad," Ryan said, looking Lauren in the eye. "Her son died because no one cared. Just another druggie."

"You care."

"Even after reading his file, it didn't really hit home."

Lauren opened her car door. "It never does until we meet the victims. It's important you understand their grief, but it's also important you don't let it touch you too deeply. You can't carry their sadness and pain. Sympathy, not empathy."

She lowered herself carefully into the car. The sofa at the Collins' house had been luxuriously deep, but Lauren found her leg aching after ten minutes. Two hours sat still, listening to Mrs Collins give them all the details of her son's life, left her leg screaming in agony.

Ryan glanced at her. "You want me to drive, Guv?"

She glared at him, and the young detective constable shrank into his new suit. Pulling away from the kerb, Lauren wove through the wide Victorian streets towards Weston-super-Mare's seafront. The Collins' family home was one of these large houses. Mrs Collins had spoken at length about how happy her twins had been growing up in the area, so close to the sea. They had good shops just down the road and the beach within walking distance.

Lauren didn't meet Eliza, the surviving twin, but she felt like she knew every intimate detail about the woman. There were family photos everywhere, and Mrs Collins obviously worshipped both children. She explained their father, who also featured in the vast array of photos, hailed from Tunisia. He'd been a doctor working for the NHS his entire career. It hadn't saved him from the cancer when it arrived.

Since Sonny's death, the young man had become a saint alongside his father. To be honest, they were beautiful children to look at, both of them striking. A male and female version of each other, with dark brown hair, eyes the colour of honey, and cheekbones Aphrodite would want to steal.

Unfortunately, Lauren had also seen the autopsy photos, and those taken at the scene on the seafront of Burnham. Sonny hadn't looked so lovely in those.

"I know mothers exaggerate their child's brilliance," Ryan said. "According to my mother, I'm on the way to being Chief Constable by the time I'm thirty—"

Lauren snorted at this.

Ryan grinned and continued, "But Mrs Collins is well over the top. No mention of the drugs or the lifestyle he'd been living in Glastonbury."

"No, I found that interesting," Lauren said, parking on the seafront. The infamous muddy sand of the Bristol Channel matched the moody colour of the sky. The sea at low tide a myth, vanished into the distance. "There're no photos of the twins from the last two years of Sonny's life. We know he had tattoos, piercings, took drugs and drank enough for the pathologist to find the evidence of liver damage, but mummy didn't want to know."

"Which makes us think...?" Ryan asked as they left the car.

"Bugger, it's cold," Lauren hissed. She limped and stumbled into the bonnet of the car. "Fuck."

"I'll get the fish and chips. You wait in the car, Guv," Ryan offered.

Lauren wanted to tell him to go to hell, but her leg had other plans. "Fine. Think about this, though, if Sonny and Eliza are that close, is she into his lifestyle as well?"

Ryan grinned again. He liked to smile, and it made him boyishly handsome, Lauren thought.

"We need to find the sister," he said.

"We need to find the sister," Lauren agreed. She watched him dash off across the road and wondered if she'd ever be able to run again. Just climbing the stairs to her flat often made her want to scream after a day in the office sitting in that bloody chair.

She sank back into the car, relieved to be out of the hard wind. It would be sweeping over Sedgemoor, smacking into Glastonbury on its way. Her flat would be cold when she got home, and dark. Maybe she'd head straight to Dale's place.

"Maybe not," she muttered, forcing herself to concentrate on Sonny Collins.

The autopsy had revealed long-term drug abuse. When the case had been opened and Sonny's bedsit searched, they found evidence of 'legal' highs imported from China and more local substances in the form of genetically enhanced cannabis. The young man's stomach contents interested her most. He'd had nothing to eat for several days, the bowel as clean as it could be under the circumstances, but for a broth of mushrooms and peyote—a lot of peyote. She knew from research that the mescaline in the cactus was the psychoactive, but you needed to consume ten to twenty grams for it to work. However, if the little buttons of cactus were potent, then twenty grams of the cactus might well send you over the edge.

The plant came from desert areas in Mexico and Texas, grew slowly, and didn't suit the British climate. Mescaline could be manufactured, but certain types of spiritual questers sought the 'organic' experience. The use of the actual plant made her antenna twitch. Someone in Glastonbury had access to a drug that was expensive, rare, and sought after. She'd talk to Dale. He and Milly had easier access to the alternative scene than she did as police. The connection did not thrill her DCI, but he knew a useful resource when he saw one, and Dale was useful.

Ryan arrived, wrapped in the amazing smell of fish, chips, vinegar, and salt. Lauren's stomach growled like a tiger.

Silence filled the car as the windows steamed up and they ate.

Ryan put down his fish long enough to say, "What Mrs Collins said about the diamond bracelet was interesting."

Lauren grunted, her mouth full of greasy, wonderful chips. When she swallowed, she said, "He probably sold it. You saw the photos of the bedsit. He owned nothing of value."

"Do we find the sister?" Ryan asked.

She nodded. "I think that's the best place to start, but we want to talk to Sergeant Webber about the peyote. He has more experience than the two of us combined. He'll know which dealers would move that stuff around."

"Won't the original investigation have covered that?"

"Blackburn ran the original investigation."

Ryan grunted. "Oh. Right."

Blackburn, now retired, had hated working the Glastonbury patch. He had no patience with those who'd fallen under its spell, then fallen down the well. Lauren had read several files of the cold cases he'd managed, and she found holes in all of them. Leads not followed up, findings ignored. Sonny Collins' case was one of Blackburn's last. Her job was to find new leads, and send them up the chain of command to see if they had enough new lines of enquiry to warrant reopening the case. So far, all her hard work had hit a wall. She wanted this one to be different. Something about that young man, left to die naked and alone on the seafront, touched her heart.

Her phone rang.

"Shit," she muttered, sucking grease off her fingers as she tried to fish the phone out of her coat pocket.

Ryan handed her a couple of paper napkins he'd swiped. Forever thoughtful.

"It's the station," she muttered, using her little finger to open the call. The screen had a nice smear over the surface. She hit the speaker. "Kennedy here."

"Ah, Lauren, good. We need you back in Glasto," said the rough cider and tobacco stained voice of Sergeant Webber. "I've a live one for you. By which I mean a fresh corpse."

~ *Chapter 4* ~

DALE'S PHONE RANG, CUTTING THROUGH his concentration as he was making his initial report for Wolski. He glanced at it and saw *Lauren* on the screen. Despite their problems, his stomach did a small flip, a Pavlovian response to the contact.

Milly glanced up from her computer.

"Lauren," he said.

His assistant tried to hide her smirk and failed.

Dale took the call. "Lauren, 'sup?"

"Can you meet me in Middlezoy?" she said.

He frowned, hearing her tension. "Hello, Dale. How are you today? I don't suppose you—"

"Cut the crap, Valentine. You know you'll say yes. Can you meet me in Middlezoy? I've a dead body and I need another experienced eye."

"I thought you were benched?" The need to find Joanna pressed inside him, like a severe bruise. He trusted his instincts, and they were yelling big and loud that this American wasn't a stray. She was in trouble.

"We're short staffed. I'm the only DI in the area. They've a big job in Bristol. The major crimes team are up there. It's people smuggling."

Dale rubbed his head. "Bloody hell, Lauren… I've a case here that needs my total dedication. A missing woman with a fake passport. Does that sound important?"

She sighed. "What? Yes. I suppose so. I tell you what, I'll tell the corpse and my team they can all wait for you. Get down here. I'll drop you a pin."

Her sarcasm and assumptions both hurt. When their relationship began, he'd been a slave to her master, and she often seemed to forget that had changed. Still, it didn't prevent the next words coming out of his mouth. "Sure." He glanced at Milly, who watched him with cat-like intensity in her green eyes. "Milly's coming. She's never worked an active murder scene before."

Lauren had already hung up. Seconds later, his phone pinged with a location. He bit back his resentment. "We're heading to a place called Middlezoy?"

"That's the Bridgwater road." Milly rose and grabbed her coat. "What's there?"

"Dead body," Dale said. "Lauren wants me to look with my ex-copper eyes on the scene. I worked on a few murders in The Met as a detective sergeant. She's only really dealt with undercover work."

They left the office and climbed back into the Audi.

"She's had the training, though, right?" Milly asked as she buckled her seatbelt.

"Of course."

"You don't like seeing dead people."

"No," Dale said, his voice tight. "However, I enjoy missing the evidence even less. Lauren's good. She ran Brook's murder very well, but…"

"She wants a second opinion on something?"

"I guess so," Dale said, following his satnav out of Glastonbury.

"What about Joanna?"

Dale paused for a moment and stared out of the windscreen. "We keep her as the priority. I've a bad feeling about her disappearance and the more we find out, the worse it's getting."

They headed towards Street, then out over the flatlands towards the small village of Greylake. It only existed because of a handful of cottages and a large farm rose slightly from the surrounding fields, clustered around the main roads from Taunton and Bridgwater. This area always gave Dale a creepy feeling. The road itself was long and straight, enabling the Audi to push the speed limit with ease, but the fast approaching winter and low wet fields made the hidden isolation of Sedgemoor and the Levels all too real. It felt like history lay in the fine mists, rather than buried in the damp peaty soil. He half-expected Monmouth's men to come marching over the narrow road as he took the turning in the dimming light of the coming rain clouds that raced towards Middlezoy.

"That's an Anglo-Saxon name, I guess," he said in an effort to rid himself of the silly notion.

"Yep, *Middle Stream Island*, or something. It belonged to Glastonbury Abbey."

Dale concentrated. The lane had a white line down the middle in places, but wasn't really wide enough for two vehicles to pass without care. On either side of the lane, more water-filled ditches separated farmland and tarmac. For him, it didn't feel safe enough, so he slowed. The dead body wasn't going anywhere.

Milly smirked.

"What?" he asked.

"If you didn't rely on satnav, you'd have found it faster going on towards Othery, then cutting back up the main road."

He took a turning onto Moor Road. "Why didn't you say?"

She shrugged. "I never get to go this way. It's more interesting."

"Thanks, Milly."

"You're welcome." She grinned at him.

"This was a lot easier before we were friends," he grumbled.

"Liar," she said.

He came to another junction, and the village lay just on the other side of the main road that he recognised. "Bloody hell," he said in exasperation.

"At least we're at the right end of the village for the address she gave us." Milly pointed ahead. Flashing blue lights made the damp, late afternoon air vivid with shocking reality. A small housing estate of red brick bungalows lay to the right, and Dale took the turning, pulling the Audi up behind an ambulance.

They left the car and headed into the small cul-de-sac. At the top of a rise police tape hung, limp and soggy with the mizzle, around a tiny home. In the back of a police car sat an old man huddled into a blanket. A paramedic knelt on the wet tarmac, talking gently. The man's hair held flashes of deep purple and vibrant blue, and Dale noticed he hugged a large crochet cushion to his chest. Dale guessed he'd found the body.

He walked up to a young female constable guarding the tape. "PC Pippa Allison, it's good to see you again, despite the circumstances." He recognised her from the summer's drama.

"Mr Valentine, Ms Wolfe, it's nice to see you as well. Detective Inspector Kennedy is expecting you."

"You on sign-in duty?" he asked.

"Yep."

"Poor you, stuck out here." He took the offered pen and signed next to the name she'd already written.

Allison shook her head. "I'd rather be with the living, thanks very much." She glanced at Milly. "If it gets too much, Milly, just come join me."

Dale glanced at his assistant. She already looked pale. "Do you want to wait here?" he asked. "We're private detectives. We're not likely to find dead bodies on a regular basis."

Milly glanced at the door to the bungalow. "It's just all a bit…"

Dale knew exactly what she meant. "Real," he finished softly.

She nodded, and he saw the threat of tears.

"Okay, stay here. Note what's happening around you so you're familiar with the police procedure for a crime scene."

"Sorry."

Dale placed a hand on her shoulder. It looked huge next to her neck. "Don't be. I didn't hire you because you're an emotionless block of ice. Rather, it was the opposite." He'd needed that contrast to help bring him back into the world.

She nodded, and Dale left her in Allison's tender care. His long legs ate up the short driveway and he took the forensic suit, gloves and booties offered by the next police officer at the door.

"Sorry, sir, we don't have any XXXL left," said the man.

Dale grunted, unsurprised. As always, his long, thick limbs made the suit three sizes too small, and his boots almost split the blue foot covers. He felt thirteen years old again, his school blazer shrinking to his elbows before his mother replaced it. She only did it because of the school's concern about his care.

He climbed into the disposable suit and covered his head with the hood. The officer who'd arrested him back in the summer stood inside the doorway. He glared at Dale.

"Nice to see you as well, Constable Lewis," Dale said, with a slight twist on the 'con' syllable. No kid on the estates of Peckham missed an opportunity to test out this slang.

Dale grinned as colour rose in Lewis' face.

"I'm in here." Lauren's call interrupted the testosterone-fuelled competition.

Dale stepped on the forensic metal plates covering a hideously patterned carpet. Lauren crouched over a young woman's body, too still for anything but death to have claimed her.

He saw a tangle of hair the colour of a field mouse, a creature he'd become familiar with since moving his office into the old barn. The hair had been dreadlocked, but not with the skill of a Rastafarian hairdresser. This looked more matted than carefully oiled and twisted. Dale had tried it once as a youngster, his Italian skin and dark curls making him desperate to fit in with his best friend Ringo, but it took a lot of patience and work. Keeping the soft, black locks very short suited his ego far more.

"Dale?" Lauren tapped on his bent knee.

"Sorry." He realised he'd been focusing on the hair and letting his mind ramble to keep him away from the obvious. The dead eyes, the blue lips, the slack mouth stained by foam and dribble. Death tears made the black mascara run towards her ears.

A flash of light arced through the room, and he blinked. The forensic photographer snapped pictures of the mantelpiece.

"What we got?" He'd knelt beside Lauren, but hadn't really noticed her yet.

She sat, her healing leg kicked out awkwardly to the side. "Well, it looks like an OD, but something doesn't feel right. An overdose for this victim feels highly unlikely."

"Explain," he ordered, pushing all thoughts away.

It had been a long time since he'd had to assess a crime scene like this one, but his training rose from the labyrinth of his mind and guided his thoughts.

The girl lay on her back, her right arm flung out as if she'd rolled over in a deep sleep. In that arm, a needle hung, the plunger depressed. Dale frowned. No other track marks. He twisted to look at the other arm, also no track marks. The feet had heavy black boots on them, expensive ones, so he couldn't tell if the girl injected further down. Christ, she was a tiny young woman. A sprite in big boots with big hair. The cloudy eyes might once have been a light brown, maybe hazel. Her jewellery looked expensive. At least for the traveller-hippy vibe she wanted. Her clothing was intact, no torn tights, so no sexual interference, at least nothing obvious. Some killers masturbated over their victims or used the oral option.

He shuddered at the dark turn of his thoughts.

No bruising to the mouth.

He glanced around and saw the works the girl had used to cook her drug of choice. However, he also saw two wine glasses on the table. Both with lipstick on the rim.

Lauren said, "We received a call at fifteen-hundred hours from the neighbour. He usually sees Adele leaving for college in the morning, and returning in the afternoon. Wednesday is her half-day, so he was expecting her around two. He thought he'd missed her leaving in the morning, despite waiting at the window for their daily exchange of a wave. He struggles to walk so doesn't go far and since Adele moved in a year ago, she's been helping him with shopping. They've become quite close." She finished softly, "He's devastated. Talking about having to go into a home now she's not here to help." She finished quietly, "Adele dyed his hair last week. He thinks it's 'groovy'."

Dale's heart ached for the old man. How terrible must it be to connect with a young person, only to lose them like this? "We can rule him out then."

"He got over here and saw her fallen body on the carpet. Tried to raise her by knocking on the window, which is all he can manage, then called us."

"So, no family to report her missing? She's been dead longer than a few hours." Dale glanced at Lauren.

"The pathologist is around somewhere. She said she thinks it's been at least twelve hours, maybe a full day. When I asked the neighbour about it, he said she'd been away with a friend for the weekend. The college had half-term, so they went down to Devon for some surfing. She returned, visited with him yesterday, said she was going to college today. She inherited this tiny ex-council bungalow from her grandmother. It's a one bedroom place."

"He didn't see anyone arriving last night?" Dale pointed to the glasses. The rest of the room was clean and tidy. No ciggie butts overflowing a foil ashtray. No empty cans of beer or cheap cider. No take-aways half-eaten. No stench. This was not the home of a typical substance misuser. The small packet of heroin, the spoon and lighter on the table looked out of place, almost an embarrassed mess invading a tidy home.

Lauren shook her head.

"Then there's this," she said, and pointed. "I wanted you to see it in place."

Dale shuffled back to Lauren's side. The room wasn't large enough for the amount of people it had to occupy while trying to preserve the scene.

"You need to move some of these people out." He made a shooing gesture.

"What? Like giants who take up too much space?" Lauren laughed. "I think they'd rather see you leave."

Dale glanced around at her colleagues. She was right, many other technicians and police officers cast him baleful looks. He ignored them, but it stung. His place, ex-Job, ex-con, now a private investigator, made many of the officers unhappy with his status as consultant. The younger members of the team took their lead from Lauren, or their grumpy sergeant, and it meant a division. One he'd caused. One that wouldn't make Lauren's job any easier.

"I don't think it's my size that bothers them," he murmured.

She ignored him and pointed at the body.

Dale drew his head back in surprise, then leaned further over the small corpse. "What the fuck?"

In the hollow of the girl's throat lay a single jewel. It picked up the light and spat it out like small darts.

"It's a diamond, right?" Lauren almost whispered.

Dale nodded. "It's a black diamond. That means it has many inclusions in the gemstone, so they treat it and turn it black, or smoky grey. Sometimes they're natural. It's not an area I know a great deal about. In fact, that just about sums it up."

"You know more than anyone else on the team."

He grunted. His paternal grandfather had dealt in antiques and jewellery, teaching the young Dale as much as possible during the periods when his grandparents became his guardians.

"It has no setting, like a chain or a ring." He examined the girl's jewellery more closely. "There's no sign this is the kind of gem she'd choose. Her stuff is all contemporary gothic silver. She's into lumps of crystal, not finely cut gems like this." He took out a pen from his jacket pocket. "See, here," he carefully nudged the gem up a little, "it's delicate, a gem you'd find in a ring or bracelet, maybe a necklace made of stones."

"So it's expensive?"

He sat back and considered. "That depends on the carats, obviously, the quality of the inclusions, the age of the cut. To me it looks old, but you need an expert—"

"So it's an antique?" she interrupted.

"Maybe. Out of its setting, it's going to be worth less than it would be in its original state. You also need to find out if it's factory or natural."

Lauren glanced up at a technician. "Okay, we're ready to move. Keep an eye out for anything that could be connected to the gem in her throat. I want those photos emailed to me as soon as possible."

Dale hid his smile. She controlled the scene effortlessly, giving orders to her staff without a moment's hesitation. He rose and left the room, glancing into the kitchen—tidy and clean—then the small bedroom. A bag lay half unpacked, a washing basket full of clothes but not overflowing, and a neatly made bed. No sign of drug use. None of the usual drug paraphernalia associated with an addict was littered around the place. No sign of forced entry. New locks, though. Lauren wouldn't have missed that, so he didn't comment.

He left the house and found Lauren on the lawn.

Climbing out of the forensic suit, he said, "This isn't an overdose. Unless her bank account shows you otherwise."

"I agree."

"Make sure they test those glasses. My money's on a date-rape drug being used, then the heroin going into her arm once she's unconscious. Or something similar."

"So someone she knew and trusted enough to share a drink with?"

"Yep."

He watched Milly, who was speaking with DC Matthews, and the conversation looked personal, not professional. Milly's shoulders were rounded, and Ryan seemed to dominate. It made Dale itch to interfere.

"Guess we'll need to start on her boyfriends," Lauren sighed. "I bloody hate domestics. They're always so depressing."

"Don't be too sure it's a man," Dale said, forcing himself to concentrate on the crime scene. "She was poisoned and…"

"Women prefer poison over violence."

He nodded. "Keep an open mind on this one, Lauren. I'll be on the end of the phone if you need to chat anything through. I've a pressing case. It's a misper and I'm worried. I can't save this girl, but there's another out there somewhere, and I think she's in trouble. Come for dinner if you want."

"The missing American? Did you say something about a fake passport?"

Dale nodded. "Yeah. I know you guys have been up to her place to check it over, so it would be good to see the file. No one thought to check under the bed."

"We don't toss a house while doing a welfare check, Dale. If she had a passport hidden, we'd not have found it, but I'll send over the file. As for dinner? Maybe it would be good to have some company for a change." A call came from the house and Lauren left to deal with a problem.

Dale returned to the Audi, considering Lauren's words. Joanna's house had clearly been searched, but not well, so who did it? And why? All of

Joanna's expensive jewellery remained. Someone else wanted Joanna found, that's what it meant.

"Your boss wants you." He approached Ryan and Milly.

The young man turned, and for a moment Dale saw something in that usually friendly face that he really didn't like. A dark possession lay behind those blue eyes and fluffy blond hair.

He looked at Milly over the roof of the Audi. "Come on, we're leaving."

Wordlessly, Milly climbed into the car. Dale turned them around and left Middlezoy, heading back to Glastonbury on the easier road.

"Want to talk about it?" he asked into the silence.

"No."

"Fair enough. Wanna know more about the crime scene?"

"Yep."

"Okay. A pleasant home. Clean and tidy throughout. Young woman, tiny little fairy thing. Good neighbour. Found with a needle in her arm and heroin in the living room, but not anywhere else in the house. Odd thing. A black diamond lay in the hollow of her throat. No necklace, just the diamond."

Milly glanced up from her phone. "Throat chakra."

Dale took his eyes off the road to stare at her. "A what?"

"You've been in Glasto long enough. You know what the chakras are."

"Only in the vaguest sense."

"Well, the throat chakra is about the voice, creativity, and you must be clear of guilt for it to be healthy. I'd have to look it up to tell you more."

"I think we can leave that to Lauren." Her depth of knowledge amused him.

"So, we in on the case or not?"

Dale slowed further to avoid the speed camera's loving attentions. "No, I don't think so. Joanna remains my priority. They'll need to trawl through the victim's past looking for a potential crime of passion, or a pissed-off family member. It's unlikely to be a stranger murder, so someone knows something."

Milly nodded. "Good, because I took a call from the business line while you were in the bungalow."

"Oh? New client?"

"Several, it seems. We've been hired to find a man who is digging holes on the Levels around East Lyng and Athelney."

"That's Burrow Mump way, right?" Dale called up his internal map of the area, trying to locate the ancient names in his head.

"It is. I'll be meeting with several people in the pub, The King Alfred, in a couple of days. I thought I might handle this one on my own. I know Joanna is our priority, but the local farming community is also important."

Dale didn't see any reason Milly couldn't handle it, so he agreed. Joanna's disappearance needed a plan, and one had formed in his head. It didn't involve Milly so, she could stretch her skills alone for a change.

~ *Chapter 5* ~

LAUREN'S DESK PHONE RANG. SHE picked it up without paying much attention to the notification. Before she uttered a word, a deep rumble snarled in her ear, "DI Kennedy, can you come into my office, please?"

She focused on the call. No one in the station had informed her the DCI had arrived from Bristol. "Of course, sir. I'll be with you in a minute." Staring at the now silent phone, her first thought was: *What have I done now?*

Trying to push the negativity away as a paranoid rambling, she rose from the desk and eyed her stick. Glaring at her leg, she said, "If you let me down, I'll fucking hack you off myself."

Ryan looked up from his work. "Guv?"

"Not you, DC Matthews. You're safe. The DCI is here and wants a word."

The young officer's eyes widened. "Is he going to take our case away?"

"I have no doubt he's going to try," Lauren said. "I'm not going to let him."

She walked, despite wanting to limp, down the short hallway to another office. As the ranking officer on duty most often in the small station, she had the largest office, which she shared with Ryan. When the DCI came to visit, he had a private office, but it had about as much room as a coffin.

The door stood open and the moment she filled it, he looked up. Detective Chief Inspector Whitfield dominated any room he occupied while at work. His intensity almost deprived her of breath every time she'd received a one-on-one interview with him. His hair resembled rusty wire wool, more iron grey these days than red, but just as tough and it formed odd clumps. With a flat face and wide-spaced eyes of deep chestnut, he kinda looked like a pug dog mixed with a wire-haired terrier. Not that any of his colleagues would say it to his face. Or even whisper it in the canteen, just in case it leaked back to him. Not a man to suffer fools in his team. What he lacked in height, he made up for in breadth, with wide shoulders, powerful arms and legs, and barrel chest. He ran marathons for fun.

"DI Kennedy, sit. I want an update on the dead girl, and I want a plan for the next stage of the investigation. Your lack of experience in this area troubles me. Convince me that you are the right person for the job."

Lauren sat. "Of course, sir." She'd mulled over several options while she'd driven back to the station, but hadn't expected Whitfield to demand a coherent set of thoughts.

She explained the crime scene and combined her thoughts with Dale's ideas about how Adele Smith died. Whitfield watched, listened, and then told her what she would actually do with her team and the case.

LATER THAT NIGHT, LAUREN SAT at Dale's kitchen table while he prepared something clever with the remains of a chicken. She felt wrung out. The morning's episode with the distressed mother in Weston-super-Mare, then being called in to supervise the discovery of Adele Smith's death, and her row with the DCI drained her resources. Coming up the hill to Dale's place felt like a refuge, especially as he wanted to feed her.

"Wine not to your liking?" He nodded at her untouched glass.

Lauren looked up and blinked. She realised she'd been slumped in the chair, twirling the glass by the stem and watching the light play on the pale liquid inside.

"Sorry. Long day."

"They take you off the case?" He stirred something that hissed and spat in his big frying pan. The smells were amazing, and her stomach rumbled. The fish and chips from earlier had long since worn off.

"He wanted to. Said I wasn't fit enough with the leg. Said I needed more experience after almost being shot on my last murder inquiry. That, as a new detective inspector, he'd like me to have closer oversight while I learn the ropes. All fair arguments and DCI Whitfield is a good bloke. I like him."

"But?" Dale dished up and her mouth watered.

"But we're short staffed and I have enough years and experience with the London Met to run a team. We might be small in Street, but I'm sure we have the skills to do a good job."

Dale smiled as he brought over two bowls. "That's good. You put it down to the skills of your team. That's what he needed to hear. You'll call in resources from Taunton and Minehead?"

"Of course. I can't imagine I'll need them. It's a small area. How's your misper?"

Dale sat opposite, and she noticed how his chest moved under the thin fabric of his expensive looking jumper. "Chicken risotto. I'm trying a new recipe. See what you think."

Lauren took a forkful and groaned. "God, I love you."

The words hung over the table as ephemeral as the light from a firework.

She felt her cheeks warm. "I meant the food."

Dale smiled, and she saw the sadness in his dark eyes. "I know." He took a breath. "As for my misper, Joanna Wolski is proving elusive. She's a trust-fund hippy, or that's how Milly describes her. Missing for three weeks, but showing signs of depression before that. Broke up with her boyfriend. He's in the States, so that's a dead end. No credit card use or movement on her bank account. Her father controls both. No unexpectedly large withdrawals in the days before we think she vanished. The only thing we found? An excess of books and leaflets about a meeting, almost a year ago, to do with Guru Raj, whatever the hell he is. A fake Canadian passport and a whole lot of cash someone missed, when they tossed the place. I'm worried about her, Lauren. There was obvious tension in her life before she vanished, and she had a plan to run. However, it obviously didn't work out the way she wanted. I'm not sure her father, who is very wealthy and powerful in his home city, is being honest about their relationship. There's something off about the way he talked me through her life. He knows too much about her. No grown woman wants her father to know everything, and he seems to think it's his right to have that level of detail."

Lauren frowned and asked around a mouthful of rice and chicken, "What does that mean?"

Dale moved his food around. "When I called him this afternoon, meaning morning in Georgia, he wanted all the photos Milly and I took of the house. Even the bathroom and bedroom."

"Could he have people in the States working on the case?"

Dale's eyebrows rose. "I hadn't thought of that. Maybe."

"What else? Something has you all tangled up. You're not eating, and you love risotto."

"You know when you deal with a case of coercive control, it's not about the actions or words, it's about the..."

"The way those actions and words come across. Like a creepy stalker saying, 'She left the curtains open. It's not my fault I was watching,' before said stalker kills the victim and runs off with their head."

Dale's mouth twitched in a smile. "Yeah. Like that. I'm getting a vibe from him. It's sinister."

Lauren chuckled. "I know you well enough to know you won't give up easily. You'll find her. We'll need to report the passport." She grunted. "More paperwork."

Their talk moved on to other things, and the evening slipped into the night with easy familiarity. Lauren considered Dale's offer of using the spare room rather than going back down the hill, but...

Something unnameable held her back. Even staying in his spare room moved things from friendship into something she wasn't sure either of them wanted, not really.

DALE WOKE EARLY THE NEXT morning with a slightly buzzy head. He'd finished the bottle of wine after Lauren had left, while pondering his future. He'd loved her once. Passionately. Now, though, he wasn't sure. They'd both changed since Ringo's death and despite trying, he still held her responsible for her part in the tragic death of his best friend.

Rising, he drank a large glass of water, dressed in running gear, and headed for the Tor. He needed to be on his game today. He had an American to find. With a headlamp on, not something he'd ever needed in London, he made it safely to the top of the Tor to watch the sun rise.

"That you, Valentine?" came a voice from Saint Michael's tower.

"Jimmy?" Dale sucked in a sharp breath, hoping his assumption was correct. Occasionally, he worried his past might wait for him up here and suck him down into the odd hill to face his demons.

"Get that bloody light out me face," grumbled the other man.

"What the hell are you doing up here?" Dale walked over to the tower.

Jimmy sat on one of the two benches built into the rough walls. "It's being off the booze, mate. I don't sleep much. Doc says that'll change. They don't want me on tablets if they can help it. Encourages addiction."

"They're right, Jimmy," Dale said. The big man looked very different to the version who'd tried twice to knock Dale on his arse, the second time he'd sort of managed it.

"Yeah. Still, makes it difficult, though." His thick, Somerset accent almost blurred the words together.

Dale watched Jimmy's face. He'd lost weight without the endless supply of cider going into his system. Dale had found Jimmy walking all over the Levels, following footpaths to unknown destinations, just to keep busy. To keep moving. From the angry, despairing man of the summer, Jimmy had become a sad, quiet man, taken to deep introspection on subjects he didn't always know how to untangle. Dale had talked to him several times and Jimmy seemed pleased to have the company.

The man adored Milly. She'd held his hand after Jimmy tried to hang himself in the abbey grounds, while they'd waited for the paramedics to arrive.

"So, what brings you to the Tor?" Dale asked.

Jimmy chuckled. "Thought I'd try talking to the old gods. Tell them me troubles for a change."

Dale laughed. "Well, if they answer you, let me know, I could do with some help myself."

In the grey light of dawn, Dale saw Jimmy frown. "What you need help with?"

"Troublesome case. A missing Yank. Well, not a Yank, more a Southern Belle, I guess."

"Hippy chick?" Jimmy's question surprised Dale.

"How'd you know?"

He shrugged. "I've lived here a long time, mate. I knows the type. You got a picture? Maybe I seen her at some point."

"Yeah, sure," Dale said, taking his phone out of his running jacket and bringing up a picture of Joanna. Jimmy had lived most days on the streets of Glastonbury, begging and drinking. He'd seen many people.

Jimmy studied the picture. "Yep. I've seen her."

"Really?" Dale asked.

"Yep. She's one of the regulars down at the community centre and she always gave me a quid in me tin when I was beggin'. She's a good girl. Nice. Stopped for a chat most times."

Dale realised he'd dropped a ball the day before. Adele Smith's murder had prevented him from visiting the community centre. "When was the last time you saw her?"

Jimmy puffed out a breath. "Must have been after they found Brook."

Dale had discovered Jimmy had two lives now. One before Brook's death, and one after. Jimmy had been in love with Brook since they'd been at school. Brook, returning to Glastonbury, his subsequent murder and the discovery of the paedophile, had tipped Jimmy over the edge and shoved him into the abyss. Now, Jimmy had social services taking care of him and gradually his life was changing. He even smelt clean.

The big man pondered for a while and said, "I seen her come out of the health food shop. She crossed over the road to give me some money, bless her, and I asked her if she was alright." He focused on Dale rather than the memory. "She seemed surprised by that. As if no one asked her it before, while meaning it—you know?"

Dale nodded. "I know. Can you pin it down for me a bit more? Tell me what she was wearing?"

Jimmy laughed. "Mate, that's askin' a lot."

"I know." Dawn light slithered over the horizon.

The other man thought hard for a few moments, screwing his face up. "Summer frock. One of them crochet shawl things. Sandals. Hair down. It was a cool day for summer, and she looked cold. I think it was during the school holidays because there seemed to be grockles and bloody kids everywhere."

"So, August?" Dale suggested.

Jimmy shook his head. "No, later. Must have been the beginning of September. That any help?"

Dale nodded. "It is actually. I'm struggling to find the people who knew her best. You are currently the last known sighting."

"The police aren't going to—" The flash of panic was clear.

"No, Jimmy. The police aren't interested in her disappearance. Her father has hired me. He's worried about her."

Jimmy grunted. Dale knew from speaking to Neil, Jimmy's only friend for a long time, that the compassion of a father was an alien concept to the broken man. Just as it was for Dale.

"You want me to ask around?" the rough voice asked in the lightening gloom.

Dale glanced at him in surprise. "Really?"

Jimmy's eyes, now a soft grey since giving up the booze and recovering some of his health, dropped to the ground. "She was always kind to me, no matter how pissed I got, I reckon she deserves some help."

"Okay," Dale agreed. "You still have your phone? I'll send you the photo I have of her." Dale transferred the image, and the pair sat out of the wind, watching the sun lift over the distant hills. Today it seemed reluctant.

Jimmy said in a hushed voice, "All those years I've wasted when I could 'ave been up here watchin' this magic every damned day."

"I spent four years in a prison cell, mate. I know exactly what you mean," Dale murmured.

He felt Jimmy's eyes on him. "Really?"

"Yep." The sudden darkness of those days rumbled over Dale like an earthquake, ready to shake his new life to its foundations—if he gave the memories the chance. He forced them away, and the world settled as the sun made more of an effort. Just like the two men watching it.

"Fair enough." Jimmy's attention returned to the free miracle of another dawn.

The sun's rays tore through distant clouds and rose to pierce the last of the night with golden splendour at last. The heavenly battle cast the wide valley in shades of green so vivid after the rainfall, it almost hurt the imagination. Fine mists wreathed over the lowest of the land and thick grey streaks marred many of the fields where the rhynes and rivers had cast their banks aside in wild abandonment of the rules. The trees and hedges made the whole look stitched together in a medley of man's attempt to control nature.

Jimmy said, "There'll be more flooding this winter and it'll be bad."

"You know this?" Dale asked.

"Farmer's son. Or I was until the old man moved us into the town 'cos he lost the farm. I always wanted some land of me own one day, but…" Jimmy shrugged his large shoulders.

Dale watched him twist his hands together. As a victim of a paedophile, Jimmy lost a lot of his life to the misery of his memories. Dale placed a gentle hand on the big man's back in solidarity.

"Why don't we walk down the Tor together?" Dale suggested.

"I've taken up enough of your time," Jimmy said.

"Come on. It'll be busy up here soon and you have a job to do. You find me information about Joanna, and I'll pay you off the books."

Jimmy's face lit up. "I'll be a detective?"

Dale laughed. "Let's say you'll be a confidential informant for the moment."

"Hey, it's a job. I'll take it."

As they walked down the big hill, Dale said, "You heard of Guru Raj?"

Jimmy snorted. "Is he another of those dickheads who'll offer you salvation and a way to heaven on Earth if you part with enough cash?"

Dale laughed. "Yeah, seems like it."

"Fucking con artists. I don't remember him specifically, but you should ask in the community centre up from Milly's place. They have people in there who knows all sorts of old bollocks."

Dale couldn't help chuckling. "Not a fan of alternative faiths then, Jimmy?"

"No. Not made up ones like that old bollocks," came the simple reply. "They promise too much and deliver nothin' good in return. You can talk to the old gods if you want, or the new ones for that matter, but flogging it for cash? That pisses me off. If that poor lass, Joanna, was tangled up with 'em, then she needs findin', Valentine."

For a moment, Dale was taken aback. "Okay, then we'll find her if we can, but mispers that don't want to be found rarely are, Jimmy."

Jimmy stopped at the bottom of the hill, his hand on the kissing gate. "She's a good person. She needs findin'."

"Alright, Jimmy. Then we'll work hard to do it."

Jimmy grunted and walked through the gate. Dale followed but didn't catch him up as the other man strode away with his mission clearly on his mind.

Dale walked home, rather than running, his muscles cold after his sit down with Jimmy. Once there, he showered, changed and ate his breakfast standing up watching his bird table out of the window. Jimmy was right, which was a startling revelation. Joanna deserved to be found. A woman like that doesn't just disappear for no reason, and if she vanishes this thoroughly, the reason isn't good. Dale knew perfectly well he'd always had a 'white knight' complex, hence his unending guilt about his shitty past. And since leaving prison, it had just grown stronger. He wanted Joanna to have left Glastonbury for pastures new and she'd be back in a few weeks full of some new mystic's teachings in her head. However, the increasing pressure of his instincts told him another story.

He needed to up his game for Joanna Wolski's benefit.

~ *Chapter 6* ~

DALE SAT IN THE OFFICE, pondering the best way to look for the missing woman, when Milly arrived ten minutes early.

"Morning, Guv," she said.

He glanced up at her. For the last few months, Milly had kept her hair under control and her clothing had become more conservative. This morning she turned up with her hair in full red-cascade mode, and she wore loose fitting patchwork trousers with a long shirt in deep blue.

"Morning," he answered with a brief hesitation in his voice. "Dare I ask what's put some pep in your step?"

She grinned at him. "Ryan came to his senses and ended things between us, so Sully is coming with me to the King's Arms in Burrowbridge. He has a driver's licence so he can sit next to me while I take mum's car."

"Right." The word drew out like a worm being pulled from the dirt by a blackbird. "Are you okay? Is Ryan okay?" Dale wondered if this would affect their relationship with the local police and by how much.

Milly cocked her head. "I think he'll be okay. He's shocked right now, but…" She looked at Dale directly. "We're too different and it made him very stressed. I think he made a mistake in finding me attractive and some part of him knew it. Those insecure feelings made him angry with me and himself, it wasn't fair to continue the illusion."

"Fair enough. Okay. Well, it seems the day for it," Dale said. He described his meeting with Jimmy that morning. "We'll go talk to Wolfie first, then head to the community centre. They'll know something about this guru even if they don't remember Joanna."

"What if the guru is a dead end?" Milly asked.

Dale shrugged. "Then we hope Jimmy discovers something."

Milly's eyes widened. "That's a bit of a risk, isn't it?"

"It's not like we have many options right now. We do not know who her friends were in Glastonbury. That's my priority today."

"If she was into the healing side of Glastonbury, and had money, then it makes sense the people at the Chalice Well might remember her. All those books might well be bought locally, so we need to check the bookshops. Also, we haven't interviewed her neighbours yet."

"We need to find out who saw her last and what frame of mind she was in. From her phone records, her last call was to her father. That was..." he checked his computer calendar, "...October the twenty-second. Since then, nothing."

Milly said, "That's almost a month."

Dale rose from his desk and grabbed his coat. "Come on. Let's go pester your father, then visit the community centre."

They left the office and headed off on foot. Parking in Glastonbury, even on a blustery, and now soggy, November day, meant spending money Dale didn't want to part with, for the sake of a few extra minutes walking. In London he'd done more walking than driving, his regular haunts easier to reach on foot or by Tube and bus. The countryside made a car essential. If you couldn't afford a car, it limited your prospects horribly.

When they reached the café, they found it quiet, existing in the hiatus between the breakfast rush and lunch. Wolfie was cleaning down his beloved kitchen. Milly's mother, Daisy, said he loved his cooker more than he loved her. The way he coaxed the old machine into life every day, she might have a point.

"Milly-girl, what you doing down 'ere?" Wolfie asked. He currently sported a white goatee. His long white hair lay at the nape of his neck in a blue hairnet. "Dale, you want something to eat?"

Wolfie spent much of his time feeding the visitors to Glastonbury, but he loved to cook for his friends even more. Dale had become a friend. A strange sensation.

"I'm alright, Wolfie. Trying to keep this under control," Dale said, patting his almost flat stomach. Since discovering the Green Man café, it had become harder to keep his weight down.

"Well, if I'm not feeding you, what is it you want?"

Sully came in from the rear entrance, having cleared the tables that sat under an ivy and vine-covered trellis. His attention drifted from the kitchen and straight to Milly. Dale saw her smile and Sully's pale face, that always made Dale think of Tolkien's elves, flushed a cherubic pink. His tongue flicked out to fiddle with the lip piercing. Wolfie grinned and winked at Dale.

Milly tried for professional. She handed her father her phone. "Do you remember this woman at all?"

Wolfie took the phone and dug out an old pair of glasses, metal framed and round. They found purchase at the end of his long nose. "Yeah, I remember her. Nice kid. American. Tipped well."

"She ever come in with any of your regulars?" Dale asked.

Wolfie considered as Milly handed her phone to Sully, asking the same question. They began a different conversation, but Dale concentrated on Wolfie.

The older man said, "She'd often come in for a quiet hot chocolate on her own, or with her fella. He wasn't as nice. Struck me he was a bit of a bully, but she had control over the purse strings. Then she started coming in on her own most days. Sometimes she'd be part of a group. The artist groups, or writers."

"No special friends? No lunch with the girls?" Dale prompted.

"There were a couple of women, similar in age, she'd come in with sometimes."

"Regulars?"

"Not really. Don't think they lived in Glasto. Think they came in for events and talks. If I see them, I'll let you know."

Dale huffed in frustration. How could a young, attractive woman be so isolated? Why hadn't anyone locally raised the alarm? "Thanks. Can you remember the last time you saw her?"

Wolfie narrowed his eyes. "That'll be… before Samhain. Maybe a few days before. She seemed off. Jittery, unhappy. But then she'd been sliding down that hill for a while. Daisy sat with her during the summer a few times, had a chat," Wolfie said with sudden amazement at his memory. "Daisy's visiting her parents right now, but Milly can give her a ring and find out what was going on. I think the girl suffered from boyfriend trouble." He pondered a bit more. "But maybe there was also something about the dad. I remember Daisy saying something about the lass feeling pressured to go home, that maybe she was being watched?" Wolfie said this last bit with a question, as if Dale could tell him if his memory was playing tricks. The man's eyes suddenly grew sharp. "I tell you what, Dale, I was in here about three weeks ago and a couple of men came in."

"Okay, not unusual in itself, Wolfie. You do own a café."

Wolfie scowled at him. "Don't take the piss, you bugger. They were asking after the girl as well." He held up a hand as Dale opened his mouth. "I didn't tell them nuffin'. What would I say? Not like I knew whereabouts she lives. They were American too, and they were big. One was alright. He had black hair, skin a bit darker than yours and he wasn't as big as you. Soft-spoken. The other bloke." Wolfie pulled a face. "He gave me the creeps. Dead eyes. They were blue, though his hair was dyed black. Nasty looking bastard."

"And they were looking for her?" Dale wanted confirmation.

Wolfie nodded. "Cause I ain't seen her. Told them I didn't know her at all. That's why I forgot about it. I find it best if I'm lying to forget everything."

Dale decided not to pursue the last statement. It would lead to a conversation he'd never understand.

It meant the end of October really was the last sighting, later than Jimmy's. Also, the possibility Joanna felt watched, and someone was looking for her. Did these men work for Mr Wolski and after they failed to find Joanna, he'd called in Valentine Investigations? It seemed likely.

Dale wished he could scratch that vague itch in his chest and mind that told him something was wrong. "You're a star, Wolfie. Thanks, that really helps."

"She in trouble?"

Dale's mind raced, and he answered with an absent, "We hope not. She's not been seen or heard from for over three weeks. Since those blokes came looking."

Wolfie's eyes widened. "That's bad news. I'll keep an eye and ear on the masses. See if I can find something out."

Dale nodded his thanks. "Come on, Milly, you know the people at the community centre better than I do."

Milly peeled herself away from Sully, and Dale didn't miss the gentle hand squeeze they shared.

Back outside, Dale shivered in the wind and the pattering rain. It made the High Street look tawdry with its alternative shop fronts and narrow road. They hurried up the hill and down a small alley. A shallow set of four steps led up to the large double doors of the community centre, an old nineteen-thirties, fake Victorian church hall. Noticeboards covered the walls on either side of pale green doors with pieces of paper smattering them like multi-coloured measles. The posters held everything from missing person images to how the astral plane can realign your life. When he'd first started the business in Glastonbury, he'd used the missing person's posters to help him find business. They never seemed to grow any less. On the noticeboard inside, which represented businesses and events the community centre supported, he saw Milly's *Valentine Investigations* poster.

"We'll talk to Grace. She knows most about what's been happening here over the last year or so," Milly said over her shoulder as they walked up more wide, shallow steps.

At the top, Dale saw a very simple café area offering soft drinks, tea and coffee at knockdown prices. They sold confectionery and crisps. Nothing fresh, nothing fancy, just somewhere warm and safe if you needed it. Mostly, the place relied on volunteers. Grace, he knew, was one of the few members of staff to receive a salary, though he doubted it was much. Milly talked about her often, but Dale hadn't met her. When he'd first arrived in Glastonbury, and set up the business, she didn't work in the centre.

The moment he crested the steps, everyone stopped talking. The slight aroma of cannabis floated about. Being a big bloke with skin definitely not of

Anglo-Saxon heritage, he stood out in Glastonbury. It meant people noticed him and the community centre often sheltered the vulnerable.

It didn't matter how hard he tried, those people with big, police-type problems picked up on his previous occupation. You could put the copper in prison, but apparently, that didn't take the smell of pig away. As always, Dale found himself trapped between cultures.

Milly smiled and nodded at various people. Gradually, the hall relaxed, and the chatting resumed. Dale looked around. The high, narrow and gothic looking plain glass leaded windows allowed some dull sunshine inside, but mostly the large space was peeled open by the strip lights hanging from beams overhead. Not glamorous or pleasant to look at, but practical and cheap to run. The heating came from the groaning radiators, the type to be found in old schools, and only really useful if you happened to be within half a metre of the cast iron surface. The tables and chairs were cheap, probably Ikea or Amazon.

Dale trailed behind Milly as they headed towards the back wall of the centre and a fire door. She knocked, Dale heard a voice, and Milly pushed hard. The door swung in and they walked into an office. Boxes lined every spare piece of space. They were stacked high on several filing cabinets, leaned away from one wall that wasn't straight, and fought for space among the box files. A desk just about made itself known under a square window, and behind the desk sat a woman.

She looked small among the clutter of paperwork and, he realised, boxes of chocolates and drinks for the community centre's café. In an outsized cardigan of brown and green stripes, with glasses perched on her head rather than her nose, she blinked at them, trying to focus away from the computer screen. Those eyes were large and pale, almost outsized. She had a small nose, but her mouth stretched across her face, with full, pale lips that turned down naturally. Her hair, the colour of dark river sand and just as dull, lay in rat's tails over her shoulders, all thin and wispy. At first glance, people might not see this woman as a classic beauty.

"Milly?" her voice was light, but deeper than many women.

"Hello, Grace. Sorry to barge in like this. You haven't met my boss, Dale

Valentine?" Milly shuffled to one side and caught a box of crisps she'd knocked with an elbow.

"It's a pleasure, Grace. I've long admired the work you do here." He offered a small wave and smile from his location, not wanting to risk his bulk disturbing the fragile balance of the room's contents.

She blinked, as though having a long internal monologue with herself, then her entire face shifted as she smiled in return.

The wide mouth, with deep lines on either side, shifted. Light infused the round cheeks, and those enormous eyes became deep, soft green as the smile spread like a happy infection. Strong, straight teeth were on display. She became beautiful in a way Dale had never seen before. She couldn't be more than her mid-thirties and that smile brought a sparkling youth to her entire being.

"It's a pleasure to meet you at last, Dale." She rose and held a hand out over her cluttered desk. "I'm sorry for the mess."

She'd barely reach his shoulder.

He chuckled. "The mess means you're busy, right? That's not a bad thing for a publicly run organisation." He found himself fascinated by her speech patterns. Something in there wasn't quite native English. She had a soft lisp, barely noticeable, and a direct expression. It made him very aware of her presence in the tight confines of the room.

"Busy?" she said, shaking his hand vigorously. "I think that's the polite term for overwhelmed. Anyway, you've rescued me from the accounts for the month, so what can I do for you? I'd offer you a chair but..." She waved a helpless hand at the buried chairs in the corner.

Dale leaned against a filing cabinet, trying to reduce his bulk. "We're here about a man you might remember."

He glanced at Milly, who removed the leaflets they'd taken from Joanna's house. Guru Raj was smiling beatifically out at them in the perfect publicity shot.

Grace frowned and took the leaflet from Milly. Her mobile face narrowed as she flipped her glasses onto her nose to examine it carefully. "When was he in town?"

Dale gave a small half-smile, a flash of movement, a predator sensing his quarry. "We think about a year ago. According to that, he did some seminars."

Grace nodded. "I remember him. My predecessor booked them in."

"Do you have a list of attendees?" Milly asked.

Grace's eyes widened. "Yes, but…" She waved a hand at the box files. "Tish wasn't known for being the most organised person in the world. Also, she had a habit of booking people into the centre to do these types of seminars without checking them out first. I'd never have let this bloke use the community centre. He was dangerous." She tapped the leaflet with a finger, her mind obviously recalling more detail. "I remember meeting him." She shuddered.

Dale's attention became focused. "What do you mean, dangerous?"

Grace heaved in a breath. "Let's go grab a coffee out there and we can have a proper chat." She squirmed her way out from behind the desk in a well-practised crab movement, and they retreated to the café. Three mugs of coffee were ordered and three slices of flapjack. Grace groaned as she bit into her slice. "I could eat this forever."

Dale watched her devour the simple food and enjoyed her effortless pleasure. Shaking his head, as if clearing it from a spell, he said, "You wanted to talk about this guru?"

Grace nodded and licked those full lips. She paused, gathering her thoughts, and focused on Dale. "I met him the first week I started here. It was a bit of a bumpy transition because Tish didn't want to retire. She didn't make it easy for me to understand who was doing what in the community rooms."

"This guru being a case in point?" Dale asked.

Grace's fingers spread over the surface of the table, and she studied them. "Running a place like this is about balancing a wide variety of people's needs. Glastonbury has been a hub of faith for well over a thousand years. You can't discount that, and what it means to the pilgrims who come. Those people might not be looking to kiss the bones of some dead saint, but they are looking for something. We offer a safe space for Buddhists, Muslims, Pagans, and Christians—of any denomination. From witchcraft to UFOs, I'm happy to host a talk, a conference, a book signing, and lessons on how to talk to tree folk. What I'm not happy to do is to promote dangerous practices involving illegal substances that destroy minds."

Dale watched the colour rise in her soft, round cheeks. He softened his voice and asked, "That's what you think this guru was about?"

Grace met his gaze and held it. "Yes. He wanted to lead his version of a prayer meeting, then a select group would go on to the guided meditation session. He was charming, handsome, charismatic, plausible, and had obviously enchanted Tish."

"But not you?" Dale asked.

A small half-smile made that mouth lift again, and she stared directly into his jaded heart. "No. It takes a great deal to charm me, and it usually involves a person having to be honest."

Dale felt a pang of disappointment. She'd said 'person', did that mean she was gay? "So you thought he lied?"

"He lied. He charged a great deal of money for these private sessions and everyone he chose came from the beautiful people in the group who'd attended the expensive prayer meeting. I sat at the back, and it made me feel sick. I almost resigned on the spot. He'd concocted some mad religion based on a mix of Zen Buddhism, Toa, western Druidism, or maybe Norse, and added a touch of Hinduism for shits and giggles. Of course, he leaves the three major Abrahamic faiths alone. Too structured, too well known in Britain. It's a lot easier to create mystic bullshit if you pick bits from faiths and beliefs that have a much smaller following this side of the planet."

"He really pissed you off, didn't he?" Milly said with a chuckle.

Grace sat back and rolled her head, obviously trying to loosen the tension she felt. "If I'm honest, and I always try to be, a lot of these groups piss me off. Those that live the faith they preach, that's a different thing entirely, but these guys," she stabbed the leaflet with her finger and growled. "These guys are bad news."

Dale leaned forwards, turning the leaflet to face him. "We're trying to find an American woman who had the money to be in the private group and she was certainly pretty enough. After the session, her family started to worry about her declining mental health. Then, three weeks ago, she vanished. Her father wants her found and I have to say, the more I hear about this guy, the more worried I'm becoming."

"You think there's a link?" Grace asked. "It's been almost a year."

He frowned. "Call it a copper's instinct. There were a lot of his books in her house and her father noticed a change in her behaviour after the sessions she had with this guru. The boyfriend left her, and she's an American heiress, so this guru may have been charming her for a long time. We need to find her."

Grace nodded. "I'm happy enough to give you the information I can, but data protection makes it tricky. I'm not sure where I'd stand."

"What about your visitors' book?" Milly asked. "Would they all have signed in for the initial meeting?"

Grace grinned, and it made Dale smile because her face suddenly took on a feral aspect. "Oh, Milly, yes, that would be a good way to get around it. The log is public domain. Give me a second." She rose and hurried off.

He noticed her jeans were boot-cut, and she wore practical walking boots that must have done some miles to look that comfortable.

He felt eyes on him and glanced at Milly. She raised an eyebrow.

"What?" he asked.

Shaking her head and not bothering to hide the smile, she murmured, "Nothing. Just remember, she believes in honesty."

Dale frowned, about to snap back that he was honest, when it occurred to him that Milly had only just discovered the truth about his past. He felt his ire sink under the weight of embarrassment. "Yeah, fair enough."

They slumped into silence until Grace returned, wielding a large hardback book like a shield, and a little out of breath. "Found it. Last year's logbook. I never thought I'd be grateful for the insane amount of paperwork they force us to keep, but this is good." She banged the book down, making several of their customers start in shock. "Sorry, guys," she said to the room. "Sorry." Flicking through pages of scribbles, she said, "Here. This is the day he first held a prayer meeting." She air-quoted the words 'prayer' and 'meeting', adding a grimace of disgust.

Dale and Milly leaned over Grace's shoulder to look.

She ran her finger down the list. "I made this obligatory right from the first day I was here. It's important to keep track of the type of customers and clients we have arriving every day. In my last place we had a lot of trouble with the local community and police, so we logged everything that happened."

Dale scanned the page, but asked, "Where were you last?"

"Birmingham."

"You're not from there?"

"No. Or here." Grace pointed. "This is when he arrived, so the names from around this point are the ones likely to belong to his group."

Milly took photos of the page.

Dale murmured, "Here. That's Joanna Wolski." He pointed to the centre of the page and an artistic scrawl. "Can we compare this to the page where he booked in the meditation session?" He frowned and took a photo of the page saying nothing to either woman. Another name on the list stood out. Adele Smith, the murder victim from Middlezoy.

Grace shook her head. "That was the problem with this bloke and Tish. I didn't want him here doing his meditation bollocks. I thought it was dangerous and the amount of money he wanted—which was five-hundred pounds, by the way—was ridiculous. He wanted to do guided meditation with the use of peyote."

~ *Chapter 7* ~

SERGEANT WEBBER CLOSED ONE EYE, which just added to the piratical air about the man. "Well, DI Kennedy, I'm pretty sure we haven't had peyote in Glasto for at least a year. Synthetic mescaline, that's different, that is, I'm sure that's been around over the summer. It usually is if there's a festival."

"This is the real thing," Lauren said.

She and Ryan were in the back room of the small station in Street. DCI Whitfield had left, making the entire staff at the rural outpost take a sigh of relief, including Lauren. As much as she liked her boss, she didn't enjoy his scrutiny. Sergeant Webber, one of the few real beat coppers left, sat warming his hands on a cuppa. He cycled into work, come rain or shine, and today it was raining—again. He'd been on sick leave during the summer, so had missed all the action around the death of Brook and the subsequent chaos. Lauren was fairly sure that if Webber had been in charge the evening Dale was arrested, it wouldn't have happened and she'd not have known he'd moved to Glastonbury. Sergeant Webber might be old-school, but he was fair and wise when dealing with the public. He also knew the underworld of this odd piece of rural England like no one else on the Force.

Webber's eyes sunk back in his head making them a hazel splodge, narrowed to the point of almost closing. His heavy brow, wrinkled by years of deep thought, concertinaed further and he scratched the steel coloured beard. "Well, yes. We had a few rumours about it… Umm… must have been about a year ago now. Lot of bother, if I remember rightly. Lot of people started causing problems on the Tor and in the centre of town." His accent came full of the willow trees and bog moors. Lauren doubted he'd ever left Somerset for longer than a two-week holiday. "We had a spate of psychiatric call outs, left us and social services in a bit of a bind for several weeks." His eyes widened as much as they could. "You on about that lad who died on the seafront at Burnham? I remember it, but it's not our patch."

"Yes."

"Shouldn't you be busy with this lass over Middlezoy way?"

"Yes," Lauren admitted. "But I needed to think about something else for five minutes and you were here, so I thought I'd ask. We never found out who brought in the peyote or who distributed it?" Knowing and proving were two different things. The police usually *knew*, they just couldn't *prove* it.

"Rumour had it there was some bloke from Newcastle, but why he'd have the stuff, I don't know. The real thing is expensive and hard to find in the UK. I'll have a think for you. See if I can come up with summat useful."

"Thanks, Sarge."

He stood up and said, "I've got the briefing to do. Want to sit in and explain about this girl…?"

"Adele Smith."

"That's it. I'm getting old. Shouldn't forget the name of a victim."

"I'll come in a minute," Lauren said. "I just need to get my thoughts in order."

"Fair enough." Sergeant Webber flexed his broad shoulders and lumbered off.

Ryan grinned. "He'd make a great gangster looking like he does."

"Except he sounds like a farmer from some parody about rural life in the nineteenth century," Lauren muttered. "I need to make some significant movement on the Smith case today. You'll have to help collate any information uniform digs out. You're my hub, understand?"

"Yes, Guv."

The briefing was just that, brief. She needed to speak with Adele Smith's family, and uniform needed to go through her phone numbers. Forensics would come back with a preliminary report, but now the body had gone,

Lauren wanted to revisit the scene. Quiet time in the house might help clear the buzz in her head. She left Ryan at the station and headed back to Middlezoy.

The crime scene tape fluttered in the chilly breeze and the sky had a translucent blue quality reminiscent of a wildness the modern world couldn't understand or remember. It made her think of hunting wolves and dark gods. The officer at the door gave her a nod.

"All quiet, PC Allison?" Lauren asked.

"All quiet, boring and bloody cold. The neighbours are lovely. They've given me tea and cake."

"They're supposed to leave you alone. They're suspects," Lauren said, exasperated with rural policing.

"Don't be daft, Guv. They're all older than my nan. I don't think they posed a threat to Ms Smith."

Lauren gave up. "Fair enough. They say anything interesting?"

Allison nodded. "Though… Can I come in and show you something?"

Lauren nodded and allowed the younger officer to take the lead. She followed the thick fluorescent police coat down the short hall towards the kitchen, but PC Allison broke off and went out the back door.

"I think Adele Smith wanted to be a writer. She has a shed back here with all sorts of books in it. Come and have a look."

Lauren frowned. "Why didn't we look at this when we found the body?"

Allison shrugged, then flashed a grin. "Don't know. I'm not the SIO on the case."

"Fuck," Lauren breathed. "I ballsed it up."

"Not really, Guv. The shed isn't on the property belonging to the bungalow. We couldn't have known. It's part of the allotments back here. It was Mr Coin that pointed out he hadn't seen our SOCO team in there and didn't I think it was important?"

"At which point you rang me immediately to tell me?"

"I knew you'd be in a briefing. Then you showed up here. So there seemed little point."

Lauren gave up. She knew Sergeant Webber wanted Pippa Allison promoted, but the police constable said she needed more time at the cliff face just doing the job. They'd offered to move her into a city for more experience, but Allison's preference was to keep things simple. Lauren didn't understand it. When they'd offered her the fast track scheme, she'd grabbed the opportunity with both hands and throttled the life out of it until it gave everything it could—which turned out to be Dale Valentine's handler. The less thought about that, the better.

They reached the shed and Allison removed a key from her pocket. "Remember the set you found by the back door? We figured they were old keys from somewhere. Or keys for someone else's house. Turned out to be Fort Knox here."

Lauren felt her eyes widen in surprise. "Wow, she took security seriously."

"Which is odd, don't you think?" PC Allison began unlocking one of three chunky padlocks.

This sense of security made the crime scene take on a new, twisted vision in her head. "Shit, she really did know her attacker," Lauren whispered. "There is no way a woman this paranoid about a shed would allow a stranger into her home."

Allison nodded, also grim-faced. "Standing still in the cold gives one time to think. If I lived alone, I'd not let someone in I didn't know for alcoholic drinkies."

"We didn't see excessive locks on the house."

"We did see new locks, though," Allison pointed out.

Lauren had to concede the point. She'd missed the locks, missed the shed, and she was beginning to think her DCI had a point. In London, she'd been part of a close team, the same in Bristol. Down here, she had little oversight and no one to help see the things she missed. Dale gave her insights, but she'd only brought him in to see the body, not do her job for her.

As much as she hated to admit it, she still had a lot to learn.

The door to the shed opened outwards and Allison flicked on a light. "I haven't been in there," she said. "I thought you'd want first look, then maybe decide to call the SOCO team back in depending on the budget."

"If this place was locked up the whole time, there's only going to be

Adele's prints in here," Lauren said, pulling on some nitrile gloves and handing another pair to Allison. Her pockets and bag always seemed to be full of gloves. "Still, be careful and if anything seems out of place, let me know."

"Oh, this is the laptop." Allison pointed with hungry glee. "It's far more modern than the desktop we found in the bedroom."

"There're some larger evidence bags in the car's boot." Lauren handed over her car keys and Allison sighed, leaving without comment.

It gave Lauren a chance to stand still for a moment. The chilly wind off the moor ripped up the small hill separating the ancient village of Middlezoy from the bog lands. It chivvied at the small shed, with nagging draughts, but the building held most of it away. The winter grasses hushed, and late autumn leaves crackled in counterpoint. Brambles climbed up the shed's rear, but the small window looked out over the moorland. In the summer, this shed must be a wonderful place to work. In the winter, it felt bleak, but still held inspiration.

Lauren saw the rows of books and pictures of mystical places and animals. The computer sat on a desk, and she went through the four shallow drawers. Nothing turned up of interest, except for a dozen leaflets. She turned to the shelves of books. Fantasy novels took up a lot of space. Lauren recognised a few of the older titles from when she'd read them as a youngster. Then an entire shelf and a half was taken up with books that promised to take you on a spiritual journey to seek enlightenment or the opportunity to visit other planes of existence. Lauren felt a little disappointed in Adele Smith.

Several of the books were by the same author and when Lauren pulled one out, she muttered, "Hello. I know you."

The evening before, at Dale's place, she'd looked through the file he'd started on Guru Raj. The handsome young man stared out at her from the book cover and when she checked the leaflets in her hand, she found one. It had the advertising blurb for a prayer meeting and meditation session in Glastonbury.

Allison came back with several bags.

Lauren turned and said, "I want all these books bagged up." She waved at the section for Guru Raj. "I'll take the laptop now. Once you've finished cataloguing everything in here, lock it up. Request a body to come pick the stuff up. Well done, PC Pippa Allison, you've found us our first proper lead."

Allison grinned. "Thought you'd be pleased."

DI Kennedy left her subordinate to the shed and hurried to her car. Glancing over to the west, she saw the gathering storm clouds of another dump of rain heading in their direction. Knowing she needed to talk to Dale, she called him while pulling out of Middlezoy.

"To what do I owe the pleasure?" he asked the moment he picked up.

"Where are you?" Lauren swung her car out onto the main road, careful of the huge puddles.

"In the office. I'm doing research on a self-proclaimed mystic called—"

"Guru Raj?" Lauren's suggestion cut him off.

Silence for a beat. "Your murder in Middlezoy?"

"Maybe. Can you come down to the station?"

Dale groaned. "Do I have to, DI Kennedy? It's warm and dry in my office, and it smells better than your place."

Lauren glanced at the laptop on the passenger seat. "I need to update my team."

"Then come and update me afterwards."

"Valentine, you are either a consultant I can call on or not. Which is it?" she snapped, exasperated with him.

Stoney silence met her outburst. "Fine," he growled. "I'll be there in twenty minutes." He hung up.

"Bastard," Lauren muttered under her breath as she drove back towards Glastonbury.

She'd loved him enough to screw up her career in London and her marriage. Her career had survived, just about, but her marriage had not. Seeing him again after two years caused her new life in Somerset to wobble for several weeks, especially as she'd been vulnerable because of the shooting. However, the spark between them flared, then turned to dust under the weight of the past. Like a meteor burning through the atmosphere, it never reached Earth. She had the feeling they both knew they needed to move on, but how? They'd shared an intense chemistry and a period in both their lives that had ended in tragedy. No one else could ever understand their history, their grief, or its consequences.

Lauren had the feeling that even if she moved on from Mr Dale *bloody* Valentine, he'd continue to haunt her present and future.

Pulling into the carpark in front of the small police station never failed to tickle Lauren's sense of humour. The place looked like a social housing building from the nineteen-sixties, with square windows, and a functionality that had become old-fashioned but loved for its simplicity. It made her think of bobbies on bicycles whistling as they wove through the lanes, waving at farmers and women hanging out their washing. Completely ridiculous, but nostalgia breathed through Somerset like a virus trying to contaminate anything new.

Dale pulled up beside her. His long, muscular body slid out of the low-slung Audi with ease. Even in winter, his skin maintained that dark Mediterranean colour he'd inherited from his mother, while his father left him with the height and breadth of a broadsword wielding Scotsman. He held her car door as she stepped out, and they took a moment. Then she registered the sadness in his eyes and knew he was thinking of his friend Ringo, and her failure to save him.

Lauren turned away first. "Thanks for coming down."

He followed her into the station, her security badge letting them through the building to the small briefing room upstairs. She'd called ahead and everyone was waiting for her when she arrived. Dale peeled away from her and remained at the back. Several faces scowled at seeing him, but a few nodded and offered a smile. Out of the eight people she'd called in to help investigate, she had seven in the room.

"Where's Ryan?" she asked the assembly.

Sergeant Webber said, "The boy is out looking for friends of Adele's at Bridgwater College. He's taken it upon himself to talk to her tutors. I said he might want to ask you first, but…" The big man shrugged his shoulders.

"Bloody hell," Lauren muttered. "Fine. He'll have to catch up after I've skinned him. Right, PC Allison found out our victim had a garden shed in the allotments behind the cul-de-sac. She used it to keep her books and for writing. The place is done up nicely and keeps out the weather. I have her laptop." Lauren held up the bag. "Who wants first crack?"

Several hands went up.

"Give it to young Robert. He's the best with computers." Webber pointed, signalling one of his new constables.

Lauren looked at the fresh-faced young man. "You okay with that?" Lauren asked.

"Sure, DI Kennedy." He came and took the laptop. "I have a degree in computer science."

Lauren shook her head. "Of course you do. Okay, we have a concrete lead. That's why Mr Valentine is with us today. He has a case of a missing American woman, and we have a dead body, the two are linked by this man," she held up a leaflet, "Guru Raj, a spiritual teacher and so-called warrior who was in the area a year ago."

"A year ago? That can't be relevant," said one of the other officers, on loan from Taunton.

"Dale? Would you like to take this one?" Lauren stepped back.

Dale rose and came towards her. "I've found evidence of this man at Joanna Wolski's property. We went down to the community centre and, although they can't give me access to the people who attended, I saw the public records of those who signed in to the initial prayer meeting. Joanna's on the list and so is Adele. Which means they knew each other."

The officer who'd questioned Lauren's link between Joanna and Adele sniffed in contempt. A middle-aged man, he had the ageing face of a petulant child. "All these weirdos know each other. It's a small community."

Lauren felt her eyes narrow. Dale might no longer be police, but he'd been one of the Met's youngest detective inspectors before being thrown into prison. He knew more about chasing down connections than this plod would ever manage.

"You're seconded to us from Traffic, right?" Lauren asked the petulant child-man.

"Yeah, so?"

"Maybe those with investigative experience, rather than filling out speeding fines, should run the briefing?" She smiled sweetly. The man's face turned puce. He was going to be a problem. "Mr Valentine, please continue."

"The people in this group paid significant amounts of money to this Guru Raj, hoping to go on a quest meditation. It's a type of guided meditation that can cause the mind to reveal anything from past lives, to communication with aliens. In this case he was supposed to be leading them through past lives and into their future while connecting with their higher selves."

Several of the officers groaned.

Dale nodded. "I know, I know, but it's like any religion, dogma or creed, people live it, and we have to respect that. Who knows, maybe they're right and we're wrong? All we're really interested in is the connection. It's important because the father of my missing woman became disturbed by her changes in behaviour after she'd attended this meditation group. When I spoke to a very helpful woman at the community centre, Guru Raj advocated the use of peyote to reach the sublime mindfulness necessary to move through time. Much of this I've cribbed from his website, which is now out of date. This guy is a predator. Grace threw him out after the first meeting, but I think we need to know where they went and what they did after that initial session. We need to track down Guru Raj. We need to find out his real name and current whereabouts. Then, we need to know who else was in that group and we need to locate them."

Lauren put a hand on his arm. "Thank you, Mr Valentine, for taking over the briefing so well."

Dale stepped back, and she recognised the look of embarrassment.

She finished up the briefing, giving specific tasks to her small team, and sent them on their way.

Once the room emptied, Dale said, "I'm sorry. I didn't mean to take over."

Lauren chuckled. "It's fine. I'm not offended. It's good. It'll help bed you in as a serious asset for the area rather than a wanna-be-copper and ex-felon, which is how most of them think of you."

"Can I go now, miss?"

"Not yet. I want you to come and help investigate HOLMES 2 with me. I have an idea." She headed towards her office, hoping the Home Office Large Major Enquiry System would spit out something useful.

~ *Chapter 8* ~

DALE SAT IN LAUREN'S SMALL office and tried not to notice how she smelt. The slight waft of Chanel No 5, combined with the lemon shampoo she liked, played havoc on his memories. He shifted back a little as she interrogated the HOLMES system. They tried various search terms to find potential links to other crimes until Dale said the obvious.

"Why don't we try the black diamond?"

"You really think it's a calling card? Seems a bit specialised for the murder of a young woman in rural Somerset," Lauren said.

"Can you think of another reason why a black diamond, out of its setting, was left on the throat chakra of the victim?" asked Dale.

Lauren raised her eyebrows. "Get you, with your throat chakras."

"Yeah, yeah, Milly told me."

"Of course she did."

"Just try it, wise arse." If she'd had pigtails in her blonde hair, he'd have pulled one.

Lauren chuckled, and he grinned. If he'd met Lauren when he first signed up to the police, maybe he wouldn't have gone bad. She had a habit of drawing the best out of him at times like this.

They waited while the HOLMES machinery did its magical work with ones and zeroes to spit out some results. The system was always refining and improving. So long as they pushed enough detail in about a crime, any other police force in the country could use many parameters to find links. It just depended heavily on over-stretched police officers, filling it out in infinite detail.

"Holy shit, it worked," Lauren whispered.

Dale sat back in honest surprise. "Wow." He leaned forward, taking in the detail. "Bloody hell, they're both names on my list of people in the community centre that day."

Two names: Simon Morton and Kayla Rennie.

Lauren sorted, selected, and hit print. The machine in the room's corner whirled to life, eager to please, making Dale start with its suddenness.

"I need to talk to this Grace woman, and we need to find out more information from her. We can't find Guru Raj's face on our database, so he's unknown to us under this pseudonym." Lauren rose to fetch the paper.

Dale leaned further forwards, better able to read the screen now he wasn't being sabotaged by Chanel. "We've a drowning in Cornwall after an OD, and Simon died in South Wales by falling off a ladder under the influence of opioids. In both cases, they found a small black diamond, one in the breast pocket of a coat, that's Kayla and the other in the front pocket of a pair of jeans." Dale looked up at Lauren. "I know you think it's bollocks, but that covers the heart chakra and maybe the base chakra as well."

"Seriously?" Lauren scoffed.

"Hey, my grandparents were high Catholics from southern Italy. That's borderline sorcery right there, turning wine into the blood of Christ."

Lauren chuckled. "I think you might *not* want to mention that if you visit the abbey grounds again. Lightning will strike you."

"This black diamond thing bothers me, Lauren. Something about it is really important and we're missing the point." He rubbed his hand over his short black hair as if trying to slide the pieces into place inside his head. The trouble was, he couldn't see the picture yet.

"Any mention of a black diamond with your girl?" Lauren asked.

Dale shook his head. "Nothing. It's weird, I'm feeling trapped inside a case I don't understand. I'm anxious about Joanna's safety, and I can't untangle her life because she didn't seem to know anyone."

"I think we go visit the community centre, dig out the rest of the group, and see if we can find anyone left alive. At some point, I need to phone my DCI to inform him we could have multiple murders linked throughout the country."

"He'll be pleased."

"Whitfield's alright. He's dealing with people smuggling and potential gang warfare in Bristol. I'm low on his radar right now."

Dale looked at her, rather than the pieces of paper she'd given him. "The one on the news? The bodies in the shipping container?"

"Yep. Ten bodies dead in the container. Four survivors. The gang warfare is over missing drug money, apparently."

"Bitcoin is easier," he muttered.

He felt her eyes bore into the side of his head. Dale knew she desperately wanted to know where he'd come up with the money for the house in Glastonbury, and how a private detective agency provided for the quiet luxury he sustained. The Crown Prosecution Service had stripped him of his ill-gotten gains before sending him to prison, so Lauren was more than curious. He didn't want to confess his complex economic plan to Lauren, mostly because he didn't really understand it himself.

Rather than sharing a car, Dale and Lauren headed into Glastonbury separately. The weather made the abbey carpark quiet, so they left the vehicles there and headed up to the community centre in easy silence. Dale took the lead as they walked in and headed towards Grace's office.

The door stood open, and Dale gave it a light knock as he poked his head around the door. Grace sat behind her desk and that amazing smile brightened his day.

"Dale, what brings you to my door again? Not that it's not lovely to see you."

"Grace, I'd like you to meet Detective Inspector Kennedy. Our work has collided, and we need some more help." Dale stepped aside and Lauren walked into the room.

He saw a flash of something sad cross Grace's face and a resigned sigh that confused him before Lauren received a smaller, more professional smile.

"DI Kennedy, it's good to meet you," Grace said, holding out her hand. "I had a feeling Guru Raj might cause me more of a problem." She looked at Dale. "I found the paperwork. I can't show you, but I can show the police." Her eyes flicked away from Dale to the police officer.

"Call me Lauren."

Grace gave Lauren a nod and handed over a file. "I've put the original contact details inside, the contract, the details of the people who signed up for the initial prayer meeting and…" her eyes flashed to Dale with a bright smile, and he couldn't help but respond, "…I have the details of those who signed up for the first guided meditation session. It's always in the paperwork."

Lauren's eyes widened. "You don't want a warrant?"

Grace's expression became one of deep concern. Dale realised almost every thought became a new and interesting physical demonstration of her emotions. "Oh, should I…?"

He grinned. "She's winding you up, Grace. It's not normal for people to be so helpful with paperwork."

"Oh, yes, of course, sorry." Grace frowned and shook her head a little, embarrassed by her naiveté.

Dale watched her, until Lauren made a strangled groan. "What is it?" he asked.

Wordlessly, she handed him the folder. He scanned the page she'd been reading and cursed. "You're right."

"I have to return to the station and run this up the chain," Lauren said, already turning away.

Dale watched his friend mentally push him and Grace far away. He reached out and grabbed her arm. "Wait, Lauren, please. Before you go, I need—"

"Not now, Valentine. I've a job to do." She pulled away and hurried out of the community centre.

Dale swore. "That woman has no sense of loyalty."

Grace cocked her head. "You've known each other for a while?"

He sighed and felt his shoulders slump. "Too bloody long. Too much bloody history, and when she does this…" He shook himself. "Never mind, it's all in the past and a good thing, too." He focused on the woman before him instead of the woman in his memories. "I don't suppose you'd like to go for hot chocolate at the Green Man?"

Grace laughed. "Wolfie is a wicked man. Where do you think this comes from?" She patted her round hips. "Just give me a second, would you?"

Dale sat on the edge of a table and watched as she hurried towards her office, the centre quiet for the moment. He thought about Lauren's dismissal of him and realised something terribly sad. Ever since they'd met, she'd done this to him, disregarded simple requests. In the past he'd made excuses. Her marriage, her job, his servitude because of his previous crimes, but here in Glastonbury they were equals. Her job relied on his help, not his obligations to her because of a contract, one signed in his blood, and Ringo's.

Tears came unbidden to his eyes as a wave of loneliness swept over him. The desire to have someone in his corner that he could trust completely as he'd trusted Ringo, as he wanted to trust Lauren, overwhelmed him. He trusted Milly, but it wasn't the same, never could be the same and shouldn't be the same. Dale quietly acknowledged to himself that he wanted a partner in life.

Grace hurried back and gave him that dazzling smile. "Just as well I don't trust the police." She waved another folder at him. "I figured you'd get the information from her, eventually. This way, we can leave DI Kennedy doing her job, and you can get on with yours." She put the folder in his hand and shrugged. "Maybe you can explain exactly what put that bee in her bonnet and why it's upset you so much?"

Dale studied her for a long moment. "What exactly did you do in Birmingham?"

A wicked grin spread over her face, turning her eyes a deeper green for a moment. "I worked as a liaison between the police and community leaders in Ward End and other Muslim districts. We were a charity run organisation trying to keep kids off the streets and improve relationships with local authorities."

Dale's eyes widened. "Wow. That's…"

"Mind shattering—eventually. I came down here to reorganise my life. It's a great deal quieter, and usually people don't yell at me so much." She managed a chuckle. "Come on, I can hear that hot chocolate calling."

They left the community centre, Grace giving her colleague instructions as to where she could be found if necessary. When they reached the Green Man, they found Daisy serving while another young woman took orders.

Dale sat at his usual table, furthest from the door, back to the wall, while Grace joined him and grabbed a menu.

"I'm starving. Do you mind if I turn this into a late lunch? I'll pay for mine, obviously," she said.

"No, I'll pay. I owe you for this." Dale waved the folder she'd given him. "And I could eat."

She smiled, those large eyes almost grey in the café's soft lighting. Outside, it rained again, thick wet stair rods of water smashing into the glass and bouncing off the pavement before forming thick rivulets dashing down the hill.

The café was quiet, free of tourists on this pre-Christmas, post-Halloween, foul weather day.

"The usual, lovey?" Daisy asked, excluding the serving girl from the order.

"Please." He turned towards his companion. "Grace?"

"Whatever he's having," Grace said. Then to Dale, she said, "I'm crap at deciding about food."

"Two specials, coming up," Daisy said. "You know Milly's out driving?"

Dale froze, horror sweeping over him. "In this?"

"She took my car, and she's gone with Sully to Burrow Mump. She's meeting with one of your clients."

"Now?"

Daisy cocked her head. "You didn't know?"

"I didn't know it was now." He looked out at the weather. "I bloody hope she lets Sully take over in this."

"There'll be flooding soon. You mark my words." Daisy returned to the counter. "Maybe give her another half hour and phone her, get her to come home before it gets dark?"

He knew this wasn't a suggestion. Milly's status as a diabetic with an eating disorder scared the daylights out of her parents, and although Dale didn't understand their over-protective attitude, or where it came from, he respected it.

"Yeah, sure. I think that's for the best."

Daisy nodded and turned back to cook their late lunch.

Grace's look of concern made him say, "Milly's learning to drive. She has a job out on the Levels. It's not exactly the weather for a learner driver."

"Fair enough. Though, she is an adult." Grace's sharp reminder wasn't lost on Dale. "Let's look at this list." She drew his attention away from Milly.

Dale opened the folder. "I guess you're no stranger to violent crime coming from Ward End."

"We usually managed to keep it out of the centre where I was based, but working with the police gave me a vision of my community that provided little room for ignorance. Mostly about the police."

He noticed she rubbed an area on her upper chest as if a memory rose from the depths she'd rather not explore in company.

Dale understood that private ache. "Sometimes I wonder if you're born with street violence in your veins, rather than finding it the moment your parents send you out into the world on your own."

"Where are you from?" Grace asked.

"Peckham."

She nodded with empathy. It was odd for him, having this conversation here in Glastonbury. Ward End in Birmingham held many of the same social and economic problems that Peckham had, maybe more so. With Grace's background and his, they had a shorthand about that life of poverty driven violence that few in Somerset could understand.

They both looked at the list, choosing to share the present, not their pasts.

Dale ran his finger down the list. "Keep this quiet, but Lauren and I found a link between the young woman found in Middlezoy and two other bodies in the last year. One in Cornwall, the other in South Wales. I shouldn't share too many details, but their names are all on this list, including my missing girl." He pointed to Joanna Wolski's name.

"I remember this name." Grace pointed, their fingers almost touching. "I also remember a newspaper report saying he'd died from exposure on the seafront somewhere." She pointed to a fifth name on the list. "Sonny Collins. He was one reason I wanted Guru Raj stopped."

Dale frowned. "Why?"

Grace leaned back. "You know I said I'd only been here a week? Well, it all sticks in my mind rather vividly. This lad, Sonny, I tried to help him. When he came to the initial prayer meeting, he had the money for the session, but he was clearly off his face. I had no choice but to let him attend. Tish wouldn't let me stop him from going. Things in Birmingham had left me feeling... insecure, I guess, so I didn't push back hard enough."

"Sonny wasn't on the visitors' log."

She shook her head. "He wouldn't sign in. He didn't want to be tracked. Tish said it was normal and waved him through."

"But he signed the paperwork for the expensive meditation session?"

Grace nodded. "Though I don't remember that bit, so it would've been Tish."

"How do you remember his death?"

"Newspaper. It stuck in my mind because Sonny is an unusual name and he's a twin. It was sad, knowing he left behind a twin." Her face dropped, sadness softening all her features. "If I'd known more, I might've been able to help him. I wasn't on my game back then, and I let him down."

Dale reached out and gently touched the back of her hand with his fingers. "Sometimes the world just takes away opportunities to save those in trouble, and we have to live with it."

She rolled her hand over and squeezed his in solidarity. The contact felt warm, dry and terribly, compellingly, safe. Their eyes met, and she smiled. "Thank you." She released him and slipped her hands under the table, dropping her gaze.

He sat back, withdrawing, shocked at the quiet intensity of their moment. "So, we have one other name on this list we haven't found yet. Charlie Brent, that's who we are missing." He'd known a Brent once. Long time ago now. A slick lawyer who'd worked for a man who'd been trying to muscle his way into Peckham's underworld. He blocked the memories from surfacing. That world didn't touch this one.

Grace moved the paperwork around as their lunch arrived. He studied her instead and felt the past wash back like a wave, cleaning the dirty footprints off the sand. She took a bite of the burger and made a soft sound of approval that hit Dale low in the guts. He coughed to force his concentration back to his brain.

Through a mouthful of veggie schnitzel burger, she said, "Here're the details he gave us when he signed up before I cancelled the event. I must have spoken to him, but I don't remember, as I had to call all of them to tell them they wouldn't find this bloody guru at the centre."

Dale looked through the details. "Charlie Brent. Lives in…" He glanced up at Grace. "Balch Road, Wells. That's nice and local. Fancy a drive?"

"Won't the police be going?" Grace asked.

"Maybe. Lauren has to get permission; it'll depend on the evidence she can give her DCI. They can't just annoy the public for no reason. I can, though."

Grace's eyes lit up. "I've never been a private detective."

He chuckled. "Well, all we're going to do is drive over there, take a look, see if anyone is in, and if they are—ask a few questions about Guru Raj and his training."

"I'm in. If I go back to the centre, I'll get sucked into something, so I'll phone Mosh and let her know she's locking up this afternoon."

"You won't get into trouble?" he asked.

Her expression darkened as she scowled. "I'd like to see someone complain about me knocking off early. I'm in there dawn to dusk almost every damned day."

~ *Chapter 9* ~

MILLY DROVE WITH CARE. THE small Corsa battled against the rain and driving wind. Sully sat beside her, calm, patient and seemingly unaware they might die at any moment. When they'd reached Greylake, she'd wanted to pull over and make Sully drive.

He said, "No. You need to learn to handle this weather. Just take it steady, concentrate, and you'll be fine."

They were heading towards Othery, and the road was awash with rain. She gripped the wheel and leaned closer to the windscreen. The tension in her shoulders made her entire body ache.

"That won't help, Milly. Sit back, relax, you're doing great."

"We're doing thirty."

"In these conditions, that's fine."

"Not according to the traffic behind me."

"Then they can overtake or be late. It's dangerous. Most of these people have bigger, newer cars with better braking systems. If you're that worried, pull over up here." He pointed to a small layby just past the speed camera's omnipotent eye.

Milly checked her mirrors, indicated, manoeuvred and pulled in. The trickle of vehicles sped up as they moved past her. She rested her head on the steering wheel and took several deep breaths.

"Well done," Sully said in his light baritone. "That was beautifully done. There's no shame in letting others pass you."

Milly sat back. "I'm exhausted, and we've only done a few miles. Ryan used to tell me to dominate the road."

"Ryan is a police officer. You need to find your style of driving, and it's probably less aggressive than his," Sully pointed out.

She turned to look at her co-driver. "You're very relaxed about this."

The rain pounded on the roof, bonnet and glass of the car. Sully shrugged. "I have every confidence in your ability to stay alive. We'll be fine. But we do have an appointment, Milly, so let's get back onto the road and finish the mission."

"Can't you—" she started, sounding pathetic even to herself.

"No. I can't."

She nodded, took the wheel and went through the 'pulling out into traffic' procedure. In the last few months, she'd tested every one of her barriers. The martial arts classes, the driving, the on-line group she'd joined for her diabetes and binge eating, the going out with men on dates thing. Each one of these would have tipped her into panic mode just a year ago. She didn't kid herself she found any of them easy, but the one thing that made them all less scary was having Sully in the background. Something about him, just like her boss, gave her the strength to face her challenges. Only she didn't have to pretend as much with Sully. Dale had expectations. He pushed her. Sully just accepted.

Slowly they drove out of Othery, up the long hill, across the top with the wind trying to shove the compact car into the hedge, and down.

"I feel like I'm water skiing." Milly panicked.

"You are. Don't worry. Just keep straight and try not to do anything suddenly."

"What if I have to brake?"

"Then keep straight. If the car twists, go with it."

"What's that mean?" she almost screeched.

Sully laughed. "Don't worry, you'll be fine. We're almost there." He pointed to the small sister hill of Burrow Mump rising before them, and its collapsed church on the summit. "Remember, traffic lights, then the pub."

"Thank God, and I'm having a pint, so you have to drive back." Her words were mutinous.

"No you're not."

"You can be very stubborn," she growled.

He just smiled that gentle, slightly mysterious smile she'd begun to care about a great deal.

When she made it to the pub, she pulled into the lane that ran beside the River Parrett and breathed. This time of year, in this weather, the wet meadows and willow trees looked forlorn as the wind and rain battered them.

The King Alfred pub sat beside the busy road, and alongside the church that replaced the one on the hill. The entire village had a strange history and romance about it that Milly loved. It was like a mini version of the grand Tor and Glastonbury Abbey just a few miles away.

"There are other cars here, so the people we need to meet must be in the pub." Sully nodded towards some very muddy farm trucks.

Milly looked at him. "When my legs aren't feeling like gone-off jelly, I'll move."

He frowned, his brow piercing just catching the sallow afternoon light fighting to get through the rain clouds. "Can jelly go off?"

She laughed, his silliness setting her at ease as it always did. Reaching for her coat, she tugged it on, and they left the safety of the car. By the time she reached the entrance to the pub, all of ten metres, she was soaked. Hurrying down the shallow steps, she pushed the door open as the wind shoved her and Sully into the bar.

Set lower than the road, the floor of the pub had a dark red paint over wooden boards. The terrible flooding of a decade before doubtless caused a significant rebuild of the old house. Milly was pleasantly surprised to find the interior to be bright, with a modern feel and a total disregard for matching furniture. Flowers decorated the old nooks and crannies, with menus for specials, traditional pub food, and theme nights. The people who ran this pub wanted it to be a destination, and it showed with the care and forethought they put into the place. It had a real family vibe, with a good mix of modern and traditional.

Sat near the fire were three older men in wax jackets and wellington boots, along with a younger man in an old army camouflage coat. Milly felt her eyes widen a little. He was strikingly handsome. Even sitting down, it was obvious the gods had sculpted the man. His long legs rested on the hearth of the fire and a tumble of black hair kissed his broad shoulders. In the firelight, his chiselled features were full of shadowed edges and smooth planes of crafted flesh and bone. When he turned and looked at the bedraggled pair, Milly saw full lips with a strong nose to balance the almost feminine grace of his large dark eyes.

She heard Sully make a soft sigh beside her. Fully aware of Sully's ability to play on both sides of the fence, she moved to block off the blond man's view of his dark counterpoint.

"Milly Wolfe, of Valentine Investigations, we spoke on the phone." She approached the only one of the men to stand up. "Mr Newberry?"

He frowned a little, taking in her short, round stature and the slight young man. "That's me," said Newberry. His voice was expensive and a little higher than Milly would've expected in a man of his size. He had a natural tonsure. The hair left to him was a well-trimmed mix of brown and grey. He might sound expensive, but the ruddiness of his skin made it clear this man walked his own fields and tended to his cattle. The handshake engulfing Milly's small palm was rough.

"I have to say, I was expecting Mr Valentine."

"I'm afraid he's working with the police at the moment." Milly's smile remained smooth and displayed none of her internal queasiness. All the confidence she'd shown to Dale about being able to handle this case alone evaporated under the cynical gaze of four farmers. "He asked me to come because he didn't want to break his promise to you about the meeting."

"He helpin' the police to do with that murder over Middlezoy?" asked another of the men. This one had the full Somerset roll to his accent and a canny, sharp expression on his small vole-like face.

Milly smiled. "Sadly, I can't say, but—" She allowed the sentence to hang, giving each man a little secret he'd feel able to hoard and take home. It wouldn't do the business' reputation any harm.

"Well, I think as Mr Valentine obviously trusts his partner, we should as well. His reputation is solid. Old Giles from Splott's Moor said you did a fine job for him when he faced the vandals and sheep rustlers." Mr Newberry moved to pull up a chair for Milly.

She felt Sully vanish from her side. Never one to place himself inside a situation not directly involving him, he drifted to the bar to order a drink.

"We are confident we can help the farming communities find modern ways to tackle old crimes." Milly sat among the men, forcing her nerves down. Silently she repeated, 'They're just people who need help. You can do this.'

On close inspection, the last man to gain her attention didn't look well. Obviously, once an oak tree, time and illness had whittled him away, making his skin sallow and cling to his skeleton.

"Let me make the introductions," Mr Newberry said. "This chap is Frasier." The vole-like man nodded at Milly. "This is Bayne." The fallen oak gave a brief nod, but said nothing. "And this fine young fella is Mark Weaver. His small holding has been most affected so far."

"It's lovely to meet you all." Milly gave them each a smile and a nod. Sully arrived with a fruit juice. She knew he'd have chosen the sugar free option. Placing it in her hand without a word, he dissolved into the background once more.

"I don't see how *she* can help," said Weaver. His handsome head gave Milly nothing more than a nod. He'd barely acknowledged her existence, something Milly was accustomed to when it came to beefy, striking men.

"I can't help until I have all the details of the problems you're facing," she countered, making sure none of the resentment at his irritation reflected in her voice. "However, if you give me those details, I'll see if I can resolve the issues you face. If necessary, in collaboration with Mr Valentine. If I think we can't help, I won't waste your time or money. So, gentlemen, talk to me."

Weaver dropped his gaze back to the log burner.

Newberry shook his head, obviously disappointed by the young man's attitude. "Ms Wolfe, it's a conundrum for us."

She let the 'Ms Wolfe' stand, wanting to keep this as professional as possible. "That still doesn't explain your problem."

Newberry smiled. "No, I don't suppose it does. We all have neighbouring farms to the River Parrett and the River Tone, mostly covering Stanmoor

Mead." He waved a hand in the general direction towards the back of the pub. "All over the moor, in our fields... Someone has... Well..." He really struggled to make the point.

"It's 'oles. Lots of them," said Frasier. "The trouble is, Ms Wolfe, these aren't small 'oles. These are big buggers, appearing overnight mostly. You'd think it wouldn't be a problem but—"

"You have cattle, sheep, machinery and a possible flood coming," Milly put in.

"'Xactly," said Frasier. "We don't have time to keep looking for these bloody 'oles. We don't have time to go fillin' the buggers in. We don't have time to figure out how they appear."

"How long have the holes been surfacing?" Milly asked, trying to keep a straight face.

"It's only been a few months," Weaver said with impatience. "Whoever it is will get bored and move on once the weather turns really bad."

Newberry snorted. "Whoever it is just cost you two ewes, Mark. I'm surprised you can afford it."

Weaver glared at him. "I don't want no bugger poking about on my land. It's bad enough I've got the bloody footpaths to deal with."

Milly wondered at his hostility. Suddenly, the young farmer muttered a foul oath, rose and left the pub without another word. She turned to Newberry.

The farmer looked embarrassed by Weaver's behaviour. "He's a man with a lot of responsibility and paltry income. His place is always the first to flood and the last to dry out. He knows how to farm this land, but he has no interest in Somerset. What income he gets is mostly from us renting his fields and using them for our sheep and the coppiced willow we grow here. He's rather unhappy with his life being derailed by family responsibility. Still, his manners could do with a brush up."

Bayne croaked, "Too much like his mother. But don't say that to his face. Hated her as well." He focused on Milly, and she saw yellowing in his eyes. He noticed her scrutiny. "Cancer." A practical word for a terrible battle. "Young Weaver came here as a favour to a dying man. His grandmother was a gypsy, but she never stayed, left his father bitter at growing up without a ma.

Young Mark, he's full of the wanderlust. He'll be gone soon enough if he can find someone to buy that land."

Newberry muttered, "Nothing to do with wanting to get back to the young beauty he's got living there then?"

Milly's head filled with the romance of the road, the handsome man in a scarlet waistcoat… She shook her head, clearing it of a child's daydreams.

Forcing herself back to the practical, she asked, "Are the holes dug mechanically, do you think?"

Newberry shook his head. "That's the oddity. It looks like they're done by hand, but it must be the work of a crazy man, because most of them are at least four feet deep. You'd need a ladder to climb out, and the ground is wet, making it very heavy. The holes would fill with water quickly."

"Some bugger is lookin' for sommat," added Frasier. "We're used to them history buffs looking for Monmouth's army, or even King Alfred's battle against the Vikings, though I don't think they came this far west, but these aren't archaeological," he pronounced the word with care, "digs. Legal or otherwise. There's no care. I seen enough of those telly programmes to know what it should be like."

Milly, well aware of her father's teachings, realised she'd misjudged Frasier. "Do you know who it is?"

Bayne smiled and the ghost of a good-looking man showed himself for the first time. "Aliens."

"Fairies," offered Frasier.

"Let's try to maintain some sense," said Newberry. He faced Milly. "Can you and Mr Valentine help?"

"I think we need to see the problem," Milly said. "Get an idea—"

Bayne reached down for a plastic bag she'd not noticed. "I have a map. You need to see it from a bird's-eye." He grunted and his face twisted in pain.

Frasier reached for the bag in silence, sorrow making his sharp features droop. "I'll do it. You rest, Ned." He patted the other man gently on the knee.

Ned Bayne nodded and closed his eyes.

Milly just knew they'd been friends for a long time, and it brought tears to her eyes.

Frasier opened a large patchwork of paper they'd made themselves using several Ordnance Survey maps from the Explorer series. These marked all the footpaths, bridleways, and lanes in detail and were very easy to read.

Newberry helped flatten it out and said over the crackle of paper, "We've marked the farms' boundaries. We've marked the holes as best we can as of last night. You'll see clusters of holes around the rivers. We have a theory he's coming in by boat down one of the rivers, though in this weather, that'll be dangerous. They aren't large, these rivers, but they are in full spate, and we have autumn tides ripping up and down from Bridgwater. You need to know, we've seen no strange vehicles, and tourists are rare this time of year."

"Never mind the bloody weather. Where's he livin'?" Frasier asked.

Milly studied the map. She noticed the holes were in the 'Y' created by the joining of the rivers, then spread up towards King Alfred's Monument, all on the side of the river away from the main road. "That's a lot of holes. Especially if he's only been doing it for a few months. You don't think it's more than one person?"

"Maybe. But I seen a man three nights ago," said Frasier. "He was tall, and I thinks he had long hair. Trouble is, we've the River Parrett Trail on this land, meanin' it's easy access to many of them fields. We brought most of the cattle in, and the sheep 'cos of the rain, but still…"

"Let me take this and have a word with Dale." Milly found herself fascinated by the detail of their map. "We have high spots in various locations that'll give us an opportunity to see for some distance. I think a simple OBS for a few nights might solve this mystery."

"Good, because the bloody police don't want to know." Bayne could barely be heard above the crackle of the fire. He sat still with his eyes closed.

Milly glanced over her shoulder and saw the darkening sky. "Well, gentlemen, if I want to get back to Glastonbury in one piece, I think I should leave. Or I'm going to need a paddle. That rain isn't letting up, and I want Dale to see this map. The moment we have a plan, I'll call you. Mr Newberry, if you don't mind being the central contact?"

"Makes most sense," Newberry stated. "Bayne's in no fit state and Frasier is helping with both farms. I'm the least troubled by all of this for the moment."

"Good." Milly rose. "It was lovely to meet you all."

When they reached the car, Sully held his hand out. "Give us the keys. You don't need to drive back in this." The rain pelted them, and dusk held sway despite full dark being a long way off yet.

Milly sighed. "You're a hero, you know that?"

~ *Chapter 10* ~

DALE AND GRACE SAT LOOKING at the house on Balch Road. The entire estate was nice and fairly new, each house had a unique finish to make the modern sprawl appear special. The house they wanted to visit was clearly expensive, and a Mercedes S-Class sat outside.

"Charlie Brent isn't short of a shilling." Grace gazed up at the impressive frontage.

Dale's eyes narrowed. "No, he isn't." The house couldn't be more than twenty years old, had wide windows and white walls. With the large front garden and quiet suburban vibe in the street, he couldn't imagine why a person who lived here would take peyote to seek a different reality. This one looked lovely.

The rain in Wells fell with less passion than in Glastonbury, so when they left the Audi, they didn't hurry to the front door.

Suddenly, Grace grabbed his arm, dragging him to a stop. "Who are we going to say I am?"

"What?" Dale already had his mind on Charlie Brent.

"Well… I'm not a detective, I'm not police." Her big pale green eyes were wide. "I need a role."

Dale tried to smother his grin, but by the look on Grace's face, he failed. "Okay, sorry. You're right. Let's tell him you're an associate of Valentine Investigations. Which is true. You're helping me figure this out."

"Okay, but what if he asks for ID?"

"Then show him your driver's licence, but I'll cover for you, don't worry." He felt an odd thrill being able to display his talents as a detective to this woman. She barely reached his shoulder, and often seemed made of mystery and shadow, rather than flesh and blood. Those pale green eyes were now wide and focused on the front door of the house with total concentration.

He knocked. A brief wait. The door clicked, then the slide of a dead bolt, and when it finally opened, a silver chain gave them only three inches of a young man's face.

"Who are you?" came a thin, almost scratchy voice.

Dale, ready with his identification, held it up. In the past, this kind of paranoia was normal. His beat in Peckham and the surrounding area made people mistrustful the moment they were born. Since he'd been in Somerset, things had changed, and he found this tension and wariness disturbing.

"My name is Dale Valentine. I'm a private investigator. This is my co-worker," Dale hesitated. He realised he didn't know Grace's last name.

Smooth as peanut butter, Grace said, "Hello, Grace Beloe. Are you Charlie Brent? It's a pleasure to meet you." She elbowed Dale away from the door. "I know he looks scary, but he's a pussycat."

Dale blinked, staring down at the top of her head. He'd been described as many things over the years, most of them unpleasant, 'pussy cat' didn't appear on that list.

Grace continued, "We're here because we need your help."

"I'm Charlie," the man admitted. "Are you vaccinated?"

Grace cocked her head, then glanced up at Dale. He pulled her back. "Why?"

Charlie looked behind Dale's bulk as if trying to see up at the street. "You better come in. I don't want the drones to circle back."

Totally baffled by the man's behaviour, Dale watched the door close. He whispered in a hurry, "You should wait in the car."

Grace chuckled. "No chance."

The door opened, and they finally had a good look at Charlie Brent. Naturally a tall man, he stooped to hide his height, and struggled to meet their gaze. Dale caught flashes of wide brown eyes ringed by dark circles.

He appeared to be in his late twenties. An untidy mop of hair the colour of dying autumn leaves lay in a tangle around a face of sharp bones, but even features. Long nervous fingers plucked at the air, as if seeking the strings of a guitar.

"Come, but you can leave your phones in this," Charlie said, holding up a box. On the front it read, *Security*, in large yellow letters.

Grace placed a gentle hand on Dale's arm and dropped her phone in the box. He followed suit. Glancing at the walls in the hall, Dale saw photos of the man Charlie Brent used to be. Handsome, fit, chiselled features with a winning smile and cocky attitude, carrying an electric guitar in front of a microphone on a stage. Also an older man, obviously the father, with a casual arm around his young son, the face recognisable but somehow out of context. Dale reached for the memory, but it didn't surface fast enough. Something to do with the name… It vanished. Not a priority right now.

He needed Charlie to feel comfortable. "You're in a band." Dale tried to sound friendly, while watching his phone being shut in a box with a combination lock. His life lived on that phone. He also used it during interviews to remember the cadence of what people said, rather than just the words.

"Was," Charlie said. "Until I realised *they* worked for *them*."

Dale wasn't sure he wanted to know, but the word slipped out anyway. "Them?"

Charlie put his finger to his lips for silence and, with a nod of his head to the right, led them down the hall to a room. The house, for all of its occupant's oddness, was immaculate. The living room had the space and feel of a pleasant family home with grown children and money to spare. Pale furniture, pale walls, colourful curtains to add that pop Dale tried to emulate in his cottage, and complementary cushions. The rug before the log burner matched everything else. The room had a lot of lamps taking away the darkness from the closed curtains.

"It's safe in here. We can talk openly." Charlie's manner relaxed completely, even his spine straightened. "My people scan the room every morning."

Dale felt like he'd walked into a Netflix series he didn't understand.

Grace sat. "It's good to have people who understand."

"They really help," Charlie admitted. "It's exhausting being under attack all the time. *They* feel it when I leave the room. We have to be so careful."

"I'm sorry, Charlie." Grace sat still, her hands resting between her knees. "Who are 'they'? I'm fairly new in town and I don't want to run across something scary."

Charlie shook his head and sat in an armchair where he could watch the window, even though the curtains were closed. "They don't live in town. They live on the other plane, but they are using people like me to come through to this reality. If they get control of me, they'll use me to hurt people of influence. I have to stay vigilant. I have to watch for them, or I'll do something terrible. Like Lee Harvey Oswald." Charlie nodded emphatically. "They used him, then destroyed him."

Dale slowly sank into the sofa next to Grace, finally catching up on the weird conversation. He wondered what Charlie's diagnosis might be, and if his questions would do more harm than good.

The thought didn't prevent him. "Can we ask you about an event you attended about a year ago? Just down the road in Glastonbury." He watched Charlie's eyes, a laborious process because they flickered about like dark fireflies.

"Glasto is the place they like the most. It's full of the energy they need. They suck it out of the Tor. Tough place to live. Real difficult." His fingers began that scratching of the air, looking for a magical riff they'd never complete without the instrument.

Dale needed Charlie on track, but he had to do it in a way that didn't trigger the man into a meltdown. More often than not, during his time on the beat in London, he'd been dealing with public order issues related to mental health problems. Sometimes diagnosed, often not. Those years taught him a great deal about how mental health could shatter like fine china against a wall, leaving bits of the person scattered all over the ground. He'd understood addiction issues, due to both his parents preferring drugs and drink to raising their children, but sometimes people broke for other reasons.

"Charlie, what happened to you with Guru Raj?" He kept his voice soft and tried to let the sofa absorb his size.

The man's eyes widened even more, and they ping-ponged around the room. "Don't… You can't…"

Grace took over. "It's okay, Charlie. It's okay. We aren't here to do any harm. We just wanted to help a missing girl. Do you remember Joanna? She's American. Nice girl. Friendly, kind."

Charlie nodded a lot. "Yeah, yeah, I remember Jojo. She was cool. Not like some of the others. Though, to be fair, he was out of order."

Grace flicked her gaze at Dale. He nodded. If Charlie felt more comfortable speaking to Grace, then Dale would let her run with it for the moment.

"Who was out of order, Charlie? The guru?" Quiet voice, quiet body language. Grace knew how to speak to the desperate, broken young man.

"Sonny. Yeah. It was him. We knew each other a bit. He comes from Weston. I haven't seen him since then." This obviously struck Charlie as odd. "Yeah, Sonny was off his face before we even started. I told him he needed to be straight first, then the trip would work. We'd find the healing path through to the other dimension and bring it back to this dimension. The healing offered by the super-beings."

Rabbit-holes. Dale had fallen down one, eaten a cake and probably a mushroom or two and now he was talking to the Walrus, or maybe the Caterpillar. He had consumed nothing other than a bit of weed for decades, but this conversation took him back to a night where he'd tried cocaine and MDMA for the first time. Ringo's idea, of course. They'd been fifteen.

Grace took a breath, as if all this was perfectly normal, and asked, "What happened to Sonny?"

Charlie shook his head. "We had to be seven for it to work, with Guru guiding us. Sonny, he made it impossible. He just lost the plot. He scared Jojo. Bad trip even before we started the meditation to open us up as vessels for the super-beings. We had no choice. He was killing the connection. So, we kicked him out."

Grace scooted even further to the edge of her seat, trying to lean into Charlie's soft voice. "But you weren't at the community centre?"

"Naw, man. The woman running it didn't want us there. Fascist."

Dale watched for Grace to react, but she held the line. Charlie obviously didn't recognise her. She asked, "So where were you when you did this?"

Charlie focused on her face. "Burrow Mump. In the church on the hill. You can feel its connection to the Tor, to the ley-line with St Michael. We used his angelic energy to help move us through the layers blocking us."

Trying very hard not to bite at the weirdness, feeling it was probably irrelevant to the dead bodies mounting up, Dale tried to draw more from Charlie. "What happened to Sonny?"

"Dunno, man. He left the circle. Guru joined with us to keep us at the sacred number and guided us through to the other plane." Charlie leaned forward, then lowered his voice to a whisper, "It was amazing."

They heard the front door rattle. "It's only me, Charlie. It's your mum," called a woman from the hall. "All good. I have the shopping, so you don't have to worry."

The door to the living room opened fully and a middle-aged woman with long white hair over her narrow shoulders stood staring in astonishment. "Who—"

"Dale Valentine." He rose. "This is my associate, Grace Beloe. Charlie offered to speak to us about some events that happened a year ago. I'm a private detective and we're looking for a young American called Joanna Wolski. Your son knew her."

The woman's strong, handsome features relaxed only a little. "He's not well."

Grace also stood. "We understand, Mrs Brent, really. We didn't know he was unwell." She glanced at Dale. "We only have a few more questions. Perhaps you would like to sit in?"

"He doesn't let strangers into the house." She eyed them, her gaze hawkish and hard.

Charlie's fingers fretted. "It's okay, Mum. These are some of the good ones. They can be trusted. Jojo needs them."

"Charlie, could you check the shopping is clear and put it away? I need a quick chat with these people." Her accent came straight out of the private school system, but something in it felt false to Dale. She watched him with all the intensity of a cat watching a mouse.

"Yeah, okay, Mum. I'll go check nothing came in the shopping." He rose and left the room without another word. They heard him muttering about spies and the rustle of canvas bags being hefted about.

Mrs Brent turned and closed the living room door with care. She then stripped off her thick, damp woollen coat. A slim woman, bordering on skinny, she wore expensive knee high brown boots, a wool skirt, a polo neck jumper and small pectoral cross over the top.

"Please call me Catherine. Mrs Brent was my mother-in-law and not someone I want to remember. The only reason you are still in my house is because my son mentioned Jojo. I liked her. We met a few times at different events in Glastonbury. You're here because of her disappearance? That doesn't sound like Jojo. She's a considerate friend. She's been worried about Charlie. I don't think she would just leave."

Dale nodded his agreement. "That's what we're worried about as well. So far, you and your son are the only people who really knew her. An event at the community centre brought us here. Guru Raj—"

The woman held up her hand. "Don't. Don't use that name in my house. The man needs locking up. He's a…" Her jaw tightened as if repressing some colourful descriptives. She sucked in a hard breath. "The man is a criminal. He destroyed my son's beautiful mind." She swallowed back the sudden shine of tears in her brown eyes. "A gifted musician, Charlie lost it all when he returned from whatever that man did to him. He was hospitalised for three months. Charlie's very vulnerable, and we're still trying to bring him back to the real world. He doesn't need reminding of that time. It won't help his recovery. If something has happened to Joanna, he doesn't know what it is."

The protective anger of the woman was understandable, but it didn't help Dale. "Catherine, your son is the last surviving member of the group Guru Raj took to Burrow Mump."

She frowned. "What do you mean by last surviving?"

"There's no easy way of saying this, but we, and the police in Glastonbury, believe someone might be targeting the people involved in that night. Joanna

Wolski is missing, four others are dead. We cannot locate Guru Raj or even find out who he really is. Charlie is our only genuine lead. He knew Sonny and Joanna. Does he know the others?"

"You are telling me someone is killing the people who went to that terrible place?" she hissed, glancing at the door behind her.

"We're not sure. The police are investigating. I'm here to find Joanna, hopefully alive and well, but…"

Catherine sank into the armchair her son had occupied. Dale realised she had the same cast to her features as her boy.

Grace sat as well, mirroring the woman. "Can you tell us anything?"

The older version of Charlie shook her head. "Not really. Something happened on that hill that Charlie can't share. He's been doing drugs for years. We wanted him to stop, but…" She looked at Dale. "His father died, and I didn't cope well. I lost sight of him and…"

Dale sat back down, placing his elbows on his knees, keeping his hands open and relaxed, but forming a loose circle. He softened his voice, his eyes, and gave Catherine his full attention. "It happens, Catherine. Parents have to let their kids find their path and sometimes they fall off it when you're not watching. That's not your fault. He's an adult. He made his decision." Dale watched her shoulders rise and fall.

"My husband and I tried to find a more spiritual path." Her left hand strayed to her cross. "When he became sick, that's how I met Joanna. At a healing event in the Chalice Well gardens. After everything Charlie's been through, my only real consolation has been my Christian faith. I don't dabble in anything else. It was a stupid, desperate thing to do going to the healing waters."

Grace said, "Faith is a difficult thing to truly understand. People can spend a lifetime trying to figure out how it does, or doesn't, fit into their lives."

Catherine nodded, then something shifted in her, returning her to the present. "Are the police going to want to talk to Charlie?"

Dale said, "Probably. Maybe go into the station in Street and ask for Detective Inspector Lauren Kennedy. She's a good person, a fine copper. She'll be able to cope with Charlie. Or maybe get her to come here if it's easier for him? If you think it's necessary, arrange for his support worker or a solicitor to sit in. I have Lauren's card." He took a small wallet from his coat pocket and withdrew a card.

"What do I do to protect Charlie?" A loving mother's large brown eyes filled with worry for her only boy.

"Just keep him at home." Dale wanted to reassure her that special precautions weren't necessary, but it would be a lie.

Catherine laughed with bitter amusement. "He hasn't left the house in five weeks. I can't even get him into the garden at the moment. He thinks, 'they', are going to come and possess him, make him hurt me and others."

Something occurred to Dale. "Can you think of a reason why people in this group are being killed?"

"Me?" She considered for a moment, obviously wanting to help. "Maybe," she admitted. She took a preparatory breath. "If the police are going to be involved, everyone will know soon enough. My maiden name is McKie." Catherine paused. She wanted him to recognise the name. He ran it through his internal database.

It clicked.

His past roared out of the darkness. A subterranean club. A room full of punters and young women. The smell of cheap booze, aftershave, perfume and sweat mixed sickeningly with sex. The violence of the raid. Blood spraying over the floor. He'd had to stop a snout from talking to his police colleagues. Dale's illegal job that night, to help Mr Roy drive McKie off his patch, under the pretence of his police badge.

He forced himself to concentrate on Catherine's words, not the past, despite the sudden nausea rising in his throat.

Catherine's soft voice filled his head. "My brother is Carlton McKie, the bank robber, drug dealer and worse. He's currently in HMP Exeter. He… Damn it." The frustration in her bubbled over. "He had some influence over Charlie. We're all 'C' names in our family. Stupid tradition, but when Charlie was born I didn't feel strong enough to fight the family. My husband was one of their lawyers. Before he died, he became convinced his illness was karma repaying him for the work he'd done for my brother." She laughed. It sounded like lemons being squeezed over her vocal cords. "Maybe someone thinks Charlie knows where Carlton left the money from his last big job."

Grace looked up at Dale, obviously confused by the conversation.

Dale tried to keep his voice calm. "The armoured vehicle raid from a year ago?" Now he knew the Brent name and the links so teasingly elusive that tickled his brain.

Catherine nodded. "During the raid, people were hurt. Carlton was arrested, but they haven't been able to prove it was him leading the team. He's on remand at the moment, for traffic offences, believe it or not."

One of the worst men Dale had come across in his time in the Met and the bastard was doing time for speeding?

"Apparently, and I only know this because my husband's firm still works for him, the police are trying to find the evidence necessary to bring more charges."

"Don't tell me," Dale said, "they're failing to find the digital forensics they need as well as the physical? No witnesses, no victims, no one willing to turn King's evidence against him?"

Catherine nodded, suddenly taking on the ethereal illusion of a penitent Madonna. "As far as I know, Carlton still hasn't confessed where he hid the cash and gems he and the team took. He'd rather do the time than drop his people in the shit. I'm worried I've missed something. You see, Carlton and I used to spend our summers here in Somerset. In a little place called Andersea and he learned from our maternal grandfather how to navigate the River Parrett, he even sailed right through to the Bristol Channel. For a few weeks every summer, Easter and Christmas, we could be normal kids. He doesn't have any children of his own, so Charlie became one of his projects. Before they sent Carlton down, he came and spent time here with Charlie, trying to 'knock some sense into him'." The words petered out.

Grace leaned forwards and touched Catherine's still hands. "Did he hurt Charlie?"

A slow shake of the head. "I don't think so, not physically, but afterwards Charlie's mental health took another turn for the worse. I tried so hard to keep Charlie clear of it all…" Her face hit her palms with an audible slap. "I failed so spectacularly it's almost funny." Quiet sobs began betraying her misery rather than any dark humour she found in the situation.

Dale usually relied on Milly for these moments, but Grace stepped up and moved closer to the grief-stricken woman.

"It's all such a mess. Even if Charlie knew where the bloody stuff was, he'd never be able to tell you now." Catherine's accent finally slipped, and he heard the hard twang of East End London. "I've worked so bloody hard to be Mrs Brent. Even sent my son to the Wells Cathedral School. I wanted him to be free to choose his own life and look at what he did with it."

Grace rubbed circles on the woman's back. "He has a lot of life ahead. Don't give up on him. You've created a safe place for him to heal from his psychosis. That's more than many get. I have the details of many support groups for people like Charlie and their families." She took Lauren's business card, ruffled around in her pockets, and found a pen. Dale saw her write an email address on the back, her phone number, and her name. "You can write to me, and we can set you up with some help. How does that sound? As for the police, get your solicitor and arrange for all of them to talk to Charlie here. Call me if you need someone to bully them. I'm very good at that."

Catherine nodded. She seemed to stare at Grace's fluid handwriting in stunned shock. "Thank you."

Dale, on the other hand, couldn't quite let it go. He felt the tingle of past, present and future blending together. It awakened his sense of adventure, but also his dread. There was more here, if he could push the right buttons to find out the secrets. He needed time to think this through. He had to keep Catherine Brent, nee McKie, on side. "If you discover anything about that night which might be useful, please call us. We really are trying to find Joanna before anything happens to her and keep you safe in the meantime." He'd learned that by putting the victim's safety at the centre of his request, he could just about make them do anything he needed. Given the time. Right now, he had to talk to Lauren.

It took a few more minutes, but he disentangled Grace from Catherine's problems and they retreated to the car. They didn't bother trying to speak to Charlie again, who seemed to have forgotten their existence.

Dale breathed out slowly. "Christ, what a mess, and what a story."

"I think she's doing an amazing job trying to support her son."

"Yeah, but Carlton McKie is no laughing matter. I tangled with his mob up in London. They are, or were, bad news." Understatement. Dale's memory flickered and shadowed rooms full of the scent of cigarettes, aftershave, hate, fear and bourbon, rose. Faces, voices, the memories of power created in the heart of man's darkness.

"You tangled with them?" Grace asked.

Dale started the car to give himself a moment. He'd forgotten it wasn't Milly sat next to him but a woman he didn't want to disappoint. "When I was in the Met." He didn't mention the off-books work he'd done to push McKie's gang out of certain parts of Peckham for a hefty fee.

Grace didn't ask. Lauren would have, she'd have needled away until she uncovered the truth she wanted. Grace had more trust, which weirdly made Dale feel more guilt.

That's because you're an idiot, bruv, came Ringo's condemnation in his head. It had been a while since Dale had thought in Ringo's voice. His hands tightened on the steering wheel.

Grace asked, "Do you think this McKie gang could be killing people in this meditation group?"

"I don't know. I need to speak with Lauren. She's going to be screaming bloody mad at me for queering her pitch in that house. If I'd known how it was going to go, I'd not have approached."

"What's the worst she can do?" Grace asked.

He wanted to say, 'Throw me back in prison', but he just slumped into silence until they reached Glastonbury. He dropped Grace off, knowing he left her confused and probably hurt by his sudden withdrawal from their shared afternoon, but Lauren's fury and its consequences dominated his thoughts.

~ *Chapter 11* ~

THE DARK WRAPPED ITSELF AROUND Dale and he sat in his office chair, staring at the blank computer screen. He'd switched it off when daylight still nibbled at the clouds. Now the rain pattered around the old converted stable and the wind tried to find new ways into the cold room. Lauren's words screamed through his mind on a loop.

When he'd rung her to explain his visit to Charlie Brent and what had happened, who he was, and the connection to the largest armed raid Bristol had seen in over thirty years, Lauren's fury turned icy.

"You thought you'd take a civilian along to question someone of interest in a murder inquiry?" she asked. He saw her Nordic beauty in his mind; it made him think of icebergs and starving polar bears.

"I didn't think it would be that relevant. I'm looking for Joanna Wolski, not casing a lead in a case that's way out of our league. The armed raid is nothing to do with us, Lauren. Besides, goodness knows how long it would've taken you to gain permission from—"

"Don't you dare, Valentine. You know police procedure. You know I'd have arranged an interview with Charlie Brent."

"Lauren," he heard the slight whine in his voice and hated himself for it. "They're going to phone you—"

"With a nicely prepared and sanitised statement prepared by their very expensive lawyer, no doubt."

He'd tried another tack, "The cold case—"

"I know about the cold case. Because, Mr Valentine, I happen to be rather good at my job and don't need the assistance of a gung-ho, self-proclaimed criminal mastermind, black-hat wearing, bloody convict." At this point, her voice had a pitch and fury he'd never heard from her before. "I put my rather tarnished reputation on the line for you, again, and you do this to me?" She paused, and the ice swept the fire away. Colder and more deadly than the Arctic Ocean. "How dare you do this to me, Valentine? How dare you?" He heard the furious tears for just a moment before she hung up.

"Fuck," he said again.

You always were a fool over that woman. I warned you, bruv. Even Ringo sounded disappointed in him. On top of that he'd obviously hurt Grace as well with his odd behaviour.

He'd been showing off. For the first time in years, since before his arrest and conviction, he'd felt good about himself and in one swift stroke, he'd destroyed it all. His company's relationship with the police might as well be dust. His friendship with Lauren, gone. Any trust they'd built now lay in tatters. She was right. He'd screwed that line of inquiry for her, and Charlie was their only witness to her cold case, Joanna's vanishing act and possibly the biggest crime the South West of England has seen. The broken mind of the young man could also connect all the victims of a possible serial killer. He'd fucked it.

Softly the voice in his head added, *You care about this Grace, that's a good thing, bruv. Lauren would never have worked out and you're lonely. Take her some flowers...* The voice petered out for a moment, then bounced back with, *Naw, man, take her a plant. She'd prefer something alive. Chicks dig that shit.*

Despite his self-recrimination, Dale had to smile at the chirpy inner voice that sounded just like his old friend. "God, I miss you, Ringo," he murmured. "What the hell am I doing in Somerset?"

The door to the office opened, and a light flicked on before he could react. He winced and turned in the chair.

"Bloody hell," Milly squeaked, jumping back into the rain.

"Shit, Milly, don't do that," Dale barked. He rose fast, sending his chair scooting over the floor.

The pair of them stood and stared at each other for a moment, as if making certain the other existed.

"What are you doing in the dark?" Milly asked. "I've been phoning. I was worried when you didn't pick up."

"Sorry, needed some time to decompress after a call with Lauren."

Milly came into the office. "What happened?"

"I've screwed our relationship with the police, is what happened."

He watched her pause as she hung the damp woollen coat on the back of her chair. "How?" she asked.

While she made tea for both of them, he explained about finding the lead and chasing it down. He described Charlie and Catherine Brent and their relationship with the infamous Carlton McKie. He did not mention his previous connection to McKie.

"You really are an idiot, Dale," Milly said, sipping her tea and watching him over the rim of her mug.

"I know. I'm sorry."

She shrugged. "It's your business that'll suffer."

He frowned. "You don't really feel that way, and you have a right to be angry with me."

She paused for a moment and put down her mug with care. "I'm pissed off I didn't get to see you interview Charlie Brent. It would've been an excellent training opportunity. However, you spent time with Grace, and I don't think that's a bad thing for you. I'm talking to you as a friend, not my employer. Lauren's not good for you. When she's around, there's a level of tension inside you that doesn't scream happiness. It screams addiction."

Dale blinked several times, trying to pull together something sensible to say.

"I'm sorry if I overstepped." Milly didn't look sorry. She had her implacable face on the one that said, 'I'm right, even if you don't like it'.

"It's the business that'll suffer most," he said.

Milly snorted. "Not from my meeting this afternoon. If we help the farming community, we're in clover, so to speak. Besides, you don't really need the business to do much more than pay me and keep you in running shorts." Her eyes took on that mischievous look he'd grown to appreciate.

He smirked. "Yeah, alright. I enjoyed the reputation and working with, but outside, the confines of the police."

"You mean your ego liked it."

Dale stood up and stretched, almost touching the low ceiling. Her words, blunt, honest and true, hit him hard, but he needed to hear them. "Come on, let's go into the house. It's more comfortable. I need to know what happened to your farmers."

"That's part of why I'm here," Milly said. "I wanted to write a report while it was fresh."

"You can do that somewhere warmer than here."

The two of them returned to the house. The integrated heating system, part solar, part gas, kept the kitchen warm. He'd have the log burner going if he wanted to entertain in the living room, but the kitchen had always felt like the hub.

Dale cooked. His great stress buster when he wasn't running. If he'd been alone, he'd have gone to bed with a bottle of whisky and stayed there, reliving every poor decision he'd made in life. Milly, she had the same knack as Ringo. She made him see things from a different perspective. One that didn't carve holes in his heart, rather, she helped him build bridges over the crevices.

Milly told him about the farmers, describing each of them and Mark Weaver's anger at the thought of the investigation.

Dale grunted as he chopped sweet peppers for a simple stir-fry. "I wonder what he has to hide."

"My thoughts exactly. Bayne thinks it's something to do with a woman."

"Would that be enough? Maybe it's a weed farm?"

Milly shrugged. "His land is wet, but very open to view. There are a few barns from what I've seen on Google Maps, but nothing I'd describe as a grow house."

"Okay, we'll shelve that for the moment. What's your plan?" Dale asked.

"Well, Sully's happy to help. I thought we could use him as a bit of a part-time gopher. He and I can do night obbos for a bit, maybe from Burrow Mump to start with. Look at the map and see if you agree."

She laid out the map the farmers had provided, and they started to plan. Dale cooked for Milly without fanfare and kept it carb low for her diabetes.

"I think you have it all in hand," he said. "If they need the boss on site, I'm happy to help, but Joanna must remain my focus."

"Without the police, how are you going to manage?" Milly asked.

"I'll find Jimmy in the morning. He'll be able to ferret out anyone selling real peyote in town."

Milly frowned. "I don't understand how that'll help find her?"

"She ran. She left her house and ran. Someone connected to that meditation, spiritual quest, whatever mumbo-jumbo you want to call it, out on the Mump, scared her. I think she knew about the other deaths, or she saw her attacker and she ran. I don't think Adele Smith was as lucky, or as savvy. We have to track Joanna's whereabouts over the previous months to get an understanding of her state of mind."

"Or she's dead and we haven't found her," Milly said morosely.

"There is that."

They slumped into silence for a while. Milly finally broke it. "Is there anything I should worry about if the police, meaning Lauren, decide you need investigating?"

Dale focused on her. "Like what?"

"Well, you've been in prison, Dale, so I'm guessing you've done some shitty things, even if you don't talk about it. Obviously, it wasn't a miscarriage of justice, or you'd explain your situation. If your previous crimes are going to come back to haunt us, I need to know. I love my job. I really enjoy working for you, but…"

"This has been on your mind for a while?" he finished for her.

"Honestly? Yeah. For a start, I know, because I do the accounts that we break even, we don't make enough for you to afford all that nice food." She nodded at the range of vegetables on the counter. "Never mind the posh car."

Dale felt the walls come up. His financial situation didn't need explaining to an employee.

You really can be a prized shit, bruv. She's your mate. She needs to know her job is secure. You need to trust.

Milly watched him. Her sharp, vivid green eyes focused on him, obviously aware of the internal struggle.

"This goes no further. I don't even want your family to know," he stated almost aggressively.

"Agreed," she said.

"It's a mix of investments. I did someone a favour in prison, and they set me up with a mix of virtual currency and other long-term share options. They manage the accounts, we split the profit."

"That must've been some favour," Milly said.

"It was." Dale thought back to that terrible night. The blood on the hard concrete floor of the prison cell had flipped his mind to Ringo's death. The consequences for the other prisoners before the guards turned up, wasn't pretty. "Tim, he was my cell mate for a while, was almost killed. He's a genius with computers and I don't pretend to understand half of what he's doing with the money, but it's legal. It's all legal. I can promise that."

"Well, I hope so for your sake, because Lauren might want to punish you for this."

Dale chuckled. "You have her pinned down, don't you?"

Milly shrugged. "You employed me because I'm sharp and I'm great at reading people. Lauren's ambitious, even if she pretends not to be. You're a tool in her box of tricks, but you're also a threat. Today, you've threatened her, and, like any ambitious person, she'll come out fighting her corner, not yours." She grinned suddenly. "Grace, on the other hand, she's a more complex person."

Dale laughed. "You bugger."

"I bet she's not your usual type?"

"I'm not divulging my love life to you, Milly."

"Supermodel types, right?"

He shook his head and collected their bowls to hide his embarrassment.

"Knew it," Milly crowed. "Beautiful women who liked to be seen with either a handsome man in uniform, or a bit of rough, depending on how you met them."

"Alright, smart arse."

"Whereas Grace isn't even beautiful until she smiles. Those big pale green eyes that shift to—"

"Alright, Milly." He didn't hide his exasperation with her. "Though I'm probably going to need to grovel there as well."

"She likes you, don't worry." Milly stood up, ready to leave.

"I'll walk you home."

Milly snorted. "Don't be daft, it's only nine o'clock. I'll call Sully. He can walk up the hill and meet me."

"You'd drag him out on a night like this?" Dale asked.

"He likes to feel he's protecting me. He's bugger-all use, but it helps give him confidence, so I'm not going to take that away."

Milly grabbed her coat and bag, already on the phone to her would-be knight in a rainbow jumper and jeans. "You'll see. It'll work out with the police. You'll find a way." She left Dale alone. He shook his head as her whistling diminished.

Dale realised he needed to tackle the case with a fresh mindset and work the angles he had for Joanna's disappearance, not the murders.

~ *Chapter 12* ~

WITH THE RAIN EASING, MORE due to arrive the following day, and the rest of the week, Milly decided to spend a few hours on watch over Stan Moor. Burrow Mump would be their observation post, because Sully promised to come with her.

Not one to deny herself home comforts if she could find them, Milly dug out her plastic bivouac, a couple of sleeping bags, packed a food hamper and made tea rather than hot chocolate. By ten-thirty that evening, they were ready to go.

"It's not raining, you can drive," Sully said.

"It's dark, I'm not driving. If you try to make me, we're not going." She crossed her arms. "I won't be safe. I need to think, and thinking stops me from driving."

Sully shook his head, but couldn't hide his smile. "You don't think when you drive? That explains a lot about your driving." He unlocked the car doors.

"Hey, that's not fair," she protested.

"Yes, it is. Get in and we'll go over the plan for the night."

"I've packed Dale's night vision goggle binocular things and we have his camera with the special night settings on it. There's a long lens in there. Also, a voice recorder should there be a problem with the phones."

"And a picnic."

"We can't stay up for hours without food," Milly protested. "You've never done a stakeout. They can be very dull. Snacks help keep you awake."

Sully pulled off smoothly, and they trundled through Glastonbury. "The boss okay with me tagging along?" He glanced at her.

"Of course. I don't think he wanted me that far from people, anyway. Not with a potential nutter on the loose. Besides, he has quite enough on his plate at the moment."

"Oh?"

"Some of it's personal. What I can say is, he's screwed up something for the police while moving along our investigation into Joanna's disappearance."

"That sounds bad."

"It won't be good until he works things out with Lauren."

"She's very…"

"Intense?"

"Driven."

"Hmm."

"Which I like in a woman," Sully added. "I like it in you, but there has to be balance, trust, and loyalty on both sides when one is more driven than the other. Or has different priorities."

Milly studied him. The sallow streetlights turned his almost white-blond hair and pale skin ghostly. Sully was easy to ignore, despite the piercings, and in the forgetting, he became the perfect observer.

"Are you giving me a gentle warning?" she asked.

He shrugged. A careful movement, just like his driving, thoughtful even. "Perhaps. I'm all in for Team Milly, but within that support, I want my needs and wishes to be remembered."

She gave him a small smile when he glanced at her. "There's no one but you, Sully. Not now. I'd like us to take things further, but we'll have to do it slowly. There was…" she breathed out. "Men have hurt me, a man, not just emotionally. I can't…"

Sully's hand came out and grabbed her knee. "I don't expect you to. I just need to know I can rely on us being a team."

"You can. While we both agree to it. We're a team."

The streetlights ran out and night swamped the small car. She asked, "What can I do to help and support you?"

"For now, I have everything I need, thanks to your parents. Maybe I need to think about moving out if we're dating formally. I don't want to crowd them, or you. Space for us is important. Maybe we can look for a place for me, but do it together. I don't want to be alone again." His gentle voice thickened. "I don't think I'm ready to be alone."

She reached out and put her hand on his thigh. "You don't have to be alone, Sully. S and M forever. Okay?"

Sully looked at her, his eyes wide. "I think you might want to reconsider that."

She frowned, then her cheeks warmed. "Oh… Oh, that's funny."

LAUREN FELT SICK. HER FURY with Dale hadn't abated, and everyone in the station avoided her eye and her office. As the police didn't directly employ him, she hadn't had to hold her temper in check for the sake of Human Resources. Basically, he'd taken the ball she'd lent him and not just run with it, he'd nicked the damn thing, then stabbed it so it deflated. Meaning no one else could play with it.

She sucked in a deep breath, held it, tried not to imagine decapitating her ex-lover, and breathed out. He knew she needed her witnesses fresh. She knew he'd let his ego take over.

Focusing on the large board she'd erected in her office, she took in the new information Dale had given her about Sonny Collins. The young man had been on Guru Raj's list, but she'd not known Sonny had been kicked out of the guided meditation session with violence, or that it had taken place on Burrow Mump.

Even as a kid, the place had always given her the creeps when they'd driven around the edge of the Mump. The ruined church on the top somehow looked far more sinister than the single tower on Glastonbury Tor. Maybe it was the soggy farmland, the endless pixie-like willow trees, or the mists that hugged the lowlands. But whatever it was, Burrowbridge village and its Mump were creepy.

Her eyes rested once again on the black diamond from Adele's death. She'd pinned up the photo of it resting on the young woman's neck.

That damn thing is more important than it looks.

Lauren turned back to her computer and pulled up HOLMES 2. She entered a search for black diamonds and thefts in the South West. How had the killer come across something so expensive? Why use a black diamond as a calling card? Who could afford to throw them away like this? Was its spiritual connection important? Or was it purely decorative? If they could afford to throw away diamonds at the murder scene, then why black ones?

She had no answers. The urge to talk it through with Dale increased her anger again, which didn't help her think.

As she waited for the ones and zeroes to line up correctly, she wondered how Ryan was getting on in finding Sonny's twin. Since seeing Sonny's name on the list for the Guru Raj, it'd become more important than ever to locate the missing woman. She'd ring Ryan once she'd calmed down a bit more. If he said something annoying, it would just set her off. Bloody Dale, bloody, Valentine.

Even the thought of resurrecting anything romantic between them now lay in tatters. Bollocks to him. She'd sign up for a dating app and have a little fun. Her ex-husband now had babies with another woman and Lauren had spent long enough paying for her stupid affair with Dale *bloody* Valentine.

The screen on her computer changed and came up with the relevant search results.

It cheered her up no end and finally pushed all thoughts of Italian-Scottish hybrid men out of her mind.

Two items.

Six months ago, a burglary was reported in Burnham-on-Sea. One item listed was a black diamond bracelet.

Also, during the largest armoured car heist Bristol had ever experienced, two dozen black diamonds vanished, along with many other gems and a pile of cash. One Carlton McKie was suspected of being the organ-grinder on the robbery with violence in Bristol almost a year ago. So far the only thing they could charge him with was traffic offences. He didn't enjoy paying his speeding or parking fines. While on remand, the team in Bristol, working with the Met in London, were hoping to uncover more evidence. Or even find the stolen gems and cash from the robbery. They knew he ran an OCG, an organised crime gang, but no one would talk, including McKie. He was just waiting them out. Without the evidence they'd never be able to charge him with the robbery, or find the rest of the gang. Lauren needed help. She picked up her phone and rang her boss.

The moment the ringtone ended, she said, "Sir, can I have interview rights for Carlton McKie?"

"Nice to hear from you, DI Kennedy." Detective Chief Inspector Whitfield sounded exhausted.

"Can I?" she pushed.

A long sigh. "No, but give me the reason for the request."

"The multiple murders I believe are connected; they could come back to him."

"The *possible* multiple murders that *might* be connected will not come back to him," Whitfield said with weary patience. "He has the perfect alibi. They have him locked up for each murder."

"He can pay—"

"Lauren, you're a solid detective. You're great at running a team. I like the work you're doing, but I only assigned you the violent death in Middlezoy, because I have no one else there. You're on cold cases. Stop digging around. Solve Adele Smith's murder."

"I know, sir, but I have viable leads that show these cases are connected, and the black diamonds are the link. They were taken during the heist. It's too much of a coincidence." She felt the frustration tighten her voice, making her sound like a pleading child in her ears.

"Write me a report. State your case. I'll take it to the Serious Crime squad dealing with McKie and his people. See what they say."

"That could take weeks!" Lauren exploded down the phone.

Silence. An arctic wind blew over the tundra of DCI Whitfield's patience and she felt it come down the phone's connection.

"I'll write the report."

"Good," he said. "You've made the initial assessment of Adele Smith's murder. Send it up and we'll have our team check over your findings. They could see something your small, and let's face it, inexperienced team down there will have missed. It's all about sharing information and using resources, Lauren. We have them in Bristol, and we have experience. I need you down there as our legs, eyes and ears, but I'll be directing things from here. Understood?"

"But—"

"DI Kennedy," Whitfield's voice hardened. "Desk duty is supposed to be just that, you tied to your desk. I can just as easily put you on sick leave. It was your decision to come back to work. This is what we agreed. You are down there to man the desk if they need CID for a case and to revise the crimes your predecessor and the previous coroner buggered up. You are not there to stir up trouble for our more experienced divisions."

She knew the tone. Lauren felt her heart burn. First Valentine screwing up her chances of talking to Charlie Brent and gaining useful information. Now Whitfield was putting her back in her box.

"Sir." The only concession she could give to her orders.

"Have a good evening, DI Kennedy. Try to get some perspective. I'm not out to damage your career. I'm here to guide you and offer my experience. Don't waste it."

"Yes, sir. Thank you, sir."

Whitfield sighed. "Just don't do anything stupid, Kennedy."

"No, sir."

He hung up. Lauren stared at the board hung on the far side of her office and seethed. She needed a plan, and it didn't involve waiting for Serious Crimes to give her permission to do her job. People were dying, and they had all been in the same place at the same time.

As she wrote the report for her DCI, a plan formed and if she needed to play nice with Valentine to get it done, so be it.

MILLY SIPPED HER TEA WHILE she watched Sully learning to use the night vision binocular things. He lay on his belly inside the small bivouac. They'd set themselves up with the remains of the church tower at their back so they could see out over the meeting point of the two rivers. With most of the leaves gone from the trees, they had a pretty good view. She didn't intend to spend the entire night on the hill, but a few hours in different locations over the next week should give her some photographic evidence that the farmers could take to the police without it costing them a small fortune. Digging holes on someone else's land had to amount to criminal damage if nothing else.

"I still think that Weaver bloke's reaction to you was odd," Sully said, head shifting from one side of the wide valley to the other as he peered through the optic.

"Dale's right. He has something to hide. We just don't know what, and it obviously doesn't have anything to do with what's been happening here with these holes. Dale thinks it's a weed farm. I think it's something else. Maybe something to do with his woman?" She tried to drag her eyes away from the back of Sully's jean-clad legs. She had to take things slowly, and being a tease wouldn't help either of them.

"Oh, hello," Sully murmured.

Milly put her tin cup of tea down. "What?"

"No, it's a cow. Sorry."

She smacked his leg. "Stop winding me up."

"Is this better than taking photos of wandering spouses?"

"It's better on my faith in humanity," she said.

Sully grunted. "Yeah, well, I don't have too much of that either. I just think there are people you can have faith in, and you need to treasure those people. Like your parents. I have faith in them." He added quietly. "And you."

She reached out and placed a hand on the tumble of almost white-blond hair. "I trust you as well."

He lowered the binoculars and offered one of his ethereal smiles. "Then we'll be okay. It doesn't matter what everyone else is doing."

Milly's gaze wandered over the landscape. The night had no moon, the cloud cover low, threatening rain again. The ground sheet they sat on didn't quite keep the damp out and the wind moved around sullenly. Her sharp eyes caught something out there, which didn't seem normal.

"Give me those," she said, waving a hand.

Sully didn't argue. He just handed over the binos. She placed them against her face, corrected their focus, and searched.

"Got ya," she murmured.

"What?"

"Believe it or not, there's a boat coming down the River Tone."

Sully sat up, turning his slim body without effort into the upright position. "Really?"

"Yep. It's moving slowly, but I can see the shape and there's someone on board." She concentrated. "Yes, that's it. There's someone there."

"Do we go down there?" Sully didn't sound concerned, just asking for her lead.

"I think we should," she said. "We need photos."

They slipped their way down the steeper slope of Burrow Mump, then worked their way along the fence and hedge towards the graveyard of the church. Milly followed now. Sully's night vision and sure-footedness made him the best candidate for the job. He helped her through the wall, towards the church building, then past it and onto the road near the bridge.

They hurried together, keeping their faces away from the odd vehicle to preserve their night vision. With the River Parrett at their backs, they kept going until they reached Stathe Road.

Milly puffed a little, trying to keep up with Sully's long strides. "We should've brought the car."

"Too obvious. Once you have your photos, I'll go get it while you monitor whatever's happening. I don't think we should approach. We don't know how this person, or persons, will react."

She'd have argued, but whoever this person was, they could dig a hole fast, which made them determined and strong. Having a shovel around the side of the head didn't seem like a good plan for their date.

Sully said, keeping his voice down in the quiet of the night, "We'll take the towpath next to the river."

"We can't see anything," she whispered. Without their torches, and so far from the houses and road, they had almost no ambient light.

Sully muttered something. "Let's take it slowly. We'll be okay. You'll be surprised at how much you can see. Just don't look at the ground directly, use your periphery, it has more black and white cells or something."

"Seriously?" Milly asked, hurrying after him.

"It's handy. I can't remember the science of it. Someone told me and it works."

She smiled at his back. The man had a stubborn streak she admired, and he really wanted to make sure she found her target. Checking her phone, she realised they'd been walking for almost thirty minutes. The narrow path followed the river, and she could see the houses on the other side of the river. How many times had those houses flooded? The insurance for living here must be huge.

A car passed on the main road, just a field away, and for a moment they had enough light to see clearly. The small boat sat on the river a few metres ahead. Milly grabbed her companion's coat and dragged him to a stop. Putting a finger to her lips, she prevented him from talking. She pointed to her ear and mimed listening. Sully nodded and cocked his head.

They waited in the dark, standing on the narrow path next to the river. The reeds sighed in the slight wind. The water soundless. This old river knew its way after centuries of travelling the same path through the wide expanse of the Levels.

Sully's hand closed over her wrist, and he pointed to their right. A muttering, a huffing, a *shook-pop* noise, Milly didn't understand. Then she did. Pulling Sully's face close, she whispered in his ear, "He's digging. Go get the car. I'll work my way closer and take photos."

His hot breath caressed her neck, making her shiver. "Be careful."

She squeezed his hand. He didn't even try to take over, or tell her how to do her job. She'd poked around after enough errant spouses to know how to be a good spy, and he trusted her to do it well. It felt odd, being trusted so completely by a man she wanted to care about romantically.

When the soft sound of Sully's feet vanished, she moved. Taking great care, she headed towards a stand of trees. Despite her inelegant appearance, Milly knew she moved with cat-like grace when necessary. Sneaking up on people had become one of her hidden 'ninja' skills and she took pride in it.

Pulling the camera around her body, its weight familiar with its long lens, she waited until the soft grunting and *shook-pop* gave her the digger's location.

Off to her right. Why? This was just a field that flooded. It held the hope of a winter crop, and nothing else. She lifted the camera, switched it to night mode, and there, with the aperture as wide as possible, she saw him. A tall man, his skin darker than hers, more like Dale's, and as she snapped images, he flicked a long black ponytail over his shoulder. He held a shovel and worked like a demon, digging deep and muttering about something she couldn't catch.

Turning, she took shots of the boat, not daring to approach in case this lunatic wasn't alone. Seeing where the boat was moored, she realised the digging-man had the perfect access to either side of both rivers without having to use people's gardens, the footpaths, or the gates on the main road. Slowly, she backed away from her hiding place and returned to the path. The digging-man didn't seem to be aware of anything else around him. Without wasting time, she started back along the towpath, moving as quickly as possible in the dark.

When she reached the safety of the car, she and Sully drove away from Burrow Mump and headed straight for the office.

~ *Chapter 13* ~

DALE SIGHED AND SENT WOLFIE a text message.

I've found him. Thanks.

Jimmy sat in the small graveyard at St James' church in the centre of the High Street. He'd taken up temporary residence under the yew tree, the thick branches keeping the ground fairly dry.

The moment Dale saw the bottle of cider between Jimmy's knees, he knew he'd made a mistake. He'd screwed Jimmy over. Sending a recovering addict to question the local dealers about the drugs they sold had placed Jimmy in an impossible situation.

Dale's only consolation? The cider's lid remained intact.

He removed the bottle and in silence offered Jimmy his hand. The big man took the lifeline slowly, as if they'd made his body from boulders too heavy to lift, and together they walked in silence up the hill. As they passed a bin, Dale dropped the cider inside. Jimmy made no comment. Reaching his house, Dale led Jimmy around the back and opened the office.

Once he had the big man settled in a chair, Dale sat opposite. Jimmy hugged his cuppa as if it contained the answers to the big questions of the universe.

"These are bad people, Dale," Jimmy said for the tenth time.

"Okay, I get it. Don't poke the scary drug dealers." Dale almost laughed. No one in Somerset could be half as scary as some people he'd worked with in London, the people he'd grown-up with.

Jimmy's eyes focused on him. "I'm serious. These guys don't bugger about. They know I've been asking questions. The only reason I'm still in one piece is 'cos I'm such a loser."

"You're not a loser, Jimmy. There aren't many people who could've survived your past."

"Freddy and Brook didn't." His heartbreak and misery leaked out of every pore, like fever sweat.

It would take time, but Dale realised he needed to force Jimmy into a different frame of mind. "What happened today, Jimmy?"

"I just..." Jimmy shuddered. "There was a smack house. That's where I found the people I needed to talk to."

Dale breathed out slowly. This was his fault. He'd sent Jimmy on a mission with no thought or protection. "Not the best place for a recovering addict."

"No."

"You saw something?"

Jimmy nodded. "A kid. Couldn't be more than sixteen. She was smoking crack. Here. In Glasto. How does that happen?" Faded, jaded, lacerated eyes met Dale's.

"I don't know, mate. I'll talk to the police, okay?"

"She needs social services," Jimmy said. "I'm going to talk to my social worker. I can't leave it. She'll end up on the game, or worse."

Dale would put money on the kid already turning tricks to pay for her smack. "I'm sorry, Jimmy, but we need to keep our focus on the mission at hand. What did you find out about the peyote?"

"Smack is everywhere," Jimmy said, not listening.

"Yes, mate it is, but right now—"

The door to the office opened and Milly arrived with Sully. Suddenly, the office felt tiny. Dale sighed, knowing he'd lost Jimmy's attention for the moment. After the greetings and Jimmy's mood lifting the moment Milly gave him a hug, Dale found two extra seats and set about making more tea. He glanced at the clock above the door. Almost two in the morning. Valentine Investigations never sleeps. He rubbed his face and blinked, trying to clear the grit out of his eyes.

Milly had her computer kicked into life and gave it food by sliding the camera's memory into its mind. She described their night, and Dale had to admit to being impressed.

"Do you think he's living on the boat? That could make life difficult," he said.

Milly shook her head. "If he is, then he's living in a smaller home than the average Londoner." She grinned at him.

"That small?" Dale smirked at her observation.

"He probably has limited places to hide the boat. We can call the river authority people tomorrow to find out where he could berth a boat that size," Sully added.

Milly fiddled with software and images popped up. They all huddled around the screen.

A tall man, wearing nothing other than some figure hugging Lycra and mud, churned through the thick soil of Somerset.

"He seemed to talk to himself, but without breaking cover, I couldn't get close enough to record anything." She pulled up one image that made the man's profile show clearly.

Dale mirrored her, "Damn me."

They looked at each other and smiled.

"What?" asked Jimmy, finally caught up in something other than his own misery.

"That's Guru Raj," Milly said, pointing at the screen.

Dale gripped her shoulder. "Bloody hell. What's going on?"

"That's the bloke that bought the peyote," Jimmy said. "It's gotta be."

They all looked at the man, who desperately wanted to rebuild a ruined life, but didn't know how. He wilted a little under their scrutiny, then rallied, "Bongster said the bloke who put in the order looked like a Paki." Jimmy caught Milly's expression and held up his hands. "Not my words. Bongster is a prick, but he knows more about the drugs' scene in the area than anyone else." Jimmy pointed to the screen. "This bloke must have found the biggest, most diverse dealer in the area and gone to Bongster, which shows some balls. The bloke is scary."

"Then what? He puts in an order for an exclusive drug?" asked Milly.

"Yep. Given enough notice, with enough cash, Bongster would've got the right stuff."

Dale leaned against his desk. "Could Guru Raj have owed Bongster money?"

Jimmy shook his head. "No way Bongster would've left it a year."

Dale hummed agreement. "So it's unlikely the drug angle has anything to do with this. This Bongster would've had no reason to go after the attendees, only the damned guru." He rearranged the mental map he had of the case, discarding drugs as an option. "The next thing we do is find Guru Raj and take his shovel off him." He pushed off the desk. "But right now, we all need some kip. Jimmy, you can take my spare room for the night. Sully, I'm guessing you're on breakfast duty tomorrow at the café. Milly, I want you back here, first thing. We are going to have to talk to DI Kennedy and I'd like a human shield."

"Oh, that'll be fun," she muttered.

The impromptu meeting broke up and Dale showed Jimmy the spare room. He really didn't want a borderline homeless, ex-junky, staying in his house, but…

You're going soft. Ringo's voice was gentle and had a hint of pride in it that made Dale smile as he lay down in his room.

"I am, mate. It's all these nice bloody people in my life," Dale muttered aloud.

It's not a bad thing, bruv.

"Maybe," Dale murmured. He rolled over and thought about Lauren. As his mind slowed, the Nordic goddess dissolved into the far kinder vision of Grace and her vivid smile.

The following morning, Dale woke to the dulcet tones of his front door being abused by a set of knuckles that expected to be obeyed. Jimmy threw open his bedroom door.

"What the—"

Jimmy's eyes were wide, and Dale grabbed his dressing gown. "We're going to be raided. It's the pigs."

"It's not the pigs. It's Lauren, being assertive because I've pissed her off.

I'd know that knock anywhere." He glanced at the clock. Seven. Then he realised he was looking at far more of Jimmy than he ever wanted to see. "Go get in the shower, get dressed, let yourself out. She doesn't need to see you. We'll be in the kitchen." He was already heading down the stairs.

Opening the front door, he found not just Lauren, but Ryan as well, looking as sleep deprived as Dale felt. "I didn't think you ever wanted to see me again?"

Lauren glared, then shoved past him. "I need coffee."

Dale glanced at Ryan, who said, "Don't ask me. She summoned me into the office at six-thirty. The guv's on a mission."

"Wonderful," Dale muttered. He trailed after the Nordic nemesis.

Lauren banged around in the kitchen.

"Leave it," Dale ordered. "Before you break something."

Pipes overhead lurched into life. Lauren's eyes zeroed on their target. "Entertaining?"

The illusion of porcupine spines rising around her, or maybe swords, came to Dale's mind as he tried to ignore the sounds of Jimmy upstairs.

"How about we try for—none of your business?" Dale studied her face. Things needed to end between them. A firm line.

He saw the threat of anger rise, then the wave petered out, washed back, and Lauren calmed. "You're right. I'm sorry. It's none of my business." She managed a brief smile.

Dale had a strange lurch in his reality, and it gave him an odd nausea for a moment.

You're letting shit go, bruv. It'll be time for me to leave soon.

He turned back to the coffee maker, hiding the rush of tears in his eyes. He could let Lauren go, but losing Ringo? No. Not yet. He wasn't ready. He'd never be ready. His hand trembled as he poured the milk.

"Why are you here before dawn, Lauren?" He sounded harsh.

"I have a lead. A solid way into this case, but I need your help," she said.

Dale felt his shoulders hunch. His mind flashed to the first time she'd said that. She'd made it clear the lives of several young women rested on his ingenuity and guile.

He finished making the coffee and her silence during the process made him even more worried about where she'd force him to go this time. One, he handed to Ryan and one to her. He made himself a cup of tea. They all heard the front door snick shut.

Lauren's dark blonde eyebrow rose in a question. "Doesn't she want coffee at least?"

The demon on Dale's shoulder bit his ear. "No, it's fine. I already paid her."

Ryan coughed coffee all over the kitchen table.

Lauren's eyes narrowed, as did her mouth.

Dale didn't flinch, daring her to make the next move.

She took a deep breath, exhaled slowly, and closed her eyes. "I'm not biting."

"Good," he murmured into his tea. "So, what do you want?"

"I want you to re-interview Charlie Brent. Then we're going to interview Carlton McKie."

Dale felt his chest constrict. "He's in a Cat B prison, Lauren. I'm not going into a prison."

"You know this how?"

"It's in the newspapers. I did a perfectly normal background check on him when we discovered his connection to Charlie through Catherine Brent. Sister to one, Carlton McKie." He didn't want to tell Lauren he'd crossed paths with McKie in London. It would lead to conversations he didn't want to have, and they weren't relevant to the current situation.

"Well, I think we have a new perspective on this case. I just need confirmation before taking it to my DCI."

Dale paused. The rising panic over her demand he visit McKie eased a little. "You don't have permission from your boss for this?"

Ryan kept his mouth shut, watching the two of them.

Lauren said, "Would I have brought DC Matthews here if I thought DCI Whitfield didn't know about my plans?"

She would, bruv, came Ringo's soft voice. *She's playing you.*

Dale shook his head, trying to find the trap. "Lauren, the most important thing in my life right now is Joanna Wolski. If I find Adele Smith's murderer, great, but Joanna is my priority." He stated this with as much controlled clarity as he could muster. He felt under siege in his own kitchen.

"What you don't know is that McKie's last heist contained a bag of black diamonds," Lauren said. "Whatever happened on Burrow Mump that night is connected to black diamonds and that means…"

"So is McKie and therefore his nephew." Dale closed his eyes. "Bloody hell."

He heard boots on metal grating as they walked past his cell door. The rise of fear each time, never knowing if the guards were coming as allies or enemies. The daily terror of having to share meals and showers with other prisoners who knew he'd been in the police, then abandoned by them and placed in general population. The slam of the cages. The lights going out. The muffled screams. The endless sobs. Those who walked the stone and metal corridors with the dead eyes of men who'd had enough, who just waited for the opportunity to die. Suicide, the only sure escape from prison.

He forced his mind back to the present, and he realised why Lauren had turned to him for help. "You can't get permission to formally interview McKie. They'll never let you. You only have circumstantial evidence he took part in the heist. That's why he's still on remand, serving time for traffic offences while they try to find a witness or victim willing to talk. The Crown Prosecution Service will never allow anything that jeopardises any other case being built by another team."

Lauren's expression softened and she leaned towards him, those big, blue eyes pleading. "This isn't about me, Dale. This is about kids being murdered because they were in the wrong place at the wrong time. Something happened on that hill that put them all in danger. We need to find out what, and McKie doesn't even know his nephew is in danger. What if one of his people is responsible, and he doesn't know? This is a way under his shell. You might be the key that unlocks him."

Dale thought about the shattered mind of Charlie Brent. His poor mother, Catherine, having to choose a name for her son that pleased her brother and the rest of the family. The insanity of that control. How she'd tried to escape by marrying Brent, but he'd become McKie's lawyer. Somerset was no longer a refuge, but was another type of prison.

"McKie won't be any help. I'll go back to Charlie. I can re-interview him with Catherine's help. That's something I'm prepared to do," he said.

"And if it doesn't work?"

He wondered how hard it was for her to be here. He'd dropped her in the shit. She'd thrown it back in his face, and made it clear she never wanted to work with him again, but the next day she's here. He knew her temper. Rage would build. Fury stoked by every misdemeanour. Then the storm would crash into its target with all the force of a hurricane. Then it would blow clear. Things would return to a new normal. The damage would be ignored, for the most part, until it became too much for the target to bear. In this case, him.

He didn't want this. He didn't want to do her bidding, but Charlie and Catherine Brent could be victims in this, and he owed them some kind of help. Charlie's broken vision of the world had to be coaxed into revealing exactly what happened on the Mump that night.

"Fine. If I can't get Charlie Brent to give me enough, I'll go see McKie," Dale said with terrible resignation.

Ryan looked shocked.

Lauren sat back and drank her coffee. "Good. I'll leave you to tidy up after your guest and we'll arrange your visiting order." Standing, she made it clear to Ryan they were leaving.

Dale stood, unable to find the strength necessary to use his size to intimidate her. His one defence against the woman and it failed every time. He'd never scare her into leaving him alone, she knew him. The old and the new. He'd gone soft, and she understood all too well how to use the guilt of his past to hurt him.

No words came as the police left his house. He just stared out of the window at the gradual lightening of another grey dawn.

~ *Chapter 14* ~

DURING HIS LONG AND VERY hot shower, Dale found some balance to his day. Lauren did this to him. She breezed into his life, delivered her rapprochement, then her orders. Once he'd accepted both, she left him to figure out the details. She was using him, as she had when he'd been her informant in London. It left a bitter taste in his mouth.

More like your soul, bruv, murmured the quiet voice of his dead friend.

Dale snorted. Ringo had rarely thought in terms of 'souls'. It goes to show that a subconscious haunting can talk bollocks, just like everyone else.

He had his orders from DI Kennedy, but the one thing she couldn't control was when he opted to visit Charlie Brent. With the weather making itself known in the form of lashing rain and wind, sent to punish the foolhardy, Dale bundled up against the bullying and headed for his car. First stop, the local garden centre next door to the DIY superstore. He bought several ferns and a rather lovely ivy, figuring that would make more of a statement than a miniature potted rose.

Then he went to one of the few independent bookshops left in Somerset. Squirreled away among books about dragons, fairies, crystal healing and divination, he found a local history with maps containing interesting walks. That would be a good bribe. He now had the apology and the bribe; next he wanted something to tell Grace he was worth the risk. She seemed a bit risk averse.

On the counter were a set of beautiful wooden candlesticks, carved from holly and a set of beeswax candles. Unique, local, made into curling spirals that spoke of endless strength and—*Just buy the bloody things and stop justifying it, weirdo.*

"Thanks for that, mate," he muttered, fishing out his wallet.

Armed, he walked over the road to the community centre to do battle.

DALE'S STOMACH TWISTED AS HE walked up the steps to the community centre. He ought to let this go. Grace was a woman of integrity. He was a man with a dirty past. She deserved better.

"Dale?"

He glanced to the right, where the meeting rooms were, and saw Grace kneeling among more boxes. "Oh, erm... Hi." This wasn't the plan. He'd wanted just a little more time to prepare for what he needed to say.

She glanced at the box in his arms. "If they're more leaflets, then take them away and come back when I'm less inclined to set fire to them."

"Have I picked a bad time to make a formal apology for my terrible behaviour yesterday?"

For a long moment, she didn't move. Then a delicate dark blonde eyebrow rose. "You want to apologise?"

"Very much."

"For what?" She still knelt among her boxes, and he still carried his. This wouldn't work unless he changed the ambiance.

Putting his box down on the high reception desk to the meeting rooms, he offered her hand. "Let me help you up?"

Those moss green eyes looked at his offered hand. Again, she seemed to pause her life while her mind made several calculations. He watched it happening.

Her hand almost flopped into his. "Okay."

Rather than haul her up as if she were a sack of dog food, he lifted her gently and didn't pull her towards him. The moment she had her balance, he let go.

Dusting off her knees, she said, "Go on then, apologise. I have work to do."

Dale frowned and felt a stab of disappointment. "You're really pissed off with me, aren't you?"

Her jaw tightened and along with it, her eyes. They became bitter, less like soft moss and more like chips of pale jade. "Yes. We interviewed two vulnerable people, gained important information for the police and your investigation," she pointed at his chest, then shook her head as if distracted by something, before adding, "then you cut me out. Suddenly, I became irrelevant. I felt used."

"I know. I'm sorry. If I may, I'll explain, then at least you'll know why I can be such a shit."

She crossed her arms over her chest and stared up at him. "Go on then, explain."

Dale realised he wanted to squirm like he used to when his Italian grandmother's gaze pinned him down, just before receiving a scathing dressing-down. "I really am very sorry, Grace. I know my behaviour was demeaning to you. I didn't think, and worse, I didn't care in the moment. I've been alone a long time and I fear it's made me unaware of the needs of others."

Grace's expression shifted. Concern flickered through her eyes. "Thank you. You understand how it made me feel to be dismissed. I appreciate that. It means a great deal."

He breathed out, and the tension between them evaporated.

She grinned. "It's hard staying mad at you when you come in here looking like a giant puppy with those big brown eyes and that face."

"You saying I look like a dog?"

"God, no, you look like a GQ model. That's one thing that intimidates me about you." The tumble of words rushed out. Her colour shot to a deep red as she realised what she'd said.

Dale chuckled. "I don't think I've ever been given such a back-handed compliment."

She tried to hide her smile by turning away. "Yeah, well, you're hard to ignore with all that going on." A hand waved in his general direction, then she gave him the hard stare again. "That doesn't mean you get to treat me like that again."

"I know. I really am sorry. Something in the interview caught me off-guard and it..." He huffed out a breath. "Look, I would love to get to know you better. I'd happily settle for friendship, but I'm looking for more. I need more. It's just—Grace, I've made a lot of terrible decisions in my life."

Her body language relaxed, and she leaned against the reception desk. "You're trying to tell me something."

He nodded. "You know I'm ex-police. What you don't know is why I left." He stopped. She said nothing, just studied him. This woman really knew the power of a good silence.

"Alright, here it goes. I was stripped of my rank, my money, my liberty and slung into Wormwood Scrubs for four years. It should've been a lot longer, but I struck a deal with Lauren's boss and agreed to work with the Met to bring down an Organised Crime Gang in exchange for my freedom. In the process of that, Lauren and I became lovers and my best friend died in my arms after we were both stabbed." He added after a beat, "In a strip club."

Her eyes widened at this last bit. "Okay..." The word sounded like a stretched piece of elastic.

"I moved to Somerset to start a new life. Lauren and I are just friends, or we were until yesterday. I'm not sure what we are at the moment. I know it's always complicated. I don't want to lie to you, mislead you, or hurt you. Hearing McKie's name yesterday brought back some terrible memories from a time in my life when I was a very bad man."

Grace drew in a long breath and let it go. "Right. I see. Well, that's..." She gave one of her defining nods. "That's alright." A smile brought her stillness to life. "I'm still married," she blurted. "It's messy, and horrid, and torrid and it makes me feel like a worthless piece of shit most of the time. I haven't been on a date in twelve years. I don't know how to do this." Her eyes were darting all over the place, hardly able to settle. This confession obviously cost her a great deal. "Any thoughts about my ex-husband make me behave like a deprived junky in fear of his dealer. He's dangerous to me."

Dale took a moment to reassess her. "You've been to some dark places."

"Very." She still couldn't meet his gaze. Whoever this bloke was, he'd done a real number on this woman.

"I don't pretend to understand. You've been through something nasty. I can promise I've never laid a hand on a woman or child with violence."

Her breathing became rapid. "I came here to start again as well."

Gently, he took her hand in both of his and rubbed her knuckles. "Grace, look at me?"

She finally settled her darting eyes on his face, but didn't quite meet his eyes. She murmured, "Prison isn't a problem for me. I've known a lot of ex-cons, most of them are very sweet. Though few of them are as charming as you." She tried a tentative smile.

He grinned. "I have my moments. I would like to take you out on a proper dinner date. Would you like to come to dinner with me, at your convenience?"

"Answer me this first. Did you know this McKie as a policeman or a criminal?"

He felt a well of sadness open up. "Both."

"Will you tell me?"

"All of it, but there's a lot to tell."

She nodded. "I will listen."

"Thank you." His relief was palpable.

She pulled her hands back, physically shifting the heavy energy between them. "What are you doing today? Still trying to find Joanna?"

Dale let her change the subject. He straightened. "Sort of. I have to re-interview Charlie Brent."

"You don't sound happy about it. I thought you said he was too delicate?"

"Apparently, the police disagree. Lauren needs more information, but she'll never be able to bring him in for an interview. Her boss won't allow it, so she's given the job to me. I can take my time, make sure he feels safe."

Grace nodded. She looked to be on the edge of a decision. "I used to be a social worker. My Phd involved the psychology of victims of abuse and drugs, how they should be treated differently to ensure their testimony is trustworthy and recorded with care. I worked mostly with vulnerable kids. I can act as an appropriate adult in interviews."

Dale felt his mouth fall open in surprise. "You couldn't've mentioned this yesterday? You're a doctor?"

"Didn't think it was important," she said with a shrug.

"Christ, Grace, this is amazing. Come and help, please. I'm a big bloody man and I know I scare people, which has its place, but not with Charlie Brent. I need a partner in this."

"What about Milly?"

"She's chasing another lead for me. Though she's going to hate me when she gets back. I have her tramping all over the Somerset countryside looking for a boat."

Grace laughed. "In this weather? Alright, let me go dig Mosh out to take over our busy café and I'll come help."

"You mean the one with hundreds of patrons?" He glanced up at the ceiling. Silence reigned above their heads in the large public hall.

Grace groaned. "Yep. That one. Give me five."

"You can have ten. I want to warn them we're on the way. Give them a chance to kick me out before we get there if they change their minds."

Dale watched her run up the stairs in search of Mosh. He realised he hadn't given her the gifts. They felt a little redundant now, so he left them on the reception desk. She'd find them later. He felt like Grace offered him the chance of something new, and very different from anything he'd tried with Lauren. It felt right.

MILLY AND SULLY TRUDGED UP the footpath from Burrowbridge, retracing their steps from the night before and going further into the unforgiving wet. The rain pounded the saturated ground. Puddles formed looping streams that tumbled into the already full river. It raged against the banks containing its frothing mass. The wind tore at the coppiced willows, their thick trunks like twisted torsos, the bark deeply creviced and almost black in the endless wet. Their branches ripped at the low sky, clawing at the clouds and whipping back and forth like tortured flagellants.

"God, I hate this." Milly huddled further into the waterproof wax coat, which wasn't waterproof, and tried to stop the run-off from filling her wellington boots.

Sully had his face to the wind. "I love it. Makes me feel alive."

"You're weird."

"If I were normal, I wouldn't be here," he shot back.

Milly smiled, despite her misery. "You know, we might end up walking to Taunton at this rate."

"My money is on Curload. Whatever he's looking for will be close by."

"Then maybe we should have driven there and walked back towards the Mump," Milly pointed out.

Sully grunted, then chuckled. "Oh, yeah, that would've made sense."

Milly shook her head, amused despite the misery of the weather. "I'm going to get Dale to come pick us up and drive us back to the car. We can't walk into this lot. It's bad enough with it being at our backs."

"I think it might be wise for more than one reason." Sully had stopped walking, and his tone was serious. He pointed. Ahead, the river had decided it didn't want to be kept under control. It had spread over the fields. The bank they walked on using the footpath, nearest the houses, rose far higher.

"It's kinda awesome seeing nature rip away our control with such ease." Milly had to raise her voice over the howling storm.

"It is," Sully agreed. Then he gripped her shoulders and turned her. "But it's even better when we find our quarry."

Milly let out a whoop. A small boat, painted in faded blue, more than scruffy, with a tiny cabin, bobbed about.

The two of them checked their surroundings. No obvious signs of people. Milly approached the boat.

"Don't." Sully made a grab for her arm. "The water is rising too fast, and I don't know how secure its mooring is to this bank." The boat twisted and tugged at its ropes.

"We need to find some evidence. Or at least find out who he is," Milly called over another noisy gust of wind. It tore at her hood, and won, so it attacked her hair. She cursed, catching at the tangled, damp red snakes.

Sully's grip tightened on her arm. "No."

She pulled away and frowned. "What's that supposed to mean?"

"I mean, it's too dangerous, Milly. I'm not letting you on that boat." This was the first time he'd tried to prevent her from doing her job.

She opened her mouth to argue when a sharp crack made them both flinch. After hearing the gunshot in the summer that almost took off DI Kennedy's leg, Milly had become nervous of such sounds. Yanking on Sully's arm in return, she dragged him towards the ground.

"It's not that." He pointed, and she watched the little boat hurtling down the river as the manic current took hold.

She gasped, glanced at him, then the boat, gathering speed. It looked like a child's toy caught in the current of a weir, twisting and bouncing off the banks.

"How did you know?" She let him help her up.

"I didn't... I just get... Feelings about things. Dangerous things..."

She stared at him in surprise. Then she realised she'd lost her only decent lead on the case. "Now what?" Her frustration at the loss, the failure at finding their suspect, made her want to scream. The bloody weather was conspiring with this deceitful guru who'd not only stolen people's money in a fraudulent attempt to show them enlightenment, but had hastened the deaths of many.

A firm hand held her shoulder. "Now, we go back to the car, go home, eat, dry off and come back later to talk to the people in the houses with gardens backing into the river. They must've seen someone, or something, coming and going from this boat."

"Oi!" came a booming voice designed to strike terror into every child on a game's field throughout history.

"He will not like my face." Sully licked his lip-ring and stepped back from Milly's shoulder, pulling his hood back up.

"Hello," Milly called, as a man who looked like he could take on the entire New Zealand rugby team all alone, strode up the steep bank holding the river back from the cottages.

"You something to do with that boat?" he bellowed over the gap between them. The river did its best to drown out his belligerence, but it wasn't up to the task.

"No. I was hoping you might help. We're looking for the person who uses it. We think they've been trespassing." Hoping Lauren would forgive her, she added, "We're working with the police in the local community."

The man's face, made of slabs that might once have been granite, but now looked like they'd been coated in fudge, folded into a scowl. "Bloody police are useless. I keep phoning them in Taunton, nothing. Bloody vagrants shouldn't be allowed to use the river."

"We're here to photograph evidence." Milly lifted the camera case.

"Well, you need to photograph his damned yurt. It's over there." A stout arm waved at a thick stand of trees. "Though why Singer gave him permission to stick the damned thing up is anyone's guess. The chap isn't even a local. You can tell."

This confused Milly for a moment until she felt that lurch in her guts that always accompanied casual racism.

Sully murmured from behind her, "Probably to annoy you, Mr Grumpy."

"Thank you, sir. We'll go check it out." She felt her teeth grind.

"Just see that Singer knows what's what when it comes to letting these foreign types move into the area. We've enough problems with refugees—"

"Sir, we work for the police. Probably best to stop that sentence before I have to report you," she barked. "Besides, I'm guessing you bought that farmhouse from a local who now can't afford to live in the area, so I wouldn't throw too many stones, or someone might throw them back." Big bastard or not, she wouldn't put up with this shit. Without another word, she took Sully's hand and strode back the way they'd come.

"You go for it," Sully murmured in quiet approval. Then he added, "Are we going to check out the wood?"

"Yes, but not looking like a couple of drowned puppies."

As they walked, they heard the man bellow into the wind. It stole his pointless words and tossed them into the tempest.

~ *Chapter 15* ~

"I'M SORRY I'VE INVOLVED YOU in this." Dale watched Grace as they pulled up outside the Brent house.

She'd been quiet on the drive over. Maybe processing his confession about prison. Maybe as surprised as he was at the level of personal information they'd shared over the reception desk in the community hall. He'd never done it before, just told someone about the major trigger points of his life. A stranger, really, and yet, Grace didn't feel like a stranger. This silence between them didn't stretch unnaturally. They just lapsed into quiet. Sharing something other than words.

He'd felt nothing like this before.

Grace took a deep breath. "It's okay. If he feels comfortable with me being there, then I'm glad I can give him that safety while helping you and the police."

He stared into the pale green eyes, now like shallow seawater. She made one of those strange smiles, her mouth mobile, her expression just a little wicked. "Stop it, or we'll never get anything done."

He felt it as well. The rising sexual tension between them. Grunting, Dale left the car. They walked up the path, the rain a hammer on the tarmac and soil, abusing them in its turn, and the door opened before they reached it.

"Come in." Catherine managed a wobbly smile. "We're in the kitchen. It's warmer in there and less formal. Charlie feels safe. He's having a good day, so you might gain some more information."

Dale nodded. "Thank you. We'll be as brief as possible. I don't want to upset anyone."

They followed Catherine down the hall. She'd dressed in pale colours, one item of clothing blending with the next, making her appear ephemeral, almost not existing in her own life. The kitchen sat at the back of the house, and despite the weather, Dale could see it looked over a well-tended and sizable garden. The kitchen itself was modern, sleek, organised and surprisingly colourful. This room felt like Catherine allowed her personality to creep out of the box she'd coutured for herself. The illusion of the nice, upper-middle class woman who sent her only son to the cathedral school. Not the younger sister of an organised crime boss.

Charlie sat curled up on the sofa with an iPad and earphones on. His face was a mask of concentration.

She waved at him, trying to draw his attention.

When he caught sight of Dale, he looked confused for a moment, until he saw Grace, then he smiled. "Hello."

"Hi, Charlie. Do you remember why we're here?" She walked over and sat in the armchair next to Charlie's sofa.

The young man nodded. "We need to talk about what happened the night my mind was opened. I get it now. I have to explain it all to you, so we can start showing the way. Without those of us who have already entered the portal explaining how to reach the next level, how can you know? I can't keep it a secret. It would be selfish."

Dale glanced at Catherine. Large tears hovered on the mascara of her eyelids. She turned away and headed for the kettle.

"Tea?" she managed.

"Thanks." Dale took a kitchen chair and moved it to sit near Grace, but keeping back, letting her take a lead for the moment.

She smiled at Charlie. "So, can you tell us what happened that night? What happened to you and the others?"

Charlie nodded, but opened something on his computer and fiddled with it while he spoke. Dale glanced at Catherine.

"It's a game he plays, helps to soothe him. We use it in therapy."

Dale turned on his phone's recording app. He'd gained permission from Catherine in their earlier conversation, and she'd suggested not mentioning it to Charlie.

The young man started to explain that strange night. "We all met in the carpark at the site of the ascension. Together we walked, hand-in-hand, up the side of the hill, each of us carrying a lamp, a blanket and water. Sonny was already wired on MDMA and weed. His sister was there. They'd put all their money together to take the trip into the alternative universe. We were scared, but excited. Guru Raj had taken a lot of time to prepare us. Had us fasting, doing meditations."

Dale broke the flow, but made sure his voice stayed gentle. "How long before the ascension were you fasting and meditating?"

Charlie kept his focus on the screen. "Three weeks. Only certain foods could be eaten. Mostly white. We had to pray for the Guru's strength so he could show us the path, walk with us. We had to sustain him as he prepared us for our journey."

"Sustain him?" Dale asked.

"Yeah, man. We had to give him money to help him. It's not like someone that spiritual can work in a supermarket."

Dale and Grace shared a glance, both full of loathing for the leaching bastard who'd manipulated Charlie.

"So we were pure, or at least most of us were. Sonny was already losing it. His sister tried to keep him on track, and she covered for him, but it was difficult. We got up there. The sun was setting but there was going to be a super moon, so we'd be okay."

Grace asked, "Were you inside the building?"

Charlie shook his head. "Nah. We were on the grass. Inside is too closed up, though I remember walking through it with Jojo. We had a wild time in the nave with the stars." He glanced up from the screen and looked at Grace. "She's a pure spirit, you know?"

Grace nodded, her hands resting between her knees as she leaned forwards. "That's why we need your help, Charlie, so we can find her. Keep going."

"Yeah, we gotta find Jojo." Charlie frowned at his computer screen, obviously trying to stay on track. "We sat around in a sacred circle. Guru Raj did a space clearing with sage and stuff, asking for the revered and ancient Celtic spirits to help us."

Dale clenched his jaw. The desire to punch Guru fucking Raj in the head overwhelming him for a long moment. Just as well he hadn't brought Milly. She'd have lost her shit over the tangling of this Celtic nonsense.

"Then he brought out a gas stove from his bag and a pot, like a cauldron with all these magical sigils on it. We talked while we waited for the brew. Guru Raj spoke prayers over the tea. He added the peyote, and we chanted to bring its power into us. Then we smoked some really strong weed and each of us drank from the tea. Things went bad with Sonny just as we were coming up. Even his sister was getting pissed off with him. She was the one who asked Guru Raj if he could make Sonny leave and the Guru become our seventh, rather than Sonny. Seven is the magic number."

Grace nodded encouragement. "It's sacred to many faiths for a reason."

This was news to Dale.

"Then it got heavy." Charlie's focus was on the game, but his knee shuttered up and down in nerves. "We had to make Sonny leave. I thought he'd make it back to Glasto, okay. Still loads of people on the road for a lift. He was well used to acid, but this stuff, it's different..." Suddenly, his eyes focused on Dale. "You said he's dead, like the others?"

"Yes, Charlie, he's dead, but no one killed him. He died on the seafront at Burnham, from exposure."

The young man's entire body twitched, his anxiety so strong it coated Dale's tongue as he breathed in, like milk past its best.

"I never meant to hurt him."

Dale scooted his chair closer to Charlie. "Listen to me. It wasn't your fault. You did not do this to Sonny. The drugs did this to Sonny."

"We came up on the peyote. We smoked more of the weed from a communal pipe. More chanting and then..." Tears streamed down Charlie's face. His mouth twisted. "Then the journey started."

Grace reached out and took the iPad from his loose grip before he startled himself by dropping it. "You don't have to tell us about the trip,

Charlie. Not if it was scary. We could do with what happened afterwards, maybe. What did you see in our mundane world while your spirit travelled? Do you know?"

"I saw my Uncle Carlton on the moor, by the river." He blurted the words out, and he appeared confused by the statement.

Dale sat up. "What?"

Charlie nodded. "I know, right? Weird. I was with Jojo. We were by the tower, making out, fuck man, she's beautiful. Share the love, you know? So we were walking through the night, through the landscape as the moon rose. It was amazing. Then we saw this light on the river and these two men on a small boat."

"How do you know it was your uncle?" Grace asked. "That's a long way to see in the dark."

"Cos we walked down there, me and Jojo." Charlie seemed to think this was the most normal thing in the world.

Dale couldn't believe his ears. "You walked down to the river from the hilltop?"

"Yeah. We were tripping, but the main part of our journey was done and when we saw the lights on the river, we knew we had to go. When I saw it was my Uncle Carlton and his mate, Blackbites, I thought *they* had asked us to deliver a healing message. I know Uncle Carlton is a dangerous man. He needs some deep healing. Also," Charlie's face became so sad it made Dale's heart ache. "Dad was dying. Mum was going to be alone. She needed a family, but a proper family, not like a crime family."

"What was your uncle doing?" Grace asked.

"We didn't get close. Jojo freaked out. They had, like, they had guns. She knows about guns because she's American. It got real messy for her. But they were digging. Which was weird. Why dig in a field for no reason? I think it was part of my lesson for the night, from the other dimension, but I still don't know why. I still don't understand. Why was my Uncle Carlton there?"

Dale had a horrible feeling he knew the answer. "Did you tell anyone?"

Charlie nodded. "Had to. Jojo was in a bad way. She had to know it was safe. We needed guidance from Guru Raj."

"And you got it?" Grace's voice dropped, a coaxing you'd use for a scared dog.

"Yeah. Kinda. I don't know. It all got a bit weird from there. Jojo wanted to leave. Eliza wasn't doing so well because of her twin. The vibe switched. The moon was so fucking wild that night. So wild." Charlie's eyes became saucers and Dale worried he'd pushed the young man too far.

Dale nodded. "Okay, Charlie. I think you've said enough. We can take it from here. We'll find Jojo."

"I've helped?"

"Loads. You have no idea, mate. You've been brilliant. Thank you."

Charlie retrieved his iPad and spoke while resuming his game. "I'm so scared all the time now. I know I've destroyed Mum's life, but I don't know what to do to get well." He smiled.

Dale had seen nothing so fragile, broken, shattered.

"You have an amazing parent there. She'll help you heal." Even to his own ears, he sounded baffled about how to handle Charlie.

Grace rolled her eyes at him and took Charlie's hand off the pad. "Listen to me. You are a strong man, who was taken advantage of by a bad one. You trusted Guru Raj. That was a mistake. Staying in this reality with your mum can't be that bad. Try to do that, and you'll be helping her, Charlie. No drugs, no booze, take your meds. You'll be okay."

"You think Guru Raj was a fraud, don't you?" A small voice, like a five-year-old trying to find out the truth.

"I'm so sorry, Charlie. Yes, he is a fraud and by giving you those drugs, he committed a terrible crime. He placed you all in danger." Grace fished around in her handbag for a moment. "Here, this is my business card for work. We're always looking for volunteers for different projects. There's a cool tree-planting one right now. Strong young men would be handy. We're all old! Come and help plant trees. You'll feel better."

"I'd have to leave the house," Charlie whispered.

"And talk to people, but I'll be there. It's fun. We're mostly older people, so no pressure."

Charlie put the card in his hoodie pocket. "I'll think about it."

Grace gave him one of her full wattage smiles and he responded. Dale doubted anyone on the earth could resist that smile.

Back in the car, Dale heard her exhale slowly. "You okay?"

"Not really. I've interviewed dozens of kids like him during the process of getting my doctorate, and it's always the same. The same visuals, the same auditory experiences, the same belief systems. The desire to be special in this mundane world. To escape responsibility. To be 'chosen'. When they come back, like Charlie might, it's a lifelong battle with the need to be special and having to live an ordinary life. I hate drugs. I hate them being illegal, so there's no control over what they're made with, or how much someone takes."

Dale had been a part of the drugs' culture his entire life, one way or another. He just didn't want to think about it anymore. He opted to lighten the mood. Smirking, he said, "I can't get over I'm going on a date with a doctor. Dr Grace Beloe."

She chuckled. "Don't worry, I still find it hard to believe. Though, it's cool, huh?"

"Very, and for the record, I agree. I've seen some terrible things on the streets and in prison. The bodies..." He left the sentence there. He didn't need to explain.

Grace shook herself all over, making the car sway a little. "Let's find something very twee, safe, and ordinary to do."

"Lunch?"

"Perfect."

~ *Chapter 16* ~

THAT AFTERNOON, AFTER DROPPING GRACE back at the community centre, Dale rang Lauren. Milly arrived, doing a fine impression of a drowned hedgehog, round and grumpy with her spines jabbing the unwary.

"We found him. Or we think we have." She plonked herself down at the desk and shook out her hair. Dale heard rain hitting the stone floor.

"Really?"

She glared at him. "What, didn't think I'd manage it?"

"Didn't think the weather would help." Sheepish, he sounded sheepish.

"No, don't suppose you did. However, Sully is part fish, so he dragged me up the river until we found the boat."

Dale leaned back in his office chair. "Well done."

"Not really. The flooding river took the boat away before I could climb on board and do a little exploring."

He leaned forward. "You what? Milly, I don't pay you to take risks like that. You don't know what kind of man we're dealing with. You didn't know if he was on the thing."

If it were possible, she looked even more pissed-off. "I wish you and Sully would stop pretending I can't look after myself and make my own decisions about my safety. It was small. He can't live on it. A mad racist who lives in Curload thinks he knows where the nasty illegal immigrant—because that's what they all are apparently—told me where the only person in the area who isn't Anglo-Saxon might be living."

He took a beat to make sure he didn't piss her off. Then changed his mind. "First, I'm sorry for caring, as I'm sure Sully is." He watched as his assistant stuck her tongue out at him and blew a raspberry. "Second, bloody well done. Mad racist aside, you had a productive morning."

"I'm going to phone Mr Newbury. Let him know the progress of the case."

Dale nodded and saw Lauren limping up the path. "Okay, but don't tell him where the guru is, we don't want any vigilante silliness. We'll go visit together. I don't want you handling that alone." He held up his palm as she protested. "No, that's my final word. Not alone."

Lauren opened the door to the office and a gust of wind, leaves, and rain came with her. "That's nasty." She almost had to wrestle the door closed. Brushing blonde hair out of her face and propping her stick against the wall, she smiled at Dale. "It's taken a lot of effort to get up here. I hope it's worth it."

He expected the usual kick in the gut reaction to her presence, but barely a ripple passed through him.

Don't screw up your freedom, bruv. The soft murmur leaked through his mind. Too bloody right. He wouldn't screw things up with Grace.

"It'll be worth the effort, I promise." He stood and walked around his desk to find her a chair. "Drink?"

"G&T out of the question?"

"You're still on duty."

She gave a heartfelt sigh. "I know. You've been to see Charlie Brent?"

"I have, and Milly has found our missing Guru Raj."

"Your favourite suspect for what, exactly?" Lauren rubbed her thigh.

Milly turned back to her computer, but Dale didn't miss the anger in her expression.

"Well, if nothing else, the man's committed fraud."

"Because he took money to guide people on a spiritual quest? Glastonbury's been making money on the back of religious quests for centuries. We can't lock him up for that."

"He's damaging property, and he gives people Class A drugs." Milly's words came out in a flurry, almost as fast as her angry fingers skittering over the keyboard.

"We'll find you the evidence, Lauren. I know you want more information about Adele Smith's killer. That's your priority. Mine is Joanna Wolski. Adele is dead. Joanna might still be alive."

Her eyes narrowed. "You make it sound like a bad thing, wanting justice for Adele."

She had a point. He chose language he knew would provoke a negative reaction from her. Pushing her away wouldn't help them in the long-term. He relaxed his stance and perched on the edge of his desk. "You're right. Adele is just as important. The computer has transcribed my interview with Charlie. I'll send you both files. You'll hear Grace Beloe asking questions. I gave her the lead because she's had a lot of experience working with people like Charlie."

Lauren drew back in her chair and frowned. "The woman from the community centre? I've met her at some function or another I had to attend as the highest ranking police official in the area. We chatted. She's..." Lauren puffed out her cheeks. "She's just an admin person."

"Grace has a doctorate in the importance of correct questioning for victims and suspects of severe drug abuse so the police can take accurate information. She's qualified as an appropriate adult."

Lauren's expression closed down. He watched it happen, her transformation into cop-mode. "Alright, give me the highlights." She hated being corrected on her opinions about people.

"Charlie and our missing American, Jojo, saw a boat come up the river. He's not sure if it's Parrett or the Tone, but my money is on the Parrett. It goes to South Perrott and comes out at the Bristol Channel. Charlie believes he saw his Uncle Carlton on the river that night, digging holes."

"What?" Lauren's one word explosion arrived with scorn hot enough to burn. "You're going to believe a drug addled addict? You think he saw his uncle from on top of the Mump digging holes in the damp soil just off the River Parrett? Why would that be relevant?"

"Charlie and Jojo freaked out because they saw guns. They had to talk to the others about what they'd seen. By this point, just so you know, the kid—Sonny Collins—had already gone, been kicked out. His sister was there—"

Lauren sat up, shaking her head. "Wait. What? Eliza Collins was part of this group as well? She wasn't on the list."

"Well, she was there. It didn't prevent them from kicking out her brother, either. Lauren, the important bit of this is that Carlton McKie could have been on the Somerset Levels burying something."

"Why would he choose here?" Lauren asked.

"Because he and his sister spent their summers here as kids. He feels safe, and he knows the area around Burrow Mump very well. His grandfather taught him to handle boats."

Milly added, "And we have four clients who are complaining about someone digging up their fields. This man has a remarkable resemblance to Guru Raj."

"Why would—"

"Think, Lauren. The police in Bristol don't know how the gang took the loot from the robbery they know McKie planned. There is no CCTV of them leaving Bristol on the roads and we know he didn't use a private plane. Why not use a boat? It's the perfect getaway vehicle if you know how to handle one. He's in prison for completely different offences. What if you've been looking on roads when you should've been looking at boats? It's not going to take much to sail down the Bristol Channel, up the River Parrett to some recognisable place, then bury a box full of gemstones and cash."

Lauren smiled, that feral hunger back. "You believe me now? You think these people are being killed by one of McKie's people?"

"I think that night on the Mump was a busy one and someone saw something that means seven people are either dead or they're on a list."

"Then you need to talk to McKie." The light in Lauren's eyes as she scented prey made Dale's stomach twist.

Dale closed his eyes and felt the tension swamp him. He wanted to curl up in a ball and hide. Instead he said, "I'll go talk to McKie. I agreed, after all. Charlie and his mother need resolution and you need answers for the victims of that night."

YOU SHOULDN'T BE HERE, BROTHER. The voice was emphatic, louder than it had been in weeks and held a note of panic the living embodiment of Ringo would recognise as his own. Dale felt the same panic at the very core of his being. He shouldn't be here. He shouldn't be doing this. He was *not* this person.

Lauren couldn't waste her time trying to gain access to a prisoner about a crime for which they had no actual evidence, just a hunch. Dale knew perfectly well she should be chasing down McKie's known associates and asking them if they left London often enough to murder a young woman. Oh, and leave a calling card in the shape of a black diamond. She should request a meeting with her DCI, McKie's solicitor, and whoever had managed to put the man on remand. She should share her information, even if it came from the mind of a broken young man. No, Lauren decided all that would take too long. She needed information now.

Dale had his own agenda. He needed to know where Joanna Wolski might be and if McKie held the key to that riddle. If he asked the right questions, this could end today, but only if his damned hands would stop shaking. On the drive down to Exeter, he'd had to pull over, and he'd lost the coffee he'd drunk that morning. He'd tried for food with the coffee, but despite the long run, he'd had no appetite.

Lauren's blackmail, 'Do as I ask, or I'll squash Charlie Brent and his mother', hadn't helped his mood. He'd hated her for that. He knew he owed the Brents nothing, but his past held them to his heart. A past full of mothers and sons paying for the foolish actions of the men in their lives. Even as police, he'd scared family members, threatened them, even hurt the ones who deserved it occasionally. There's nothing like having a police officer, one working for the bad guys, put the screws on you for a bad debt, lost drugs, or just for stepping out of line. What would Grace think if he ever dared to tell her the whole truth?

He hadn't slept, running through those memories, feeling the sorrow of a man who'd laid down his guns. Those weapons were hard to pick up when they held the weight of guilt and regret.

Dale stood outside the prison, pockets empty except for his identification and phone. He'd left his wallet in the car and hidden the keys. He didn't want the prison officers going through his stuff. Paranoid perhaps, but he hadn't served his full time and in the darkest hour of the night, the old fear rose. The tentacles of his Lovecraftian monster letting him know he had yet to pay his debt to society.

The panic bubbled, surfaced for a long moment, tightening his chest and making his vision blur.

"First visit?" came a voice from his right.

Dale stood on the quiet leafy road that sat below the prison. He looked to his right, then down. A small man, held together like desiccated leaves, skin almost transparent and slightly yellow, peered up at him.

"Here? Yes." He answered in a measured way, the panic washing back in the face of the watery brown eyes.

"I've been visiting men here for years. Spent some of them on the inside as well." The man chuckled, a sound of old tobacco and cheap whisky.

Dale grinned. "Yeah, I did my service in The Scrubs."

"Ah, that explains the fear I see in you." The old man had the softest, palest of Irish accents. "I come and visit those who have no one. The guards give me a nod to the men who are suffering, and I lend an ear, a friendly face. A connection to the outside world."

"That's good of you." The two of them began the walk up the steep slope to take them to the visitors' entrance to the prison. A vast Victorian edifice— they really liked to build their prisons to last—of red brick and sandstone windows.

"This place isn't the prison it used to be." The old man wheezed, and Dale shortened his stride. "Too many drugs, too many suicides, not enough help for those who are facing long-term sentences."

Dale gazed up at the heavy frontage, built like some hybrid between a castle and a school. "It's a difficult transition." They hadn't given him the privilege of coming to a place like Exeter, a place where prisoners can learn what the next five, ten, fifteen years of their lives are going to be like. He'd done his research, of course. Exeter had a mix of Cat B offenders. He'd been in a Cat C prison in London. These guys were long-termers but not the really nasty ones, just those foul enough to keep locked up years, not months.

He walked in through the main door with the old man leading the way. A group of women, some with children, were already in a queue waiting to be searched.

Dale felt it seep into him. The smell: institutionalised men and cleaning products, coated in cheap food. The terrible scent also contained black despair and anger. Colours hit him next: muted green and pink layered over naked brick. A flash of tinsel or glitter from a child's toy clutched in a nervous hand. A scream of neon Lycra straining over thighs and bellies that didn't visit a gym. The bleak acceptance of the visitors that someone they cared about had made a mistake and it wasn't just the criminal paying the price.

He'd had no visitors in four years.

Locked up twenty-three hours a day inside a building where almost everyone hated him.

He stood in the line and closed his eyes. He needed a buffer against the reality of the moment. So, he began building the image of his bird table and that damned cheeky robin that scolded the blackbirds, sparrows, and tits.

That's when it changed for him. He'd be leaving this place. No one would beat him in the showers; pay the guards to look away in the common areas, the mess hall, the exercise yard. He'd survived prison, and that man had found peace among the apple trees and boggy soil of the Somerset lowlands.

"There you go," murmured the old man in approval.

Gates opened, gates closed. Metal clinked and clanged. A strange dislocation of memories, terrors, and judgements. He'd learned that he deserved every damned moment he'd spent in that place.

Strange hands searching his body. His flesh crawled. They eyed him, the colour of his skin, his sheer size, the dark eyes, the expensive jeans and shirt. He knew he should've dressed down. They found nothing. Whatever Lauren wanted from him, if they mentioned a strip search, he'd be gone. Never again would he suffer that humiliation.

Walking. Heavy corridors. The weight of history a burden. Ten thousand souls, broken and damaged beyond repair, rippled through the bleak corridors, ghosts to join the living. The few, the lucky few, who'd survive and thrive after prison, never left an impression on those thick walls, only those trapped in misery. It didn't matter what colour they painted the bricks; they were black with it. Not the clear, deep black of the night sky, the black of peat, of coal, of the devil himself.

"Mr Valentine."

Dale looked up, surprised to hear his name. "Yes."

"This way." A bored prison officer, big over the shoulders and through the belly. He pointed to an entrance that would suck Dale deeper into the maze.

He pushed open the heavy fire doors. They looked like ordinary doors, the kind you'd find in a hospital or school, but these were heavy with large locks on them that could snap closed from a distance. Just in case of madness or desperation. This room, the one that connected the inside world and the outside, it smelt of cheap perfume and desperation.

A man sat alone and upright. Tall and slim. An older version of his sister, the mirror of his nephew. A handsome man if it weren't for the cruelty leaking out of him. Dale could almost see it, like the auras people babbled about in Glastonbury. A haze of smoky grey and pus yellow.

Dale again felt something shift inside him. The man who'd run up the Tor that morning during the grey light of dawn vanished. Like a conquering trick. As if he'd never existed.

He walked through that large and noisy hall like a predator. A killer. A stealer of babies. A crusher of lives. The child who grew up in London and stole money to buy food for himself and his siblings. The pusher, dealer, dirty cop, prisoner. The hunter and destroyer.

The man at the table watched him approach and one savage recognised another. McKie's expression became wary. Dale knew he was searching his memory for the face, which of his enemies Dale might work for, but he didn't know, and it scared him. McKie didn't remember meeting the dirty cop who helped Mr Roy drive the gangster out of Peckham.

A quiver of joy at the man's fear made Dale check himself. He wasn't here to hurt or hunt, he was here to help Charlie Brent and to find Joanna Wolski.

"Carlton McKie?"

"Who are you?" Slim hands rested on the plastic table top.

Dale folded himself into the small chair attached to the table and the ground. "My name is Dale Valentine. I run a detective agency."

McKie was wary and confused. "That doesn't answer my question." Hard London accent, but with a hint of Scots. His sister did better at hiding her past.

"I'm here because your nephew and sister could be in danger."

The sharp jaw tightened, and the hands balled into fists. The scarring of past fights made the skin oddly smooth, considering the bloke had to be in his fifties. "No one touches my family."

Dale held up a hand. "I'm not here to threaten you, Mr McKie. I am here to ask for your help."

McKie barked a laugh. "Not much I can do from here."

"I think you're wrong." A flare in those hard eyes. No one told this man he was wrong. Dale added, "The police can't ask these questions. That's why I'm here."

A frown now. McKie sat back and crossed his arms. "What do you want?" The gambler in all criminals sensed a deal to be made.

"The night you took a small boat up the River Parrett in Somerset, they saw you. Charlie saw you."

McKie snorted. "I've never—"

Dale held up his hand. "I'm not police. I don't care why you were there." He'd always been good at lying. "What I care about is who else knows those idiots were up on the Mump that night. People are dying. The police think it's linked to you and your friends. Those that helped you create your dragon's hoard of prizes that you didn't earn."

McKie watched Dale. He felt the examination like an evil plastic surgeon might examine a woman's face, before turning her into a living doll.

"You saw my family?" McKie asked.

Dale gave a single nod.

"How's Charlie?" McKie sounded fragile, that interested Dale.

"Healing. Slowly. Your sister is an amazing woman."

McKie's eyes narrowed.

Dale chuckled. "Not my type."

"Only two things in my life are worth anything, my sister and her kid. I'll do anything to help them." A grudging confession.

"I understand." Dale leaned forwards. Checked the room for guards. They were watching, but they weren't close. "Could your associates be capable of removing potential witnesses to protect your legacy?" He'd chosen his words with care.

McKie knew it. "My legacy." Scorn for himself. He took a breath and Dale watched the dark inside the man fall away, just for a moment. "No one in my crew would hurt Charlie, and we didn't know a bunch of fucking hippies on a hill had seen us. I was lifted in the month afterwards, but Charlie's psychosis had really set in by then and my sister was frantic. Charlie tried to tell me what he'd seen." A black dog's barking laugh. "Wanted to know if I was an emissary from the other dimension. Poor bloody kid was raving. I didn't tell any of my people when I figured out what the hell he'd seen. No one has ever interviewed me about it, so the police don't know there were witnesses. Why do you think Charlie's in danger?"

Dale considered the man's statement. As a professional liar and a professional seeker of the truth, he knew a tall tale from an honest one. McKie knew nothing about the murders.

"One of the worst things about being in prison is not knowing what's happening to loved ones on the outside. Those we've sworn in our hearts to protect. So, I'm going to tell you what's happening, and I'll tell you how I'm going to protect your family."

For the rest of the visiting hour, Dale talked and McKie listened.

~ *Chapter 17* ~

A SNARL-UP ON THE M5 going east meant Dale didn't hit Sedgemoor until sunset. Colour raged over the autumn sky. Deep grey storm clouds, darkening blue from the horizon to the zenith, the orange and red a scream from the dying sun. A stolen, vanishing sun. A vanished daughter, Joanna Wolski's pale beauty, haunted every mile from Exeter to Glastonbury. Dale had to update her father, but not tonight.

His grip on the Audi's steering wheel made his knuckles pale and his fingers ache. He focused only on driving. After leaving the prison, he'd walked Exeter for hours. Switched off his phone, becoming lost in the ancient, medieval heart of the city. He found the swathe of green outside the cathedral and stood in awe of its ancient splendour. It whispered of times he didn't understand, but he felt its peace wash outwards.

He wasn't ready. He had no forgiveness in his soul able to accept that lure of potential mercy. The broken ruins of Glastonbury Abbey suited him far more. He walked on, into the estates that bred the most common inmates of the prison. Small-time thieves, pushers, users, abusers. Grime, familiar and safe. The multicultural elements were nothing like London, just a shadow in comparison, but still there, still normal for him. He didn't stand out like he did in Glastonbury. Even with the designer jeans and hand-finished leather boots.

By the time he returned to the Audi, the car forever patient and forgiving, he felt no peace but had a driving need to go home. He had to remember the man he'd been yesterday, last week, last month. Not the one who'd walked out of HMP Exeter. Not the one who'd walked out of HMP Wormwood Scrubs. The man who'd failed to keep his best friend alive.

Dale needed help, but he didn't know where to go, who to trust, who could bring him back...

Lauren? The idea died before it was really born. She'd understand, to an extent, but she had little sympathy and no real awareness of life in prison, of what drove him to be the corrupt police officer she'd used so readily.

Milly? He couldn't lay this on a child. Her entire world existed in the soft folds of Glastonbury's hills.

His thoughts turned to Grace. Could he do this to her?

The phone rang on his car's internal system. He glanced at the screen. Grace. He wasn't ready.

"Damn it." He pulled over into someone's driveway, too strung out to talk and drive at the same time. Accepting the call, he managed, "Hi."

"Dale." A long pause. "You okay?" An honest enquiry. He heard her integrity in that simple question. Grace helped people. She knew how to help people. A woman who wanted to understand what made men like him do crazy, stupid things that landed them in trouble.

"I'm not okay, but I will be. How are you?" He stared up at the last rays of the dying sun as they turned the bellies of the storm clouds angry red.

"Worried about you. Milly said you had to go interview someone in Exeter prison."

"She shouldn't have said that."

Grace ignored him. "Apparently, you haven't been answering your phone, and she's panicking about you tripping-out on past lives, or something. She talks a lot when she's trying not to panic."

Dale chuckled despite himself. The ties and connections to Somerset repairing, growing stronger, pulling him back from the ocean of his past, to the safe harbour of his present and future. "Yeah. She does that when she's worried."

"Can I phone her and tell her you're okay?" Grace asked.

"Yeah. Sure. I'll be home soon." A long pause. "Um, Grace..." He lost his courage.

"I'll text you my address. Come for dinner. It won't be fancy, but it will be good food. I like to eat."

Dale bowed his head for a moment. "Thank you."

"Drive home safe and I'll see you soon."

A text message appeared with a postcode and Dale plugged it in. The map showed The Roman Way. It ran up and around the farside of one of Glastonbury's special hills. He'd run it many times, but if the Romans built this road, they had no concept of space. The Audi growled up the street, taking up far more room than a Roman chariot ever would have done. At the moment, the back of the dragon that gave the hill its shape didn't matter to him, only the thought of reaching those soft, moss-green eyes and the gentlest smile he'd ever seen. When he reached the address, he breathed out. A small, old, council looking house, very square, off-white, damp, and rather sad around the edges. The paint didn't cover the window frames. The door, when he reached it, had rot in both bottom corners.

He knocked, hoping the thing wouldn't fall in under the pressure.

"Coming." The lively call made him feel... What?

Safe, bruv. That's what safe feels like.

The door opened; Dale summoned a smile. He'd stopped off at the supermarket and had a bottle of red and white in either hand.

Grace laughed. "My reputation precedes me, I see."

"I wasn't sure what we were going to be eating."

Her eyes widened. "You mean there's a wine that's supposed to be drunk with a specific food? I thought you just necked it to get pissed." She smacked her forehead with the palm of her hand, leaving a puff of flour on her temple. "Well, that's where I've been going wrong all these years."

Dale took in another deep breath and released the mould of dark that had followed him back from the prison.

He also smelt the kitchen. "Is that chicken pie?" The lure, after a day of fasting, had him over the threshold faster than Grace could move back. He almost ran her over, thrusting both bottles into her hands.

"Boots," she yelled at him.

Somehow, she sounded just like his Italian grandmother. Dale yanked off his boots while he moved, a well-practiced move from childhood. The carpet was clean, though old, the hall narrow and crowded with a mountain bike leaning against the wall.

He stopped in the doorway to the kitchen. Chaos reigned supreme.

"I haven't had time to clean up yet. I'm making bread as well." Grace moved past him and looked small suddenly, her confidence gone. She seemed embarrassed. "It's not much as houses go, but I've rented worse and it's dry, mostly." Her smile wavered.

Dale considered his next action for all of five seconds, which felt plenty long enough. He approached Grace, making her eyes widen with a mix of alarm and desire.

"Yes?" he asked as he cupped her small face in his big hands.

She nodded. "Please."

He gently drew her into a kiss. His first after Lauren. It had been so long. Such a very long time. She tasted of butter and roast chicken. She felt like warm bread and hot chocolate, like summer days in a meadow, spring sunshine and autumn winds. Her scent, natural of course, drove him wild and as his kiss deepened, his arms drew her closer. She clutched at him and gave back all he requested. Right there, he felt it in his core, right there he glimpsed the future, and he held it in his arms.

When he finally gave her back to the world, she wobbled a little on her feet. "Well, I wasn't expecting that."

Dale didn't have grown-up words. All he wanted to do was go caveman on the poor woman, throw her over his shoulder, and carry her off up the stairs.

"I like chicken pie," he managed.

Grace laughed. The tension didn't leave them, the desire didn't vanish, it just morphed into something safer. They ate, they drank, they tumbled into bed.

DALE HUMMED A TUNE HE'D name *the Joy of the Roman Way* as he strolled away from the community centre, having walked a blushing Grace to work. He'd forgotten how wonderful intimate human contact could be, especially with a woman like Grace Beloe.

He'd pick her up a breakfast bap from the Green Man, dig out Milly, and catch up Lauren on the news—from McKie, not about Grace. First, though, he needed to shed the ridiculous grin he'd been wearing since he'd woken up in Grace's bed.

The day promised rain. In fact the High Street of Glastonbury was naked of punters with a zombie movie, end-of-the-world vibe. None of the tourist shops were open. The flooding on the Levels made it harder to reach the town.

He turned the corner to go into the Green Man café from the back entrance, knowing locals had first call on the kitchen during the off season trade, when his world turned black.

A weight shoved him between the shoulder blades, hard and heavy. Dale stumbled into the wall, smashing his face and shoulder. He tried to shout and turn to fight, but another heavy blow caught the side of his head, making the blackness spark and shimmer. Rough hands trapped his arms and hauled. Dazed, blinded by a hood, his hands already cuffed in zip ties, men grunting with effort and cursing, dragged him. Vomit rose in his throat. He battled it back. For years, he'd trained for just this kind of attack, but panic hit him hard. Nothing happened. His body didn't respond. The world shifted. He hit a floor, cold, hard, uneven. The door slid shut with a roll and a clang. Utter darkness.

An engine rumbled, he tumbled over as it headed up the hill at speed.

A soft whimper and a half sob.

He wasn't alone. Rolling onto his knees, spreading his weight to remain upright as the vehicle lurched around a corner, he tried to shake the hood off. It wouldn't come and he realised someone had zip tied it around his throat. Not tight enough to do damage, but he'd never be able to pull the hood off. Whoever had him knew what they were doing.

Old enemies? Police? London coming down to Somerset to make a point about how rural life made a man weak?

Another whimper.

"Who is that?" he snapped.

"Dale?"

He'd know that voice anywhere. "Oh, God, Milly."

A bigger sob. "I can't see." Her voice, high, small, thin, a taut wire.

He shuffled closer to the voice and bumped into the smaller body with an *ooff* from both of them. With his hands cuffed behind his back, Dale could offer no real comfort, but he felt her press her head into his chest. He bent over her, offering what protection he could from whatever they faced.

"You're wearing a hood?" he asked.

Milly sniffed. "Yeah."

"Is it tied around your throat?"

"Yeah." An edge of panic.

"That's good, Milly. That means they don't want us to see them, which means they probably plan on scaring us and leaving us alive."

"Is that supposed to be a comfort?" she almost shouted.

He thought it was, but clearly she didn't. Milly's reaction was probably the sensible one.

"When did they take you?" he asked.

"Just as I was leaving to walk up to the office," she replied, her voice a little less shaky. He felt her trembling, though.

"When did you last take your medication?"

She managed a soft, amused snort. "Don't worry. I'm good on that score, despite being terrified witless."

"Did they say anything to you?"

"Only to stay silent or they'll hurt someone. They asked a few questions."

Dale wriggled again, until he sat more comfortably beside her, her shoulder touching his upper arm. "They didn't say anything to me. These guys are good, efficient, professional."

"You're trying to comfort me again, aren't you?"

"I'm guessing it's not working."

"Not really."

Silence for a bit. The van rocked, curled through lanes, rumbled up hillsides. It smelt of nothing more sinister than metal, exhaust fumes, and cleaning fluid. Actually, come to think of it, smelling this strongly of cleaning fluid might not be a good thing.

Milly said, "You went AWOL yesterday. Grace rang me in the end. Not cool, Guv."

"I know, I'm sorry."

"You shouldn't have gone to Exeter on your own."

"I know. I'm sorry."

"You okay now?"

"I was on cloud fucking nine until this happened," he said, feeling nothing short of glum. He'd just wanted a few hours where he could enjoy the dazzling lightness inside his body. The amazing gift Grace had given him, that they'd shared. But no, he couldn't even be allowed a few hours.

"Do I want to know?" Milly asked.

"Probably not. However, I know McKie isn't the one killing these people. He didn't know Charlie and Joanna had seen him."

"You believed him?"

"Very much."

Silence for a bit, but he knew that silence. It was 'Milly's planning on asking me questions I might not want to answer', silence.

"What was it like? Talking to him?" she asked.

There we go. "I won't lie and say being in there was easy. It wasn't. I spent most of the day walking around Exeter trying to get my head straight. It was like two of me existed in the same space. The past me, the one that would fight my way out of this van, regardless of the cost to you, and the present one, that just wants us to get out of this in one piece." It was the best way he had to explain what had happened to him yesterday.

"The disconnect was so profound I… I kinda lost all cohesion for a while. Like I did when I first left prison, and didn't really know who I wanted to be, just knowing I needed to be different. When I left The Scrubs, it was fast. They did the deal in days. It shocked me. I always thought, presuming I lived long enough, I'd have months or years to prepare the new version of the man I wanted to walk out of those gates. I had days, and he was a wisp, a ghost, inside me. A barely formed construct who wanted to do the right thing, but didn't fully understand what that might involve."

Silence.

Dale had to fill it. For the first time he had to give her more information than she'd asked for. Like a dam leaking water, it began as a trickle until the moment it burst. "I was scared and alone for four years. Tim was my cell mate for a while. He was in for cybercrimes. They had caught him hacking government servers. They'd wanted to throw him into a high max prison like Belmarsh, but Tim had contacts and money, real money, hidden away. He received a reduced sentence and a Cat C prison. What he didn't bargain on was how pretty and small he was, how fresh and drug free."

"The other prisoners…?"

"They tried. A few times. The last one, I lost it. I just… They'd hurt me too often for me to see Tim suffer. I don't mean they raped me. They weren't stupid. To get that close for long enough was too dangerous with me, but Tim? He was like a damsel in a castle."

"And you became his knight?" she asked.

Dale huffed. "More like the big bad dragon come to finish."

"What did you do?"

He sighed. If he told her, she'd be an accessory after the fact. "You don't want to know." He rubbed his fingertips together. They felt numb except for the slip and slide of blood that he knew wasn't his and didn't exist. Not in the present anyway.

"Okay." She sounded sad. "Do you really think we'll get out of this alive?"

"I do. I think we just stay calm. Do as we're told. Answer questions."

"Who did this?"

"Let's hope we never find out."

The vehicle slowed and pulled over, making them rock forwards and slam back into the side of the panel van.

"Oh God," Milly whispered.

Dale shuffled around, putting himself between her and where he thought the doors were. He felt her legs open, so he shuffled back until her knees pressed against his flanks and his bound hands rested on her belly. She trembled.

"Just don't make too much noise, Milly. Let me do the talking."

"I don't want to die."

He wanted to answer her, but he heard footsteps crunching and a soft curse, followed by, "I bloody hate the countryside." He knew that accent.

North London and English, no other accent like Russian or Arabic. How many enemies had he made that would do this? That would risk this? Taking him was one thing, but taking Milly made little strategic sense for professionals if he wasn't around to pay a ransom.

He took a breath. Hamster-wheeling thoughts about the who, the why and the what, wouldn't help. He didn't know, he couldn't plan, he couldn't anticipate, he had to take some of his own advice and just stay calm.

The back door to the van clicked open, rather than slid. "Get out," came the order.

He tried to say, "Not until—" But he yelped as two powerful pairs of hands yanked on his ankles and dragged him out of the van. He hit the ground arse first, then shoulders and his head cracked on the bottom of the van.

"I said out."

Dale's head swam off for long seconds as he heard Milly, from a great distance, trying to apologise. He lay in mud. It was cold, clammy and stank of farm waste.

"Just stay there," came a rough order from some distance away.

Those hands, again two pairs, hauled him up.

"Fuck, you stink now, mate."

The man shoved him hard, and Dale stumbled forwards a few steps until he fell to his knees.

"That'll do."

Something hard and small and round pressed against the back of his head, just behind his ear. "Oh fuck…" For the first time genuine terror scorched through his body.

"Dale?" Milly called out, her voice a soft pleading. She'd heard his fear.

He tried to swallow.

"Are you listening?" came the question in hard English.

"I am," he managed, willing his body away from the gun but unable to move.

"We will say this just once. If you obey, you will both live. If you do not? We will be back, and nothing can protect you. Is this understood?"

"Yes."

"Say it correctly."

Dale knew this was a controlling tactic for everyone in a position of power. "I understand you are going to give us an instruction and if we obey, you will not return. If we don't. We die."

"Good boy. I'll be forced to kill your girlfriend and Milly's boyfriend. Maybe her parents. Is that crystal fucking clear?"

Whoever this was knew their lives intimately. "Yes, sir." Dale felt the gun ease off the back of his skull, and he risked a deeper breath. His heart rabbited in his chest and even if he could get up and free his hands, he knew he'd never be able to fight. Fear dominated every heartbeat. Somerset wasn't supposed to feel like this.

"Stop looking for the prizes won in Bristol. Do we understand each other?"

Dale blinked several times. He'd not expected this. "McKie sent you?"

The gun returned with more force, making his body bend and a roaring voice bellowed in his ear, "Do not mention that name again!"

"I understand, I understand, I understand," he almost wailed. He felt tears and snot under the hood. He didn't care.

"Say it!" came the same bellow.

"Don't look for prizes from Bristol. I get it. I get it."

"Good. Count to one-hundred." The gun left the back of his head, and he heard sucking footsteps move away. "Don't make us come back. Fucking boglands. I bloody hate cows."

Dale counted as the van started up and pulled away. He kept counting until he felt hands on him again and almost fell over in shock.

"It's me. It's me. It's me," Milly said. She pulled at the hood, and it slipped off. "They cut my hands free before they left." She sank into the mud next to him and threw her arms around his neck.

It rained on them. The sun felt like a hollow administrator to the day, just going through the motions of giving light behind the clouds, but no warmth. Dale sobbed; Milly wept. They remained in the mud for a long time.

~ *Chapter 18* ~

DALE CALMED FIRST. "LOOK INSIDE my coat. There's a penknife in the pocket, Milly. You can cut me free." He felt trembling fingers open his coat and fish around. She took hold of the knife, and he heard her try to breathe through her panic and fear.

She muttered, "I'm safe, I'm whole, I'm going to be fine. This is just a blip in the road. I'm a strong and capable woman. I am not a victim. *I am not a victim.*" This last affirmation sounded as if it came through clenched teeth.

Christ, what was this mantra? What had he done to her? Had he made her feel like a victim?

"I'm so sorry, Milly. I'm so bloody sorry." He felt her sawing at the plastic cuffs with the little knife.

"Not your fault." The plastic gave. "Ah, got-ya."

She cut the tie around his throat, and he took the knife off her so he could do the same for her throat. No obvious bruising on her pale skin, not yet, it just looked sore. While he sliced, both of them still in the mud on their knees, she smiled for him. They were both tear-stained, filthy, soaking wet.

Dale had never been so scared. He'd had knives held to his throat, guns pointed in his face, baseball bats—which could be the worst of those options—battered into his body, but this brief trip down into hell scared him more than any of that. Why?

He knew the answer. He'd gone soft. The cider orchards, thick loam of this land, and gentle mists, took his edge and dulled the blade. Nothing here spoke of the dangers people faced in Peckham when they walked on the wrong side of someone's gang. He'd done plenty of that, but prison, Ringo's death, moving down here, it took his steel edge and softened it. Unaware, he'd fallen into a way of life which almost ended up with Milly being hurt, or worse.

That came as another shock. The thought of losing Milly hurt as much as losing Ringo. How could he survive such grief a second time? Such guilt?

"This is my fault," he said.

She shook her head. "You never wanted to visit McKie in prison. This is Lauren's fault. She pushed you into it." Milly cocked her head, her red hair a soggy fizz in the rain, clumps of mud stuck in the tendrils. "It's not even her fault. Not really. It's McKie's fault."

"I'm happy to blame Lauren," Dale muttered, rubbing his wrists back to life and wiggling his fingers. No blood on his palms. Not his, not Ringo's, not anyone else's.

Milly struggled to her feet first and offered him a hand. "You're bleeding. Did they hurt you?"

Dale tested the place the van caught his scalp, just above his neck. "They caught me a few times. I think I'm alright, though."

"If you've had several knocks on your head. We should get you to a hospital."

He rubbed his hand over the short hair and checked his fingers. Only enough blood to show a graze. "I'll be fine." Then he looked around. "Where the hell are we?" His eyes flickered to his fingers again—no blood. Not rushing fluid coming out of holes in the body. *It's going to be fine.*

Milly walked, or rather plopped and sucked, her way through a field gate to the road. "Ah, as far as I can tell…" He watched her frown and push her hair back as the wind caught it again. "Um, we're in the peat cuttings. But where? I don't know. I can't even see the Tor in this weather."

Dale struggled up to his feet. His vision spun, but he kept breakfast down. Reaching the lane and watching the mud slide off his expensive Italian, hand-finished boots made him feel glad to be alive but sad for the demise of his favourite footwear. His jeans were filthy beyond saving, and he didn't have much hope for his coat either. A man his size had limited options.

These things were hardly a priority. Why did his mind always do this to him? Filling his head with irrelevant details. The most important mission was getting out of this weather and not freezing to death or drowning.

"We have to get moving. Can you walk okay?" He looked at his companion in misadventure.

She nodded. "I can walk."

He checked his pockets and grunted. "They really didn't mean to kill us, did they?"

"What makes you say that?" Milly asked.

He waggled his phone at her and pointed to the other side of the lane. Milly's rucksack, this one in rainbow colours, sat on the grassy verge. Her crow of delight raised a smile, and he closed his eyes for a moment, just feeling the wind and rain on his face.

Again, his mind played through the press of the gun against his skull. The heat of the man's hand. The strength in those brutal fingers. A terrible cold, disinterested voice delivering orders. A strange lack of communication between the kidnappers. It spoke of practise.

He took a calming breath, trying to find his centre. They were both alive. He had to hang on to that fact and remember it, burn it in so the terror would fade more quickly.

Milly dug out a bottle of water, two cereal bars, and a Mars bar. "We're going to be okay." A slight quiver stained her voice. He gave her a smile as she handed him the water after taking a gulp.

"Remind me to be abandoned on a desert island with you," he said, trying to lighten the moment.

She waggled her eyebrows at him and grinned. "We have apps. We can do this. Find a location on a map, call someone." She began to walk, talk, and fiddle with her phone. "Full battery, that's good. Who do we call? Lauren?"

Dale felt his eyes widen in alarm. "God no. She'll overreact. We need someone who won't panic."

"Sully or Grace?" Milly asked.

"I don't think Grace has a car." He didn't remember one outside the house, just the mountain bike.

"Sully then. He can borrow Mum's car."

The rain lashed at them. Milly shivered.

"Walk on the other side of me." Dale tugged her around his body. "Stay close and I'll break the worst of it for you."

She looked up, raindrops making her lashes shine. "You know this isn't your fault, right?"

"I think you should consider a new career."

"Never," she told him. "I'm good at this. We're good at this. I enjoy helping people and you make it easy for me. I can't hold down a normal job with normal people."

"We just got kidnapped and threatened with death, Milly." He needed her to process this and quickly, but being blasé about it wouldn't help either of them.

Milly put down her phone and drew him to a halt. "Listen to me, Dale Valentine. I will *not* change my life because someone scared me. Never again. I'm going to be very jumpy around white vans for a while and big men in leather jackets with London accents, but I'll be fine. I am not a victim. Neither are you." She poked him in the chest.

He nodded for her, put an arm around her shoulders, and gave her a quick hug. "You're amazing."

"I know. I'll cry about it all later." She went back to her phone, muttering something to do with 5G.

Dale thought about how she'd phrased her words. 'Never again' had been in there. Who had made Milly Wolfe a victim? How had she been broken so badly she'd never left Somerset when the woman was clearly a genius? He'd never asked, but he could imagine. He'd seen her fight in the dojo. Her grim determination.

"Oh, I know where we are." She interrupted his thoughts. "We're near the Railway Inn. I'll call Sully now and we can keep walking."

"There's a pub? Out here?" Maybe in the summer, in the sunshine, it could be nice. Right now, it looked like something out of a very wet post-apocalypse film. The leaves had been stripped, the grass lay tangled and dying, the fields a dark quagmire where they dug for peat.

If they'd been shot and dumped out here, in the peat, they might never have been found. He wondered how many bodies lived under that thick soil. Isn't this the type of place people used to be sacrificed?

"There it is." Milly pointed down the road.

"Don't think they'll let us in looking like this," Dale said as they hurried towards civilisation.

"Do you think Guru Raj is in danger from these men?" Milly asked.

"Why would they know how to find him?"

Milly gazed up at him. "They asked me, before they took you, and I..." Her eyes dropped. "I was scared."

Dale took hold of her shoulder and turned her to face him. "That's not on you. It was the right thing to do. I think we need to find him before McKie's men do, that's for certain, but whatever his fate, he created it. Right now, that's our first job. I gave that bastard McKie way too much information yesterday. He'll have worked out most of this without you. I should imagine you were just confirmation for them. He..." Dale realised what an idiot he'd been. "I just wanted him to understand we had his sister and nephew's best interests at heart. I'm a bloody fool."

She didn't look convinced by his words. "You were overwhelmed, and I doubt you were thinking clearly. Give yourself a break. Lauren shouldn't have insisted you talk to him. For all we know, she has an agenda we haven't understood yet."

"Like what?" They reached the pub, realised it was closed, but sheltered under the eaves. It really would be a charming little place in the summer, or on a winter day with frost on the ground. It had elements of a modern fairy tale location.

"Well, you don't know what other departments might ask her to do, using you as a resource. Like she did in London."

Dale gazed through the thickening rain. "She wouldn't..."

Milly leaned against him for warmth. "You sure?"

He opened his soggy coat and pulled her against his chest. The coat didn't come close to wrapping around them both, but it comforted them to be snuggled up.

"Sully won't be long," Milly muttered, her teeth chattering.

Dale grunted, still thinking about Lauren's agenda in all this. Could she really be that duplicitous?

There were many scenarios where that might be the case, but, surely, they'd become friends, equals even. Respected colleagues, maybe? She wouldn't use him to further an agenda he didn't know about, one that would help his career, but leave him and Milly in danger. No. Surely not.

The circle of his thoughts turned into a spiral and as Dale watched the rain waiting for Sully, he realised he could believe Milly's version of events all too easily. He'd known Lauren for years. She could be deeply empathic, and when you needed a strong arm in your corner, she'd be there, but...

Her ambition had turned into armour a long time before she'd met him, and that armour protected her conscience whenever she had a tough choice. Like choosing to keep secrets about a case and using him as bait. Her work with him had given her a promotion. He only had her word that she'd requested a quiet life in Somerset. Of course, down here, she had a far smaller pool to make her own. Rural DI could become a rural DCI with little more than the right closure rate for a small team.

"He's here," Milly said, pulling out of Dale's coat. It left his chest and belly cold. His heart had already turned to ice.

Milly sat in the back of the car.

Sully sat in the driver's seat, eyes wide. "What the hell happened to you two?"

Dale glanced at her and shrugged.

She explained. He noticed she sanitised the dramatics. Left off the hoods. Didn't mention the gun. Had she seen it? He hoped not. The feel of it left a cold patch on the back of his skull, just behind his right ear. If he reported this to the police, they'd find nothing. Glastonbury had very little CCTV and none for the community centre. The camera outside the pub and bank wouldn't catch the angle. The van covered his abduction from public view, and they'd just find a burned-out shell somewhere near the motorway. As a professional, it's what he'd have done. First, though, as a professional, he'd finish tidying up the mess.

"We need to find Guru Raj," he said, cutting across Milly. "We need to find him now. If these people found us that easily, then they'll find him. They have a vague location." He didn't mention it being Milly's confession. She didn't need the added pressure. "We have to get to Curload. I didn't give McKie details, but he could have rung Charlie or Catherine from prison and discovered what questions we'd asked."

Sully slowed down as they took a series of wobbly humps in the road. "Um, wouldn't it be better to go home? Get dry, eat, call the police?"

"No. Curload. Now. We should get Charlie into safe custody as well."

"He'll never leave that house," Milly said. "The people who just took us wouldn't hurt him."

"No, they wouldn't. You're right. They want this bloody guru for trying to dig up their treasure. Also, they didn't kill the other people in the group. Until I went to HMP Exeter, they didn't know they'd been seen. I've led them to Guru Raj. We have to go get him now. Charlie's in danger from whoever is killing people from the meditation group."

Dale knew he'd made a terrible mistake. He'd put Milly's life in danger and this Guru Raj would likely die if they didn't reach him first. Why had he done it? Why had he gone into the prison and just spilled his guts to McKie? What did he honestly expect the man to do? Millions of pounds worth of gems and cash had vanished during the raid and Dale had sent up a flare showing him all the players on the field. Prison wouldn't stop him from reacting to the threat. This was an unforgivable error in judgement.

"Milly?" Sully asked.

"He's right."

"You're both soaked, and filthy—"

Dale snapped, "And they will tear this guru to pieces if these guys find him. Curload, Sully. Get me to Curload or I'll drive."

"You can't take the car—"

Dale scoffed. "You think I don't know how to take a moving vehicle off someone?" He didn't, but Sully couldn't know that. He gave the younger man the benefit of his stare. One that he knew burned the steel out of tough men.

"Okay, Curload it is." The younger man shrank in on himself, pulled over, turned the car around and headed off to the other side of the Levels.

Dale twisted in his seat, which made his head throb and his right eye close for a moment. He didn't quite suppress the grunt of pain.

Milly scowled at him. "That wasn't very nice."

"I know. I'm sorry. Sorry, Sully."

The younger man waved it away. "It's your health at risk. Not mine." Still, he didn't look happy. Dale realised he'd lost the man's trust and he'd need to build it back.

"Milly, find this yurt's location if you can. I need a few minutes to think."

He closed his eyes and realised the crack he'd taken from being pulled out of the van hurt his head more than he'd confessed. Classic concussion: nausea, headache, blurry vision, wobbly body, exhaustion. He needed to be in the hospital.

A gust of wind and rain hit his side of the compact car and it rocked, then slid. Sully cursed, steered into it, and regained control. Water cascaded over the road and down it, creating weird illusions on the tarmac. The pixie-headed willow trees craned their heads to watch them pass. The clouds lowered over the moor, trying to squash the little vehicle under the deluge. Dale realised he'd made a mistake. This downpour wasn't just bad, it was dangerous. It changed nothing, though. They needed Guru Raj, and they needed him alive.

Sully drove through Ashcott and onto the main Taunton Road. Things became a little easier until they were once more crossing the flat lowlands of Sedgemoor. Red flood signs littered the road, shouting their warning and joining in the road closed signs to form a slalom. Sully drove around them.

"This is not a good idea," he muttered.

The little car rocked in the wind and Dale cursed. He wished they'd taken the time to go home. The Audi would have handled this. The three of them slumped into silence and concentrated on helping Sully stay on the road.

"I really am sorry about this, Sully," Dale said as they aqua-planed through the junction to take them towards Athelney.

"Well, if we drown here, then that's going to be on you." Sully kept hold of the steering wheel with such intensity, his knuckles looked like carbuncles on the plastic.

"You're doing really well."

"I took an advanced driving course in another life," Sully almost whispered, as if words were too much.

Milly dared to look away from the road. "You've never told me that."

"Well, I have now."

They crept up the lane. The wind and growing darkness hid the narrow slice of tarmac from the car's wheels just as much as a blinding rain. Houses on either side of them broke the weather slightly, but not enough to make life any easier. The occasional recycling bin dashed past them, and a branch hit the back of the car so hard it made them all yelp in shock. The car lurched forwards as if being swatted by a dirty old geezer in a pub.

"How much further?" Sully obviously fighting his rising panic.

Dale knew McKie's men had a big transit van, or something similar, so they needed to be aware of its arrival. It would stick to the road with more ease, but the wind would batter its larger frame. Maybe thugs from London wouldn't know how to drive these very narrow byways of the old world?

"Oh! Stop! This is where we were on the path when that horrid man told us about the yurt," Milly cried out, then muttered, "I can't believe I can get internet in this weather. Amazing really."

"Great, Milly, but where exactly?" Dale said. He realised he was shivering, badly.

"Oh, well…" She pointed in the direction she'd turned her phone, off to the right. "That's where the man said the house was."

"Stay here. Keep the engine running. See a tsunami of water on the way, drive off." He opened the car door and stepped out into the storm.

~ *Chapter 19* ~

THE MOMENT HE LEFT THE safety of the car, Dale stumbled. A small, but strong hand grabbed him to correct his balance.

"Seriously?" Milly's eyes were bright in her cold, pale face. "Like you can do this on your own."

He didn't have the strength to argue. Together, they plunged into the storm and walked up the gravel drive. Dale preferred not to think about how dreadful the walk turned out to be for them. His perceptions were playing with his mind. The world around him made little sense. The wind screamed at the trees bordering the fenced area, and in turn they howled and lashed at the sky. When he tried to focus more than a few metres ahead, the gathering shadows of an early dusk crawled over the ground and lurched upwards, smothering the light between the dark trunks.

A gust of wind hit him and knocked him sideways, the ground lurching. Water ran into his face, stinging and making him blind for long seconds. When his vision cleared, he saw Milly crouched on the path, trying to stay upright. All around them, the water rose and lapped at their narrow track. They were mere centimetres away from being a part of the flood.

Then, for one moment, the wind stopped. The rain continued to fall, but the overwhelming torment of the weather eased. Milly rose and looked at Dale. They started to hobble-run towards the gate.

"There," Milly cried out. She pointed to a small gap between the enormous trees. Without leaves on them, Dale had no chance of identifying them.

Amongst the thick, smooth trunks, a flash of something white caught his attention.

"It's canvas." Dale reached the gate, a simple farming affair, and kept hold of it as they stepped through, just in case the wind returned as quickly as it had vanished.

Hurrying now, the last dredges of their adrenaline pulling them towards their goal, they reached a tiny clearing. In it squatted a small yurt. The round canvas home was no more than five metres in diameter.

A tangle of outdoor living gear, including a long-handled spade, torn branches and other debris, littered the site. Dale decided they didn't have time to mess about.

"Anyone home?" he called out.

Milly's phone chimed. She took it out. "Shit, Sully's just seen a transit van drive past the turning. They'll find this place in no time."

"Damn it." He decided to do this old-school police style, the way they'd raid a dodgy flat or bedsit.

He didn't bother asking a second time. The low wooden door to the yurt gave easily under the heavy kick from his boot at the handle.

"Hey! You can't do that!"

The moment the door opened, Dale charged inside. The light wasn't great, and he couldn't see most of the yurt, but it looked dry, covered in rugs. A log burner gave it welcome warmth and the walls inside were like a huge wooden lattice. A man sat in a large armchair with a stack of books beside him.

Dale stood to his full height and dominated the small space, his head almost touching the ceiling this close to the entrance. "You're coming with me."

The man rose. Dale did a quick threat assessment. Maybe five feet ten, basic construction, thin but strong, with wide shoulders, narrow hips, skin darker than his, face more aesthetically pleasing than the average. A Bollywood look to him. Dale had dated several women of Indian heritage over the years, and he'd watched his share of Indian films. This bloke wouldn't be the star, but he'd be the best friend.

"We're leaving," Dale told him, crossing the small gap and grabbing the man's upper arm.

"What? Wait? Who are you?" The accent came from Birmingham, thick and pure.

Dale would bet all his wealth on this bloke using a very different accent when hooking his punters. "You've pissed off the wrong people and they are about to find you. Come with us or you're going to die a painful death. Besides, the river is about to explode, and you're not high enough to survive." While he spoke, Dale dragged the smaller man over the floor.

"What? What are you—"

Milly grabbed the man's coat and threw his boots at his chest. The man caught them. She said, "You've been searching for a hidden hoard of gems. The men who hid it aren't happy. They're coming. We're here to save you. Get moving."

In a blur, the fake guru was dragged out of his house, none too gently. Dale didn't have the energy to piss about. He used pressure points in the man's upper arm to force compliance. Easy enough to overcome if you knew what was happening, but this bloke had no idea. He yelped in shock every time he tried to pull away. Only going along with Dale's intentions made it painless. Holding his coat and boots, the fake guru hurried to keep up, sloshing through the mud in thick socks.

Dale watched the trees, knowing he had very little time to reach Sully. He didn't want to play with the blokes in the van, and he didn't want to drive away while trying to escape them. They needed this to happen fast and easy. The way this day was going, he'd be lucky to have either fast, or easy. To have both would be a flat out miracle.

The man made protests, voiced his innocence, yelled about kidnapping to the rising wind that once more tried to tear trees from the ground. He yanked back against Dale, jarring his head and making his brain explode in pain.

"Enough!" Dale bellowed. "You either do as I ask now, or I'll fucking drown you. I know you are Guru Raj, the man who took a bunch of whacked-out kids onto the Mump and filled them full of Class A drugs. You're in deep shit. I am your only way out. Do you understand?"

Dale realised he was only five centimetres from the other man's face. All his frustration and rage at being caught, the endangerment to Milly, not being able to fight back, having a bloody gun pressed into his skull, poured out with more ferocity than the river trying to break free of its confines.

From nowhere, the trusty little car appeared on the gravel track. Sully opened the door. "Get in, they're coming. I saw them trying to find a place to turn the van around. We have to hurry. The river's about to explode."

"My yurt," the fake guru moaned as they watched the water tumble over the high banks.

Dale placed a hand on the man's thick black hair and pushed him into the back of the car. Then he climbed in. The space would be hard for two miniature poodles to share, but two big men?

"I'm in a Buster Keaton movie," he muttered, his elbows pressed against his knees, his head bowed.

Milly scrambled into the front, water beginning to slosh around the wheels. She scooted her seat forwards to give Dale a little more room. "Get us out of here."

Not wasting any time, and being a great deal less cautious, Sully drove. He tore down the narrow lane, now a shallow river, water spraying everywhere. Soft, heart-felt prayers to various deities fell from his lips as they retraced their steps. Dale looked over his shoulder, the twist making him grunt in pain. The white van was behind them.

"Head back to Glastonbury," Dale ordered. "We can lose them in Othery, maybe."

Milly twisted and gasped. "Or maybe they'll drown." She pointed to the riverbank rising on their left.

He struggled to turn again. "Oh my God."

The river burst through the artificial bank and hit the van. It slew sideways and fell off the narrow road. It remained upright, but the water raced off into the fields, sweeping the van along.

"Keep driving," Milly almost screamed. "We're just about high enough to be protected." The water wanted the lowest places first, and they'd risen a few feet up the small gradient by being ahead of the van.

Sully muttered, "I don't want to know. I have to believe we can do this."

The main road beckoned. They hit the wider slice of tarmac running through this ancient flood plain. As they rose up the hill, the engine straining with so many people in the small vehicle, everyone relaxed. Dale heard Sully make a sound close to a sob.

He reached out and gripped the narrow shoulder. "Hey, you did good. Really good. I've seen police officers crack with less stress while driving city streets. You're a natural. Get us home now." Dale would've offered to drive, but it was taking all his concentration to stay alert with Guru Raj in the back of the vehicle.

Large brown eyes, a few shades lighter than Dale's, kept looking at the back window. They were framed by ridiculous lashes some women would murder a man for possessing. "Will those people be okay? Shouldn't we call the police or something?"

Dale leaned closer into the side of the car so he could look at the fake guru without squinting. "You want to save the lives of men who were sent to break your bones?"

"Well, we don't know—"

Milly twisted in her seat and smacked the fool on the leg. He yelped in shock. She snapped, "That's the least of what they'd have done. They kidnapped me and threw me into the back of that van, thinking I knew what you were looking for. I was hired to find out who's been digging holes on people's land and why. You are an evil little troll monster for putting me through it. This is your fault." She pointed at a growing bruise on her jaw and throat.

Dale hadn't noticed it. He growled. "They hit you?"

Milly glanced at him. "I didn't think it wise to mention. You have a tendency to overreact. We needed to get out of the van alive and in one piece. Besides, they had a gun." So she had known about it. Did they threaten her with it as well?

Sully cut in, "You never mentioned a gun." He took his eyes off the road and the little car wobbled. He returned his concentration, but muttered under his breath and kept shaking his head.

"If they get out of that flood alive, I'm going to fucking kill them," Dale snarled.

He'd been on the back foot from the moment this damned case started.

He'd acted like a fool. Allowing Lauren to bully him into going to the prison proved to be the worst mistake. He hadn't thought through the angles as McKie sat there, absorbing all the information Dale spewed out. He deserved to pay for his mistakes. Milly didn't.

Dale leaned away from the window and into the fake guru. "Who the fuck are you?" he barked in his face. "I want a real name, or I'm taking you to the police right now and I'll have them run your prints."

The younger man flinched and tried to become part of the metalwork and glass. "I really don't know what you're talking about. This is nothing to do with me. I'm just a Brummy down here living a quiet life. I have permission to be on that land. I haven't been digging—"

"We have pictures," Milly snapped. "We also have your picture all over the leaflets you gave everyone a year ago."

Sully drove into the Glastonbury. "Where to?"

"My place," Dale said. "You can drop me and Mister Genius here off, then take Milly home. Get warm and clean. You can come back once I know she's tested her sugar levels and she's okay."

"'She' is right here." Milly glared at him.

"And *she* isn't thinking straight. I can see it, Milly. You're about to crash. Look at your hands. Hell, I'm about to crash."

Tears sprang into her eyes, making the sharp green of them shine.

He softened his voice. "Hey, we've had a helluva day. Let's take some time, regroup, get Lauren in, and go from there. We need to interview this idiot and have a bit of a think. You did good today."

He felt the fake guru watch this interaction with interest. If the little prick thought he could use his con-artist's skills on Dale, he'd be sadly mistaken.

Sully drove through the weather-beaten and empty streets of Glastonbury. Dale spared a thought for Jimmy and hoped the man had found somewhere warm and safe to hole up. Though, when they reached the cottage, Dale saw a large hulking shadow in his tiny porch.

They stopped the car and Milly had to climb out to allow the men to struggle from the back. Dale cursed. "Next time you come to rescue us, we're using the damned Audi."

Sully grinned. "I'm up for that."

Dale's back cracked as he straightened, and every muscle felt like a block of ice. Turning to allow fake guru out of the car, he realised the prick was already trying to make it through the hole and obviously wanted his freedom back. He moved like a snake.

Dale reached out and grabbed the man's jacket. "Jimmy," he yelled. "Come make yourself useful."

A large shape, more crinkly plastic over layers of dark clothing, than a man, lumbered up the footpath. "Guv?"

"Take this inside. Don't let it escape. It's a slippery little bastard." Dale handed over the fake guru. He made some protests about his civil liberties, as a hand, even larger and heavier than Dale's, clamped on the man's long black hair and twisted.

"You're coming with me," Jimmy growled as he took Dale's house keys.

"Get home, rest if you need to, then come back." Dale spoke slowly into Milly's eyes. They were a little hazy from shock and probably the mother of all sugar crashes. "Let Sully look after you. Please, Milly. I need you back here on full form. If that takes a little time, it's okay."

She nodded, and he watched her register the state her body and mind had fallen into during the drive home. "You need to watch for concussion," she sounded slurry.

"Yeah, I know. Jimmy's here now. I'll call Lauren and if I get stuck, I'll call Grace."

"Call her anyway. She's probably wondering why you didn't show up with the coffee you bought this morning. I heard you ordering as I left home."

Dale blinked. "Christ, I'd forgotten about that. She really is going to be worried."

The others left and Dale returned to the house. He'd developed a disturbing limp and hoped it would wear off with a hot bath. He almost groaned at the thought of an hour in his enormous tub, preferably with Grace.

Glancing through his kitchen window, he saw Jimmy glowering at fake guru, who sat meekly at the table. Dale thumbed through his contacts, knowing his priorities were off, but right now, he didn't care.

"Grace?" he said the moment the call went through.

"Yes." Colder than the flesh on his bones.

"I'm so sorry. It's been a terrible day so far." Then he realised what he'd said. "Except for this morning. Waking up was amazing, coming into town was wonderful, the rest has been shit."

A long pause. "Work shit?"

"It's a very long story, but yes, it's because of work. I was…" He barked a short laugh. "I was kidnapped, along with Milly."

"You were what?" Her incredulousness almost made him relax.

"Yeah, I know. I'm home now, safe and sound, but get someone to take you home. Don't walk up that hill alone. I'd be there if I could, but the day's not over." His stomach made a protest at also being practically ignored since dawn. "When things calm down, I'll call and explain. Just know, I am so sorry. I'm not that kind of player, not anymore."

"I'm not used to men saying sorry." Her voice was small, and he hated himself for it.

"Sadly, I'm well practised at it and I'm willing to admit when I've screwed up. Let me take you out to dinner soon and spoil you rotten." He liked that idea.

"I'm not a toy or a dog to play with when you want. You get that, right?" He heard the accent she kept buried under her very correct English. It sounded vaguely what? Norwegian?

The way her thoughts had twisted during his absence disturbed him. "I'm aware, Grace. As I said, I will explain. It was out of my control."

She muttered something he didn't catch and as he glanced through the window again, he saw Jimmy about to take the fake guru's head off. "I gotta go. I'll call later." He hung up and, without another thought, strode into the house.

"Right, you two, pack it up. Jimmy, step back. You," he pointed at fake guru, "sit back in that chair before I let him loose on you for good."

"You can't hold me like this," said the man, grunting as Jimmy helped him back into his chair.

Dale turned his back and made another call. It took three rings before he said, "Lauren, I have the man we're looking for. Come up, bring handcuffs, he's being difficult. I'll explain when you're here."

"You have Dean Greene?"

"If that's our fake guru's real name, then yes, I have him here."

"Give me ten." She hung up.

Dale turned back to the man in the chair. "Dean Greene is it?"

Those big brown eyes turned murderous. "That's not my name."

"The police seem to think it is."

"My name is Nissim Doshi," he said, holding his head up. "Dean Greene is the damned fool name my parents chose to make me sound Western. They wanted us to blend in. Ridiculous people." His Brummy accent had vanished under an Indian one that Dale thought sounded just as fake as when Ringo attempted a black American gangster aged ten. Dale had taken the piss until he'd packed it in.

"You be sure to tell the police that when they arrive." He looked at Jimmy. "Why were you waiting for me?"

"Why do you look like a drowned rat that got stuck in a sewer?" Jimmy replied.

Nissim laughed. "Yeah, you smell like one, too."

Dale's desire to burn off some of the day's tension almost overwhelmed common sense. He wanted to punch this smarmy bastard and watch his pretty nose explode.

"This overall effect is because of you." Dale pointed at the prick in the chair. He refocused on Jimmy. "Why are you here?"

"More intel on Joanna. I thought I'd explain in person. When you weren't here, I figured I'd wait. Nothing else to do." A momentary pause. "Intel's the right word, right?"

Dale watched Jimmy's face. The man's eyes darted around, looking for something to focus on rather than Dale. It made him calm. Something wasn't sitting right with Jimmy. "Yes it is. What intelligence do you have, Jimmy?"

"If the Old Bill are coming, I'll leave you to it. Wasn't urgent." The big man shuffled his feet and glanced out of the window at the never ending rain.

"What's happened, Jimmy?" Dale forced himself to take a softer approach.

Nissim moved. Jimmy's hand clamped once more on the man's shoulder, making him yelp. He didn't reply to Dale's question.

"What's happened, Jimmy?" Dale asked again, wondering if the day would ever end.

"My stuff got thrown out. I got nowhere to go and..." The big man couldn't meet Dale's gaze.

"You need a place to stay?" Dale asked, working hard to keep his tone even.

Jimmy shrugged.

"Make yourself useful. I need a quick shower. Don't leave when Lauren turns up. Keep him still. I'll cook once all this," he waved a vague hand at Nissim, "is sorted out."

~ *Chapter 20* ~

WHEN DALE REACHED THE SHOWER, having peeled off his soaking wet, filthy clothes, he discovered he hurt everywhere. He'd been battered in the past, and seriously hurt in prison, but this cold gnawed at his bones and added to the external injuries. As his fingers and toes warmed up, they stung with pins and needles, and he flexed them slowly. He knew Jimmy would keep Nissim in the chair downstairs. The big man felt like he owed Dale and Milly, so he'd do anything to help.

"What the hell am I going to do with him?" Dale mumbled into the water. He wanted to make a difference in the world. He wanted to help people, but he wasn't planning on being sainted. Giving Jimmy a room in his house felt like a step too far. If Dale wanted to share his space, it wouldn't be with the ex-junkie.

He shouldn't be thinking about Jimmy. He needed to focus on Joanna Wolski. She was his priority. Jimmy could stay for the moment, and he'd talk to Grace about finding him new accommodation. Maybe she could help. Obviously, the new social worker hadn't given Jimmy the support he needed.

Okay, decision made about the immediate problems, he could focus on something else, while he scrubbed farm crap out of his body and washed his head wound. No blood there, but a fine and squishy lump.

Grace. He'd stepped over a line and onto an emotional landmine. No matter how unintentional, he'd obviously hurt her. First question, as always:

was she worth the effort to fix the problem? Callous, but his checkpoints were clear with new relationships, and he wouldn't change them now.

Except you're approaching forty and still single. There might be a reason for that…

Ringo's voice sounded smug. Dale ignored him.

He thought back to the previous night. She'd listened to him. Really listened as he tried to explain how prison changed him. How he'd been so desperate to escape, he'd snapped Lauren's arm off when the police offered him a way out. He hadn't gone into all the messy, and sometimes gory, details. He hadn't spoken about Ringo in any depth, but he'd given her the broad strokes and she hadn't run away.

She'd shared some difficult confessions about her ex-husband and his effect on her life. Also, her miscarriages. Grace knew grief. She was clever, compassionate, funny, and honest.

"Of course she's worth it, you damned fool," he muttered, finally feeling a little warmer. He'd pursue her, regardless of how angry she was right now. He'd make the effort and try to fix things. Again.

Two decisions down. Good.

He pulled on a clean pair of jeans, a black t-shirt, a thin black jumper and a navy Arran sweater. Then a good pair of thick socks. He dug out the painkillers and swallowed two. Human, he felt human again. Hearing a car pull up outside, he returned to the kitchen just as Lauren arrived with her detective constable in tow.

"What the hell happened to you?" she asked the moment she clapped eyes on Dale.

"McKie, thank you for that brief excursion into hell, by the way. A couple of his heavies took Milly and me this morning. Ripped off the street, hooded, bound, and I had a gun pointed into the back of my head. Seems they wanted this idiot's location—"

Ryan blurted out, "Is Milly okay?"

"Fine. She's with Sully. He found us."

"Of course she is." The police officer checked himself. "So long as she's okay."

Dale frowned, confused by the young man's obvious distress. He shook his head, setting off the headache again, and continued, "Milly gave them Nissim's location." When the young man half rose out of the chair in protest, Jimmy forced him back down. Lauren's eyebrow rose, but she didn't comment. Dale said, "We knew it would take time for them to narrow down the search. The long and short, we almost died in the process because of the flooding, but we took Nissim. He's your problem once I have any information he can give me about Joanna Wolski."

All eyes focused on Nissim Doshi, who flagged under the pressure.

The Brummy looked at Lauren. "If you're police, you have to know they took me from my home against my will. These men—"

Lauren held up a hand, cutting him off. "I've had a really shitty day. I've been up to Bristol and had my arse handed to me by my boss. Listening to you bleat about what Mr Valentine, may or may not, have done is of no interest to me. He's a consultant, working for us, so you're just going to live with whatever's happened." She focused on Dale. "I have," she checked her watch, "eighteen hours left to make significant progress on the Adele Smith case. Whatever this idiot has done—"

"Adele?" Nissim piped up like some gopher, hoping for an easy meal. "I know an Adele and a Joanna." He made a small yelp as Jimmy's hands tightened on his shoulders.

"Talk to them about Joanna," Jimmy suggested.

Dale hid his smile. The big man certainly had his uses.

Nissim's dark eyes flickered around the room, calculating his chances, his angles. Lauren looked bored, but Dale knew this was one of her ploys.

"Well?" she asked, dragging out one chair. She couldn't quite hide the wince as she sat, and he wondered how bad her day had been with her DCI breathing down her neck. Lauren's ambition made this case important to her, something he understood, but were he and Milly going to be victims?

Nissim tried to shrink away from Jimmy's paws and Dale nodded at the big man to let the fake guru go—for the moment. Jimmy stepped back and Nissim straightened his clothing, fussed with his long hair and tried for the beautiful boy look when he smiled at Lauren.

Her eyes narrowed.

Dale chuckled. "She won't fall for your charms, Nissim. Don't waste them."

The man glared at him. "Like you'd know anything about charm. Adele and Joanna are two of the people who attended my sacred spiritual quest course about a year ago."

"The one where you took peyote, sent a young man mad, who later died, and you all witnessed a crime without reporting it?" Lauren shot back. "Let's not forget one of those women is missing, and another has been murdered. Two more have died under mysterious circumstances. Was that you, Mr Nissim Doshi? Did you kill Adele Smith?"

This tactic surprised Dale. Lauren should've taken Nissim into the station under caution, and given him the right to reply to the charges, or call his solicitor. Though this idiot would need a duty lawyer, Dale doubted he had the money to keep one on standby.

"Um, Lauren, shouldn't you—" he tried.

She put her hand up and kept her focus on her quarry. "Well, Mr Doshi? Did you know about the complaints stacking up against you in our files? We have several colleagues in Birmingham who would like to talk to you. Apparently, this whole," she waved a hand to encompass Nissim, "*thing* you have going on with being the grand poo-bar of some fake faith has upset many people. Some of them have parted ways with a lot of money. Where is that money, Nissim? What have you been doing?"

The colour drained from Nissim's face. "I haven't killed anyone," he squeaked. "Can I have a drink?" he asked, his accent switching back to full Brummy. "I'm gagging for a beer."

Dale glanced at Jimmy. "I can do coffee."

Nissim collapsed into himself, like a dying exotic flower. "Black, three sugars, unless you can make it properly with oat milk."

Dale shook his head. The cheek of this little bugger. "Black it is." He turned to the machine on his counter and woke the beast.

"If I tell you everything, will you let me go?" Nissim asked.

Lauren snorted and coughed. "Yeah, the police will let you go because you give us information you should have shared a year ago. Fuck off. If you cooperate, I'll let the Birmingham team know."

"Fine." Nissim sighed. "I have a deep awareness of the universe—"

"No," Lauren said. "No hippy-dippy bullshit. I want facts."

The man looked annoyed now, deprived of his showcase. "I offered a group of people a special experience on Burrow Mump. It was supposed to be in the community hall, but the new woman there wouldn't let me charge and wouldn't let us use the spiritual cleansing rituals."

"You mean Grace Beloe?" Lauren asked.

It gave Dale a strange thrill to hear her name.

"Yeah. She thought I was a charlatan."

Jimmy growled from his corner, "You are."

Nissim ignored him. "We took peyote. A magical plant that took us to the next plane—"

"Facts," barked Ryan, who was making notes on his pad.

The man huffed like a petulant three-year-old being denied sweeties. "We took the drug and people started tripping," Nissim snapped. "Some of them handled it better than others."

"Sonny Collins?"

Nissim's eyes widened. "How'd you know about him?"

"We've been talking to another of your victims."

"They aren't victims." Nissim threw his hands up and those enormous eyes flashed in horror.

"Adele Smith is dead, murdered. Simon Morton, Kayla Rennie, both dead, currently mis-adventure, but I'm opening their files as well. Sonny Collins, dead. Joanna Wolski is missing. *You* are my prime suspect." Lauren jabbed a finger at Nissim, all pretence of boredom gone.

The man finally realised how bad things were for him. "What? No. No." He waved his hands in denial. "That can't be right. Sonny's sister wanted him to leave. She… Eliza was worried about him from the beginning, but they had the money, and it's not my job to make sure they aren't on something before the ritual starts. He knew the rules. I made it very clear. I had waivers. Eliza wanted him kept safe. Made me send him away. It's her you should talk to, not me."

Dale said, "We would if we could find her."

Nissim's eyes widened.

"She's missing as well." Dale's statement seemed to flatten Nissim.

His reality closed around him. Dale recognised the panic. He'd felt it. Despite knowing he was guilty, Nissim began clutching at those straws, hoping one was strong enough to pull him out of the shit. The trouble is, straw doesn't survive a storm, it bends and breaks, dropping you deeper and deeper every time you open your mouth.

"He…" Nissim was touring his memory now, not making up stories. "He wouldn't go until she made him be quiet. Like you would a horse or something. She gave him a bracelet. Her bracelet. Said he could give it back when she'd returned from the journey. It would bring her home to him and keep him tethered for her."

Dale's heart leapt, and he shared a long look with Lauren. He gave her a nod.

Lauren asked, "What kind of bracelet?"

"I dunno."

"Bollocks. You know the value of everything you look at."

A flash of anger passed over the young man's face. "Fine. Black diamonds. They were real ones. It would've been worth a few quid. She told me they shared it. Something they inherited from their grandmother who claimed to be a witch. She worked here in Glastonbury with the Dion Fortune crowd during World War II."

Dale almost asked what the hell he was talking about, then realised they'd drift too far off topic. He'd ask Milly later.

Lauren sat back. "So the last time you saw this bracelet, it was on the wrist of Sonny Collins?"

"Yeah, why?" asked Nissim.

"You have found no diamonds on the Levels, even with your nightly adventures?"

Nissim became forlorn. "You know about that, then. No. I keep dowsing for them. I know they're out there, but I can't find them. I've been living in that bloody yurt hoping I'll figure it out."

A squall of rain hit the cottage so hard it startled everyone. The lights flickered, then died.

Pitch black filled the kitchen. With the endless cloudy days, the solar batteries were empty of juice. The room faced away from the road, backed onto the extensive garden and the abbey grounds, they had no ambient light. A shuffling and scuffling sound, like a giant rat moving around in a cereal box, made Dale lunge for a shifting shadow, only to collide with Lauren.

"Ryan, take hold of the man," a desperate DI Kennedy cried out.

Dale heard his back door slam. "Shit, too late. Jimmy, front door. Get him before he reaches the road."

"Guv." Jimmy stumbled into something heavy, and Dale knew he'd collided with the dressing table.

Lauren couldn't run, so Dale headed for the back door and made it through. He heard a woman's voice and a car door close. Making it to the road, the rain almost blinding him, he watched a set of tail lights blur in the downpour. The slippery bastard was gone.

Lauren hurried around the corner. Her stick tapping on the ground. "Get in the car. We'll—"

"There's no point, Lauren. He's gone. I didn't catch a registration or make, or even a colour. You can't see bugger all in this. Get back in the cottage before we drown."

~ *Chapter 21* ~

THE ELECTRIC HAD COME BACK on within ten minutes, and Dale made the most of it before it switched off again. He had Ryan and Jimmy help him in the kitchen, then search for more candles. Lauren did nothing but pace the kitchen. She'd screamed at the storm in the garden for a good five minutes and returned to the cottage soaking wet. He'd offered her a towel and some dry clothes. Dale then did his go-to stress buster. He prepared a quick meal of sausage, egg, beans, and chips. Ryan and Jimmy sat eating, eyeing Lauren warily. The sausages were amazing, but Dale was fairly sure he'd met the pigs while out running, the meat was that local.

"Lauren. You can't go anywhere in this weather. Your plods are trying to keep people from drowning. We'll just have to reassess in the morning. Sit, eat, before you fall over."

"That bloody man is going to cost me my career."

"That bloody man won't get far." Air fried, fresh chips were the best. He heard another car pull up outside and glanced at Ryan. "Sounds like Milly is here." She'd called a few minutes before, and Dale gave her the good news about Nissim's flight. The resultant explosion of frustration ended up making them both laugh.

Ryan's eyes flicked to the back door, seeking her out for a moment, but he shrugged and returned to his food. It felt good having the young detective constable with them. The lad was clever and fast. He'd lunged for Nissim the moment the lights went out, but he'd missed. Seconds later, he'd lost his balance as something heavy knocked into his leg. They guessed Nissim sank under the table and simply crawled to the back door. They'd all blundered about expecting him to run upright.

Dale had to admit, he admired Nissim. It showed some balls to escape like that, but who picked him up? A random stranger stops in this weather to pick up a dark-skinned bloke who isn't wearing a coat while running from something?

Milly came into the kitchen. "You look better."

"You too," Dale agreed. She'd obviously defrosted like he had, and she'd eaten. "No Sully?"

Milly flicked a glance at Ryan, who focused on his chips. "No. He dropped me off. Says he needs some time to recover and they're putting together care packages for those who are flooded out. Some people have turned up at the community centre. Grace is down there."

Lauren stopped pacing. "Is that Grace Beloe?"

Milly's gaze flickered between Dale and Lauren.

He took control before something stupid happened. "Grace has been helping, you know that. She's been talking to Charlie."

"Yeah," said Milly with a frown. "About that. Grace got a call from Catherine Brent. She thinks Charlie might be missing."

"What?" Dale felt that sickening plunge rip down his spine. Call it premonition, or copper's instinct, maybe even paranoia, but this wouldn't be good news.

He glanced at Lauren, who nodded. They agreed, and suddenly they'd found a thread to pull.

She ordered, "Valentine, call Brent. I'm going to try the station. Then call the community centre, find out if Charlie's there."

Dale walked into the living room with his phone, Milly coming in behind him.

She touched his shoulder and whispered, "Grace said to stay safe, and she'll talk to you soon. She's worried about you."

Dale felt a surge of warmth flood his insides. The goofy grin on his face spread, even as he tried to smother it. "I'll call her now."

Milly shook her head. "Don't bother. Seriously, I've just come from down there. Charlie wasn't in the centre. She'd have told me. Though, a couple of the farmers we've been working for turned up. I explained about Nissim. They're happy enough. I didn't see Weaver, though, which is odd, because his farm is the lowest among that group. They will not be happy that Nissim's gone."

"Yeah, well, I'm not happy about it either. Who the hell would pick him up in this weather?"

"Did he know anything useful?" Milly asked.

Dale gave her a quick update about the black diamond bracelet.

Her eyes widened. "You think it's Eliza Collins? The twin? She's been dismantling the bracelet?"

"Not sure. We need to get to Weston and re-interview the mother. I'm worried about Charlie as well. Let's talk to Catherine and see where it goes."

It took two rings before a breathless, "Oh, Mr Valentine, I'm so relieved to hear from you."

"Catherine, I heard from Grace at the community centre you've been worried. Why didn't you ring me directly?" he asked.

"I just… Carlton rang from prison," she whispered, and he heard heart-breaking shame in her voice. "He… He told me I wasn't to speak to you, but I'm so worried about Charlie."

"You've done the right thing, Catherine. What can you tell me about Charlie's last known whereabouts?" Dale's sense of impending doom heightened.

She took a breath, gathering her thoughts and he could almost see her trying to remove the emotion to give him the valuable facts. "This morning a girl, well, young woman really, came to visit Charlie. Said she was one of his fans and she'd tracked him down through another of the band members. She gave me names. It all looked legitimate. A nicely dressed young woman, with long, thick, black hair, no tattoos or piercings, I could see. She had amber eyes and seemed lost, vulnerable. I let her in. Charlie, after meeting you and Grace, seemed happy to talk in the kitchen. He was so normal for a while…" Her voice cracked and Dale's heart wept for her. "I needed to do some shopping, so I thought it would be safe to leave them together. With the weather being bad, everything took much longer than it should and when I got home, I knew something awful had happened." She hiccupped as she tried to regain control.

"It's okay, Catherine, I'm right here," Dale murmured. "I'm going to do everything I can to find him."

"I came back and... and the house was a mess. The kitchen, the living room. I thought it might be Charlie having one of his attacks. Afterwards, when he does this, he locks himself in his wardrobe. I bought him an extra big one and made it a kind of safe room. Even had heavy duty tinfoil nailed to the wood inside. It's where he can go when I'm not there and he feels attacked."

This woman deserved the mother-of-the-year award, Dale thought.

"But I didn't find him there, or anywhere. I talked to the neighbours and despite the rain, Mr Watkins, who has been a dear friend throughout this, said he saw Charlie leaving with a woman in a red Fiat Punto. He couldn't see the registration plate, though. I called the police but..."

"I know. You don't have to tell me what happened."

"Then I called Grace. Carlton said I wasn't to talk to you, he can be..."

"I know exactly what he can be, don't worry. It's okay, Catherine. You've given me some great information. I'm going to go now, so we can start to action it. I have the police here and they are going to help. Floods or not, we'll find Charlie."

"Promise?" she asked in a small voice, so small he thought of dormice.

"I can promise I'll do everything I can." He wouldn't lie to her. He'd made that mistake before.

"I understand." Her sadness made him close his eyes.

"I know you do. We'll talk soon. That I can promise."

"Thank you, Dale."

"You are very welcome, Catherine."

She hung up.

Milly gripped his wrist. "It'll be okay."

"I hope so." His thumb rubbed over the blank screen. "I really hope so." They returned to the kitchen. "Lauren, I have a vehicle for you to check and we need to get to Weston-super-Mare to talk to this mother of the twins. I want to interview her."

He went through his conversation with Catherine Brent and Lauren phoned in what details they had about the vehicle. A red Fiat wasn't much to go on, there must be hundreds in Somerset alone, but timing could help them. In this weather, there wouldn't be as many vehicles on the road. CCTV had to have picked them up somewhere.

Lauren hung up the phone. "Come on. We're going to Weston."

Ryan rose from the table.

"No," Lauren said. "I need you back at the station. Dale can drive me. They're inundated down there."

"That's a PC's—"

"Ryan, I'm sorry, but we're a small team. Get your head in the game. They need you on the streets."

Dale watched Ryan's colour change. He felt for the lad, but Lauren was right he'd be more use working with the Fire and Rescue Services.

"Report to Sergeant Webber. He's desperate," she said, slinging her coat over her shoulders. She looked at Dale. "Well, come on then, you're driving."

He scrambled for his keys, and he grabbed his Belfast jacket this time.

Milly called out, "He has a concussion. You can't let him drive."

"He'll be fine." Lauren strode back out into the storm.

Dale glanced at Milly. "Be safe. This is going to be a rough night."

She nodded, her expression one of genuine worry. "Call me when you reach Weston and when you come home. I need to know you're okay."

"I will." Dale gave her a smile. Friends meant people who worried about him. It felt good. He glanced at Jimmy. "Keep her safe. Stay here. Understood?"

"Guv," Jimmy nodded.

Dale walked out into the storm again and felt the sharp needles of rain hit his face and the lump on the back of his head. He pinged the locks on the Audi and Lauren lowered herself with care into the sleek interior.

He climbed into his driving seat and took a moment to appreciate being in control. "Let's go."

The drive to Weston-super-Mare happened in silence. Not an uncomfortable one, but subtly different to the many other occasions they'd shared a car. Lauren delivered instructions, the satnav not coping with the weather. Dale took it steadily, but the drive over the hills wasn't anywhere near as traitorous. The wind and rain might batter them, but the roads were clear of water. Debris lay everywhere, despite it being late autumn many of the trees still had leaves on them and the wind tore the limbs off, hurling them at the ground.

The town of Weston looked like a weather war-zone. As they drew closer to the seafront, Dale's headlights picked out the vast waves crashing onto the shoreline. "I didn't think that was possible here."

"High tide, I guess," Lauren said. He didn't miss the fact they both sounded a little anxious.

"And it's a full moon." When she glanced at him in confusion, he clarified, "Tidal surge up the Bristol Channel."

"Get you, Mister Local." She grinned.

"Milly likes to torment me with facts about Somerset. Sometimes, I even pay attention."

Lauren chuckled. "It's a shame about her and Ryan."

"Yeah, but it would never have lasted. They're too different. He'll recover."

"It's funny how differences matter when the pressure's off," she murmured.

He pulled up outside a large Victorian red brick house. "I agree, they do. They matter a great deal."

For a moment it hung there, between them, the corpse of what they'd once shared. The burning flame of passion that almost ended his life and had ended Ringo's. Then, like the phantom it was, the corpse dispersed.

"Come on," Lauren said. "Let's go frighten some truth out of a grieving mother."

"You fill my days with joy, DI Kennedy."

"It's always a pleasure, Mr Valentine."

They left the safety of the car, and Dale helped Lauren keep her balance as they battled up the drive. A security light hung under the eaves of the small entranceway. He banged on the door. "Mrs Collins, it's the police. Please open the door."

The heavy wood entrance cracked open, and Lauren stepped into the light. "Mrs Collins, it's DI Kennedy. I'm here with Mr Valentine, a consultant with the Somerset and Avon Constabulary."

The woman's eyes, blank and staring, barely registered them as she pushed the door closed, removed the chain and opened it fully. "You better come in."

Dale, never having met the woman, was surprised to find she had skin like porcelain and eyes the colour of under-ripe hazelnuts. He'd seen the photos of Sonny Collins and the twins had inherited their father's colouring, much like Dale inherited his mother's Mediterranean genetics. Mrs Collins also resembled a wrung-out dishcloth of indeterminate age. She looked small, withered, and as if all the weight of the world lay on her thin shoulders as her body grew weaker under its relentless pressure.

"What do you want?" she asked, leading them into the living room.

Dale saw photos everywhere of the twins, but especially of Sonny. A candle burned on a table that now resembled an altar, but the house felt cold.

"We need to talk to you about Eliza," Lauren said. "And your mother."

Mrs Collins' eyes sharpened at last. "I don't discuss my mother. She's dead, and that's an end to it."

"It's not, though, is it?" Lauren pressed.

Dale cut in before Lauren dismantled any good-will the woman had towards the police. "Mrs Collins, there's a storm out there and it's cold in here. Do you have a problem with your heating?"

Lauren glared at him, but he ignored her.

The older woman shrugged. "I can't get the logs in, they're too heavy, and the boiler is on the blink. They won't come out. It never works in this weather, there's a draught. It needs a service."

He nodded. "I tell you what, why don't you make us a cuppa, and I'll see to the logs and the boiler? No point in me being here if I can't be useful."

Lauren's mouth dropped open, but he shook his head. They needed the woman's trust. If Eliza had killed Adele Smith and the others, then this woman was looking at a world of pain in the near future. He didn't need to make it worse.

The woman's shoulders lifted a little. "Really? That would be very kind."

"It's no bother," he said, making sure he matched her public school accent as closely as possible for a Peckham bred oik. "Show me the logs first, then you can chat with DI Kennedy here while I have a bash at the boiler. Or at least give it a good hard look, you know, what with me being a man and all." He offered one of his smiles and caught Lauren rolling her eyes behind the woman's back.

"Oh, that would be so kind. It's been impossible since my husband died. This house is just too much, but the twins didn't want to move."

"I understand, Mrs Collins," Dale said, wondering how a parent could be so blind.

"Call me Ann, dear."

"Ann," he said. "Lovely name."

He followed her through the house. Everywhere, pictures of the family and the children hung from walls and stood on flat surfaces. All lovingly polished. The paintwork looked tired, and Dale noticed a place in a doorway where the family had marked the growth of the twins. The highest was Sonny's, for his sixteenth birthday. In the back of the house was a room that resembled a shed and here were the logs. He lifted the basket and carried it back to the living room.

"Lauren, you know how to do this better than me, why don't you set the fire and we'll look at the boiler?" he suggested.

He saw the argument in her eyes. She knew perfectly well he could lay a fire. "Fine." She managed a tight smile.

He once more followed Ann, and they headed into the large kitchen. He saw the large gas boiler on the wall. If he were being honest, he had almost no idea what to do with the thing, but he could make a lot of noises about it, and maybe there was just a chance he might figure it out.

Ann Collins relaxed. She put the kettle on, and they talked about the storm. He said they'd seen the waves and feared for the seafront. They discussed climate change as Dale lifted the front of the boiler off and looked at its intestines. He'd seen his grandfather fiddle with these things, and had vague memories of carbon build-up around the pilot light.

Finally, she gave him the opening he needed. Ann said, "Sonny and Eliza were so close growing up. They'd have loved to see those waves."

"It must be hard for Eliza, losing Sonny," he said, taking out his penknife and giving the gas jet a poke.

A long sigh came from behind him. Like bagpipes dying in the cold of a Scottish winter on the side of a road, having been hit by a truck.

"She can't come back."

He stopped and turned; the movement awkward from his position on the step-ladder. "Come back from where?"

Ann focused on him. "Grief. She can't come back from grief. She's full of this terrible icy rage. I see it in her and I can't reach her. Honestly, I never could. I was always closer to Sonny." Her eyes filled with tears. "What a terrible thing to say."

"It's not. Things happen. We love our kids, but we don't always have to like them." He often thought this was his mother's motto.

She gave a wan smile. "Eliza can be very hard to like sometimes. She has the sharpest tongue. It's like she was born with razors in her mouth. Things changed for her when her father passed. They were thirteen."

Dale returned to… well, whatever he was doing. "A difficult age."

"I was weak. I know that now."

He clicked a button he noticed on the panel below the gas jet. It sparked and went *woof*, making him start back. In seconds, the boiler, deep inside, gave a second, deeper *woof*.

"Oh! You did it," Ann exclaimed.

Dale chuckled. "Yep, I did. Let me show you, so you know for the future."

"Oh, Eliza understands—"

"Please," he said. "You need to know how to do this. Empowerment and all that."

"You remind me of my husband."

"Tell me about him." Dale listened as she described her husband. He started to understand the family dynamic. The woman loved her men, but

Eliza was a mystery she couldn't unravel. Ann had dedicated her life to providing a family home to the men in her life, and she didn't understand why Eliza wanted something different.

When he had the boiler's cover back on and screwed in place. He showed her the control panel and how she needed to use the ignition button if the pilot light went out.

"That's it?" she asked.

"Sometimes. Doesn't mean it doesn't need a service, but it might just be a simple fix."

She beamed at him. Dale saw Lauren watching them from the hallway. She gave him a brief nod, giving permission for him to keep pushing.

"I don't suppose we could see Eliza's room?" he asked. "We're trying to find her."

Ann frowned. "Why are you looking for Eliza? I thought you were here about Sonny?"

"We're worried Eliza might be mixed up in something because of the night Sonny died. Since DI Kennedy started looking into your son's death, I've been investigating the disappearance of a young American woman, Joanna Wolski." The name obviously meant nothing to Ann. He added, "They knew each other. We now know where Sonny was before he died, and we think we know how it happened. We just need to find Eliza before she does something terrible."

"Like what?" Ann whispered, her eyes widening.

"We're not at liberty to discuss it," Lauren said, walking into the room. "But we want to find Eliza to make certain she's safe, that's all. We have some questions for her, but it's mostly about safety at this point. Anything you can tell us would help."

"Like what?" Ann asked again, her desperation raising her voice.

"Can we see her room?" Dale pressed.

The woman looked from one to the other, her body shrinking into itself once more, as if waiting for the final blow.

~ *Chapter 22* ~

THE ROOM LOOKED PERFECTLY NORMAL for a young woman in her early twenties. Smart, organised, a desk under the window which looked out onto the garden, with a space obviously meant for a laptop computer. The pictures on the walls made Dale think of dark fantasy lands where fairies bit you rather than saved you. Lauren opened the wardrobe and, apart from some obvious office clothing, most of the space emphasised Eliza's darker, more sullen nature.

"She's vegan, so the leather isn't real," Ann said from the doorway. "I keep hoping she'll grow out of the gothic look, but maybe she will now she's lost Sonny. The last time I saw her, she looked very smart."

Lauren turned from riffling through layers of shoes and boots. "What do you mean? You said the other day, you hadn't seen her for weeks."

"Oh, yes, that's right, but the day she came home." Ann's tired face softened. "She was so kind. We had takeout and shared a bottle of wine. Apparently, work wanted her to go up to London for a few weeks, but when she came back, things would be different. She said it was time to move away from the past."

Dale could practically see Lauren's frustration with the woman mount towards fury and accusations of obstruction and wasting police time.

"Where does Eliza work?" he asked, trying to head Lauren off.

"Oh, she has an office job with the local council. She's on some work placement scheme where she's rotated through various departments to learn how they function. Then she'll settle into the department that's best suited to her."

Dale glanced at Lauren. They had a moment of unity. The job didn't exist. Eliza Collins spent her days planning her revenge.

"We've been told Eliza had a rather beautiful bracelet," Dale said.

Ann smiled. "Yes, though she was forever lending it to Sonny. He liked to be," she shook her head and smiled, "gender fluid in his dress. Another phase, no doubt. My mother left it to her in her will, a black diamond bracelet, necklace and earrings. They're quite valuable."

"Where does she keep them?" Dale's stomach twisted into knots as more of the evidence formed a noose around Eliza's freedom.

The mother, unsuspecting of the Sword of Damocles hanging over her head, crossed the room to a chest of drawers. The fine-grained wood glowed softly in the light, the Edwardian craftsmanship obvious. Ann pulled open the top drawer and took out an old black Chinese lacquered box with a crane and a tree painted in exquisite detail on the lid.

Ann opened it and frowned. "Oh, the bracelet isn't here. That's odd. She must be wearing it."

Lauren's expression turned grim. "Ann, we really need to find Eliza. Is there anywhere you can think of that she might go if she thought she was in trouble?"

"I don't really know."

Dale sensed the growing panic in the small woman. "Were Eliza and Sonny into all this spiritual stuff because of their grandmother?" He'd been looking at the bookcase and handed Lauren one of Nissim Doshi's—aka Guru Raj—books.

Lauren's expression tightened further.

Ann nodded. "When my mother died, which was just a few years ago, she left Eliza the jewellery and Sonny her old house." The woman blanched as the attention of both investigators ramped up.

Dale tried to keep his voice even. "What old house?"

"I guess it'll be Eliza's now. I... Since Sonny's death, I've lost touch with so much. Eliza took over the paperwork—"

"Where's the house?" Lauren asked, her voice strained through a sieve of self-control.

"Oh, it's near a place called West Yeo. It's in the middle of nowhere. The farm cottage is very basic, no real plumbing, kitchen, there are holes in the roof, and it floods. I should imagine it's close to collapse."

"Did you grow up there?" Dale asked.

"Goodness me no. After my father died, and I married, mother went deep into her spiritualism and said she wanted seclusion for her studies. She was one of the youngest members of the team who are said to have helped defeat the Nazi's spiritual invasion. I'm not sure how much of that I believe, but the children loved her stories."

"I assume you have a postal address for this property? And a phone number for Eliza. We might be able to find her via her mobile's location." Lauren managed a smile that reached her eyes.

Ann looked a little startled, but nodded. "I'll find it. But Eliza won't be there. She's working away from home. I told you, she's in London. I called her." She frowned and gave Lauren a glare.

Dale shouldered his way between the two women. "Let's go find that address and we'll soon clear this up, Ann. If something has happened, and Eliza is in any form of trouble, we need to check all options. Especially in this weather."

He followed the woman downstairs. She still held the jewellery box, clutching it to her small chest. They went to a telephone table in the hall, the landline obviously still in use. In the table's drawer, Ann removed a small black address book. Everything about this woman screamed analogue.

As Ann handed Dale the small book, she said, "That police woman thinks Eliza's done something terrible, doesn't she?"

Dale wanted to lie to her. He felt a deep compulsion to protect this frail creature, as no doubt her husband had done for years. She lived in a time that no longer existed, one of cocktails at five and dinner at seven.

He also saw in her eyes the soft pleading for the truth. Pity filled his heart. "I think you should be prepared for some difficult times ahead, Ann. I have contacts which include some very good criminal defence lawyers." He handed her a card. "You can call any time and either Milly, my co-worker, or myself will pick up. We'll help if we can. Right now, we really have to find Eliza before she does something else. Just one more question. What kind of car does she drive?"

Tears welled in Ann's eyes. "It's a Fiat Punto, a red one. She and Sonny bought it with their own money. They were really proud of it."

Dale nodded. "Okay. I'll call you the moment we find her."

Ann clutched his hands, the alabaster skin making his look even darker than usual. "Please find her. Even if she's done something terrible, tell her that I love her, and I'll do all I can to help."

He nodded, feeling more than a little overwhelmed. How could this tiny, bird-like creature survive yet more grief and guilt?

They left Ann Collins in her large mausoleum of a house, her entire face and body closed down, her mind numb. Dale felt desperately sorry for her, but Eliza needed stopping before she did something to Nissim and Charlie.

The storm raged as Lauren struggled to hold the door of the Audi safely while she lowered herself into the car. "Why can't you drive a Land Rover?"

"Because I don't like them. I like these." He closed her inside the vehicle, then hurried around the bonnet. The silence, even with a few moments in the wind and rain, shocked him.

"We need Eliza's laptop," Lauren said as Dale drove carefully out of the street. "There wasn't one in the bedroom. It means she's living somewhere else."

"We need Eliza. She's obviously our prime suspect. I just hope she hasn't killed Joanna as well." Dale thought about the pretty American and the ethereally beautiful twins. What a terrible waste of life. As a dedicated martial artist, he understood the spirituality of his chosen arts, the way the martial form and the transcendence of physical meditation can lead some people to a higher awareness of the world around them. Many warriors who dedicated their lives to the martial life became monks, surrendering their weapons for peace.

He'd read the books in prison when he could, looking for a deeper understanding to his existence. He'd lost count of the times he read *The Five Rings* by Miyamoto Musashi. He grasped many of the concepts, but some eluded him, and Dale knew there was no shortcut to receiving a sense of grace in your life. If these people were experimenting with strong psychedelics to reach a higher plane of understanding, then they were cheating. Monks, medicine men, shamans, and others spent their lives dedicated to a path of self-awareness. Why anyone thought taking drugs would get them there faster, he didn't know. Taking drugs for fun was one thing. Taking them to lead you to another dimension on some spiritual quest made no sense.

Lauren interrupted his internal rant. Quietly, she said, "This isn't going to have a happy ending."

"No, it's not."

"I wish it was one of McKie's thugs doing this," she murmured.

He glanced at her and saw the forlorn look on her face. "The job sucks sometimes, doesn't it?"

Lauren sighed. "It really does. She's just a kid."

"She's a murderer, Lauren. We both know it and she might have two more victims on her tally sheet by now. Three, if she's done for Joanna as well."

Rubbing her face with her hands, Lauren growled, "Fucking mess." She sighed again and picked up her phone.

Dale listened as she phoned through to the station in Street to rouse some bodies for a search of the West Yeo property. He stopped paying attention to her as he struggled to navigate the streets of Weston with the weather and flying objects making people drive erratically. The pavements were almost empty and many in the lower-lying streets were piling up sandbags. They were planning for nature to commit to a full frontal assault.

Lauren hung up. "Almost everyone is out dealing with the flooding. West Yeo is part of Burrowbridge, did you know that?"

"Where Burrow Mump is? No, I had no idea. Won't it be flooded as well?" He felt the wind catch the low-slung car as he drove up and over the bridge spanning the M5. Forcing the car to slow again, he breathed carefully. He really was too tired and hurt for this.

"We have to get over there," Lauren muttered.

"I agree, but two of us, one with a gammy leg, and one with a possible concussion, isn't enough personnel for it to be safe."

"We'll get Milly over."

"So she can deal with a murderer? I don't think so, Lauren. We're private detectives, not police, not the damned army. We find missing persons, missing cats, missing husbands." He paused and thought about what he'd do in her situation. "You need nearby bodies to move to the location of Eliza's cottage. If we clear that area, we have a chance of finding her and making it look like a police operation to keep people safe from the flood. It'll be less confrontational."

Lauren considered his advice. "Or I could get an armed response unit down from Bristol?"

"You could do that," he said, increasing his speed as he hit a good stretch of road. "But she'll either run or kill. Besides, it'll take them hours to get down here. The M5 looked empty. There must be a stoppage somewhere."

"They could fly—"

"No one is flying a helicopter down here in this storm." He considered their options. "I'll phone Milly, you call Ryan, see where he is and PC Allison, she's handy with problem people. Milly can meet us with Sully and Jimmy if he's still at my place."

"This is so frustrating," she growled, even as she called Ryan.

Dale put his Bluetooth in his ear and called Milly.

"Hey, Guv, how'd it go?"

"Good, we have a location. Trouble is, the local plods are overwhelmed. Where are you?"

"I'm at the community centre with Grace. Why?"

"We need bodies out at West Yeo, it's—"

"It's part of Burrowbridge, I know."

"Okay, Eliza has a cottage out there, practically a ruin. We think that could be her bolthole. We need bodies to help form a perimeter so we can close her down. I need you to find Jimmy, if you can, Sully if possible and anyone else you think can hold their own, take orders and be sensible. We are saving lives, not trying to take this woman in some Butch Cassidy ending."

"I'll see what I can do, though things here are pretty hectic. The low-lying traveller sites and tourist campsites have flooded, they've come into town looking for help. We also have Mr Newberry, Bayne and Frasier here with their families. The farms are underwater, and they wanted to leave before the lanes became impassable. Grace is chatting with them, and their wives are helping organise the kids. Dad's come over with food."

"Do what you can. We just need a few more people," he said. The sound of children's voices in the background made him grateful he wasn't there. He wondered if he should phone Grace, but one glance at Lauren put the thought out of his head.

The DI said, "Ryan is with Allison. They're going to meet us in Othery. If we can get down there, we'll take their *Land Rover*," she placed a heavy emphasis on the words, "to West Yeo. From the map, there's almost nothing there. A set of offices in an old farmhouse that belong to the Environment Agency and a few small cottages. The postcode is a largish area."

"Do you remember the old days when a postcode meant a single block of flats or a street? Rather than miles of empty farmland and a few addresses down tracks barely fit for cows?"

Lauren chuckled. "I'm from here, remember? Going to the London Met was the shock of my life."

"How do you want to play this?" he asked, lifting his speed as the weather dropped from catastrophic to merely dangerous.

"Whoever makes it down to West Yeo, we use them to block the entrances to the property once we find it. Then you and I go in and try to see if we can find them. From there…"

"What?"

"Well, Dale, you're far better at the softly, softly than I am. If she comes out swinging, we take her down. If we think you can talk to her, then we'll use that option."

"Living here has mellowed me," he admitted.

"I don't think it's Somerset," she said. "I think you were desperate to leave London. You were exhausted."

He maintained eye contact with the road, her perceptive comment reminding him all too clearly how close the two of them really were and how his attraction to Grace might hurt Lauren. He'd chosen to think of her as too tough to care, but she did care about him. She cared a great deal.

"Lauren, there's something you should know…"

He felt her stiffen beside him. Even in the dark, he saw the tension.

She said, "No. I need to focus on Eliza Collins, not Grace Beloe."

He opened his mouth, then snapped it shut. How the hell did she know?

Lauren sighed. "Fine, once I realised you'd met her, I knew you'd be attracted to her. She's clever, sweet, and the total opposite to me." Lauren realised what she'd said, "Except for the clever bit. We're both clever. My point is, when I met her a few weeks back as part of a police and community thing we both attended, I liked her. Then I discovered she was single and straight and sane. Oh, and age appropriate. Difficult to find in Glastonbury."

Dale laughed despite his growing concern over where Lauren was taking this conversation.

"It's easier talking to you about this when you're driving. And it's dark." Her voice dropped. "I wanted it to work between us, but we don't have that trust. We never will." She fell silent.

He considered his words carefully. "What happened to Ringo was not your fault. It was not really my fault. Ringo switched his phone off and we couldn't find him, despite telling him how dangerous it could be until you rounded up everyone in the gang. He died because he wouldn't listen. He never did. Something in me broke that day and it's never going to heal. I want to leave it all behind me. I want to start again. That's not possible with you."

"So do I. Once I've done a few years either in Street or Bristol, whatever the DCI decides once I'm fit again, I'm going to ask for another transfer—"

"Lauren—"

"No, listen. My career is so important to me, Dale. I ruined my marriage, you, the chance to have kids and a normal family life. I want to be good at this and you can help get me there."

"Meaning what?"

"Meaning we keep it professional; we keep it friendly, and you get to have Grace in your life without feeling awkward around me. Then you'll have your little happy family thing going and I'll be running Somerset and Avon Police by the time I'm fifty."

He laughed. "You know it'll be called something else by then."

She groaned. "I know, right? All those letterheads and badges changed. All that money…"

The street lighting made it possible for them to share a smile.

"This was all very grownup," he said.

Lauren snorted. "Trust me, when you've been through a divorce with a lawyer as a husband, sensible is the only way to manage relationships. I can't be doing with the drama, and I love you as a friend, Dale, but it's only ever been a drama between us."

"It really has." He knew he failed to hide his relief, but it didn't matter.

"Okay, now that's done, the elephant can wander off and bother someone else. We can focus on finding Eliza Collins."

They made it to Othery as the wind and rain eased considerably and the hint of a moon appeared. The police Land Rover sat outside the graveyard at the top of the hill and Dale saw several people collected around it. He pulled up, and leaving the vehicle, breathed in cold, wet, but calm air. From their location on the hill he could see the darker shadow of Burrow Mump and its church, then an odd shining darkness broken by strips of jagged matte.

"It's all flooded down there." DC Ryan Matthews approached.

"We've no choice. We have to get down the hill." Lauren struggled into her big coat.

"I know. We've another vehicle from someone at the community centre. Sullivan drove it over. He says he's done the advanced driver course and can handle it."

Dale heard the doubt and felt the need to defend Sully. "It's true, and he's good. Very good. Better than some coppers I've driven with who've had years more experience."

"Then we'll take both vehicles. Anyone know the area well?" Lauren called out.

Milly stepped out of the shadow and smiled at Dale. "That'll be me." She held her hand up. "Dad and I used to go mushrooming down there."

"Do we want to know what kind of mushrooms?" Lauren didn't bother hiding her amusement.

"That's probably not a good question to ask, DI Kennedy," Milly said. "From memory, the cottage we're looking for is located at the end of this track." She waved them over to the front of the ancient Land Rover.

"You borrowed this off one of your farmers, didn't you?" Dale eyed the ancient beast.

She grinned. "They think I'm lovely. Newbury, Frasier and Bayne have moved their livestock onto higher ground or put them into sheds, but Frasier has his grandchildren staying with him and Bayne's wife needs help with his care, so all three of them came into town. We haven't seen Mark Weaver, which is odd. They're quite concerned about him and this woman they think he has staying with him." She frowned and shook the thought away.

"We'll do a welfare check on them if necessary after we've found Nissim and Charlie safe and well," Dale said.

Milly nodded in agreement. "Before we left, I had a quick conflab with the farmers, and we think this is the most likely place." She pointed to the paper map that several large stones held down.

Dale peered at the thing in the darkness until Milly switched on a powerful torch, making them all step back and blink.

"Sorry. Forgot to warn you. Lambing lamp." She pointed again.

At the end of the lane that followed the River Parrett towards Bridgwater, he saw a footpath marked in dotted red. About two hundred metres from the main tarmacked road, a small building was indicated by a pale pink square.

"There're some stables nearby, but other than that, the place is quiet. It's on a ridge, so it should be free of the flooding for the moment. We can take that ridge to the cottage. This area is above sea level. The surrounding farmland is several feet lower."

"How many bodies do we have?" Dale asked.

"Jimmy and Sully are in the vehicle," Milly nodded.

Dale looked through the windscreen of the old, grey four-by-four, and saw the two men watching everyone. He nodded.

"But that's all?" he asked her.

"Other than Ryan and Pippa," Milly said.

Lauren interrupted them. "Let's get down there and do a risk assessment first. Then we can make some decisions."

~ *Chapter 23* ~

MILLY SAT IN THE BACK of the old Land Rover with Jimmy. She watched her boss with concern. Dale wanted Sully to drive, he said cranking his way through a complex differential gear box in a car older than him, wasn't good for his sanity. She thought he looked too tired and ill to be doing any of this, and the day didn't appear to be ending.

Still, he and Lauren seemed to get on okay, which was an improvement on her and Ryan. He'd broken up with her, so why was he being such an annoying brat over Sully?

Milly shook her head. A tendril of red hair snaked over her face. She picked it up and shoved it back into the band at the nape of her neck. She knew why Ryan was acting the fool. Within five minutes of them breaking up, she'd started something with Sully, and that something was special. She'd tried normal with Ryan, but normal would never work for her. Sully just fit. He let her be the person she wanted to be, and it would never occur to him to make her have a more normal life. One that didn't involve chasing potential murderers around a floodplain in the dark.

Water rose over the road as they dipped down into Burrowbridge, but the fields contained the worst of the flood. The houses of Burrowbridge were safe for the moment. Even the low-lying pub looked dry. At the traffic lights, they turned right and headed down the lane that mirrored the river. The thought of being trapped by the swirling, dark and heaving mass of water charging down towards the distant sea made her feel queasy.

"And it's not yet high tide," Jimmy murmured next to her.

The dark hid so much, but when the moon gleamed off the tumultuous mass, it appeared otherworldly. This river was mostly benign and, if she were honest, a bit ugly, but like this—when it was in full spate—it made her think of dragons and darkness heaving out of the centre of the world and seeking vengeance.

"You think it'll get worse?" she asked.

"Bound to. No easy job farming here," he murmured.

"You'd like it, though?" she asked.

Jimmy smiled at her. "I'd love it. Not sure I remember enough now, but I could learn. Not much chance given the price of land round here."

She patted his knee. "You never know, Jimmy. You could start by working on some of the farms."

He snorted. "They'll not trust me."

"I could talk to them. Explain a little."

He nudged her shoulder, almost squashing her into the door. "Not your job to look after me, Milly."

"Eyes up," Dale said from the front. "We're close."

The two Land Rovers, one with police markings all over it, pulled into the path they'd seen on the map. Things looked different in the dark, during a flood. Milly climbed out of the big vehicle, her rainbow coloured wellington boots sinking into the thick soil. Sully came to stand beside her, his fluffy coat making him look bulky.

"This is going to be almost impossible," he said.

They peered out over the Levels. As the clouds released the moon, the light made vast swathes of the land look like sheets of silver tied together by the tangle of pixie-headed willow trees.

She pointed. "That's the cottage."

It sat on a raised dais of earth. Milly thought it might even be the remains of some ancient hillfort. Many of the older farms in the area had…

"Milly." Dale's bark broke her mental meander.

She focused and walked over to him. "What's the plan?"

"I don't know. Lauren wants to go in. I think we should approach with more caution. We don't want people to fall in the water and the place is almost surrounded."

"It looks like a moat."

"I'm going to try to talk Lauren into being sensible."

Milly chuckled. "Good luck with that."

He grunted. "Just keep everyone here until we've made a decision."

She gave him her best cockney twang. "Sure thing, Guv."

As he walked away, she heard him mutter, "I wish she wouldn't do that."

Within moments of Dale joining Lauren, she heard them arguing. The police had to consider risk assessment, and as Eliza was a prime suspect in at least three deaths, and one known kidnapping, then they had to believe she was dangerous.

Milly also wondered if Nissim was working with Eliza. A reach perhaps, considering the evidence, but a possibility to be pondered. If she mentioned it, they'd never decide on who was doing what, and everyone was going to freeze to death.

"Bollocks to it," she muttered.

"Bollocks to what?" Jimmy asked.

Sully took his shoulder off the Land Rover and joined her wordlessly.

"Come on. The three of us can look in the house and report back."

Both men stared at her.

"What?" She waved a hand at the 'grown-ups'. "They could argue until the sun comes up. We just want to know if she's in there. We can't see any lights from this angle, but that doesn't mean she's not holed up in some back room. The gable end of the house is facing us."

Jimmy and Sully shared a moment in silent contemplation of being led by Milly into a potentially hazardous situation, and just shrugged. She grinned, knowing she had their loyalty.

With their torches off, they walked quietly away from the four people surrounding the police Land Rover, arguing over tactics.

The ground underfoot stretched in unpredictable slides of mud and grass. Rising water lapped just a few centimetres below the path. The drowning pixie trees wafted their thin arms in the remaining breeze, clacking together, but other than that, the world held a disturbing lack of noise. Helping each other, they made it to the side of the house without incident.

"I'll go first." Jimmy tried to whisper, but his big voice didn't understand the concept.

"No." Milly pulled him back. "I'm the least likely to cause a threat. I'll go first."

"Dale won't—"

"He's not here, Jimmy," she hissed quietly. "Please, let me do this. If I see anything dodgy, I'll need you to come help while Sully runs back to the others. I can't run in wellies. He has proper boots on and will move faster than we will." She pointed at Sully's well-made walking boots.

"Milly's got a point. She's not quick on her feet," Sully admitted.

She glared at him, but arguing felt pointless. Slowly, she left the safety of the others and crept around the corner of the old house. The grass tufts around the front wall were thick and old, but well shorn by grazing animals. Milly guessed the rabbits liked it here. Not a great place for hunters. There were brambles in the mix, and these snagged on her jeans. The pervasive damp climbed inside her clothing and began sucking the warmth from her skin and bones. She'd been so cold and wet earlier in the day that she'd needed half an hour in a hot bath just to stop shivering. And now she felt the chill returning.

Reaching the first window she saw no glass, just empty holes, withered and dying as the surrounding wood rotted away. Seeing no light, she peeked inside. Not a damned thing could be seen, but puddles of rainwater on the ruined wooden floor. Reaching the front door, she realised it stood open, at least a little, the rot and decay making it impossible to close. This place would be worth some serious money in this location. The views must be amazing.

She paused by the door, listening hard. Nothing but the soft breath of wind and her heartbeat reminding her that fear had its place in her armoury of self-defence mechanisms.

A crack behind her almost ruined Milly's jeans and her sanity.

"Sorry," Jimmy growled in her ear.

"Shit," Sully added. "I slipped."

They'd come up behind her. To be honest, she'd ignored Dale, so their insubordination shouldn't surprise her.

"Just let me breach the house," she whispered. In need of her torch now, she pulled out her tiny Maglite and stepped into the darkness. The smell of rotten wood, wet stone, rain and something foul reached out to greet her, welcoming her into the confining black. The narrow cone of light lit the floor, littered with dead leaves, animal spore and…

Footprints. Clear footprints smearing the detritus of years. The hall was tiled, but with the miasma of age, the colour or design was impossible to see. Her eyes flicked ahead; her ears strained. She licked her lips, then trapped the bottom one between her teeth to prevent herself from talking aloud, just to feel some comfort. God, it was cold in here. Cold, dark, grave-like. The walls felt heavy and wet, as if they just wanted to fall down, tumble into the soft peat of the ancient bogs surrounding the cottage, to lie forgotten.

She saw a room to the right. The door stood open and the flash of something bright shocked her. So far everything she'd seen matched the muted colour-swatch of a rotting corpse.

The floor sagged under her weight as she stepped into the room. The torch licked the rotting boards. Light flickered over a shape she recognised, but it made little sense, until she took another step and the beam hit the body.

"Oh no." She sucked in a hard breath. Screaming would panic everyone and if Eliza were nearby, she'd vanish. Milly had to keep control. She had to keep the fear at bay. This was no different from any other body. No different.

Except it was because she knew this body. She'd helped to save this mass of bone and muscle and conscious thought. He didn't deserve this. Wanting to take another step forwards to check if he might still be alive, she paused. He wasn't, couldn't be, with that hole in his throat. The second mouth to which her torch seemed perversely attached. This was a crime scene.

"Milly?" Sully hissed.

"Go back," she said aloud. "Go back, get Dale, get Lauren. We have another body. It's Nissim. Yes, he's definitely dead. Yes, it's another murder." How did Eliza do this? How was she so full of hate for these people that murder was her only expression of grief?

Milly felt her knees beginning to give way. She clutched the door frame, panicked about fingerprints, and finally realised she wore gloves. Woollen gloves to match her rainbow wellington boots. Tears sprang into her eyes. Nissim would never see her silly gloves and wellies. He'd murdered no one, he was just a con-man and thief. Not a good way to make a living, and no telling how much damage he'd done to people in the past, or would've done in the future, but he was just a normal bloke. Now, he was dead.

Her breathing shortened.

"Hey, Milly, it's alright." A thick, low burr of words. Two large, powerful hands gripped her elbows and guided her back, away from Nissim.

"We shouldn't leave the body." She resisted the gentle tug.

Jimmy looked down into her face. "I don't think it'll bother him, girl. He'll be alright now." With great tenderness, he herded her outside, back into the chilly night, and Milly let out a gasp of sudden pain that flared from the bottom of her guts. It hurt so much she almost dropped to her knees.

Dale crouched beside her, a strong arm around her shoulders and his woody scent making her feel safe. "Hey, it's okay. It'll be okay. Though I wish you'd learn to listen to me."

"I just wanted to see if she was there."

"She's dangerous and you go charging in?" His chiding was gentle but firm.

Milly pulled away, suddenly aware they were all treating her like a child. She was a professional woman at work. "I'm fine. It was just a shock. I seem to remember you didn't do too well after you found Brook."

She noticed Jimmy flinch at the dead man's name.

Dale rose with her and stepped back, obviously sensing she'd done with the tea-and-sympathy part of the proceedings. "Fine, but we are going to have words about you following protocol. You placed yourself, and half our team, in a dangerous situation. The police have procedures for a reason, and we need to accept that."

"You're going to lecture me about procedures? After some of the stunts I've seen you pull? Where was the procedure when you and Lauren faced an armed man and accused him of murder? I was the only one able to save your damned arses," she yelled at him. Was that rain again or tears on her face?

"You're in shock—"

"Am I fuck. I'm furious," she shouted. Waving a hand at the cottage and its grizzly remains, she said, "This shouldn't have happened. How the hell did she know we had Nissim at your place? Who was she following and for how long?"

"Valentine, you need to see this," Lauren called from the doorway of the cottage.

"We aren't finished," Dale warned Milly.

She huffed out a breath, not trusting herself to answer, and watched him stride into the house.

Milly turned her back on the house and stared out over the water-crushed fields. She didn't think any of them would have done any better with their first corpse. Finding a dead man in that horrible stinking darkness with his throat gaping open… Suddenly, her stomach rebelled. She stepped to the edge of the grass and threw up.

"Fuck," she gasped as her stomach eased its cramps. A bottle of water appeared under her nose. "Thanks."

"I wasn't any better on my first dead body," PC Allison said. "Old lady, a week dead. We'd gone to check out the smell. Sarge Webber warned me what it was likely to be, but it didn't make any difference. It was bloody August as well. Hot and humid. I still taste it sometimes in my throat. At least we didn't have to move her."

Just the thought of it almost made Milly want to puke again. "Thanks for that, Pippa."

"You're welcome. Thought you'd like to know, there's another gemstone on the body, this time on the third eye."

Milly straightened. "Really?"

PC Allison nodded. "Same as the others. Figured it was important."

"Just clarification at this stage, I suppose."

"Interesting she chose the third eye for the teacher of the group." Allison sounded clinical and detached. Milly envied her that ability.

The two women stood side by side, looking out over the fields. Milly liked

Pippa Allison. She suddenly wanted to reach out to the other woman. "I know I've split with Ryan, but maybe you and me could go for a drink sometime?"

She felt Pippa's eyes flicker towards her without the other woman moving. "Yeah. That would be good. I don't have many people outside the Job that understand what we face."

"Me neither." Milly managed a smile.

"What's that?" Allison pointed into the moon's soft glow as it struck the land.

Milly craned her neck forwards. "Not sure." She turned. "Sully, don't suppose you have a telescopic lens on you somewhere?"

He trudged over, having been helping set up cordons for Lauren and clear paths for the forensic teams when they showed up. Opening his rucksack, he pulled out a camera with a long lens on the front. "Try this, but it has no night vision."

Pippa Allison looked down at it. "You carry that around all the time?"

He shrugged. "It's heavy, but very good."

Milly lifted the camera to her eye before Sully—without saying a word—removed the lens cap. She gave him a sheepish grin, then focused on the shift of shadows she and Pippa noticed.

Two people. One smaller, but seemingly in control. They struggled up a rise in the land, on a footpath heading towards a series of farm buildings. In silence, she handed the camera to Pippa.

"Bollocks," the PC said, thrusting the optic back at Milly. The woman hurried off to find her senior officer.

Milly handed the camera to Sully. He focused with practised ease. "Shit," he muttered.

"It's them, isn't it? Charlie and Eliza?"

"I guess. It's not likely to be anyone else." He fiddled with a few settings on the camera and rattled off a series of shots. "They might not work, but who knows in this light?"

"She's heading towards that maze of farm buildings. We need to get over there." Milly's gaze remained on the distant figures.

Sully looked at her. "Your boss has just reamed you out for not listening to him. Do you really think it's a good idea? You like your job and the look on his face made it clear he's not a happy little rabbit."

Milly laughed at the thought of a rabbit with Dale's expression when he was cross with her over something. "He's not going to sack me."

"I hope not, for your sake."

She looked around and found Jimmy, who stood, obviously totally out of his depth, near the farming Land Rover. "Come on, we can catch them up in the truck."

"Milly…"

"You're not going anywhere," boomed Dale's voice. "Nowhere." He strode out of the farmhouse like a huge avenging angel, coat blowing back in the soft breeze. "Show me what we're dealing with." He held out his hand for the camera, which seemed to shrink as he took possession. Scanning the buildings, he asked what they'd seen, and Milly obliged.

He glanced back at the cottage. "It might not be them, but it needs checking. Don't go anywhere and I'll talk to Lauren. Give me a few minutes." He called to Jimmy. "She is not to leave in that truck. Understood?"

"Yes, Guv."

He gave Milly a smile of victory and returned to the cottage, spoiling the overall effect of being the big man by slipping in the mud.

Milly huffed. "Bastard."

~ *Chapter 24* ~

"SERIOUSLY?"

Dale understood Lauren's frustration. Leave the body and issues of scene contamination could jeopardise the case for the Crown Prosecution Service. The defence team, for whoever they charged for this murder, could claim continuity of evidence was destroyed. Rendering that evidence, inadmissible. On the other hand, if she stayed with the body, she'd be allowing a bunch of civilians to chase down a dangerous suspect. Whichever way she did this, there would be problems down the line.

"Split your team," Dale suggested.

"What?" Lauren's exhaustion was clear.

"When was the last time you had a decent meal and a good sleep?" He wanted to help, but he knew they were out of their depth. They needed more people.

"What month are we in?" she mumbled.

"There's dedication to the job and stupidity, Lauren." She scowled at him, but he ignored her, thinking through the problems. "We'll split the teams. We can leave Ryan here as your detective constable with you, because you can't run. I'll take PC Allison, who can make a formal arrest. If I have Jimmy, Sully and Milly with me, I can form a cordon with that quantity of people."

"Leave Allison, take Ryan."

"You sure?" Dale asked.

"Yes. Stick the lights on the police Landy, it'll help the other teams find us. We'll have more help soon from the surrounding area. I'll send them up to your location if you need them."

"Okay. I'll keep in touch." He waggled his phone at her.

She gave him a quick nod and Dale left her with the remains of Nissim Doshi.

Taking the older vehicle, Sully drove them further up the West Yeo Road towards the tiny hamlet. Nothing but wet fields and trees to see in the moon's strong silver light. It might be romantic if they weren't trying to catch a killer.

Seeing Nissim's body hurt Dale. Would Nissim's mother weep for him, despite his wicked ways? Of course she would. She'd still love the mischief filled boy who she'd fed and clothed, washed and cared for when he was sick. Dale had to force himself not to think about the terrible sadness heading towards that family like an articulated truck.

He'd never been great at dealing with corpses, but he'd noticed all kinds of detail while trying to avoid looking in the face of the young man and those large, still brown eyes. The careful placement of the black diamond. The sticky mass of blood they'd managed to avoid, thanks to Milly's warnings. More blood flared over the walls as the knife sliced, and the heart pumped. The velocity of blood inside the human body always shocked him. It painted everything it touched, depending on how hard it was working. Nissim must have felt great panic, his heart going fast, so he knew he was going to die.

Tape held those elegant hands together and bound his feet. He couldn't have fought to save himself.

Pieces of broken tape lay in the corner furthest from the body and he'd seen larger footprints in the dead leaves. Those feet had scrambled at one point. To escape the blood? Or perhaps to escape the killer? Dale guessed she'd cut Charlie free and dragged him out of the cottage, after setting the scene with Nissim's corpse.

What did she say to them? Did she explain why she wanted Nissim dead? And if she had killed Joanna, where was she? Dale needed the broken woman to tell him where they'd find Joanna Wolski. He felt an overwhelming sorrow at failing Joanna.

They pulled around a corner and the road dipped into dark water. Sully drove forwards with care, keeping the vehicle steady and straight as they approached a ninety-degree bend. The big, old diesel just churned her way through the black mass. Dale realised Sully must be using the hedges to navigate because the road was invisible. One wrong decision and they'd end up in one of the flooded rhynes.

The farm buildings drew closer, and Dale tried to concentrate on how best to deploy his people. He should leave Milly with the Land Rover, but she was one of his assets. Clever and intuitive, she'd be wasted if he left her in the relative safety of the Landy. Jimmy, he was needed in case Dale wanted extra muscle. Ryan was the arresting officer if they found Eliza Collins. That meant Sully should remain with oversight. He had the camera, knew what he was doing with it, and would be as much use in a fight as a frog.

Decisions made, Dale began giving orders. He started with Sully. "I'll need you to stay with the Land Rover and keep oversight on the scene. Keep your phone open to me and we'll conference with Milly and Ryan. You'll need to keep full awareness of the entire area. Do you understand?"

"I think that's best." Sully didn't put up any argument. Dale admired his ability to let go of any masculine inclination to charge into battle.

"Jimmy, I want you with Milly as physical backup."

"Right oh," came the rumble from the back.

"Milly, you'll take the buildings on the right and do a full sweep of each. Remember how we practised sweeping rooms?" Dale asked.

"Yes." She sounded nervous.

"Good, then go with that, but adapt as needed, considering the size of these barns. You hold command of your area. Ryan, we'll take left because that's where we last saw those people. Remember, all of you, this woman has killed at least four people with some damned clever planning. She's now desperate, and she has a hostage. We do nothing to endanger Charlie Brent. He is innocent in this, and his mind is fragile. We have to take great care. Eliza is going to be highly reactive and primed for violence. Charlie is our priority. We need Eliza alive. We're still missing Joanna Wolski from the group on the Mump that night. Also, remember the conditions out there: cold, wet, slippery underfoot. We don't know if there are animals in these barns or dogs in the local area. Please, be aware." He tried to think of anything else he'd tell a team of trained police officers doing a sweep in hostile terrain. Though this place was nothing like the factories and storage units all over London he'd raided. He finished with, "The most important thing is all of us coming out of this in one piece. I want everyone alive and healthy. Remember that."

A series of nods from his people. They left the safety of the vehicle and split up into their teams. He watched Milly, with Jimmy's bulk two steps behind her, take the track to the right-hand side of the extensive farm buildings.

"Come on," he said to Ryan.

The young police officer didn't argue. Dale wondered if he'd have been as happy to follow the orders of a civilian when he was first promoted to detective. He doubted it, but by then, he'd already been on the take in a small way, so obeying the rules had never come naturally.

Dale approached the largest farm building first. He saw security lights, alarms, and heavy padlocks on the huge double doors. These were modern barns. He said into his Bluetooth earpiece, "Milly, the larger barns look like they have heavy security on this side."

"Same over here. No sign of forced entry. I'm not setting off the alarms to check, but there doesn't seem to be an easy way into any of these sites. No animals. I think they store farm machinery and from the smell, animal feed or something."

"Look for older buildings. I have a stable-like thing down here," Dale whispered. "I'm approaching now."

He heard Milly go still on the other line.

Sully whispered into his ear, "I can see movement near your location, Dale. There's something flashing in the small stone barn. I guess it's a torch."

"Roger that," Dale murmured. All his instincts prickled. Clouds stole their light again, and he blinked, trying to keep his vision clear. He signalled to Ryan to break right behind the low stone barn. This must've been one of the few remaining farm buildings from the days when these lands were first drained for farming. The roof looked solid, and the path well worn. He took each step slowly, keeping his torch off.

The wind shifted slightly, and he caught the sound of a voice. A woman's voice.

"I tried. I really tried to tell him, but Sonny doesn't listen to anyone. He's impossible to control. He never listens to our mum, and I just want him to listen to me. He has to stop. He has to stop spending our money on his dope and we have to settle down. We have to grow up, get normal jobs, be normal people. That's the only way he can save himself now. Then, down the line, when we have families, we can go back to the quest. You know?"

She spoke about her twin in the present tense. Not a good sign. Her words were rapid fire, like a machine gun letting loose with no control on the trigger. Stream of consciousness thought.

He heard a soft male voice he recognised. "I get it, Ellie. I really get it. We should talk to Sonny together, get him to see sense."

Dale breathed out. Charlie was alive. They'd not found a weapon at the site of Nissim's murder, so odds on she still had a knife. He crept closer to the front of the building and saw Ryan crouched at the opposite corner, looking to him for orders. The rain started again, still soft right now, but for how long?

He whispered into his phone, "She's in the barn. Call Lauren. She has Charlie Brent, and he's alive."

Eliza was ranting again, "He just won't stop." Dale heard her tears. "He won't stop with the drugs. I get it. We want to see what Gran Collins saw during the war. We have the same gift. She told us it was because she was a twin. She lost her brother. Did you know that?"

Sensibly, Charlie stayed quiet. Dale crept up to the first half door. It looked in good condition and he saw the straw had escaped. They must keep some animals in these smaller sheds. Dale hoped they were small animals that didn't react to violence. In the window sat a gas fuelled light, casting steady, but strong shadows over the back wall like a cinema story in silhouette.

"Sonny is fascinated by Gran and her stories. They talk for hours about it all. How to reach the higher plane. How to see the other worlds. We're going to make it. Together we'll make it—"

Dale risked a quick look over the door. Ryan crawled closer. Dale held his hand up, silently requesting he remain still. Ryan would have to move around a large pile of brambles and rubbish. Too much risk of noise. He saw Charlie sat in the straw, his hands bound, and his face covered in blood and the remains of tears. Other than that, the lad looked okay. Eliza paced in front of him, directly on the cobbled floor. She held a large knife, kitchen probably. Available in any homeware shop.

He tried to think through his next action. Interrupt her flow and gain her attention long enough to allow Charlie to run for Ryan? Or wait until the cavalry arrived?

Looking back, the way he'd come, he saw distant flashing blue lights heading in their direction, but they were miles away. Milly and Jimmy were coming. He noticed their shadows moving among the other buildings.

"Sully, I'm going in. We can't afford to make her panic," he whispered.

"I'm not sure that's a good idea."

"Just tell them where I am when they arrive." Dale removed his ear piece knowing he'd have Milly ranting at him any second.

Eliza was now pacing, and her rant seemed to be more intimate, not needing the audience of one. When she turned her back for a moment, Dale lifted his head. The movement caught Charlie's attention. The lad's eyes widened, but he clamped his mouth shut, not giving anything away.

"We will reach nirvana. I know it. Gran will be waiting for us. I can feel her in here." Eliza banged her heart, then her head. "Sonny just needs to knuckle down, do the work. That damned fool knew nothing. He lied to us. All of us and he made me hurt Sonny. I hurt Sonny." She turned and screamed in Charlie's face. "I hurt Sonny!" The knife slashed the air.

Charlie threw himself back in the straw and Dale burst into the stable. Eliza turned, lifting the blade. Twisting, Dale shifted his weight back, slipping slightly and missing the knife's plunge.

Ryan wasn't so quick on his feet. He'd come pounding in behind Dale. Didn't see Eliza lunge at the bigger man. The tip of the knife sliced into his soft chest, finding the narrow space between the stab vest and Ryan's neck. Dale saw it all happen. Saw Ryan's eyes go wide. *The blue switched to brown, the pale skin to deep russet-brown, Ringo lay in his arms bleeding to death. Hot, wet, stuttering breath, bubbles of blood.*

Ryan dropped to the floor. Astonished by the knife. Eliza screamed and yanked the blade back. Blood arched out, casting black shadows in the hard light of the gas lamp.

"You won't stop me saving Sonny," Eliza snarled in Ryan's face as he tried to grab at her.

The words dragged Dale back from that damned pavement in London. He rushed at Eliza's back. She turned and with her entire body, she threw herself into his. The treacherous ground shifted once more, and her weight tossed him into the wall of the stable. His shoulder and spine seemed to separate for one long, agonising moment. It felt like a lump hammer was being used to cut up his body into smaller pieces. Air rushed out of him, and it hurt so much his legs went weak.

Eliza lifted the blade to stab down. A blur of colour behind Eliza's snarling face shocked Dale. Milly's rainbow glove grabbed the hand with the knife, and Eliza's entire body moved in an arc away from Dale. He watched Milly try to find Eliza's elbow for a take down, but in the crazy light she struggled. Dale pushed the pain back, rushed in, and dropped an elbow onto Eliza's small back. His right arm felt like caged lightning. The fingers numb, unresponsive.

"Ryan!" Milly cried out, dropping to her knees next to the fallen police officer. She grabbed at his neck, pushing into the dark flood. Ryan gasped and gurgled.

Dale, kneeling on Eliza's back, heedless of the crack as a rib gave under his weight and her scream, struggled out of his coat. He pulled off his jumper, then his shirt. His right arm wouldn't respond quickly enough, and he tore the fabric. Throwing it at Milly, he barked, "Use this to stop the bleeding. It's a silk blend, less fibre contamination for the wound."

She didn't look like she understood the words, but she'd already snatched the shirt from his hand. His vest stuck to him, damp with sweat from nerves. A vast shadow appeared in the doorway.

"Jimmy, I need a hand." Dale fought to control the struggling woman under his knee. He watched Milly battle to stop Ryan's bleeding.

In seconds, the big man took in the scene. He headed for Charlie, which caused the younger man's eyes to widen in terror, and lift his hands to push Jimmy away. The big man swatted the bound wrists, took hold of the dropped knife and cut Charlie free.

"Help me with her," he growled at Charlie and pointed to Eliza. Turning in the straw, he took hold of Eliza as Dale relaxed his control over her arm. Jimmy grabbed her by the neck and lifted her off the ground. She stood limp in Jimmy's grip and stared into the distance, eyes vacant. She didn't look at any of them, merely stood staring at the far wall, breath whizzing out of her chest.

Dale moved to Milly's side. Blood covered her hands. The ground looked like someone had washed the old cobbles in red paint.

"I can't get him to wake up," she said, voice hard and frantic.

"Let me see." Dale peeled her hands away. If Ryan died here, he didn't want Milly's hands to be on him. She didn't deserve that feeling of responsibility and failure. The weight of it never left; the guilt of it haunted you forever.

She'd pushed down hard on Ryan's chest. Dale's larger hand covered the area, and he checked Ryan's neck for a pulse. Weak, frantic, a panicked creature no longer able to do its job as the volume of liquid in its heart dropped, the sealed unit of the body broken open.

"Is he...?" Milly sounded about five-years-old.

"Not yet." The grim realisation coursed over him that DC Ryan Matthews probably didn't have long. His skin took on a bluish tinge as oxygen became an issue.

Ryan's eyes flickered open. He tried to cough, but a gout of blood spilled out of his mouth, making Milly yelp in shock.

"Hey, look at me, Detective Constable, you're going to be fine," Dale told him.

Those big blue eyes filled with tears. Confusion and fear drove him to struggle against Dale.

"Hush," Milly said, stroking his cheek. "Hush, it's alright. We're here to help. The others are coming."

That gaze turned to Milly and Dale wanted to snatch her back, but he couldn't let go of Ryan's wound. The young man's eyes turned hazy, unable to focus.

"No, no, no, Ryan, don't, don't leave. We are friends. You are my friend. Please, don't leave me. Fight, Ryan, fight, your mum, think of your mum…"

Dale felt hot tears on his cheeks as he watched Ryan's pupils dilate, go wide, and every muscle in the young man's body diminish as the energy left.

"No…" Milly watched her friend die.

~ *Chapter 25* ~

BACK AT THE POLICE STATION in Street, Dale sat in reception with Milly's parents and Sully. The mood was grim. Every police officer who walked past Dale scowled, and he knew the only reason he had any liberty was Lauren's intervention on his behalf. She still functioned, but he knew her well, probably better than anyone else, and her grief rose like a towering wall of water inside her. Only her dedication to her job held it back, but it would break, and she'd shatter.

DCI Whitfield and another detective inspector had arrived when Lauren called it in, interviewing all of them and taking statements. Dawn had come and gone. They were now waiting for Milly to finish her statement. The entire night felt unreal. If he didn't have dark stains on his jumper and a ruined shirt in an evidence bag somewhere behind the locked doors, he wouldn't believe it had happened.

Eliza had vanished to a hospital for a check-up before they could interview her. Dale had lost access before asking where she'd hidden Joanna Wolski's body. The American must be dead.

Charlie proved more lucid than Dale expected and explained exactly what happened to him, Nissim and then poor Ryan. He sat on the other side of the small reception space with his mum. He'd given a full and frank statement, writing everything out.

Eliza had threatened him with the knife and told him that she'd wait for Catherine and kill her as well. He'd gone willingly, trying to protect his mother. She'd forced Charlie to drive to Glastonbury and park up the hill from Dale's place, waiting for them to return so she could make them tell her where Nissim was staying. Then the blackout happened and with her car being the only thing in the area with a light on, Nissim had arrived in her sights, a bird ready to be taken.

He hadn't recognised them when he'd climbed in the vehicle. Charlie drove, the knife pointed to his side, unable to say anything. Nissim had asked to be taken to Taunton, to the train station, but with the flooding and the rain, he'd been easy to confuse. They ended up in West Yeo before Nissim realised what was happening to him.

Eliza had given Nissim a bottle of water, spiked with GHB. Dale guessed she used the same substance on Adele Smith. After that, Nissim became pliable. She'd taken them into the filthy ruin, tied Charlie up, then Nissim and waited for him to come around. After that, things became much like they'd been in the stable. She'd talked to her dead brother, Sonny, for some time, asking him to forgive her, that her sacrifices might appease him. When Nissim woke, he panicked. He said some horrible things to Eliza, and she'd lost her temper. Charlie tried to stop her from killing him, but he didn't know how. He'd watched Nissim die, and finally realised the significance of the black diamonds.

When Eliza had a moment of lucidity, she knew they had to leave West Yeo, but the car had sunk into the mud and Charlie couldn't coax it out, so they ran. She held the knife, and Charlie knew the longer he survived, the more of a chance his mother had to save him.

The door to the police interview rooms and offices opened. Milly walked through with DCI Whitfield. She didn't lift her eyes to Dale. She just walked into the arms of her parents, then pulled Sully into the hug. Dale felt the cold of the dawn wind as they turned their backs and walked out, sheltering their daughter, not saying a word to him.

Whitfield watched them go. "She's given a full statement. It matches everything else." He turned his eyes on Dale. They were old eyes in the face of a man who'd seen too much of humanity to ever have any hope in its goodness. "You shouldn't have been there."

"DI Kennedy had little choice. The weather spread you too thin. People on the Levels and Sedgemoor were under threat. We didn't know we'd find Eliza Collins at that location. It was an educated guess."

Whitfield licked his lips and stared out of the door again. The wind chased some leaves about on the damp tarmac of the car park. "You used to be Job?"

"I did. Until I fucked it up." Dale felt an overwhelming sadness coming off Whitfield. He knew why. The DCI had to do the worst job in the world, tell a family their loved one died in the line of duty.

"Did you think Charlie was in danger from the knife Eliza Collins held?"

"You already asked me this."

Whitfield focused on him again. "This time you aren't on record."

Dale glanced at Charlie and his mum. "Yes. I ordered…" Dale paused for a moment. "No, that's not right. I asked Ryan to stay back. I didn't know he was behind me. If I'd known, I'd have made a different decision. Moved differently." Dale looked at his hands. "Taken the fucking knife myself."

Charlie stood up and approached the DCI. "He couldn't have stopped her. He really didn't know the police officer stood behind him. Mr Valentine saved my life. She was going to kill me. It was just a question of time. That's my honest assessment of what I saw, and I'm your only witness."

DCI Whitfield sighed. "I know. I just…" He wiped a hand over his face. "I just wish it hadn't happened. Lauren's in pieces."

"I can take her home," Dale said.

Whitfield shook his head. "No. I don't think that's a good idea. I don't think you're good for each other." He turned and left the reception area with a final word. "We might need more information from all of you, so don't leave the area."

Nothing in the world felt right to Dale.

He'd saved Charlie, caught Eliza, but it was for nothing compared to the grief Ryan Matthews' parents would feel for the rest of their lives. Dale knew Ryan had a sister, a large extended family. Then there was Milly. His clever, brave, sensitive assistant. Assistant? Hardly. She'd saved his life, but she'd been too late to save Ryan, and Dale knew how that would break her heart. They would all pay a price for this night.

"Dale?" A soft hand on his arm.

He dragged himself back to the present. "Mrs Brent, sorry. Catherine. Do you need me to—"

She stopped him. "If you need to talk to someone outside of all this, then call me. I'm a good listener and I don't judge. Just ask Charlie."

They both looked at the young man, who was staring up into a tree full of starlings making a racket about the storm ending.

"He's different today," Dale said.

"It's like a duvet's been taken off him. One that's been smothering him to death for the last year. I'm hoping I have my son back."

"Take it steady."

She nodded. "I'll try, but he's so together suddenly."

"I think Eliza lifted a mirror to his mind, and what he saw scared him. Maybe he realised how worried you've been listening to him."

She managed a smile. "Do you really think so?"

"Maybe. He needs to stay away from drugs and booze, though."

Her smile turned rueful. "If I catch him with so much as an alcho-pop, I'll kill him." The smile faded. "I hope your friend recovers."

Dale nodded and opened the car door for her. He watched Charlie climb into the other side. The young man nodded to say thanks.

Driving back to Glastonbury hurt. Dale's shoulder felt like he had a forge set up in the joint and some vile dwarf was in there hammering away, forming shards of steel to stick into his back and arm. The paramedics had checked him at the scene and advised he needed an x-ray. But when Dale saw what he'd hit on the wall, he suspected he just had terrible bruising. When Eliza had barrelled into him, Dale had fallen against a large ring set high and protruding a long way from the wall, obviously meant for tying up animals, probably horses. He'd been unlucky.

Driving up the hill, he just wanted to be alone, to lick his wounds, feel pity over Ryan, and to remember Ringo. Stabbing someone was just too damned easy. The go-to weapon for every wannabe and career criminal.

The dark mood, expected and familiar, jolted in shock when he reached his cottage. He saw something that made him smile so naturally, the feelings of darkness melted away like a summer mist under the burning sun. Grace leaned against the wall with Jimmy, both of them huddling inside their coats, but chatting happily. She threw her head back and laughed at something Jimmy said, making the big man blush in happiness.

Dale parked in the drive and left the car. He longed for their warmth to shelter him.

Grace approached, put her hands on his chest, rose on her toes and kissed him. "Jimmy told me what happened. I'm so sorry, Dale. He said DI Kennedy let him leave the scene. He came to tell me you needed help." Her joy of moments ago washed back in concern for his needs, but he saw it there, waiting to be released when the time was right.

Dale covered her hands with his and pressed them into his chest. Her big, pale, moss green eyes swam in sympathy as he nodded. "It's been a terrible night, but I think I could do with some company. How goes things with the flood?" He wanted a distraction. A link to the real world outside of death.

A long groan came from Grace, and she began regaling them with the madness of trying to keep farmers, worried about pregnant ewes, separate from animal rights campaigners who believed all meat was murder. The joys of Glastonbury's diverse population.

It didn't escape Dale's notice that Grace kept hold of his hand as they walked around his cottage to the back door. Her grip was firm, as if to silently speak the words of solidarity she knew he wasn't ready to hear.

He cooked for them. The normality of being in his kitchen, safe and warm, bringing him back from the edge. Every time he thought about Ryan's parents, his hands would shake and this terrible pain in his chest flared. He'd seen Ringo's family deal with that grief, and the memories still haunted him almost as much as Ringo's voice. The voice who'd gone silent since Ryan's death.

After he'd eaten, Dale sat on his sofa, Grace tucked under his arm, and they fell asleep. When he woke, he found a blanket over him and Grace gone, but someone had plugged in his mobile and it vibrated on the table next to him. Did Jimmy do all this for him?

He picked up his phone without being able to focus on the screen. "Valentine Investigations," he mumbled.

"We need to find Joanna. Dead or alive, we have to find her," Milly said. "Ryan died for nothing if we don't find Joanna, and I have an idea."

"Are you—"

"No, not even slightly, but I have to do this. I have to find Joanna Wolski. *We* have to find her."

He thought about the image of seeing Milly with her parents in the police station. Their deep and constant love for their daughter, and how close she'd come to being on the wrong end of that knife, like poor Ryan. Is this how Joanna's father felt? Dale found it hard to understand. His relationship with what remained of his family could best be described as tenuous.

"It wasn't your fault," she whispered. "It wasn't my fault. He didn't follow orders. He didn't follow protocol."

"I know."

"So we keep going. I'm going to fall apart later, when I have time."

"Alright, how can we find Joanna? The police have Eliza and I'm sure they'll be looking for Joanna right now. We're redundant." Dale roved through his mind, trying to see a link he'd missed that Milly hadn't.

"Bugger the police. They won't get anything from that fucking loony." Her bitterness didn't surprise Dale, but her choice of language did. "It's my farmers, Dale. My farmers hold the key. Call Grace and see if they're still in the community centre. I'll meet you there and explain in more detail."

The phone died in his hand. He looked at it in astonishment, then allowed himself a soft chuckle. From the first, Milly had surprised him with her strength and the hard determination that brought her to his door. She'd never be diminished for long.

He rang Grace. "Morning."

He saw the smile on her face when she said, "Sorry I left like that. I didn't want to disturb you and it seems Jimmy put us to bed."

"Really?"

"I didn't cover us in a blanket and put our phones on charge. I'm not that organised."

"It seems to be the morning for surprises. Milly wants to know if you have any of those farmers she's been helping down at the centre."

"Erm…" Dale heard her moving around and soft breaths. "We have some people and one man with his wife. The others left to check on their stock. Mr Bayne and his wife are waiting for an ambulance. He has cancer, apparently."

"That'll be the one Milly wants. I'll be down in a minute. Quick shower."

Grace made a warm sound. "Sounds like fun."

Dale groaned. "Don't do that, Grace. It's not fair."

She chuckled and hung up on him.

When he reached the community centre, he saw a flow of people coming and going through the narrow alley. The large double doors at the end were both open, despite the cold and lowering grey sky. Just what the county needed, another dump of rain.

"Coffee." Milly came up behind him and thrust one of her large travel mugs into his hands.

"Oh. Thanks." He tried to see her face, but she'd left her curtain of curls down. It meant she'd be able to hide more easily. "Erm—"

"Not now, Dale. We have work to do," she stated, climbing the steps to the upper floor of the centre two at a time.

He followed, wondering how much she'd had to fight Sully and her mother to leave the Green Man café. Grace met them at the top of the stairs.

Following instinct, Dale bent to kiss her cheek in welcome. Grace, startled, flinched back for a moment, then went for it. The clumsy double movement set them both off balance and they bumped heads, not lips.

"Damnit." Dale almost spilt coffee down himself. "I'm just not that slick anymore."

"I was never that slick," Grace said, rubbing her head.

"We'll get better with practise."

Grace blushed. "We're going to practise?"

He chuckled and gave her a one-armed hug. "A lot."

Milly stalked past them. "We have work to do."

Grace threw her a worried glance. "This way. I have Mr Bayne somewhere quiet." She led them across the floor. People who'd needed a warm, safe and dry place for the night sat around looking exhausted and blank-eyed, doubtless wondering what state their homes might be in this morning. Spare blankets, sleeping bags, mattresses, and airbeds were folded or stacked in corners.

They followed Grace to a small antechamber and Dale saw Bayne for the first time. He sat beside an older woman, who had a wide florid face and what must have been high, rosy round cheeks in younger years. She now looked exhausted, drawn and worn to the wick. Her hands, resting on her lap, had thick fingers, the callouses ingrained but the skin and nails scrubbed clean. Her body blended together, breasts, belly and thighs, in the design that comforted grandchildren and small furry animals. Her eyes, though, held that terrible contradiction. They spoke of loss, and an echoing sadness she'd never fully escape.

Grace took the lead. "Mrs Bayne, I have the detectives here to speak with your husband."

Mrs Bayne raised a brief smile and nod, then glanced at her husband. A sallow, jaundiced man, whose hollow eyes roved in his skull.

"I wanted to die on my farm," croaked Mr Bayne, "but that bloody old weather beat me to it."

"Don't, dear. You aren't going to die in the hospital. It's just a check-up." His wife stroked his hand.

Dale knew it would hurt him if she patted it. Even the light stroke made him wince. He'd seen his grandfather like this. The mighty mountain of an Italian rogue laid to rest as little more than a sea-ravaged sandcastle.

Bayne lifted a thin lip, as if attempting a smile for his wife. "I know, love. I know."

He did too.

Lifting eyes haunted by a future without him, the farmer took Dale's measure and gave a brief nod. "Grace tells us that your associate found the man who's been digging holes."

"She did. He's been… Um…" Dale winced.

"Murdered from what I 'ear," Mrs Bayne glanced at Milly. "That right?"

"Yes, though not for digging the holes. It's a bit of a story, but the basics are pretty clear. About a year ago, a robbery took place in Bristol, but rather than escape on the roads, or by plane, they took to the River Avon and came down the Bristol Channel. Then up the River Parrett." Milly frowned. "On the face of it, it seems convoluted, but they avoided all cameras, which is pretty clever. They buried their loot on the Levels. A group performing a ceremony up on Burrow Mump in the old church saw them."

"Should have knocked that bugger down. Attracts all kinds of weirdos," Mr Bayne muttered.

Milly didn't comment, which Dale considered tactful of her, considering many of those 'weirdos' were friends who frequented the café.

She said, "Some people on the Mump saw the treasure being buried, but one of their number died that night having been thrown out of the group." She paused.

Dale, recognising her shift in tone, gripped her elbow in solidarity. "The young man who died from a drug's overdose and exposure on Burnham's seafront had a twin sister. It seems she took revenge, blaming the other people in the group for her brother's death. Nissim, the guru who organised the spirit quest, became your digger of holes. He also became the penultimate victim of the woman whose twin died. Nissim realised the significance of what they'd witnessed that night. A small boat and two armed men digging in one field, but he couldn't remember exactly where they'd hidden the gems and cash. He'd understood exactly what he'd seen, but the others considered it a fevered drug-induced trip. By some weird twist of fate, one of the young men in the group is the nephew of the man who organised the robbery, and another of the group is still missing."

"Which is where I think you can help?" Milly said, now recovered. "You mentioned a few times that Mark Weaver is refusing to leave his land and 'some young fancy woman with a bloody strange English accent' is now living with him."

Mrs Bayne frowned, but nodded. "Well, it was me, really. I seen 'er. While I been out on the farm. She's like a willow twig with this cloak of black hair. Really pretty, but moves like a fox being hunted by hounds. All scrunched up and scared. She can't 'ave been with Mark for long. I'd have noticed. I spoke with her a few times. She don't enjoy coming into town."

Dale opened his phone and pulled up a photo of Joanna. "This her?"

Mrs Bayne took the phone from his hand. "Reckon it is."

Milly looked at him and the pair shared a moment of victory.

Dale asked, his accent slipping into the hard London he tried to avoid when speaking to witnesses or locals. "How do we find this Mark Weaver?"

Mrs Bayne looked a little startled. "He owns Tappingwall Farm, but I'm not sure you'll get down the drove. If the tide's come in, then the floodwater has nowhere to go."

A commotion from behind them intruded.

Grace touched Dale's arm. "It's the paramedics for Mr Bayne."

Within moments, two professional medics were in the room, and everybody faded into the background. Milly whispered, "I want to say goodbye to Mr Bayne."

Dale didn't know what to say. He had the feeling the man wouldn't make it back to his farm, which cut deep for some reason he didn't understand. Shouldn't a man who'd toiled and worked the land for decades be able to slip into that peaty soil with his final breaths? Rather than dying among strangers in a room full of beeping machines and the smell of chemicals designed to hide the miseries of the human body? Had we sanitised our endings too much? Is that what made him sad? Or maybe it was the blood of another young man covering his hands during those last moments of a life snatched away by violence?

Dale allowed the grief to wash through him, feeling the sharp thorns spike his heart.

He turned away from Milly and Grace, and stared hard at a wall covered in music posters from past gigs in the towns and the festival. He focused on the rainbow coming out of the prism from Pink Floyd's Dark Side of the Moon. The colour, against the black, the straight lines of broken light, the memories of the weed smoked while listening to music his grandfather loved, it soothed him, and the dark washed back.

"Come on. We have a woman to find," he said.

With a brief wave to Grace, they left the building and hurried to the carpark by the abbey's entrance. The rain drove downwards to the ground like a teenager with anger management issues. It hit so hard, it bounced back. They ran. The Audi pinged in welcome the moment Dale was within range, and they threw themselves into the dry confines.

~ *Chapter 26* ~

ONCE THEY'D SETTLED INTO THE car, silence took over.

Dale didn't know where to start, so he opted for the simplest solution, ignoring all the elephants.

He drove back out towards Burrow Mump until the Road Closed signs became impossible to ignore. Mostly because the water stretched out over the tarmac and raced off into the distance.

"Shit," Milly summed up. She wore her rainbow wellingtons and Dale wondered if she'd had to wash Ryan's blood off them.

"We can get to the farm via the footpath. It's higher than the road."

Milly glanced up at the ruined church, poking over the naked trees. "I suppose we don't have much choice. Though why they'd stay out there is anyone's guess."

"Unless they know where the money and gems have been hidden." Dale turned the big car around with some difficulty on the narrow road.

"You can't really think…?"

"Why not? Joanna was there that night. This Weaver fella knows his land. What if they've been looking as well? Maybe they've already found it?"

"Bloody hell."

Dale pulled into the Mump's carpark, and they left the confines of the warm Audi.

"We're going to have to go up and over the Mump to reach the farm," he said.

Milly groaned but did up her coat and tucked her hair into a pink beanie. Dale found his black beanie and strode on ahead.

The path up the hill was treacherous, with tiny streams rushing through the sodden ground making it slick and sticky all at once. The muddy track was almost impossible, so they had to use the sheep-shorn grass.

"Dale, I can't manage it," Milly called out from behind him.

He turned and squinted through the sheets of tumbling drops. Milly had her fingers dug into the side of the steep hill. Her wellingtons, though lovely, weren't designed for this kind of work. His thick soled walking boots dug deep, keeping him stable.

Until he tried to reach her. The slide and sudden yelp of indignant surprise at the speed of his downhill skid make Milly laugh into the rain.

Dale sat in the mud and groaned. "Bloody hell."

"At least you don't look like an incomer anymore." She wiped tears from her eyes.

"I don't look like much of anything," he grumbled.

He watched Milly close her eyes for a moment and take a deep, wet breath.

When her eyes opened, the green shone hard and bright. "It's good to be alive."

He gave her a single nod of acknowledgement. The unspoken words understood. "Yes."

She held out her hand, and together they made it to the top of the hill. The other side of the Mump proved impossible for any kind of managed descent. They half-slid, half-stumbled downwards, until they met the path leading from the back of the churchyard. It made Dale a little queasy to see the water rising among the gravestones. Just the thought of what lay underneath…

Milly had her phone out, trying to shelter it under the rough canopy of a yew tree. "This way," she said, pointing.

They trudged along a ridge that was the footpath running alongside the river. The world around them shocked Dale. He'd never seen a flooded landscape in real life, and despite the dim light of a soggy day, it was dramatic. A vision of apocalyptic proportions covered the once beautiful green of the low-lying fields. A sheet of grey water, tinged an unhealthy brown and pierced by barren trees, smothered the world for miles in every direction. They were the only people visible. The main road was gone, the village of Burrowbridge, the pub, the church, where they'd been the night before, all islands and, sometimes, finally submerged.

"My God," he whispered.

"Welcome to climate change. This used to happen once in a lifetime, maybe. Now, it's most years." Milly stood beside him, clearly just as awestruck by the devastation.

Dale shook himself. "Which farm is it?"

Milly pointed. A farmhouse rose from the gloom, sat on a rise in the land that lifted it from what once would have been marshland. Dale realised a dwelling could have existed on this site for thousands of years, long before the Romans came to Britain, or the Vikings invaded. This current home looked bleak and alone, made of dark stone and dark slate. It wasn't an attractive place to live during a flood, the colour was just a few shades darker than the sky and the drowned world.

Heads down, they trudged on, and Dale tried to consider what they'd be facing.

After ten minutes of slogging through the weather, on what was actually a well-maintained footpath, Milly pulled him to a stop. "That's the white van that chased us."

He tucked Milly back behind him, the movement so ingrained he didn't realise what he'd done until she harrumphed, and returned to her previous spot.

"Are we sure it's the same van? Neither of us were really able to take a photo," he said quietly, as if someone might hear them. Though, the rain would cover an army invading right now.

Not a bad idea, an army. He could do with one. Pulling out his phone, he planned on calling Lauren and requesting just that, when Milly put her hand on his arm and shook her head.

"Don't. They can't help. The chances of them ever listening to either of us again are zero."

Dale ground his teeth. "I know, but we can't do this alone."

"We have the element of surprise." Then she cocked her head. "Listen."

Dale twisted his right ear away from the wind and towards the cottage. "Dogs?"

"Lots of dogs. Dogs who are in a shed just over there," Milly said, pointing to a small stone barn.

"Are you suggesting we release the hounds, and they go off to war?"

She shrugged. "Why not?"

"Because they're just as likely to attack us without proper training."

He wanted to run now. In places like Peckham, dogs are weapons, not just pets. He'd watched, helpless, as one of his colleagues had been mauled by two dogs during a drugs raid. In those days, the Job had mattered to him, and he'd only served for a few weeks before it happened. The mess those dogs had made of that big-arsed police officer filled Dale with dread. He'd been threatened with dogs a time or two as a kid, and seen police handlers release dogs into dangerous places to clear out the bad guys. Dogs were scary.

He shook his head. The fear instilled by angry beasts so deeply ingrained it made his knees go weak. "No. We aren't doing that."

"Why?"

"We just aren't, okay? There has to be another option."

A woman's long scream of pain ripped through the wind and rain. Dale ran before he thought of a reason not to, and Milly pounded along behind him. Reaching the farmhouse he saw the front door open, mud trailed over the threshold. There were shouts, more screams, hard thumps Dale recognised as a beating. As he moved down the hall, he saw an old umbrella stand and propped up inside it were two golf clubs. He yanked out the larger of the two with little idea of its technical use beyond being able to do a lot of damage to small joints. And skulls.

Following the sounds of a scuffle, more cautious now, he moved silently down the hallway towards what he presumed would be the kitchen. He didn't feel Milly behind him and wondered where she'd gone. If she had any sense, she'd be phoning someone, anyone, to get them help.

At the end of the narrow hall, a door stood open, and light poured out along with heat. He saw old rugs, old armchairs by an Aga and one raven haired woman tied to a normal kitchen chair, while a big raven haired man sat slumped, tied in another. Blood dripped onto the old tiles, and a puddle of vomit stained the floor. Two big men were pacing, obviously the same ones who'd grabbed him and Milly.

This is fucking insane, bruv, piped up Ringo from the back of his mind.

I know, Ringo. I know. But I can't leave them like this, Dale thought in return, well aware he was arguing with himself, but scared now and trying to find the 'right thing to do'.

You've no choice, mate. You gotta smack the monkey to train the donkey, came the helpful advice.

Yeah, I know that, dickhead. I just need to work out the best way to do it.

Charge the bastards. Scream real loud. Shock and awe, bruv, like they do in the movies.

Dale almost snorted. That had always been Ringo's problem. He thought he lived in a gangster film, and the anti-heroes would win, because they really had hearts of gold under all the grime of their wasted lives.

Bollocks to this. If he waited any longer he'd lose his bottle.

One of the bastard thugs was wearing a red scarf, the other a blue beanie hat. Red was obviously in charge. He'd make the decisions. Blue was gearing up for another round of—let's persuade the farmer to talk—by removing his coat and rolling up his sleeves.

Joanna Wolski sobbed. Mark Weaver moaned and dribbled more blood onto the floor.

The real danger in that room came from the leader of the two men. Dale also knew they were armed with at least one pistol, the memory of it making the skin behind his right ear tingle in panic. He had to get that gun.

Which is when he saw Red take his coat off, and the shoulder holster come into view. Joanna screamed and fought against her restraints again. Mark tried lifting his head to check on her, and Dale winced. These guys really knew how to give a man a beating.

"We don't know what you're talking about," Joanna yelled. "Please, dear God, just let him go. We don't know anything." Her southern American accent came in thick with her panic.

Well, it was now or never. He rolled his right shoulder, pulling on the terrible bruising to gain some extra leverage. Dale lunged into the room with the golf club over his head like a katana. He swept it down as he'd done thousands of times into the dojo with a bokken, the wooden training sword, and caught the man with the gun across the shoulder. The man stumbled and on the backswing Dale caught his right hand as it reached for the gun. He heard bone splinter.

Blue yelled and charged Dale. The back door flew open. Milly charged in with two savage dogs on leads almost yanking her over the table they wanted the intruders so badly. Blue turned to face this new threat. Dale took full advantage of his shocked reaction to a small, red-headed woman trying to control two dogs as they barked like the hounds from the Wild Hunt, and brought the club up in a short arc to smack Blue on the back of the head. The *thunk* was sickening, as was the crack when the front of Blue's face hit the table before the floor. The man went down like some malicious, sadistic child had cut his strings.

Then the dogs turned their attention to Dale. He readied himself with the golf club.

"Fly, Beetle, hold," Joanna snapped. They ignored her. "I said Hold!" she bellowed at the dogs. The pair looked at her, then looked at Milly. She grabbed a handful of something from her pocket and threw it on the floor. Both dogs engaged their noses and snuffled about looking for the prize.

She stared at Dale, her eyes very wide. "They really like cheese biscuits."

Dale burst into laughter. He breathed out hard for a few seconds until Red moved his left hand to the holster. As big as the bloke was, he didn't match a pissed off Dale Valentine.

"Don't even fucking think about it." He lifted the golf club. "I can't miss in this kitchen, and you can't run. You run and you'll fucking drown if you go out there and make a single mistake. Let's just take a minute and think about this. I know you're a professional. No one here needs to die today."

"My boss—"

"McKie is a fucking idiot. Whatever he buried out there is gone under metres of shit and water. Before you do anything stupid, just ask yourself one question: If these two found those gems would they still be living in this shithole during a fucking Biblical flood? None of us knows where they are. Whatever McKie left here, it's turned to mush in this weather."

Blue groaned. Dale put a boot on his back. Red moved his left hand back to cradling his right.

"What now, tough guy?" sneered Red.

Dale smiled. "Now we play tidy-up." Dale didn't move his eyes from Red and put a bit more weight on Blue. "Milly, tie the dogs to the front rail on the Aga."

She coaxed the dogs with more crumbed biscuit, and put them by the Aga, in what was obviously their sleeping area. Then she made sure they were secure. Dale realised the leads were nothing more than the plastic string farmers seemed to use for everything.

"Good, now cut Joanna free. Joanna, I need you to help Milly tie these two up. You used a firearm in the States?" he asked, suddenly inspired.

Joanna blinked a few times, obviously trying to reassess her reality. "Yes, I can shoot. He's got a Glock 9mm in that holster. It'll carry fifteen rounds."

She knew more than he did.

Dale nodded. "Okay, then you get the gun. You're in charge of keeping them in your sights. I'll help Milly. Do not shoot me. I'm one of the good guys. My name is Dale Valentine." He allowed his eyes to flick to the woman as she rose from the chair. He met the steady gaze of a self-possessed person who understood violence.

She approached Red, which made both dogs go into full alert mode. Milly returned to them and put her hand on the quick release knots holding the dogs. Red understood the threat and let Joanna remove the firearm.

Dale watched her slick movements as she cleared the barrel, checked the magazine and lifted the weapon in a two-handed, balanced stance.

She curled her lips. "Give me a fucking reason, dickhead." Her finger strayed to the trigger in a smooth movement.

"Joanna." Dale spoke with more authority and calm than he felt. "If you do this, you will go to prison for life. British prison. For life. No chance of parole. Please, unless he gives you a reason, don't kill him. If you're good with that thing, then I'm more than happy to see some holes, but not in the house, you don't want the blood on your floor. It never comes out."

The colour in her naturally warm-toned skin, darkened further.

Then Milly moved. She stood in front of Red.

Dale felt the panic rise in a rush so hard and fast he wanted to puke, but Blue was waking up and he couldn't take his damned foot off the man's back.

Milly held her hands up. "Don't, Joanna. He's no threat now. Don't kill him. Mark is a good man, and he's going to need you. He's really going to need you after this."

The war in the young woman's eyes raged for several terrifying seconds until her finger eased back to lie alongside the barrel of the weapon. Her arms and stance didn't change but the atmosphere of violence washed back.

Dale breathed out. "You got more of that string?" he asked Milly.

"Baling twine," she said automatically. Then glanced at him, a little sheepish, and pulled two more neatly tied bundles out of her pocket. Together they tied up Blue's arms and hauled him off the floor and onto a chair.

Then Dale cut Mark free. The man's face was a mess, but the thugs were used to giving a beating for information, which meant the victim had to speak and see. Mark had nothing more than a broken nose, split lips, and a nasty gash over his eyebrow that bled. There'd be severe bruising to the chest and belly, maybe the kidneys. Dale half lifted him out of the kitchen chair and led him over to the dogs and a more comfortable armchair.

Milly gave Mark a glass of water. He wasn't quite with it enough to follow events, but Joanna backed up until she stood in front of him with the gun.

Dale leaned against the table and looked at Red. "I think you know how this is going to work," he began. "I want you to take your monkey here, and leave Somerset. I want you to give Mr McKie a message from me, something like: 'Ere be Dragons." He mangled the rural accent.

Red's eyes narrowed, like they weren't small enough already. "What the fuck gives you the right—"

Dale took some photos of Red with his mobile. "I have these stored on the cloud already. I have the police on standby because I do private consultancy work with them. They like me. They don't like Mr McKie. He's never going to find that money. You know it, I know it, you're just here because the bloke is in a panic. I get it. I do."

"You don't know who you're fucking with, mate," snarled Red.

"I know," Dale said. "Trust me. I know. But we need to resolve this before anyone gets themselves shot. I'm guessing that lady over there isn't going to be interested in taking prisoners. She'll kill you and let the flood water do the rest. She isn't stupid. Before you know it, you'll be in the Bristol Channel and then you're gone at low tide. They will never find your bodies. I'll help her if I have to. The money isn't here. The madman who tried digging holes we collided over earlier? He's dead as well. He never found your loot."

Joanna gasped and just for a moment the gun wavered.

"His name was Nissim Doshi, and Eliza Collins killed him," Dale said all this for Joanna's benefit. "There is no one else left alive, except for this woman, who saw whatever McKie hid that night. Leaving now is the only way McKie *might* get out of prison."

"They're all dead?" Joanna asked. "I... I knew about Simon and Kayla, I thought... I thought it might be someone looking for the money. After the trip and my comedown, I put it together. Then something really weird happened, and that's why I ran. I needed somewhere safe to hide. Mark and I met when I rented his caravan and things... But I couldn't tell him about that night, about what we did, what we saw... I didn't want him put in danger."

Mark made a noise. "Well, that worked didn't it, Jojo?"

She turned to look at him, the weapon dropping for a moment.

"Don't do that," Dale snapped. "Either do your job, or give me the damned gun."

She returned to Red, who'd actually tried to move across the room towards her. Joanna snarled and strengthened her stance. The threat was enough, Red backed down.

Red looked at Dale, ignoring her. "What's the plan?"

"You pick up your mate here and fuck off. Nothing more complicated than that. Get out of Somerset, go back to your nest and stay there. When McKie wants to know what's happened, just tell him the entire field, or riverbank, or wherever this bloody stash is, has gone in the flood."

Red snorted. "He'll never believe that."

"Make him. Or you're going to find a world of pain down here. I'm serious about the police. I work for them, and you can't make me disappear without them coming to look, never mind my associate over there. You're professionals, I can see that, so whatever they're paying, it isn't enough. None of us knows where this money is hidden."

Red's shoulders relaxed for the first time. "I fucking hate the countryside." He pointed a finger at Dale. "I also hate you. Pain in the bloody arse you've been all fucking day. Night. Whatever the fuck it is." He sighed. "Fine. I'll figure it out. I told McKie his plan was too bloody complicated, that we'd lose the gems and the cash down here. He said he knew the area too well for everything to be lost. That boats were the best getaway vehicles. Then the stupid fuck got lifted because of non-payment of speeding fines." Red shook his head in disbelief at his boss' stupidity. "I ask you, non-bloody-payment of a speeding fine. He told us to come down here, get the stash, move it, but I couldn't find it. I hate this rural shithole." He crossed the room. "Then we find out, after you visited the boss, that we have a poaching problem that needs solving."

Dale moved back towards Joanna. She stepped forwards with the gun, like a highly trained soldier. He found it disturbing to be honest. The fluffy hippy vibe with the clothes and hair didn't match the trained killer look in her eyes.

Red dragged Blue up, and they backed out of the house. Joanna and Dale followed.

She whispered, "I can't keep this up much longer."

He didn't know if she meant the tough woman act, or the weapon. He needed both. "Just keep focused on them leaving without this going pear-shaped. Okay?"

"Okay."

Blue climbed into the van, Red took the wheel, though he'd never change gear with that hand. After a few false starts, some shouting and a nasty grind of the gearbox, they pulled out of the farmyard.

Dale watched, concerned. "Can they get out okay in the flood?"

Joanna nodded and lowered the gun. "Yeah, yeah, they came in on the old farm track, it's high enough." She folded at the waist, a wet rag suddenly, and tried to take a deep breath. "Oh fuck, oh fuck, shit, fuck, oh fuck."

Dale leaned over and took the gun from her limp hand. He removed the magazine, and put it in his pocket, then stuffed the gun in the back of his belt.

Next he rubbed circles on Joanna's back while she learned how to breathe again.

~ *Chapter 27* ~

DALE KEPT PACE WITH JOANNA, who moved like an old woman, spine bowed, legs stiff, as if she'd been holding all the terror in her joints and they'd corroded in one brutal day. They made their slow way back to the kitchen. Milly sat with a bowl of hot water and clean cloth, helping Mark clean his face.

"Jojo," he cried out, and tried to stand. The pain of the sudden movement made every fibre of his body rebel and he fell back into the chair with a cry.

Joanna Wolski pushed Milly out of the way and began to clean her lover's face.

Dale headed for the kettle, filled it, and started making tea for everyone. The actions were meant to soothe the household, including the dogs, who watched Mark with as much concern as Joanna.

The silence gathered around them, and Dale allowed it to grow. One thing he'd learned as a detective was the value of silence. It often revealed cracks an experienced interviewer could exploit.

As he'd planned, Joanna broke first. "Who are you? What do you want with me?"

Milly stood with her back to the sink, just watching. He noticed she tucked her hands behind her back, as if to prevent them from shaking.

Offering her a cuppa, he asked how the others took their tea. He made it calm and quiet, bringing the energy of the room down.

He offered Milly a smile and a nod. "You did well with those dogs."

She chuckled. "Yeah, surprised myself with that one. Who knew my secret stash of biccies would come in handy for training silly old collie dogs?" The smaller of the two, as if guessing she was being spoken about, wiggled her way back to Milly, nosing at her coat pocket. "I'm so sorry, sweetie, I don't have any more."

"You can take her. She's bugger all use as a sheepdog and we're leaving," Mark mumbled through damaged lips.

Joanna and Mark sat by the Aga glaring at their saviours.

"Alright," Dale said, "it's time for some home truths. Joanna's father has hired us to find her, and now we have. We also found your fake passport and your cash." He watched the pair closely.

Wild panic flared in Joanna's eyes. Mark tried to straighten, as if to protect her. Dale held up his hands to maintain the calm.

"Stop, wait. I'm here to talk. All I ever promised him was I'd find you. I said I'd tell him if you were alive. I am not contracted to tell him where you are. If you don't want to be found, then that's okay."

"How the hell am I meant to believe you?" Joanna's eyes were desolate with dread.

"Right now, you don't have a choice. Let's just talk and figure this out. A lot has happened, and you need help. Those men might not be the last McKie sends."

Joanna put her face into her hands. "I'm never going to get away from him."

"We'll figure it out, Jojo. I promised to protect you and I will." Mark seemed oblivious to the stupidity of the statement.

Dale shook his head. "Let's start with what I know. You ran from your bungalow that your father pays for, and you've touched none of the money he sends. You also stopped all contact with him. Previously to that, you'd prepared a slush fund and a means of escaping the UK without being noticed on your genuine passport. However, something happened. I think it was seeing a report about the two dead people on your spiritual quest with Guru Raj, but one was in Cornwall and one in Wales, so…"

"It wasn't them that made me run," she said. "I knew about them, wondered if it was because of what we saw that night. I'm not stupid. I know a threat when I see one. It was Eliza that made me run. She turned up at the house. I didn't like her from the start. She made me nervous even when we did that senseless quest." Joanna shook her head. "I don't know what I was thinking, taking peyote with complete strangers. Stupid move."

"It brought us together," Mark mumbled.

Joanna's face softened, and she held his hand. "Yeah, it did. That's the only good thing to come out of this." Looking at Dale, she continued, "It's a bit of a muddle, even now. You see, I don't drink alcohol, and when Eliza came, she brought a bottle of wine. I invited her in, asked after her brother. She said he was fine, but I remembered seeing something in the paper about Sonny Collins being found on some beach somewhere. Sonny's an unusual name in the UK, so it kinda stuck out. You know? It also meant three of us were now dead. I'd seen the reports online about the other two."

Dale nodded.

"Anyway, it all felt off, and when I said I didn't drink she started being weird. I took some purified water from the fridge, and poured us some. Then, I turned my back to find us something to eat. I had some nice vegan cheese. When I glanced over my shoulder, I saw her pouring a liquid into my glass. She wanted to roofie me. It's something I notice. I've been trained."

"It's what she did to Adele Smith," Milly said.

Joanna's face crumbled. "Adele's dead?" She looked at Mark as if for confirmation. "Why? What about Charlie? He's so sweet."

"Charlie's okay. The others are gone. She killed them and a police officer during the arrest process." Dale fought to keep the emotion from his voice.

Joanna's mouth dropped open. "No. I mean... She was a box of frogs bonkers, I'll swear to that in court, but she killed all the others?"

"Yes." Dale needed the rest of the details. "So, she tried to roofie you, then what?"

"I pretended not to notice. She started to ramble on about her brother. I realised her reality made no sense any more. It took a while, but I found an excuse to leave the room and I ran. I thought she just wanted to rob me. Which, frankly, wouldn't have been much of a problem."

"Why not go to the police?" Milly asked. "It could have saved lives."

"My dad," Joanna said. "If I'd gone to the police he'd have found out. He watches me all the time. I've found cameras in the houses I rent. He monitors my phones, computers, everything. If he knew about Eliza trying to drug me, then she'd be dead. He's had people outside the house, watching me, I'm sure of it. Christ, if only I'd let him hurt her." The look of shocked horror on her face couldn't be faked. "Oh, what have I done?"

"Your father would have ordered her death?" Dale found this hard to believe.

The man had obviously been a control freak, but he was a legit business owner. Milly had done a full background check.

Mark spoke properly for the first time, his Somerset accent thick and sure like the land he farmed. "The man has ties to right wing insurgency groups, like the Proud Boys. Them buggers who stormed the White House."

Milly and I shared a long look and she shrugged. "It didn't show up, but I wasn't looking for terrorist connections. I just wanted to make sure he existed and had the money to pay us for any work we did. He had no criminal background and when I did a search in the local news, he came up as a philanthropist."

Joanna murmured, "He is. He's all those things. He's also been controlling my every move since I was a kid. I came to England thinking I could escape. Glastonbury seemed like a good place to hide, but he found me here. Then he promised to back off, but I found out he'd just upped the subtlety of his spying."

"Why employ us to find you? Why not use whoever he had spying on you?" Dale asked.

Joanna shrugged. "He doesn't necessarily need boots on the ground. Besides, the people watching me, wouldn't have been detectives. They'll just be thugs. They wouldn't know the area. All my father has to do is gain access to satellites, phone records, internet and when he controls the money…" She sighed. "In the past, I got a job to try to sustain myself, but they 'let me go' because I didn't have the 'correct paperwork', which was a God-damned lie. He's a prick. Ego manic. Narcissistic. Self-righteous. Prick. I honestly thought

I'd be saving Eliza's life and mine. I took what cash I had already and just ran. I've been planning the escape for a while; it was just a bit sooner than I wanted and a bit less structured. I was hitchhiking out of the area when Mark picked me up." She smiled at him. "I've been hiding here ever since. My father hired you, Mr Valentine, because you're local and you know the people to speak to. You became his boots on the ground. If you've talked about me over the phone, and my location, he'll already be on the way."

Dale let out a breath. "That's why you know how to use the gun."

"Yep. I've been trained in all firearms and many types of explosives since I was a kid. I've done all the survival training—everything they teach those right-wing nutters. I was given my first gun aged eight. I hate them."

"You're a damned fine shot though," Mark said in admiration.

"He doesn't know you're here," Milly said. "We won't tell him."

"Milly—" Dale began.

She turned to look at him. "You know as well as I do, we're not handing her over. She's dropped off the map, let her stay dropped."

"Tell them the rest," Mark said. "We can't keep it secret anymore; we need help."

Joanna nodded and stroked Mark's hair as she spoke. "Mark hates being here. He hated growing up here and he feels just as trapped at home as I did. The farm's been in his family for generations, and when his father became too old to run the place, he wanted to sell up, but there's a codicil in the will. If he wants to sell, it has to be to someone local and no one local has that kind of money, not for the whole farm."

"My father was a canny old bastard who hated me as much as I hated him, and the damned arsehole wanted to saddle me with this place for as long as I had my youth," Mark snarled.

"So, Mark can't sell. I've run out of cash. We… When the other farmers wanted to find the man digging the holes, I worked out exactly what had happened that night on the Mump. I realised at last, what Charlie and I saw, wasn't a part of the trip. It really was his uncle on that boat. So, we started digging for the gems as well."

Dale sat back in his chair, dumfounded. "You've been looking as well?"

"Yep."

"Did you find them?"

Joanna shook her head. "No and now you've found me, we have to go. My father will figure it out. I don't know how, but he'll find me here. Mark's life will be next, and I'll be dragged back to the States. Do I look like the kind of person who would survive a lifetime shackled to a group like the Proud Boys?"

Dale had to agree with her. Joanna was clearly more inclined to strong socialism. "You need cash?"

"We want to go to India," she said. "We can hide there. Less technology in the rural areas. We can get new names, new everything, and just vanish. I want to do some good in the world, so does Mark."

The farmer nodded. "I trained in sustainable farming for marginal land and the people who have to find a way to make a living off nothing. I wanted to work in places being destroyed by climate change to help people find a way to feed themselves when they get hit like this." He waved a hand at the outside of the house.

An idea began to form in Dale's mind. "Can you split the farm up?"

Mark tried to frown but the bruising made it impossible. "What are you talking about?"

"Surely someone can buy the farmhouse and a bit of land, but the rest can be sold separately?"

"I'd have to check with the lawyer, but... who'd want the land?"

Dale shrugged. "Don't know—yet. What if someone local bought this place for the price your father wanted, he came from a farming family in Glastonbury, and he can prove it? Maybe a group buy out?"

Mark made the mistake of snorting. His nose started to bleed again. "No one can afford to do that."

"I think I know some people who can."

"Forgive me, mate, but if you're talking about you buying this place, you don't look Anglo-Saxon, never mind Somerset born and bred."

Dale laughed, while Joanna blushed at Mark's words. "You're right. I'm not local in any sense, but I know a man who is and he's homeless. I have the money for a small holding." He glanced at Milly and winked. "Jimmy has the knowhow to run the place as a tenant."

It took a while, but he eventually convinced them he was serious. He needed to talk to Newberry and Frasier, see if they wanted the larger fields. Dale would be part of a syndicate made up of Somerset farmers. That should satisfy the terms of the will.

They'd need to get the paperwork signed off fast. Joanna had to move somewhere safe, out of sight and away from CCTV, but they could organise it. New passports would be difficult, but he'd arrange it through contacts in London. It could be done. Difficult, but possible.

By the time they finished making plans with Joanna and Mark, night smothered the land, but the rain had stopped. Joanna drove them back to the Audi in the carpark.

Dale's plan also involved blackmailing a very scary, very rich, American. "I'll need that evidence sooner rather than later. He's going to want an update on the case."

"You really think you can lie well enough to make it look like I'm one of Eliza's victims, they just haven't found my body?" Joanna asked for the hundredth time.

"I think I can swing it," he said. "I need to talk to my police contact. If I can't, we'll think of something else. Missing in action is the best we can do without a body."

She nodded. "Thank you. I'm so sorry I didn't go to the police."

"Under the circumstances, I can understand why. You were trying to protect people from your father."

"Will you and Milly be safe?" Joanna asked.

Dale looked at Milly. "I'll make sure of it."

~ *Chapter 28* ~

DALE WOULDN'T BE ASKING LAUREN for anything. He didn't trust the system to set up Joanna and Mark with identities safe enough that they couldn't be bought by someone with the power and money Wolski held. He'd use a different source.

When he dropped Milly at the Green Man, her final words were, "I'll see you tomorrow morning, nine sharp, Guv."

The wave of gratitude he felt towards her shocked him. How close had he come to losing her forever? Should they sit down and have a thorough heart-to-heart about all the issues this convoluted case brought to their door? Or should he leave that to the other people in her life? After all, she had a much wider support network than he did.

When Dale reached his cottage, he saw the lights on in the kitchen, which meant Jimmy was home. Unable to process that fact, Dale headed for the office, pulled the blinds down, and only switched on his desk lamp and computer. He accessed the secure private channel Tim set up for him to use and sent a simple message:

Need your skills, buddy.

An almost instant reply came back:

Big Man, how are you?

Dale thought about this for a moment. A long list of words came to mind. He wrote:

Everything is fine.

So? What do you need from me if everything is fine?

Little shit. You could get nothing for free from Tim.

It's for two clients. They need to disappear. Male and female. I'll send you ages and photos. Take the money from the pot. Also, I'm buying a farm as part of a syndicate, so I need cash and quickly. Can we make all that happen?

A long pause ensued. Dale tapped his fingers on the desk's surface, waiting. Then…

Yep. I can do that. We need to cash you out anyway. I've some new options to explore for growth areas.

Dale had little idea what the hell Tim was on about, so just typed:

Okay, I'll send more information when I have it. Thx.

TTFN

Dale smiled and shook his head. Tim lived by far too many of Winnie-the-Pooh's concepts of existence. Being a tigger in prison had almost ended his life. Almost. Tim would make sure Joanna and Mark vanished from the world to be born anew as other people. Dale would return to the farm tomorrow with burner phones, then stay away, so he couldn't be followed.

The problem he now had was how to deal with Mr Wolski and any potential threat to him, the business and anyone connected to it.

Dale needed the kind of evidence a man like Wolski understood. It wouldn't be easy to find or the people who hunted groups like the Proud Boys would already have Wolski under control. He leaned back in his chair and closed his eyes. Maybe he just needed to sleep, eat, relax and let his damned mind switch off?

His phone buzzed. However tempting it might be to ignore it, habit made him reach for the thing. A text from Lauren.

Can we talk?

Oh.

He rang her back. "Hey."

"Sorry."

Oh dear. "Where are you?"

"At the flat."

"Come up. I'll cook. Jimmy's here, but he's surprisingly good company when he's sober. You need the distraction."

"I need to talk."

"No, Lauren. You need to live. Right now, you need to live." He felt Ryan's slick blood on his hands and wanted to puke. "Come up. Bring comfy clothes and some chocolate. We'll eat, watch a film and relax."

"With Jimmy?"

"Yes, with Jimmy."

"No, it's fine. I'll—"

"If you don't come, I'll send him down to get you."

A heavy sigh. "Okay." She hung up.

Ryan's death would have all kinds of emotional impact on Lauren, especially after arriving too late to save Ringo and all that had triggered in their lives. Then there would be the knock-on effect to her career and the decisions she made as Senior Investigating Officer. Her boss, DCI Whitfield, wouldn't be taking the blame for dumping her on her own in Street and expecting her to handle a serial killer with a team stretched to breaking point. No, he'd be blaming his DI and Valentine Investigations. He wouldn't be entirely wrong, either.

Dale knew he'd made mistakes. He'd just wanted to find Charlie alive. He'd wanted to bring Eliza in alive, and those two facts meant Ryan had died. If Dale had waited, Ryan wouldn't have tried to back him up by coming into the stables.

"What a fucking mess," Dale murmured. Ryan would've been a good copper, a good man for the right woman—not Milly—and a good community leader. The world was poorer for Dale's decisions, and it hurt. He'd have to work through it, but right now, he had to help Jimmy and Lauren. Two people he cared about in his makeshift family.

He locked the office and went into the kitchen.

MILLY SAT IN THE AUDI the following morning and tried to focus on the problems Joanna and Mark had at the farm. Things at home were complicated. Her parents loved Dale, but he'd been responsible for her being there when

Ryan was killed. She hadn't told them she'd wrestled with the knife-wielding murderer. When they heard about that, which they would eventually, this being Glastonbury, the emotional blackmail would start all over again.

"I'm moving out of the Green Man," she said into the quiet of the car.

Her friend and mentor looked like a man who'd done ten-rounds with an emotionally incontinent vampire. Namely DI Kennedy on a bad day.

He glanced at her. "Really? Why?"

Milly shrugged with one shoulder. "It's time. I want my life to be mine. Saying that, Sully's coming with me. I'm not sure who they're more upset about losing, to be honest."

He laughed and the tension in his shoulders appeared to thin. "So Sully's moving in with you?"

"Yep. I want a pay rise, and I want a new job title."

"You want?"

"Yep."

"Aren't we supposed to negotiate?" Dale obviously felt a little lost.

"No. I know what I'm worth, so do you. I want to be an associate, not an assistant. We'll still be Valentine Investigations for now, but I want full partner status within two years. I want my pay rise to be twenty percent and overtime at—"

"Whoa there, Sherlock. What about a full partner in two years, pay rise of fifteen percent and overtime at the standard rate, but I'll think about expanding expenses to help you with a car?"

"Really?"

He glanced at her. "Did you just blag me?"

She grinned. "Yep."

"Damn it. Do you accept the terms?"

"Oh yes, especially about the car."

"It can be a tax deduction, I guess." The Audi prowled down the still empty road as they repeated their journey of the day before.

"Are you okay?" he asked at last.

Milly stared out of the window and thought about how to answer. "No. I don't think I am, but I will be. I'm seeing someone I can talk to about this and other stuff. He'll help me navigate Ryan's death, my place in it, and what it all means to me. He's good. I think Sully's in shock. I'm worried about him, but he'll get through it. He knows I love this work, this job, he's in my corner, so he'll be okay. I love him. He makes the world shine for me, and I've missed that for a long time. Ryan never made me feel like that. He was a good man, though, and I'll miss him very much."

"Yeah."

Her boss, the great communicator.

She said, "You going to see Grace again?"

"Tonight, I hope, but I guess that depends on how Lauren is coping."

Milly shook her head and tapped the back of his hand where it rested on the gearstick. "Don't do that. Don't become Lauren's crutch. She's a danger to your future happiness. Grace is a good woman. Don't fuck it up for Lauren."

"I know. I just… I feel like I owe Lauren."

"No, I don't think you do."

They parked at the head of the lane that would take them to Tappingwall Farm and started walking. The flood water had risen and settled. The grey skies were gradually giving way to blue, and the storm had melted into a benign and watery sunlight.

"Are you really buying this place?" Milly asked, baffled by the decision.

"I think it's an excellent investment."

"No, Guv, it's not."

He laughed. "Maybe not, but it's a good way to get Jimmy out of my house doing something useful. He wants a farm, which I can't afford, but I can if I'm buying this house and just enough land for a small holding. He'll be a tenant, that's all. Though, if we have animals here, I have the feeling we'll have to help with the paperwork."

"Which is code for, 'Milly, can you fill out this government form on sheep dip and worms?'"

"Pretty much, I guess." He looked at her. "Do sheep get worms?"

She laughed at his alarm and patted his shoulder, then described as many diseases as she could remember that came with sheep, cattle, horses and everything else on a farm.

Dale's response was, "How do farmers make any money at all?" He looked a little pale at the prospect of watching his impulsive decision drive him into bankruptcy.

Milly chuckled. "I'm not sure, to be honest."

They'd arrived at the farmyard and the two collies raced up to Milly on a quest to find out what she had in her pockets. Without realising it, she'd dug out a flapjack and started dividing it up between the three of them.

Joanna came out of the imposing house. She made Milly feel like a dumpling. The woman just knew how to move and dress, even in old farming clobber, that made her look like a princess slumming it. Milly tried to come to terms with never being *that* woman, but it wasn't easy.

"You have news?" Joanna asked Dale.

He nodded. "Let's go inside and we'll need Mark here as well. I'll talk you through the plans."

"He's been in touch with a…" she struggled to remember the British name, "…a conveyancer?"

"Good, that'll make things move more quickly. I spoke to the others and we're forming a company that'll buy the property, then we can split it up later. Within a few days, we can start filling out forms. Without mortgages being a problem, this'll be done quickly, but I'd like you and Mark moved as soon as we can."

Milly trailed behind them, taking in the house. It would be big for Jimmy on his own and lonely. She wondered what he'd really think when Dale presented him with the house. He ought to know what was being done.

Everything moved so fast around Dale when he decided on a course of action. The man made a decision, stuck to it, and rarely shared a single iota of information other than what was necessary to get the job done. She admired it, the stubborn drive of his ambition, but it also left her feeling adrift in his plans. An unnerving sensation.

The house was bleak, no doubt. Mark Weaver obviously hadn't decorated after inheriting the place and it reeked of neglect. From what the man had said, it wasn't a happy place to grow up and you could feel it in the walls. The wet outside didn't help. However, when she walked into the living room and saw the open fire, then the view out over the Levels, Milly realised its potential beauty. This could be an amazing family home.

But would Jimmy, with all his demons, survive here alone?

"No, he wouldn't," she murmured to the empty room.

Dale Valentine made things happen. The man was a catalyst for change. Milly wanted a change in her life, so she'd ride this wave and see where she landed. Decision made, she headed for the kitchen so she could learn how to make two people vanish off the planet without killing them.

DALE WONDERED HOW TO BROACH the most troublesome part of his plan. Joanna Wolski gave the impression of being a sensible person, but a year ago she'd taken peyote on the nearby hill to be part of some mad spirit quest.

He opted for straight forwards. "There's just one more thing."

"Oh?" Joanna asked, her eyes narrowing.

Dale took in a breath. This would be a risk. "I need to stop your father coming here to further investigate your disappearance, and death, at the hands of Eliza Collins. Just as a backstop in case he threatens me or the others. She'll never be charged for you disappearing, but he'll see her go to prison for the other crimes, and that might be enough. I need a bit of security."

"Okay, I'm assuming you have a plan?" she asked.

Dale saw Milly watching from the corner of the kitchen. He didn't really want her knowing any of the details of what he had planned. The implications were too serious if... when... it went wrong. If she didn't know, she'd be in less danger. Even the small amount she knew, with her formidable and ever-expanding skillset, could catapult her into a dark world she'd never escape. Trouble was, he needed her help, and he trusted her.

He plunged in. "Joanna, I need evidence to keep your father at bay. Stuff that will prevent him from coming after us. Just enough to make sure that getting on a plane, or paying someone to do it for him, would be a very unwise move."

"You're going to blackmail my father into leaving us alone?" Joanna laughed, and it sounded like smashing glass. "Are you mad? Have you got any idea how bloody powerful he is?"

"Have you any idea what I would do to protect my people?" Dale countered.

Mark breathed in and nodded. "He's right, Jojo. You need him to act as a barrier, here in England, and to do that, he needs to build a wall."

Dale watched Joanna Wolski carefully. He knew she could run back to daddy, pay whatever toll he put on her for running, and life would return to normal for her. She'd leave this damp, old-world town called Glastonbury, and return to her wealthy life in Savanna.

Joanna said with care, "I can call his ex-wife. She's not my mother, but at the end, when I realised what he was really like, we grew close. I helped her escape. When she left, she took some evidence about his businesses that he doesn't know she has. During the divorce, she told me that I could use it when the time came, when I was ready to run for real. It'll take a few days, but if I can find her, she'll help."

"Good. I can use a contact I have to deliver the information to Mr Wolski if necessary."

"Don't you need paying?" Mark asked.

"Oh, he'll pay me. He might not know he's doing it, but he'll pay what he owes." Dale knew he'd certainly owe Tim for his help. Despite all the blah, blah that Tim liked to splash about regarding his black hat hacking skills, the man was a white knight in waiting. One look at Joanna Wolski and he'd agree to help. Dale knew exactly which of Tim's big red buttons to push.

THE NEXT FEW DAYS WENT according to plan, for Dale, at least. It devastated Wolski, his daughter's part in the terrible aftermath of Eliza's revenge, but he bought the lies. Dale had a folder tucked away on a very private cloud account that would ensure his future security from the dangerous American, but he didn't think he'd need it. Of course, if Wolski discovered his daughter was alive and on her way to India, things would be very different. Dale had closed his computer, shutting off the video call, just as Wolski broke down in noisy tears. Maybe, when he stopped grieving, he'd find the holes in Dale's plan, maybe he wouldn't. Only time would answer that one.

He spoke to Lauren at length, and there would be a full investigation into Ryan's death. She was facing some pretty heavy disciplinary charges. She looked terrible. Haunted by what had happened and the operational decisions she'd made. They'd put her back on leave and she'd gone home to her parents' place outside Langport.

Milly's statement, Charlie Brent's and Dale's, had all backed up her version of events. They kept Jimmy's involvement to a minimum. He wasn't exactly reputable. DCI Whitfield also faced questions, but Dale warned Lauren her DCI would throw her under the cattle truck if it came to a choice between his pension and her career. Sadly, Lauren agreed. She seemed very alone. Her career showed she was a risk taker, and the events of the previous summer with the shotgun wielding paedophile wouldn't help her reputation.

When he broke the news to Jimmy about Tappingwall Farm, the big man had burst into tears, run from the house and vanished for two days. Dale panicked and went to visit Neil, the only other friend Jimmy had in this world, and discovered Jimmy at the other man's house. The two of them sat with the big man and explained slowly how this wasn't charity. It would be a working smallholding and Jimmy would be a tenant. It was a way for Dale to invest in the area.

"Besides, for a while at least, you'll have Milly and Sully with you. If that's okay? They want to rent a room off me. Oh, and the farm comes with some livestock and two dogs. That's the end of my farming knowledge," Dale added with a soft smile.

"Milly's going to be there with her fella?" Jimmy asked.

Dale nodded. "They'll have a car, so you won't be cut off from Glastonbury and you'll have company. When you're ready, we'll talk about transport."

"I don't understand why you're doing this for me," Jimmy said. "I really need to understand."

For a long moment, Dale said nothing. He just stared out of the window at the dark evening. "If you want the truth, Jimmy, it's because a very dear friend of mine died in my arms. I was a bad man in London. I want to make amends and you need…" Dale focused on the big man. "You need a friend as well. I can do some good. So, can you live on that farm? We just need to give each other a chance."

Jimmy nodded and a soft smile eased the anxious expression. "Friends who give each other a chance to find a little redemption in this world. I like that."

"Yeah, me too. So, you in?" Dale stood and held out his hand. Jimmy rose and took hold. They shook, and the deal was done.

Author Thanks

Many thanks for reading. If you have a little time, I would appreciate a review. I really value my readers' thoughts about a book. It often helps me craft future stories. They are vital for indie authors like me.

You are always welcome to get in touch directly at

joe@joetalon.com

www.joetalon.com

Insta @JoeTalonBooks

Follow on BookBub!

I have free stories for you as well, all I'd like in exchange is your email address and you can unsubscribe at any time.

I'd like to keep in touch. The newsletter goes out fortnightly and has deals and steals for you in each one. There is always a library of new authors to try for free and more free stories from me, pre-order deals and more!

Or you can join my Facebook group: Joe Talon Books. There will also be an opportunity to join my *Advanced Reader Team*. You make this job worth it. Thank you.

I also have FREE AUDIO files for the novellas if you fancy those instead: https://soundcloud.com/ This is where my narrator hangs out.

Your Free Book Is Waiting

When the police offer you a deal to escape prison, you take it. Right?
Dale Valentine, understands the system, he once wore the uniform, carried
the warrant card.

Now, he's just a tool for the police as they hunt the worst criminal gang
that London has seen in a long time. It's Dale's job to infiltrate, manipulate,
and report back to his handler, Lauren Kennedy.

Only this job might just end up with him dead, and sixteen girls sold into
slavery if he can't figure out how to save them.

Impossible odds become normal as Dale earns his freedom and the future
he craves away from the dark streets of London.

Get a free copy of the prequel

Here:

A Prison of the Mind on Story Origin

ACKNOWLEDGEMENTS

MY GRATITUDE AS ALWAYS TO my editorial team; David Luddington, who pulled together the threads I'd missed, and Jeff Jones for proofreading a dyslexic's mess with patience. Any mistakes are mine after the fact.

Also, Glastonbury, the mysterious and magical town that is wildly independent and always has been, even during the medieval period. Any references to real places are made with the upmost respect. If you are ever in the area, do go for a visit, it's an amazing town. Having lived on the Levels for several years and watched them flood, I just had to write a story about it.

Then to my ARC team, my Facebook group and my newsletter guys—The Taloneers. Thank you. The support you've shown and your willingness to try this new series has been very important to me. I hope you've enjoyed the second book.

Dale's first adventure with DS Lauren Kennedy

Your Free Book Is Waiting

When the police offer you a deal to escape prison, you take it. Right?
Dale Valentine, understands the system, he once wore the uniform, carried the warrant card.
Now, he's just a tool for the police as they hunt the worst criminal gang that London has seen in a long time. It's Dale's job to infiltrate, manipulate, and report back to his handler, Lauren Kennedy.
Only this job might just end up with him dead, and sixteen girls sold into slavery if he can't figure out how to save them.
Impossible odds become normal as Dale earns his freedom and the future he craves away from the dark streets of London.

Get a free copy of the prequel
Here:
A Prison of the Mind on Story Origin

Here's the first Dale Valentine crime mystery.

FOR WHOM THE WILLOW WEEPS

DALE VALENTINE, TRANSPLANTED FROM SOUTH London to the heartlands of Somerset, often feels like the locals keep their secrets in the sap of the apple trees. It's his job to draw them out.

When he receives a call to his small investigation agency from another transplanted soul, he meets the victim of a disturbing poisoned pen letter campaign.

Only the letters aren't to the people in the house, they are aimed at the house.

With the help of his assistant, Milly Wolfe, he soon uncovers a tragic and unresolved death.

Twenty-five years before, a boy was killed and left under a willow tree, surrounded by meadow flowers. And when a second murder happens in the same location, he has to uncover the terrible secrets hidden in the damp and lonely soil of an old farm.

A new crime series from the best-selling author of the Lorne Turner Supernatural Thrillers.

For Whom The Willow Weeps on Amazon

SEVEN TEARS OF HEAVEN

A man who poisons minds. A young missing American. Mysterious holes on farmland about to be flooded. And three dead bodies.

The call from Mr Wolski disturbs Dale. He understands a father's concern for his missing daughter, but Wolski hovers on the side of obsession. His daughter, Joanna, vanished from Glastonbury almost a month ago. It's the job of Valentine Investigations to find her.

It should be easy to find a young woman with an American accent in rural Somerset.

But no one has seen her, or heard from her.

The more Dale and Milly uncover about Joanna Wolski, the more they worry about her safety.

Then Detective Inspector Lauren Kennedy discovers one of her cold cases, and a fresh corpse, are linked to the same meditation group as Dale's missing person.

The killer's calling card, a single black diamond, throws up more questions than answers.

Does Glastonbury really have a serial killer in its midst?

Who will be next?

And where is Joanna Wolski?

Seven Tears of Heaven on Amazon

AN AGONY OF LIES

A call from an old friend fills Dale Valentine with dread the moment it ends. His past is coming to Glastonbury and he's not sure he's ready.

As a professional investigator, he knows ex-convicts are rarely truthful if a lie keeps them out of trouble. This one is driven by panic.

After all, what happens to hackers who discover government ministers are lying? Rarely anything good.

As paranoia seeps through the rural town, Dale needs to uncover the real power behind the throne. A solar farm's links to the politician weave a path through the ancient landscape to foreign powers that fill him with dread.

When the politician dies, the lies start to fall apart and Dale finds himself at the heart of a dangerous game.

Can Dale and one jaded police officer, save Glastonbury and a disreputable hacker, from big business corruption and greed?

And if he can't, who will become the sacrifice?

An Agony of Lies on Amazon

The Lorne Turner Supernatural Mysteries Start Here!

COUNTING CROWS

ON A FOG-BOUND MORNING, LORNE Turner stumbles over a murder of crows feasting on the body of a dead man.

It soon becomes clear it's a ritual sacrifice.

But why? Why here? Why now?

Most importantly, why is Detective Inspector Tony Shaw ignoring the ceremonial element? What do the police have to hide?

Lorne knows the darkness is rising, he feels it scream a warning through his nightmares.

Corruption, greed and the abuse of occult mysteries lead Lorne into a world he never thought existed. Trained to stand firm against terrorists, he must now fight the ghosts of his past, and the darkness of a madman.

An old soldier once more goes into battle. What will break first, his mind, or the bodies of his enemies?

Counting Crows on Amazon

MONEY FOR OLD BONES

LORNE TURNER NEEDS A BREAK, so when he's offered the job of security guard and handyman at an old rectory in the Lyn Valley he takes it.

He thought he'd gain a little space and perspective. A little quiet from the noise in his head, from his demons, from his beast. Sadly, The Rectory doesn't provide the haven he needs.

As the rain falls, waters rise, and old graves move.

The grave of a witch, who cursed the village. The grave of a soldier, who tried to escape the Hanging Judge after the Monmouth Rebellion. The grave of a priest, broken by love and grief.

When the whispering of Exmoor's dead turns into a scream, Lorne has to act.

The original families of Scob must face their debt.

Lorne, Ella, Willow, and Heather need to find a way to balance the scales before more lives are lost.

Can they survive the haunting misery of the old bones? Can they save each other from the beckoning darkness?

And the rain. Always the rain.

Money for Old Bones on Amazon

DEAD OF THE WINTER SUN

LORNE IS BEGINNING TO UNDERSTAND that the dead might not stay in the graveyards where they belong. He also knows it's time to start facing this disconcerting reality in the same way he faced his enemies in battle.

So, when Eddie Rice buys a rundown cottage on Exmoor, and an old graveyard, which should be empty, things become increasingly weird. It isn't empty for a start. Not of bodies, or the whispering dead.

After an elderly woman is murdered nearby, Lorne, Ella and the others begin to uncover a plot that links this quiet corner of the world with Cold War espionage. Soviet secrets unravel and the more Lorne discovers the closer to breaking point he gets.

The Winter Sun burns in his blood, eating his mind. Can his desert hitchhiker save him? Or will his sanity fold under the weight of Cold War madness?

Dead of the Winter Sun on Amazon

SALT FOR THE DEVIL'S EYE

LORNE'S HOME IS TURNING INTO A dream. He's happy and at peace for the first time in his life. The nightmares are releasing their grip on his mind and he's learning to cope with the whispering dead.

Sadly, that's not the case for everyone.

An old friend calls about a missing boy from a traveller's camp on the Quantocks. They've been living on the site of an ancient hillfort, near the burial grounds of long forgotten souls.

These people don't trust the police, but they do put their faith in an old soldier to bring their boy home.

When Lorne discovers this disappearance has a link to his childhood friend vanishing, more than thirty years before, his oldest fears start to rise and take form.

The ancient sites of the Quantocks, the modern world of Hinkley Point's new nuclear reactor, and ex-police officer Tony Shaw, start to weave a tapestry of darkness that threatens all the peace Lorne's worked so hard to find.

Salt for the Devil's Eye on Amazon

Bad Waters Run Deep

LORNE ISN'T CONVINCED HIS NEW psychic detective agency is a good idea but when he receives a call from a boarding school, sat in the shadow of Clatworthy Reservoir he reluctantly agrees to help.

The wisdom of teenagers has caused a problem at the school. The students decided the Ouija board they made in class might be fun to use, but when their call is answered, everything changes.

The results have opened a door Lorne has to close or lives will be lost.

The team discover a dark secret. The rising waters of the reservoir that flooded an ancient village called Syndercombe concealed a twisted, evil mind who took the opportunity to hide his dead.

But his evil didn't surrender when age robbed him of life and he's returned to the school, seeking new victims for his twisted desires.

If Lorne, Heather and Ella can't stop the rising evil in the reservoir then more than just the water will be polluted, the souls of the innocent will be lost to the bad waters of Clatworthy.

Bad Waters Run Deep on Amazon

The Alchemist's Corpse

THE COLD OF WINTER WRAPS sticky fingers around Exmoor as Lorne, Ella and Heather learn of Saint Decuman and his healing well in Watchet.

It seems the old saint is trying to send a warning to those able to listen, the elderly of his ancient parish.

When Lorne and Heather offer to help the spooked pensioners, little do they realise they're walking into a warzone.

The local motorcycle gang, The Devil's Mercenaries, are now peddling designer drugs. While a new cult, The Watchers, is offering a different kind of high.

Lorne, Ella and Heather must untangle the links between an old alchemist, the designer drug and the cult before the hauntings claim more lives.

War is on the horizon for this small seaside town and Lorne is a man who knows how to kill. The question is, can he?

The Alchemist's Corpse on Amazon

THE SPIRIT GLASS

AS MYSTERIES GO THIS ONE doesn't look too bad. At least on the surface.

Lorne's obligations to a department within military intelligence are called in when Ms Pilar Sanchez turns up with her men-in-black.

She leaves behind a box full of photos and secrets. He's tasked with clearing out any mystical or esoteric objects in the cottage of a dead artist who lived nearby.

The cottage is full of paintings and statues of a figure that is ill defined and yet hauntingly beautiful. A creature of dreams.

Those dreams lead Lorne and Heather to uncover an entrance to an ancient mine working.

Within the darkness they find a woman, they find a cage, and they uncover a terrible secret.

Freeing the suffering creature, Lorne does the one thing he vowed never to do. He unleashes hell on the innocent.

It's not just them that pay the price this time. The question is how high will the final cost be for the team?

The Spirit Glass on Amazon

THE DEAD ALSO HAVE SECRETS

A SYRIAN FAMILY ASK LORNE Turner for help when they take over an old hotel and open it for visiting spiritualists. It turns out they are more progressive than their first paying guests.

The invited medium is an American woman and Lorne knows something about her story is wrong. She's vulnerable and he must find out why.

After being forced off the road, then shot at, Lorne reaches out for help.

The team gather and soon realise they are in the middle of warring extremist factions within the Christian faith. The Vatican on one side, the Dominionists on the other.

But they aren't fighting over him, they are fighting for an ancient relic that was stolen by pirates centuries before and thought lost at sea.

When both sides realise Lorne's uncovered their secrets he is cut-off and hunted.

He has to find a way to save himself, his people, and stop the relic from falling into the wrong hands. He just has to decide who that is and how to prevent it. If the wrong group gain the power it offers it could unleash a darkness not seen in millennia. Thousands of children died then, Lorne's not about to let it happen again.

The Dead Also Have Secrets on Amazon

Two novellas and the start of Lorne's mysterious journey into the supernatural

Your Free Book Is Waiting

Lorne Turner, a broken soldier, arrives home for the first time in twenty years
to an empty, lonely farmhouse on Exmoor.
The coming days reveal the despair of a farm drowning in debt.
The coming nights reveal something far worse.
Lorne doesn't know if the noises, the *crack, crack, crack*, are the wind
ravaging the moor, memories savaging his mind or the ghosts tearing the veil,
begging for help.
This novella is Lorne Turner's first mystery.
If you love spooky stories, then you'll love Joe Talon's Supernatural
Mysteries.

Get a free copy of the prequel
Forgotten Homeland here:
www.joetalon.com

Another Free Book Is Waiting

After ten months of being alone on his moor, Lorne Turner receives a panicked call.

He needs to rescue some teenagers from an act of stupidity. Nice and simple. Fast rope down to a cave entrance, see if they are still alive, and get them out. Piece of carrot cake for an ex-operator.

When Ella Morgan is also 'roped' into helping, Lorne begins to understand the importance of friendship outside the military. The pair descend into the cave complex and that's when Lorne realises the dead don't always whisper. Sometimes the dead scream!

This short novella takes place before Counting Crows and gives us an insight into how Lorne and Ella first begin their friendship. It's also how I first started to get to know the pair. I hope you enjoy it as well.

A Meeting of Terrors Free on Story Origin

Printed in Great Britain
by Amazon

45190597R00169